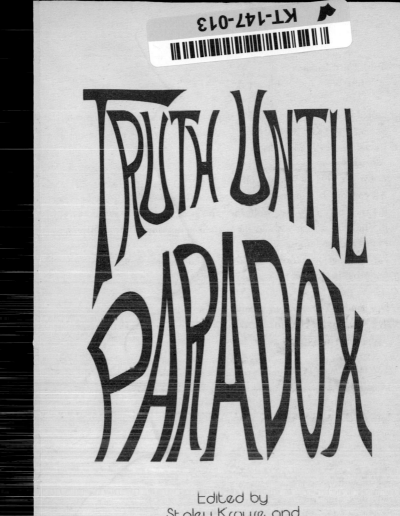

Truth Until Paradox

Edited by
Staley Krause and
Stewart Wieck

Truth Until Paradox
A White Wolf, Inc. Publication

Edited by Stewart Wieck and Staley Krause with Erin Kelly, Cynthia Summers and Kim Shropshire.
Interior Art by Mark Jackson
All rights reserved.
Copyright 1994 by White Wolf, Inc.
All contents herein are copyrighted by White Wolf, Inc. Mage(TM) is a trademark of White Wolf, Inc. This book may not be reproduced in whole or in part, without the written permission of the publisher, except for the purpose of reviews.
For information address: White Wolf Publishing, 4598 Stonegate Industrial Boulevard, Stone Mountain, GA 30038.

White Wolf Fiction:
Publisher: Stewart Wieck
Executive Editor: Staley Krause
Art Director: Richard Thomas
Graphic Design: Michelle Prahler
Marketing: Wes Harris
Sales: Michael Krause

TABLE OF CONTENTS
■ ■ ■ ■ ■ ■ ■ ■ ■ ■ ■ ■

THE CRYSTAL MESSIAH
∎∎∎∎∎∎∎∎∎∎∎∎

Philip Nutman

The day after the earthquake rocked San Francisco, I awoke with ground glass beneath my eyelids and a fractured skull. As I cried out, I didn't comprehend how the world as I knew it had changed forever.

Face down and fully clothed, I raised my head from the futon and groaned so loud a deaf, dumb and blind kid in Oakland could have heard me. It felt like the grandmother of all hangovers was beating my skull with a broom handle which was weird as hell because I hardly drink and can't stand getting drunk.

I couldn't remember what had happened the night before. As I pulled my body into a prone position, I realized I was still clad in my black leather biker's jacket, ripped jeans and scuffed-up Tony Lama boots with the killer Cuban heels. I caught a vague recollection of drinking a token Sam Adams or two with Art Baisden while talking about the latest CD-ROM developments in his cluttered Fillmore apartment.

I remembered him taking a deep toke on a joint as fat as his fingers, then asking if I wanted any. I declined.

"This is gonna turn things *around* ...," I remembered him saying before someone set off a flashgun in front of my dry, prickling eyes. I vomited all over the rare *Swamp Thing* issues Art had lent me and last night's dinner deposited itself on a splash panel of *Arcane*. I heaved again, as dry as the

Mojave desert this time, and belched.

"Sheeeiit ... what did I do?" I mumbled, trying remember the night as I sat up on my bed.

I didn't have a clue. My reflection in the full-length mirror looked as contrite as a Roman Catholic schoolboy who'd been caught writing raunchy graffiti about the convent nuns.

"Aww, hell on wheels!" The digital bedside clock clicked to 10:25 A.M.

I was going to be late for work.

On auto-pilot, I stumbled towards the bathroom, then stopped, confused.

I was already clean ... fresh — I didn't need to shower ...

The faucet behind the glass switched on suddenly and I jumped backwards in surprise.

What are you doing? I thought. *You don't work right at the best of times.*

The shower stopped as suddenly as it had started.

Groaning, and not thinking about it — other than I was going to be late for work — I stumbled towards the door, grabbed my bicycle in my left hand, and somehow made it downstairs without falling ass-over-elbow.

As I mounted the ten-speed and pushed off down the street, I smelled rain in the Bay Area air, but I didn't care. All I wanted was to get to the store within 5 minutes of opening before the returns piled up, four feet deep.

I work as assistant manager at The Videodrome, the hippest video store in San Francisco, and Monday mornings were the worst way to start the week. Everybody returned their weekend tapes, ready for their next fix of fill-in titles until the new releases hit the racks on Wednesday. The store opened at 11 a.m., but I was supposed to be there at 10:30. Jeff, the other assistant manager, was off today so I was flying solo. I had to get the computerized registers up and running and ready for business — no easy feat considering Al, the elderly owner, is too cheap to update the system and it takes

15 minutes to run the tape inventory before the system logs on.

I didn't think about it then, but the bike flew like the wind, almost as if I had willed it to get me to the store in record time …

■ ■ ■

Kublek shuddered beneath his purple silk robe.

"He has Awakened," he stated softly. "The Time is here."

He sipped coffee as he turned to his foot soldiers, trying not to grimace in front of them. Reality tasted unduly bitter this morning. The Sleeper was Aware earlier than anticipated, and Gregor Kublek hated to be caught off guard. Unpredictability and chance were facets of life the Technocratic conventions despised, and as a senior scion of the New World Order, it was Kublek's responsibility to anticipate and confine potential wild cards such as James Labac before they could disrupt the status quo.

Like an earthquake tremor, the psychic shockwave of Labac's Awakening had shaken the foundations of Kublek's morning meditation. An icy shower of water to his glowing, transcendental state, the ripple had drawn his essence back into his human form with the velocity of a World Trade Center elevator plunging to ground zero, its cables cut.

That had been twenty minutes ago, and he tried to suppress a shudder at the memory. He could not reveal his disquiet in front of Overstreet and his men.

"Try the home address first," Kublek said, handing Labac's dossier to the former CIA agent. "If he's not there, go to his place of work. Use force if you have to, but be as discrete as possible."

Overstreet took the folder, scanning the details, then turned to his black suit-clad men, giving each one of the four a photo of the subject. Rogers pressed the button to summon the car to the Executive Level of the

TransAmerican spire. Kublek waited until the doors closed before reaching for the container of Maalox in his desk. Taking a deep draught, he sighed. 50 years an Adept, but he still suffered chronic indigestion in times of stress. He despised human frailty.

The computers had predicted Labac would not Awaken before the winter solstice. Time and again, his Brothers had run the figures through the matrix; each time the probability factor had predicted no sooner than December first at the very earliest.

But it had happened. Something had triggered the boy's Avatar.

Were they losing their command of reality? The unexpected yet concrete evidence facing him stretched the limits of his rigidly conditioned precepts, and the logical conclusion was not something he wanted to consider.

Outside the mirrored glass, storm clouds lowered.

They had to reach him before the Others ...

■ ■ ■

A sharp wind blew off the Bay, whipping up urban dust devils along the street as Royle drank deep from the half-pint of Night Train Express clenched in his grime-encrusted fist. Time-it-was-a-comin', ho-ho-ho, so the Masters promised. So crystal clear, the taste obscured the sick sweetness of the crap he was drinking while in the guise of a bum. Give me the juicy tang of a placental-laced testosterone and estrogen Bloody Mary any day, his fragged memory gibbered.

Rum and smoke. Vocal chords and tonic.

"Shut up," he muttered as he drank. His seven other personalities were silent for an instant.

Be like that then, said one of the Voices.

No need to be rude, said another.

"Aaah, fuck off," Royle growled. "Get out of here. If I

want your critiques, I'll ask first."

Clinical psychologists would label him a Multiple Personality. The truth was more dramatic. What had once been Drew Royle, Underground Cartoonist, was now a Psycho-Hydra-Morp, eight souls, personalities, appetites, contained within one shell. All had sought the Truth but had embraced Darkness in favor of the sterility of the Light, trading their souls for knowledge beyond imagining. Now they were fomori, a once-human agent of the Mage Orphrence, Arch Deacon of the Nephandi, who amused himself by redesigning pathetic human flesh and broken souls into new, more elaborate entities.

Royle ignored his protoplasmic siblings, hawked up a bolus of phlegm and spat into the gutter, then pulled the Swiss Army knife from the inner pocket of his filthy denim jacket, carving a silhouette of *Cheech Wizard* into the skin of his withered left arm.

"Yabba-dabba-do-time ...one banana, two banana, three banana, four ..." He giggled as he stood, kicking over the empty bottle.

The other seven argued among themselves as he swayed on his feet.

Truth was, Time was here. The one called Labac had Awakened, and the Nephandi hungered for his Avatar. The magnitude of Labac's potential power, if harnessed by the Dark forces, could be the hammer with which the Demon Hordes could smash the defenses of the sterile, dreamless scientific minds of the Technocracy, leading them to the ultimate source of power The Earth's succulent resources

But the fomori knew nothing of this, only that success promised reward, failure unspeakable punishment.

Royle's forearm pulsed with pain. It felt good. He could smell the blood, taste the promise of chaos to come. He laughed like a hyena, performed an insane Irish jig along the curbstones, and set off in the direction of Pacific Heights.

■ ■ ■

I reached the store in record time. Every stoplight had turned green as I approached — at least something was going my way. But as I peddled down Market Street, I could see a line of customers already outside the store. At least ten, if not more. Damn. I'd have to hand write receipts while the system came on-line. Hopefully, Al wouldn't show up until lunch time and I'd have everything in order by the time he got there. He's the most pedantic, particular old coot I've ever worked with. He wants everything done his way, even down to how you count the small change while cashing out the till at the end of each shift.

"Sorry we're late opening," I said to the crowd as I brought the bike to a halt.

No one complained, which was a relief.

As I unlocked the door and flipped off the alarm switch, I noticed a girl with long hair which was as richly rust-brown as the bark of a redwood. Goddamn, she was beautiful. Where had she been all my life? Was she a new customer? I'd never laid eyes on her before. I smiled at her as I opened the door, but she ignored me with the practiced aloofness most Goth girls affect — and everything about her shouted Goth. She was around 5'2", slim but curvy, clad in a black, low cut skintight body suit beneath her leather jacket. Her face was as pale as a winter moon. The only color was her hair and the full-length ox-blood Doc Martins she sported. And her eyes — they were as green as jade. She looked a little like Death from *Sandman*.

The crowd of customers filed into the store, depositing their returned tapes in the main drop box. I noticed the tape she was carrying was a copy of *The Crow*, Brandon Lee's last flick.

"What did you think of the movie?" I asked.

She continued to ignore me.

Oh, well ... two could play that game. I set about my opening ritual and ignored her in return.

Kara Turner walked the aisles of *The Videodrome* pretending to ignore Labac, partly out of nervousness but mainly out of disappointment. This was the One Roberto had seen in his vision quest before the Nephandi had killed him? She almost hoped it wasn't Labac, that he was off sick and this was another shift manager. From Roberto's description, she'd imagined someone taller, with long black hair, lithe, muscular, with a tattoo or two — not this nondescript guy with short, straight receding hair and the inane grin of some hick who'd just stepped off the bus from South Dakota.

James Alexander Labac. The name summoned images of power. It whispered leader, but the smiling guy who opened the door didn't even radiate much of an aura, let alone real class. Was this the James Labac who'd made *Boulevard of Broken Mirrors*, the short film which Roberto had dreamed before they stumbled across the real thing at a screening? He *couldn't* be the one, *could he?* Appearances, of course, could be deceptive. But if this wasn't Labac, then where was he? Sick, or had either the Technocracy (or *Gaia forbid*, the Nephandi) gotten to him already? Kara didn't want to even consider that option, so she pretended to peruse the Japanese animation section while keeping the clerk in sight out the corner of her eye. She hoped she had reached him in time, but couldn't ignore her disappointment. Still, every time she dared glance in his direction she saw a glimmer of potential. Disappointment, be damned. She hoped she was right.

An instant after I switched on the computer, a customer approached, tape in hand.

"This copy of *Trauma's* defective," he said. "Ten minutes in and there're constant dropouts. I want a free rental."

"Let me see," I replied, taking the tape and popping it in a player. Dividing my attention between the computer and the tape, I was only vaguely aware of the bum who had just entered the store.

Kara felt the tiny hairs on the back of her neck stand up on end, turned towards the store entrance, and gasped.

He looked like a Tenderloin hobo but his aura resonated like a Fourth of July fireworks display of conflicting shades, the frenetic nimbus of a mentally unbalanced Sleeper who'd been exposed to some kind of Magick. Or worse ...

A *fomori* ...

■ ■ ■

I fast-forwarded ten minutes into the tape. It looked fine to me.

"There doesn't appear to be a problem —"

A high pitched scream cut me off mid-sentence.

The bum stood in the middle of the store, mouth open, a noise no normal person could express streaming from his vocal chords.

Everyone froze. I saw a look of terror flash across the girl's face. Then the derelict turned, shoving the Hitchcock rack to the floor.

"Hey!" I shouted as he began to dance. No, 'dance' is the wrong word. He started to rotate like a whirling dervish, spinning, twirling so fast he dissolved into a blur. Tapes started to lift off the shelves like iron filings drawn to a magnet as the hobo transmuted into a human tornado.

My jaw dropped in disbelief. The tapes hovered above him, moths around a candle flame — then spun off at lethal speeds.

One hit a suited customer in the chest. The crunch of ribs snapping resounded unnaturally loudly as he somersaulted backwards into the rack of Cantonese horror movies. Another tape shot across the store in my direction, hitting the guy who wanted a free rental in the back of the head. I flinched as something hot, wet and sticky sprayed my face and my vision turned red.

"Get down!" the girl shouted.

The complaining customer slumped over the counter, and through the blood I observed the tape a copy of *Lonely Are The Brave* protruding from the back of his skull.

Wiping the gore from my eyes, I saw the girl pull something from inside her jacket and hurl it into the maelstrom which had been the bum.

As the ersatz wino first transformed, Kara had hesitated for an instant, her mind numb at the thought that she and she alone had to face down a fomori. There was no doubt as to the true nature of the figure conjuring an energy vortex in the center of the store.

If she was going to make a move, it had to be now. She slid a silver dagger from the pocket of her leather, shouted a warning to Labac, and threw the blade with ease. Months of practice paid off. The blade entered the funnel, severing the fomori's spine.

The whirlwind ceased in the blink of an eye. Tapes hung suspended in the air for a second then crashed to the carpeted floor.

I was too stunned to heed the girl's cry. My legs had turned to lead, frozen to the spot like Talos in *Jason and the Argonauts*. But I didn't topple and crash to the ground as the bum did.

Whatever she'd thrown at him halted all movement. He suddenly stood on tiptoe, a clumsy ballerina, his back arching at an unnatural angle as he frantically reached behind to claw at his filth-encrusted shirt. His face appeared to change as his mouth opened, closed, opened like a guppy. He revolved a complete 360 degrees before folding to his knees and pulling the dagger from his flesh. He pointed at me with his left arm, mouth still frozen in a silent scream only the dead could hear. Tapes tumbled around him as his face morphed into that of an old man, a young Chinese girl, a black gang-banger, a middle-aged woman.

I blinked, a cacophony of agonized voices echoing loudly in my ears.

Then, brakes screeched outside the store and a long, black limo mounted the curb. Instinct propelled me backwards as the car plowed through the glass doors. Through the voices shouting, arguing, agonizing in my head, I heard one of the customers cry out as a series of stuttering noises tore from the vehicle.

As I peered over the counter and the customer's corpse, I saw five black suit-clad men with matching mirror shades spill forth from the open doors of the limo. Each carried a MAC-10, and the sound I'd heard was automatic weapon-fire channeled through a suppressor. In the space of a minute, reality had turned from a normal Monday morning to out-takes from a Sam Raimi movie, and now The Videodrome resembled a scene from a John Woo flick. The lead man-in-a-suit turned in my direction and opened fire again.

I ducked. I'd watched enough action movies to know when to hit the deck. As I threw myself to the ground, I saw the other suits spray the store. Customers screamed. Computer screens exploded over my head, showering me with glass. In unison, the overhead TV sets surged with power, tubes blowing out in a electronic cannonade.

Between the voices in my head, the soft splat of silenced gunfire, the shatter of exploding glass, and the screams of dying customers, a locus of calm descended, opening like a lotus blossom in the eye of the storm of violence. And I heard her voice, so calm despite the chaos. The tone was refined, the inflections English.

"Where's the rear exit?" She asked.

I started to speak, but the image in my head answered for me.

"Good. Crawl towards it. Now." She saw me hesitate. "*Do it!*"

"Who are you?" I asked.

"*If you want to live follow me.*"

I didn't need any encouragement.

At that moment, one of the suits appeared around the counter, the muzzle of his gun dropping in my direction. I rolled to one side and closed my eyes tight, expecting to feel bullets strafing the length of my body.

What occurred next defied reason. Hell, everything that happened to me that Monday defied reason.

As I lay there, suspended in the mid-breath between life and death, I heard the whir and click of the laser disc player situated behind the counter as the disc-loader opened. Looking up, I saw the disc levitate from the player and begin to spin. Then the disc shot off like a UFO, and decapitated the suit.

His body wavered for an instant, blood gushing like a geyser from the severed carotid arteries, then topple towards me.

I moved like a fox with the hounds fast on his tail, shooting around the right angle of the counter, intending to make a run for the rear exit.

And stopped dead.

Directly in front of me, blocking my path in the children's section, the bum or what had been the bum stood on skeletal, rickety, scaled legs.

There's a fun Japanese sci-fi movie called *Zeram*. It's too goofy in parts to be a classic, but it features an alien monster which gives Carpenter's *The Thing* a run for its money. And what stood before me could have been the star of a sequel. The legs were as thin as pipe cleaners, the pelvic cage a crescent moon of undulating muscle stretched tight over Gigeresque bone. The waist tapered in with the masochistic shape of a Victorian lady imprisoned in a whalebone corset, funneling out into a Y-shape of body builder musculature that belonged on a Rob Liefeld superhero; massive pecs, bulging biceps that threatened to split the skin which struggled to contain them. But the forearms tapered down into the delicate wrists of a teenage girl. The hands, if you could call them that, were exaggerated craven's talons. But it was the head that made me gag — make that *heads*.

The neck was as thick as a tree trunk, at least a foot in length before separating into serpentine lengths of throat. Eight of them. Each had a different face. An old man, a Chinese girl, black gang-banger, a street urchin, punkette, gaunt junkie, aging hooker … and the bum.

"Eat It." One of the heads said.

"No. We need It."

"Waste the mofo —"

"Come to momma, honey pie."

"Shut up, morons!"

The heads argued among themselves as the creature lashed out its right arm, showering Barney and Disney tapes across the store. I looked to my right. The suits were moving towards the creature, guns up, expressions zombie-blank as they advanced and opened fire.

"Move!" the girl's voice cried inside my head.

I dove between the creature's legs as the fusillade of bullets hit home. Some slugs ricocheted off bone, others slapped into muscle. Several split some of the heads. The hooker's face came apart like an over-ripe cantaloupe. I didn't stop to see the others splatter, but felt bone fragments and cranial matter rain down on my back as I headed straight down the comedy aisle towards the girl.

"Come on!" she shouted as we ran for the emergency

exit.

Behind us, the creature screamed.

We burst through the door, setting off the alarm. The girl turned and raised her arm, hailing a taxi. Murphy's law, you can never find a taxi when you want one, especially if it's raining, but damn, I was glad to see this one. As it pulled to a halt, the girl spun to face me.

"James Labac?"

"Yeah. How do you know —"

She hit me with a right hook and the lights went out.

■ ■ ■

Kara regulated her breathing as the taxi sped down Lick Freeway towards Candlestick Park. It took every ounce of her concentration to control the driver and scan the surrounding streets for potential threats. Escaping from the full frontal assault of the Men in Black was one thing; temporarily restraining the fomori was another. She hoped her minor use of vulgar Magick wasn't sufficient enough to warrant arousing a Paradox Backlash. Kara had to face the full implications of her situation. She was on the run with the Exalted One, most of her Clique was dead, either at the hands of the Technocracy or the Nephandi, and she had no place to go.

For most of her 24 years, Kara had been a loner. Even amongst the Clique she'd felt separate, despite her relationship with Roberto. Her life — especially her previous mundane suburban existence in the English Home Counties — had been empty, filled with suffocating hours of loneliness. Sixty seconds, sixty minutes, sixty hours, weeks, months of betrayal, rejection, scorn. Endless days and nights, the passing of which were indelibly marked into the skin of her forearms, her inner thighs a thousand tiny razor blade scars measuring ennui and spiritual entropy to an endless soundtrack of The Cure, Joy Division, Sisters of

Mercy, The Danse Society, and Wasted Youth.

But that was Then and this was Now.

She was alone again.

Alone with the dead weight of James Labac slumped beside her, wheezing softly between the lips she'd bloodied with her punch. She saw the sign for Jamestown Avenue and it pushed into the driver's mind. His foot touched the break as he signaled left.

Damn. Her plans had dissolved like a watercolor left out in the rain.

Plans? What damn plans? You didn't have any to start with, girl!

That much was true. The fact she'd gotten this far was a testament to coincidental magic. But how much farther she could go remained to be seen.

■ ■ ■

News of the massacre reached Gregor Kublek as the last drop of blood splashed across the walls of The Videodrome.

Rogers, Bullock, Newman, DeGrassi, and Feil ... all gone. They'd been good men, but they were just foot soldiers, unquestioning servants marching to the call of the Order, and hence dispensable. There were five hundred of their ilk in California; five thousand more if one cast one's net as far as Minneapolis or Tulsa.

Foot soldiers should have been sufficient to pull Labac into their web, but the unexpected appearance of the fomori had scattered the plan like ashes to the wind. And then there was the girl to consider. Obviously a Hollow One. No threat there. Those who dwelled on the fringes of the Traditions were nothing more than wishful children finger-painting on the walls of an empty playroom. But Kublek was thankful for small mercies. From Rogers' report, spoken with his dying breath, it appeared the girl had saved the One from the fomori.

Labac was too valuable to lose to the Nephandi's obscene, perverse ways. His power, if it were truly as potent as predicted, would better serve the needs of the Technocracy. If he could not be persuaded to see things their way, then death was the only option. Labac was a wild card, one that could not be allowed into the hands of either the Traditions or the Nephandi. All the signs indicated he could be the One the death-loving children who called themselves Euthanatos had been cultivating as a messiah, refining an Avatar through successive cycles of death and rebirth. *If he were the One*, the repercussions could rock the Technocracy's foundations as surely as the recent earthquake had shaken the city's foundations.

The gravity of the situation demanded a less subtle display of force, Kublek acknowledged. The option gave him little solace.

The assistance of Iteration X, the militaristic masters of cyborg technology, was necessary.

■ ■ ■

My jaw throbbed with a dull ache as if I'd just had a couple of teeth removed and the dentist hadn't used enough Novocain. Opening my eyes, I saw Death and thought I'd died and gone to comic book heaven. But her hair color was wrong, and I quickly remembered what had happened. Or as much as my disturbed mind would allow. It seemed like a dream within an nightmare.

Her fresh scent and a hint of Patchouli was comforting, sensual. The sensation of my head resting on her thigh was pure delight. I could feel her essence through the black lycra encasing her firm legs, sensed rather than felt the taut muscles under my head. I tasted female pheromones on the tip of my tongue, intoxicated by our proximity. Every sense heightened, I came to full consciousness, nerve endings flooded with hyper-awareness.

She gasped as I sat up.

"Wipe that stupid smirk off your face," she said. "It makes me want to throw up."

"Thanks," I muttered, rubbing my jaw.

We were in Candlestick Park, seated on a small incline under a tree.

She stood, and began pacing. "You don't know, do you?"

"What? That I'm with the most beautiful girl I've ever laid eyes on?" I tried to smile, but my swollen jaw flared a warning.

She groaned. "Oh, shit. You don't have a damn clue, do you?"

Her right hand strayed to the necklace dipping enticingly between her breasts.

"You *are* James Alexander Labac, right?"

"That's me."

"What does Magick mean to you?"

"Siegfried and Roy," I replied. "The Amazing Randi. Bill Bixby in *The Magician*."

I thought she was going to hurl at my last comment. Instead, she worried her bottom lip with her teeth while she nervously fingered the necklace.

"Really funny. I mean Magick with a 'K.'"

"Like Crowley and that kind of stuff? *Love Under Will*. The O.T.O. The Order of the Golden Dawn?"

She nodded. "At least you know something."

"Victorian Parlor psychosis. Repressed fantasies. Sax Rohmer and W.B. Yeats pretending they were part of something more arcane than the Freemasons. Whichever way you spell it, a bunch of 19th century bullshit."

"Bloody smartass," she spat. "You think this is a game? Roberto's dead at the hands of the Nephandi, the Clique destroyed, every twisted faction in this city out for your blood —"

"I don't care if your boyfriend's dead. Your so-called friends have desert —"

"You know, don't you?"

"What?" I didn't know what the hell she was talking about.

"I said Roberto's name, and you knew immediately." Tears welled in her eyes. "Stupid bastard."

She stooped into a crouch. I didn't know if the last comment was directed at me or not. Her hands stroked the dry dirt next to an exposed root.

"You're adopted," she said suddenly. "Your parents are Rachel and Louis Labac. He's French. A millionaire industrialist. She's from New England. Amherst. Old stock. They spend most of the year in Hawaii, pay the rent on that over-priced apartment you live in."

"You my parole officer or something?" I shot back, my voice laced with vitriol.

She recoiled like I'd slapped her. My tone, the sense of command, surprised even me.

"My turn," I said. "Your name's Kara Turner. The only daughter of a Buckinghamshire stockbroker who hanged himself when you were sixteen. After the funeral, you pulled all your savings from the National Westminster in High Wycombe, where you lived, and bought a one-way ticket to New York. You worked the bar in a number of downtown dives until you started shooting heroin. You nearly O.D'd at The Vault, but got your act together. You're a vegan, your star sign is Pisces, and you fell in love with Roberto the moment you met him —"

"Still love him, you asshole," she fired back, then sighed.

"You are the One, aren't you? No one knows about my Dad. But you … can see inside me."

I looked down, embarrassed. I knew what seemed to be a million tiny facts about Kara, from her favorite song to the day her period was due.

But how?

My head started to spin so fast I could have been on a carnival ride.

So many questions. Feeling so close to her despite the animosity and resentment crackling like static in the space between us, emotions fueled by fear and a disturbing attraction. The touch of her thigh still warmed my bruised face. Her smell tantalized my nose.

As I looked at her, and she raised her face, those intense green eyes meeting mine, I was vaguely aware of a helicopter circling over Hunter's Point. Kara hesitated, tried to speak. Words weren't possible, but the tears were. I could hear them crest from her eyelids, roll down her cheeks as clearly as I heard the bay waves lap the rocks half a mile away.

"Are you familiar with Numerology?" she managed to say while choking back a sob. She wiped a hand across her eyes, trying to gather her composure.

"The Power of Numbers? Yeah, I've read about it."

"James Alexander Labac," she said, sniffing. "Add the letters of your name, it comes out to seven, the number of the Mage. Add the combined value of your birthdate —"

"July 9th, 1970."

"— it adds up to 22, also a number of power."

"James. A mutation of the Hebrew, *Jacobus*, meaning 'supplanter.'" I added smartly.

"Alexander. Greek, meaning 'defender of men.'"

She paused. "What triggered your Awakening?"

"My what?"

"What did you do to stimulate your Avatar into awareness? Roberto theorized something would act as a catalyst, but the vision he had wasn't clear—"

The helicopter's drone suddenly grew louder, fracturing the conversation, and we both looked in the direction of the noise.

The helicopter swooped low and two figures tumbled out, gracefully pirouetting to the ground twenty feet below them; marionettes with invisible strings. Kara's eyes flashed like neon. "HIT Marks! Run!"

Now what?

As the figures landed, they both cast off their long leather dusters to reveal advanced weaponry and started up the hill towards us.

"Run!" Kara screamed, but I reached out and held her hand. She tried to pull away but my grip was firm.

A preternatural calm surrounded me as I felt my conscious mind submerge under a wave of instinct. From deep inside me an *a priori* response rose to the fore. I drew Kara into my arms as I projected a transparent blue energy cocoon around us. My consciousness split into a parallax viewpoint, and I watched the scene from a high angle, as if I were no longer in my body.

The HIT Marks hesitated, then opened fire. Heat-seeking bullets homed in on us, their lethal velocity suddenly halted as they connected with the plasmoid wall of the protective field. Kara shivered with fear beside me, and my conscious self trembled in sympathy.

This wasn't happening. None of it was real. Art, always the joker, must have slipped me an hallucinogen, his idea of a prank. But the scene below me, in front of me, was all too real. This wasn't a sequence out of *The Fantastic Four*, and Sue Storm wasn't the one protecting us with a force field — I was, drawing power from the earth beneath my feet.

My body stiffened as I inhaled slowly, deeply, drawing Chi, the life force, into the depths of my Chakras, filling my energy channels. Exhaling, I pushed outwards, the energy field expanding, rippling out like a silent nuclear blast. The energy waves sliced through the HIT Marks, severing flesh from bones reinforced with Titanium, disintegrating bio-microchips, melting wet ware circuitry.

Kara gasped, and I cried out as my consciousness plummeted back into my body. For an instant I felt like I'd leaped off Niagara Falls, my falling body pummeled by tons of icy water. I spasmed, fell to my knees, and looked up. The helicopter hovered low overhead, and I could see the co-pilot pointing in our direction, his face a mask of disbelief. He gestured frantically for the pilot to take the chopper up and away. It banked sharply to the right and headed off over the Bay, disappearing into the dense storm clouds suddenly coalescing around the park.

"What … what did you do?" Kara asked, dazed.

"I don't know," I replied, staggering up on rubbery legs. "But I think we better get going."

I started to walk down the incline towards the remains of the HIT Marks, Kara following hesitantly behind me, obviously wary of the still twitching body parts. As we approached the one nearest us, its eyes opened, the right pupil dilating into a red dot. White mucus bubbled from its mouth. Guts, both organic and plastic, leaked fluids into the soil. The air was thick with the smell of oil, blood, and something unidentifiable. Servo motors whirred, then clicked off as a final death spasm trembled through the severed torso.

"A cyborg," Kara said, although I'd already guessed that. "Hyper Intelligence Tech Mark V's. It means Iteration X are on your tail as well as the New World Order."

I looked blankly at Kara. "George Bush and Dan Quayle?"

"No, not governmental puppets — the real thing. A division of the Technocratic Conventions. Remember Orwell's 1984? Big Brother? The Order controls the State, the media. Everything you hear, read, or see is their propaganda."

I turned to Kara, grasping both her hands in mine. "How about speaking in plain English? You've got a lot of explaining to do."

She tried to pull away as our eyes met, but my grip was firm. A connection linked our minds, and I was suddenly swimming in not just the facts of her life but the emotional whirlpool of her memories. The sensation was so intimate it transcended sex. It was both beautiful and unnerving. I saw things no one other than Kara had seen from her exact point of view. Memories of parties, of making love to Roberto, of ritual, of the friends who were now dead. I let her hands go.

For an instant, I couldn't speak. The connection made words redundant. But we weren't safe here in the open.

"Come on," I managed to say.

Kara blinked at me as if waking from a dream. "Where?"

"Let's go get something to eat," I said as I continued walking. "I don't know about you, but I'm starving."

■ ■ ■

Kara was scared. Not just because of Labac's seemingly smug indifference to their predicament. She had already lost one lover, and now she was falling in love with the man sitting in front of her. As absurd as it sounded, she was in love with James Labac. Something had happened. Roberto was right. Labac had power, and the more time she spent in close proximity to his Avatar, the deeper the feeling grew. It wasn't the caffeine high of adolescent infatuation, nor the intense union of two hungry souls joining beneath passion-tangled sheets, but a spiritual love so pure, so clean, that thoughts of physical contact drew waves of guilt as much as pleasure.

Labac deftly plucked the last piece of sushi from his board, dipped it in the dish of tamari, and swallowed the slice of uri in two bites. Kara had hardly touched her lunch special. Adrenaline still pulsed through her system from both the encounter with the fomori and the intensity of her brief mind meld with James. The sushi had been his idea. Raw fish was the last thing she needed.

"Are you going to eat that?" he gestured with his chopsticks. It was the first thing he'd said since they'd ordered.

"No," she relied softly, pushing her food in his direction.

Labac signaled the Japanese waitress to order more sake.

Kara hated the restaurant, although the music playing on the CD-juke was okay. Cat Rapes Dog faded, and Transmission by Joy Division started up. She looked into her lap, tears in her eyes. As if sensing her sadness, Labac reached out to caress the back of her left hand.

She looked up hesitantly, both not wanting and deeply desiring to lock eyes with him again. Their eyes met for an instant, then he directed his attention to the window and the parade of people walking by.

"Kara ..." he paused. "I don't understand any of this ... and I need you to explain ... as best you can."

His facade of smugness had dissolved, revealing naked uncertainty, the face of a lost little boy wandering unfamiliar streets, searching desperately for a way home. A maternal emotion flared inside her. She grasped his hand. "I'll try."

Labac continued to look out the window, avoiding her eyes.

"You're an Orphan, both literally and in our terms. You don't understand what's happened to you. You've Awakened. It was inevitable. But someone accelerated the process, used a catalyst. You can use your power to shape reality —"

"I don't understand but *I know* ... I feel something . .. more alive than ever ... I look into your eyes and I know you. I can feel your essence ... *become* your essence."

He paused, staring into the middle distance, holding a thought. Whatever it was, was unpleasant.

"I can feel concepts ... the Nephandi ... Tass, Quintessence ... but I don't understand them," he said. His face changed, a tremor of revulsion sweeping across the surface like a windswept sand dune. He looked down at the sushi. In the blink of an eye, Labac was elsewhere.

The restaurant faded like a mirage, replaced by an endless white beach. Beneath his toes the sand was alive. He could feel every grain; and every piece was either an idea, concept, thought, feeling, or sensation. The sand was Quintessence, the raw matter of the universe in condensed form; the beach the palpable shape of the universe, stretching further than the average human mind could conceive.

Labac stooped to scoop up a handful of the fine grains. In his hand, the pile shaped itself into an elaborate sand castle he'd once built as a child on vacation. And this was Tass, Quintessence stored in physical form.

He let the grains slip through his fingers, the Tass dissipating, yet its energy undiminished, as he turned to the endless horizon line. Far, far away down the beach's gentle slope, a sea of darkness lapped at the shoreline. He started to run towards it. And as he ran, it drew further away, as if the sea were retreating from him. He ran faster, his legs pumping harder, feet pummeling the sand. The faster he ran, the further away the onyx sea appeared, leading him, drawing him, down the beach which turned from sand to pebbles, to sharp rocks, to jagged teeth lacerating his skin. Labac stopped suddenly, an intense static roar filling his ears, a deep black noise which pierced his skull. Then he smelled them. *The Nephandi* ... waiting, hungry, beyond the horizon line, waiting to break through the barrier to feast on the Quintessence, their breath that of gas chambers, of charnel houses.

"No," he whispered, squeezing shut his eyes.

■ ■ ■

"... you all right?" Kara's voice echoed, sounding as if it came from the end of a long tunnel. Labac opened his eyes and was back in the restaurant.

He gasped for breath. "I need ... to put this all into context," he said loudly, color returning to his face. His voice dropped as the waitress brought more sake. Labac took a drink, then looked up at Kara, trying not to make the connection.

"The world's changed, hasn't it?" He paused. "No. The

world's always been this way. *I've changed.* Like I was sleeping all these years and what I thought was real was just a series of interconnected images — scenes from a film directed by someone else — dreams programmed by others. This morning I woke up, and now the dream's over. I'm alive at last." He picked up his tumbler of sake, toasting himself. "Here's to the rest of my life."

Labac downed the drink and smiled.

Kara was amazed at how fast he was figuring things out, how easily he accepted his Awakening. Her transition from Sleeper to Orphan had not been easy. The smug expression was back on James's face, but he wouldn't have much of a life left unless they came up with a plan.

"You seem to instinctively grasp so much," she said, "but there's more, much more than I know or understand or could try to explain. I'll have to do the best I can, but we don't have much time. We need a plan, and we've got to find somewhere safe."

She looked out the window, hesitating, not daring to suggest …

"You want me to enter your mind again, don't you?" Labac stroked the back of her hand. "Do you think that's smart in a public place?"

"We don't have much choice. What else are we going to do, go find an alleyway? Look, it's the quickest way for you to learn, but —" she broke off, worrying her bottom lip with her teeth, "please, don't feel you can just plunder all my memories. Only take what you need. There are some things I'd like to keep to myself."

"I'm sorry. What happened before … I didn't know it was happening. I didn't mean to … the memories of your father —"

"Just do it, okay?" She squeezed his hand, and looked deeply into Labac's eyes.

■ ■ ■

As he entered the room, all eyes turned towards Kublek. Varbage of Iteration X squinted at Kublek through his dense optical filters, barely concealing the contempt churning in his bioelectronic chest. Itsumaki, the Syndicate representative seated beside him, nodded respectfully, a crisp white linen suit covering his Yakuza tattoos. At the furthest end of the table sat Driebeck and Shooter, Void Engineer and Proginator, respectively, sullenly whispering between themselves. *Probably arguing scientific minutiae as usual*, Kublek thought as he sat down.

"Gentlemen, thank you for your swift response to my call," Kublek started. "This Emergency Symposium is now in order."

"Why has Labac Awakened so soon?" Varbage jumped in before Kublek could continue. "We had time to plan — *had plans* — and now where are we? Your welcoming committee, dead."

He pointed at Kublek. "Two HIT Marks destroyed by an Orphan. He hasn't even been sentient for a day, yet he's capable of all this—." Varbage threw his arms up in the air.

"The predictions weren't wrong," Shooter interjected, deliberately lowering his voice to force the others to listen. "The premature Awakening was an accident, a fluke. We know who is responsible, and why."

"Why wasn't I informed of this sooner?" Kublek demanded, his face flushing with anger. "I am responsible for this operation, and —"

"No one is questioning your authority," continued Shooter. "We only learned the identity of the responsible party an hour ago, barely minutes after you called. Needless to say, the party is now in our custody and is being cloned as we speak."

"Who?" Kublek leaned across the table, clenching his fist as if he were about to punch Shooter.

"And why?" added Varbage.

■ ■ ■

Kara had become the sea and I was swimming her oceans.
Instead of fighting the waves of memory or the undertow of
emotions, I let them carry me on their ceaseless tide, mindful
this time to swim in another direction if the emotions were
too personal. I tried to steer clear of Roberto, but it was
impossible; his involvement in her life and their love for
each other had a direct bearing on my situation and our
current predicament. I let the sexual memories wash over
me, through me, and did not linger on the details. By now,
I was more concerned with what she knew of me and how I
had transformed from Sleeper to Mage.

I knew now what I was, if not *who*. I knew more than I
ever comprehended I knew. I learned a language to speak,
a new vocabulary of understanding.

Awakening. Avatar. Ascension.

My Avatar — my soul — had been freed from the
blindness of deception, and was now on the path to
enlightenment, capable of sculpting reality into a perfect
shape.

Dynamic Reality. Quintessence ... the world was no
longer mundane, but an endless flow of dynamic potentials,
and through learning, study, experience, I could become an
index of those possibilities. For every cause, and effect and
even the tiniest act of creation — a half-finished thought
— added to Quintessence. Circles. Cycles, wheels within
wheels. Yin/Yang. Everything made sense.

I saw Kara's Awakening, only "seeing" isn't adequate to
describe the sensation. "Feeling" is inadequate, too. I was
more than her memories; I became them. Awakened in New
York during rehabilitation following a near-fatal overdose.
The path for Enlightenment leading her westward, like a
pioneer of old. Through Kansas to Phoenix, from Arizona
to Nevada, where an encounter with the vampiric Kindred

in Las Vegas had almost sent her into the clutches of the
hellish Nephandi. She'd have died then, three years ago,
were it not for the intervention of Simon, a musician who
had belonged to the Cult of Ecstasy. He had turned his back
on the bacchanal debaucheries and other excesses of the
Cult and now roamed, a solitary ascetic troubadour, with
no allegiance to any Tradition.

Simon had friends in L.A. It seemed as good a place as
any. Within days of arrival, sharing space with Kimberly
D'Arc and her brother in their downtown factory loft,
Roberto entered the picture.

Roberto Wiseman. Poet. Musician. Former Marine.
Son of an Italian mother from Naples and a Jewish father
from Vienna, South Dakota. They called him "The Wise
One.". Like Simon, he'd been initiated into the Cult of
Ecstasy on Awakening, and he, too, had turned his back on
their hedonistic lifestyle in a need for something more. He'd
traveled the length and breadth of the country, hitchhiking,
scratching out a living any which way he could, either with
his guitar or by washing dishes, more often than not. One
night in Kentucky, he heard voices in his dreams, and those
voices led him to Serena, the Dreamspeaker. From that time
on, Roberto discovered the deeper meaning he had been
striving for. As a shaman under Serena's tutelage, he
communed with Gaia, danced on fire, climbed on air, and
began the Vision Quest.

Kara's memory of what Roberto had told her was vague
at this point. It seemed he had been reluctant to go into
details, but while out in Utah, he'd had a series of visions.
In one, he'd seen himself as the Deacon of a Cabal composed
of members from all branches of the Traditions: Akashic
Brothers sharing their Zen teachings with Euthanatos
disciples, Hermes children collaborating with Hollow Ones,
exchanging their arcane occult knowledge — the whole
spectrum. The focus was not on dissatisfaction with any one
Tradition, it was the merging of the spheres of experience

towards one Avatar, one holistic Ascension. Another vision revealed the true meaning of this union — not merely to unite or to form a cohesive front against the stranglehold of the Technocracy, the dark desires of the Nephandi, or the insane, nihilistic urges of the Marauders. The meaning, written in signs, symbols, and portents, indicated a time of Great Darkness was coming, an Armageddon which would destroy Mage and Sleeper alike. The Ascension war was pure folly; Ascension would be rendered meaningless in the face of utter extinction. Gaia — the Earth — would die, and with Her, the light of Quintessence would be gone forever.

There was yet another vision, one he had been able to share in part with Kara as a result of their union. The memory was so clear, so potent I could smell the scent of fresh mown grass as they sat in a South Pasadena park, could feel Roberto's gentle hands as he looked into my (Kara's) eyes, and shared the vision.

A great and almighty Darkness, a transdimensional cancer of entropy and decay, touched the outer ripples of awareness, eating away at the illumination, corrupting the Avatar mosaic. Its pernicious influence spread ... then stopped, its progress halted by a burst of blinding radiance. And in the center of that radiance stood a figure. A man.

And that Man resembled me.

Only it was more than me. He was not the James Alexander Labac of flesh, but rather, a figure of crystal, light radiating from its heart. The face looked like mine, but the image wavered and I couldn't confirm what I saw.

The vision was so intense I recoiled, breaking the connection with Kara.

"Are you okay?"

"No," I mumbled as my stomach churned, raw fish and rice wine bubbling like a witch's cauldron in my gut. Waves of nausea pounded in my head.

"Excuse m—"

I made it to the restroom just in time and was violently sick.

■ ■ ■

The symbiosis they shared had magnified tenfold during the mind meld, and as Kara sat beside Labac on the Turk Street bench, she could taste the after-bite of bile in his mouth. The color was finally returning to his face, which, as she studied him carefully in profile, she noticed spoke of a quiet nobility and inner strength. He'd hardly said a word since they'd paid the bill and left the restaurant. Words, however, weren't necessary. She understood his confusion and the weight of responsibility resting on his shoulders. From video store clerk to Mage to Messiah all in a few hours. It was enough to crack one's sanity.

"Too many damn questions," he muttered, staring intently at the cracks in the sidewalk. "It's giving me a king-sized headache."

Kara reached out her hand, softly squeezing his to reassure him he wasn't alone. The base of her skull flared with simpatico tension.

"I don't know who we can turn to. Who — if *anyone* — could give guidance. Our Clique was pretty much made of Outcasts. Everyone, apart from me, had been a part of another group, and all were dissatisfied. Simon had little faith in integrating with others in the Traditions. Roberto tried on many occasions to bring groups together, to get people to listen to him, but the politics ... " She waved a hand dismissively. "Forget it. No one seems to be able to transcend their differences unless they're caught up in a direct conflict."

Labac nodded. "How did Roberto learn it was me?"

"He had other visions. Not complete ones, just fragments, sometimes nothing more than random images: a man and a woman arguing as they drove through the

Hollywood Hills, A young boy looking down at the lights of L.A., James Dean and Jim Morrison seated at the bar of the allnight cafe in Hopper's *Nighthawks At The Diner* —"

"What?!" Labac's interrupted her, incredulous.

"Yes, scenes from —"

"My movie," Labac finished for her. "He saw *Boulevard of Broken Mirrors?*" Kara nodded. "Only he saw all that before we caught it at the short film festival."

"You saw it, too?"

"Yes. I really liked it. Why'd you drop out of film school?"

Labac shook his head, a slight smile on his lips, still angered and delighted that his film had affected her so much. "I'd never have believed it. Mind you, after this morning I think I can believe anything. If Al and Tipper Gore walked naked down Castro Street leading a nudist parade, I wouldn't bat an eyelid."

He paused, the smile fading, a serious frown creasing his brow as if he were in pain as he addressed her question. "I lost all faith in the power of movies to change people's lives for the better, to enrich reality by being creative. The movie business doesn't want creativity, doesn't want to take chances." He shrugged.

"That was the nascent Mage in you. The desire, the need, the vision to Ascend. You were just looking at the world from a Mundane perspective," she replied.

"As soon as we saw the film, Roberto was certain you had to be the one in the visions. It wasn't difficult to find out all about James Labac. Discovering where you'd gone after you dropped out of USC was a major pain, though. While I don't believe in coincidences any more, I do think it was dumb luck that Simon ran into your old roommate at The Way Down, a few nights after the screening, and they got to talking movies —"

"Roommate?" Labac tensed. "Who?"

"Rick, of course. Rick Garris."

Labac's face drained of color.

"What's wrong?"

"Describe him."

Kara hesitated. His aura had turned a violent shade of purple flecked with black. "I never met him, but … Simon said something … um … oh, yeah. He had really long hair."

"How long?"

"Like down to his ass. Simon said he'd never seen a guy with such long hair. He wore it in a braided ponytail."

Labac stiffened. "And what did this 'Rick Garris' do?"

"Computer software designer, I think."

He stood up so suddenly Kara gasped. Every angle of his body vibrated with barely controlled anger, his aura a strobing kaleidoscope of conflicting colors. He looked up at the dark clouds leaden with the pregnant promise of rain; then turned, hailing a cab.

"Wait! Where are we going?"

He didn't answer; the sky did. Lightning split the sky somewhere out over the bay, a thunderclap rumbling in on its heels.

"Rick Garris is dead," Labac answered through clenched teeth. *"He died two years ago."*

"What?!" Kara shouted back as a second bolt of lightning whiplashed almost directly overhead, the accompanying thunder a sonic boom.

"He died in my arms. Suicide. Only I found him too late." He looked around, searching for a passing cab. "Taxi!" He shouted, as he spotted one turning the corner.

"What happened?" Kara could feel the pain inside Labac as sharply as if someone were opening her sternum with a bone saw.

He shook his head. "Details don't matter. Hollywood ate his soul."

The cab pulled up at the curb. Jim opened the door, waving her in first as the sky opened up like a biblical deluge.

"The corner of Lombard and Van Ness," Jim told the driver as he slid in beside Kara, who looked at him, bewildered.

"Where are we going?"

"We're going to visit 'Rick'," he said, gritting his teeth.

■ ■ ■

The fomori watched the cab pull out into a gap in the traffic, hesitating only as long as needed to be discrete, then mounted the Kawasaki Ninja, turning the engine over with a swift downward kick. It had spent its life — its old life — as conspicuous as an ink blot on a businessman's white silk shirt, but being black with a pale, Caucasian birthmark had made Andre Devaux more than noticeable, it had marked him a freak. At six feet and seven inches, his height had only made his life worse. The taunts, looks of revulsion, the beatings. Drugs and the search for arcane knowledge had provided brief solace. Then *they* came to him and the fabric of his existence was reshaped, the tapestry of his flesh rewoven to their exotic designs. A'Duhl, as he was now known to a chosen few, preferred his new life, his skin of black leather and the helmet which perpetually covered his head.

A'Duhl directed the bike out into the traffic. Beneath the mirrored visor, his luminescent blue eyes glowed with excitement.

Soon. Soon he would feast on the girl's succulent flesh, sucking her Avatar into his hollow, hungry bones.

■ ■ ■

The Emergency Symposium was in disarray, and Kublek could feel his control slipping through his fingers like grains of sand. It was obvious the Void Engineers and Progenitors had their own agenda concerning Labac and damn the rest of the Technocracy.

"Such power," Varbage muttered to himself. "He could be the One."

"Until we have him in our hands, we will not be certain," Itsumaki added. "Ultimately, it makes no difference. We can — and will — control him."

Itsumaki didn't care so long as the Syndicate could capitalize on Labac's talents, put him out on the road playing Vegas, Berlin, Miami, like that puppet Copperfelt. The Mundanes, thinking the performer's act was all illusion and derring-do, paid over $100,000 million last year to watch something they could barely dream of, let alone figure out how it was done. The Syndicate took 80% of the profits. They were satisfied. Varbage only cared about the potential weapons technology which could be integrated with Labac's wild card talent. His litany of Psi-cannons and Ecto-Plasma-Guns bored Kublek, who could understand the Progenitor's interest in Labac — the cloning potentials were enormous — but what could the Engineers want from him?

"Of most pressing importance is where he is," Itsumaki said loudly, stopping Varbage mid-rant.

Shooter's cellular trilled before anyone could reply. He flicked open the phone and listened, a smile crawling across his lips like a charnel house maggot.

"Mmm," he mused. "Good. Very good."

He placed the phone down on the table, slid it towards Kublek.

"Our fox has been sighted. Time for you to send in your hounds."

Kublek picked up the phone, containing his anger at Shooter's impudence. One day, *very soon* ... Shooter would wear scars instead of that supercilious grin.

As they ran up the steps towards Art Baisden's

apartment, Labac's aura flared with such violence that Kara couldn't breathe. His adrenal rush was hers, but his uncontrolled anger frightened her. When he'd entered her, she had tasted his essence, drank deep from the quantal positive energy flowing through his spiritual body. So gentle, so compassionate. But this … this incipient violence, so merciless, so nova-hot …

She tasted blood, vomit, sushi, sake, and the desire to tear flesh from bone. The passions were so strong she became almost sick to her stomach.

A plump Hippie opened the door to the apartment as Labac reached the top step.

"Hey, Jim —"

Before the figure could utter another word, Labac sprang into the opening, punched Baisden full in the face, and nearly busted the door off its hinges as he landed, legs spread, straddling the prone figure on the floor.

"What the fuck happened last night?" He asked in between gritted teeth.

A spear of ferocious anger plunged deep into Kara's forehead as she reached the landing, Labac's emotions exploding inside her, and she collapsed onto the floor.

■ ■ ■

Control escaped me with every breath as I stood astride Art's overweight body, watching blood leak from his broken nose, his left hand squeezing the bridge as he tried to stop the flow.

"Aww, you *sonofabitch!* — that's the last time I let you get stoned at my apartment! What you hit me for, you crazy bastard?!"

Art wiggled on his back, snaking from between my spread legs like a floundering Manatee in a silk kimono. "Owhh, I think you broke my nose, you loony-toons bastard."

"Good," I said, noticing Kara had fainted. I picked her

up like a sack of laundry and propped her up in the old, over-stuffed armchair next to the small hallway. She murmured something as she started to come around.

Art pulled himself up, clutching the radiator for support with one hand, his nose with the other.

"I want answers, and I want them now," I said, slamming the door behind me.

"Jesus, what's bugging you?"

"What happened last night?"

"We smoked a joint, drank a couple of beers, talked — don't you remember?"

"No. And? —"

"I showed you the prototype Virtual Reality program I've been working on."

"So?" I was beginning to get impatient.

"You really got off on it," Art said. "You've got a hell of a punch, know that?"

I sighed, trying to control my anger. "Sorry," I said with no sincerity.

Art shook his head to throw off the shock. His long ponytail whipped behind him. Kara groaned, coming to.

"Let me get a Kleenex, then we'll talk," he said.

He headed in the direction of the small bathroom opposite the bedroom, and I turned to check on Kara. I caressed her cheek. She flinched at my touch.

"You okay?"

Her eyes fluttered as she floated into full consciousness.

Art returned, dabbing his nose. "Thanks, this is all I need."

"What's the theme of the VR?"

He blinked. "*Personal Quest*. It's a cyber-interactive program. You mentally project an image and the pick-up makes it 3-D, then extrapolates the symbolism, indexes Jungian archetypes, peels away the camouflage and hey, presto! — instant therapy. You were really getting off on the mandalas, though."

"I don't get it." My mind was split between wanting to beat Baisden to a pulp because he'd been passing himself off as Rick and learning more about *Personal Quest*. Instinct told me it had triggered my Awakening. But something about Art's tone said he was holding back.

"I took wet ware capabilities and turned them into an external bio-neurological format. It's less expensive, easily accessible, and is gonna make me rich. It's like neurolinguistic programming, but works on a whole other level. Forget Tony Robbins and *Awaken the Giant Within*. Like Coke, this is the_*real thing*." Art gave a lupine grin, licking his lips; the Big, Bad Wolf had just eaten Red Riding Hood and was deeply satisfied.

"Okay. Next question. Why have you been passing yourself off as Rick Garris?"

"I don't know what the hell you're talking about," he replied, as Kara mumbled something behind me.

Kara opened her eyes, gasping as she looked at Art Baisden.

"He has no aura," she said, shaking herself fully awake.

"Huh?' I replied noticing Art fumble in the folds of his kimono.

"He's a clone," Kara explained. "That means —"

"Nothing," the Baisden-clone interjected pulling out a 9 mm Beretta, "except new and improved. And on the right path."

"Progenitor scum," Kara spat.

The Baisden-clone smiled. "Hardly. Cleansed of dangerous thoughts, given direction."

"What's going on?" I asked. I knew Baisden was up to something, but this was more than I bargained for from a guy who'd always seemed as harmless as a pet hamster.

"Simple. You will join the Technocracy or perish, reduced to a pile of genetic sludge in a DNA tank after they have extracted your Avatar and harnessed your energies. You," he waved the gun at me, "are too powerful to be allowed to stand outside the Order of the way things must be. Baisden — I — was a fool to think that by triggering your Awakening and fulfilling the Prophesy, introducing a wild card into the deck, that I could change the status quo —"

"What Prophesy?"

"It's rumored the Euthanatos have been leading a soul through many reincarnations, cultivating a messiah," Kara explained.

"Absolutely right," the Baisden-clone concurred, the wolf-grin back on its lips. "I was initiated after a near-death experience, learned the Truth, and began to participate in the process of Good Death —"

"Murder," Kara interjected, scornfully. "That's all it is; pleasure in killing innocent people."

"Exactly. But no one is innocent — the flock of humanity are guilty of squandering the gift of life," he sneered.

"Soon, however," the Baisden-clone continued, "I learned the real intent behind the beauty of execution."

"The Prophecy," I said.

"Right," he replied.

"And you are the fulfillment of that Prophecy. And I couldn't allow anyone to stand in the way. Even my brothers were wrong. They saw a Messiah who would unite; I saw an agent of change, a catalyst for chaos that would unite all in the Ultimate Death. I certainly couldn't permit that fool Roberto to get his hands on you, bring you to awareness, convince James Labac he was the Messiah to all Mages."

"Motherfucker!" Kara screamed. "You betrayed us! How —"

"Your friend, simple Simon," he replied quietly, turning to face her.

"But ultimately, it's of no consequence what happened to Roberto or the rest of your pathetic Clique. My actions were right for the wrong reasons. Now I know better."

The fomori reached the landing, hesitating outside the door. Its hypersensitive ears could hear the conversation within, but its attention was focused on the girl's smell. The Masters hadn't allowed him to consume a soul for months but had promised this one if he delivered the Other.

His internal mouths salivated etheric acid beneath his leather skin as he knocked on the door, straining to speak with atrophied vocal-chords.

███

As the Balsden-clone's attention shifted from me to Kara, I exhaled slowly, releasing my anger. I inhaled deeply, summoning energy. Every instinct screamed escape. The gun didn't bother me, but who knew what else the clone had up its sleeve? The forces of the Technocracy were building around us as surely as the storm outside. We'd walked into a trap, and I sensed the jaws closing. The clone wasn't explaining to gloat or confess; it was stalling for time.

"Simon was weak, his will so easy to manipulate," the clone sneered at Kara. "The perfect Judas goat."

Deep inside I knew I had the potential to be whatever I willed. But before I could decide a course of action, there was a knock at the door.

"UPS," called a muffled, barely human voice.

Then the door exploded in a hail of wooden splinters.

███

Kara stood, her dizziness completely gone, exorcised by anger and a sudden insatiable desire to rip the vile human facsimile limb from limb. The fact it wasn't the real Baisden didn't matter; he had suffered only Gaia-knows at the hands

of the Technocracy and their machines. She hoped it had
involved agonies beyond description. But every muscle in
her body strained at the desire to pulp the sneering figure
in front of her.

As she took a step towards it, a wave of concussive power
threw her to the floor, shards of pine lancing her leather-
jacketed back.

■ ■ ■

The force of the etheric blast hurled me against the wall,
my head smacking against the glass of the framed
Maplethorpe print above the bookshelves. The Baisden-
clone stumbled back against the computer monitor,
knocking it to the floor. It almost dropped the gun as it
struggled to stand upright. The bookcase crashed forward
as I used it for leverage, pushing my back to the wall as I
turned to face the intruder.

Fomori, my mind echoed as the figure standing in what
was the doorway unzipped its leather racing biker's one-
piece, revealing raw, suppurating musculature. It was
exposed, cancerous nerve endings, a nest of pouting vagina-
like mouths spotting the weeping torso like sexual stigmata.
Protoplasmic tongues the length of moray eels emerged from
the orifices, sniffing blindly at the ozone-laced air, then
snaked forward, exposing rows of tiny sharp teeth as their
gland-like faces opened.

The clone's face froze for an instant, then the fomori
advanced. Baisden fired in quick succession.

I dove to the floor, covering Kara's back with my own.
Shards of wood pierced my flesh. My hands cradled her
head, turned her face to mine as Baisden screamed above
the percussive report of the gun.

Kara's eyes, wide with shock and fear, searched my face
for reassurance.

Quick, my mind spoke to hers *think of some place else.*

What?

Where do you feel safe?

"Lookout Point," she said, her voice cracking as the fomori stepped over us, its protoplasmic parasites funneling into the clone's flesh, ignoring the bullets slapping into exposed innards.

Good. Visualize. Think. 'I want to be there. gazing at the Pacific'.

"Hhh?"

Do it!

"Lookout Point," she said before I kissed her, our minds focusing on her memories of sea and sand, of whitecaps dancing in the ocean as an over-ripe blood-orange sun sank on the horizon.

I kissed her as I pulled my arms around her. Her lower lip bled as our tongues entwined. The taste of copper flooded my senses, silencing the clone's screams as we dissolved down to particle level, transformed to pure light ...

Two Months Later.

We escaped a fate worse than death that fateful day, and found ourselves sprawled on vibrant grass, miles from the slaughter at Art Baisden's apartment. We spent the night entwined in spiritual passion, our sweat-soaked bodies concealed by a clump of bushes, cocooned in an energy aura which kept the elements at bay. The following morning, we fled San Francisco.

Or at least we tried.

Kara's talents were many, car theft among them, and, after hot wiring a Geo Metro, we headed north. Across the Oakland bay Bridge, bypassing Berkeley, heading for Interstate 5, and several hours beyond that, Mount Shasta.

I knew then all the stories, the rumors I'd heard, were true; tales of the Sasquatch, of Pagan worship, and mysterious lights in the night sky.

Mount Shasta was a Mother Node of Quintessence, and the perfect place to hide, learn, and grow.

It was also an obvious place for the forces massing against us to investigate. Yet my naivete, and, I'll admit, hubris spurred by my newly realized potentials, blinded me to that fact. However, certain fortunate events halted our progress. But that is another story — one which resulted in our return to the Bay area.

The hows and whys don't need to be explained here.

We returned to San Francisco and adopted the guise of a Mundane couple — after all, who would think that the Mage whose powers the Technocracy and the Nephandi fear and seek to use for their own ends is the T-shirt seller who lives in a small apartment on Noe Street?

So we hide, and we wait for the day when we must act. That day won't be long in coming, but right now we have other matters to attend to.

I know now that I am not the Crystal Messiah of Roberto's vision. That formidable destiny awaits our unborn son, Christopher, who kicks softly in Kara's belly. I was but the funnel of genetic and spiritual energy; Kara is the vessel. From the moment of conception, as she felt my sperm fertilize her egg, we have known. At that precise nexus of merging came the knowledge.

And now we wait.

THE GREAT ESCAPE
■■■■■■■■■■■■■

Edo van Belkom

There were more than thirty minutes until show time, and the Pantages Theater was already half-full. From his backstage dressing room, Romano Minardi could hear the buzz of people growing steadily louder, could feel the air becoming thick with expectation. The feeling had always excited him, sharpened his magick, made him look forward to performing. Tonight, however, his excitement was tainted by a slash of worry. Mixed in with the usual anticipation, there was also a sickening feeling — a feeling of dread.

"Go see if he's out there," Romano said sharply from his seat in front of the makeup mirror, his ever-present cigarette dangling from the corner of his mouth.

Roxanne May pulled at her rhinestone-studded red dress, making sure it hugged her figure like a second skin. "The show's been sold-out for weeks, Roman." She adjusted the dress one last time. "There's no way he could have gotten a seat up front."

Romano butted out his cigarette in the overflowing ashtray and immediately took a fresh one from the crumpled pack on the vanity. "Yeah, but with the earthquake on Friday and the fog closing off the bridge, all kinds of people won't be showing up."

She took a few slinky steps toward him, then bent over his shoulder and looked at him in the mirror. "Stop worrying," she said. "He won't be there." She ran her fingers gently over the taut muscles of his back.

Romano tilted his head forward, allowing Roxanne's fingers to creep up over his neck and shoulders. For a moment he started to relax, Roxy's fingers working a magic of their own on his stiff, tense muscles. He breathed easier for a few moments, but Roxy's efforts weren't enough to stem the tide. The feeling of worry, perhaps even fear, rose up again from somewhere deep inside of him, washing over him in a wave.

He clenched his fist and slammed it down onto the vanity. Jars toppled. Lids bounced and rolled. "Dammit, Roxy! Just go and see if he's there."

Roxanne pulled her hands away from him as if he'd suddenly become scalding beneath her fingertips. "All right, all right," she said, turning for the door.

She left the room without another word.

Romano sat back in his chair and inhaled deeply on his cigarette. He'd been on tour for the past six months performing his particular brand of magic and illusion to sold-out theaters across the country. Tonight's show was the second in San Francisco and the second-to-last of the tour. Tomorrow the show moved to Los Angeles, where the tour had opened, for one last show. Then, with the tour completed, preparations would begin for a prime-time network television special that was scheduled for February's sweeps week.

But first he had to get through the last two shows, starting with tonight's. Normally, this evening's show would be just another performance — a two and a half hour mix of pounding rock music and sex appeal that made use of sleight of hand, age-old illusions and just a touch of coincidental magick. But ever since Seattle and the appearance of the man in the dark suit, Romano had been on edge. He'd tried to tell himself that the man in the dark suit was a fan, or an illusionist in his own right trying to learn something new about the art. But after the man in the dark suit had watched four consecutive shows in four different cities, each time from a seat that was exactly front-row center, Romano knew exactly what he was.

A Technomancer come to shut him down.

Romano took a long drag on the short stub of his cigarette and pinched off the butt with the tips of his fingers. Less than ten seconds passed before he lit up another.

He had kept his use of coincidental magick to a minimum, using it only in his finale, and even then not for more than a second or two. He had hoped to get through the tour without catching the attention of the Technocracy, but Arthur Gardner, the tour's road manager, had added extra shows in Milwaukee and Toronto, extending the tour by a week and giving the Technocracy more time to become aware of his use of magick.

Still, Romano was stubbornly confident that he could finish the tour untouched by the Technomancers. Part of him knew he was being foolish, but another part of him — a stronger part — knew it couldn't be helped. He was consumed by his desire to complete the tour and the television special — two crucial steps on the way to his Ascension — and he wasn't going to let anything stand in his way, not even a dark-suited Technomancer.

The door opened a crack, then slowly swung wide on its hinges. Roxanne stepped into the room, her pale lips pressed together into a tight, white line.

"Well?" asked Romano.

She closed the door behind her, turned to face him, and nodded. "He's out there. In the middle of the front row. He's just sitting there, not moving. Not even his eyes."

"Shit!" Romano turned back around, his head coming to rest in his upturned hands.

Roxanne was silent a few moments, then rushed across the room to be by his side. "Don't do the show, Roman," she pleaded. "I don't know what that guy's doing out there, but he gives me the creeps." She folded her arms across her chest as if to stave off a chill.

"I'm still doing the show." Romano's voice was impassive.

"But you don't know what he's doing out there. He could have a gun on him. Maybe he's just waiting to shoot you during the middle of the act."

"No," said Romano. "He's not going to shoot me."

She leaned over his shoulder, squinting her eyes against the rising cigarette smoke as she looked at him in the mirror. "How can you be so sure?"

"I just am."

Roxanne stood up, one hand on Romano's shoulder, the fingers of the other raking through his hair. "All right, then. If he's not stalking you, what is he doing?"

Romano had explained the mage world to Roxanne many times, but like most acolytes, she didn't always understand it. Some things she comprehended with ease, while others were absolutely incomprehensible to her. For a moment he considered telling her that the man in the dark suit was a talent scout of some sort, or maybe a big New York agent, but lying to her now didn't seem fair. Instead, he opted for the truth.

"He's a Technomancer," he said.

Roxanne continued to stroke his hair in silence, thinking. "Is he part of that stuff you were telling me about? The Teck-naw-cra-see?"

"The Technocracy, yes."

She twirled a lock of his thick black hair for a few more seconds, then abruptly stopped. "That still means he's here to get rid of you," she said, a sharp edge of realization in her voice.

"Maybe."

She stepped away from him and began pacing the room. "You can't do the show," she said matter-of-factly. "It's too dangerous. I'll just tell them you've taken ill and can't perform."

"No!" Romano cried, getting up from his chair. "I have to do the show. I have to complete the tour!" He paused for a moment, realizing he'd been shouting. "It's a necessary step toward my Ascension." He turned away from her to butt out his cigarette.

"Your Ascension?" she said. "Is this Ascension of yours worth the risk?"

"Yes."

Roxanne just glared at him, as if she'd come up against this sort of wall before. "I can't believe how stubborn you're being — even when you know it might get you killed."

"I can't help it. I'm a fanatic, a perfectionist. I can't leave something half-finished," Romano said smoothly, starting to put on the charm. "Besides, there's nothing to worry about, Roxy." He put his hands on her shoulders and held her at arm's length as he spoke. "There's nothing this mage can do to hurt me, not even in the final escape."

"Are you sure?"

"He's been in the audience the last four shows, but there are almost a dozen coincidental variables in the final escape, plus one that I've never used before. That's more than enough to see me through to the end of the tour and the TV special."

"Why don't you do the escape without your magick?"

Romano thought about it, going through the escape sequence in his mind. "No, it can't be done. The escape was never designed to be accomplished without the help of some coincidental magick. Anyway, even if it could be done, it's too late in the tour to start trying it now."

Just then, the dressing room door opened, and a young man popped his head into the room. "Five minutes!" he said, before quickly closing the door again.

Roxanne looked at him, chewing her bottom lip.

"Don't worry," he said, smiling. "Everything is going to be fine."

She attempted a smile of her own.

They came together in a tight embrace, neither of them wanting to be the first to let go.

■ ■ ■

"Ladies and gentlemen," said the emcee. "The Pantages Theater is proud bring you a master showman, a world-class illusionist and an escape artist who knows no rivals." A pause. "Accompanied by his lovely assistant Roxanne... Mr. Ro-ma-no Min-nar-deeeee!"

Romano stepped onto the stage to the sound of wild applause. He gestured to Roxanne with a dramatic wave of his hand, and she posed for a moment, gave a slight bow, then extended her arm in Romano's direction. He raised his hands above him, bowed deeply, then quickly started into the show, moving to the rhythmic, mood-setting music that would play continuously while he was onstage.

As he turned and headed downstage, he caught a glimpse of the man in the dark suit sitting in the front row, unmoving, as patient as a cat. The sight of him unsettled Romano, causing him to miss a step and stumble. He quickly regained his composure, promising himself not to look out into the audience again.

After all, he didn't have to. The man in the dark suit would always be there.

Until the end.

With the little misstep behind him, Romano settled into the first half of his show, which was composed of several standard illusions (performed with the trademark Minardi flare) and a final daring escape — the Chinese Water Torture Cell escape made famous by renowned escapologist and conjurer Harry Houdini.

The water cell wasn't a particularly difficult escape, but it did require the escapee to be able to hold his breath for an incredibly long period of time. The trick had never given Romano trouble. For one, he had trained himself to hold his breath for well over three minutes. Second, the water inside the tank was always ice-cold, slowing his heart rate and metabolism enough to give him an extra few seconds to complete the escape. But in addition to those safeguards, his Sphere of magick was Time. If he ever did get into trouble, he could always slow down time around him, giving him as much time as he needed to escape from the tank. Fortunately, he'd never had to resort to that, but knowing the safety net was there gave him the confidence to perform the trick flawlessly every time out.

The theater was silent, the audience holding its collective breath as Romano's ankles were fastened into the two hinged stocks which would become the lid of the cell. Then he was bound in a straitjacket (an improvement on the Houdini version), given a pair of goggles and hoisted up — feet first — over the stage. Then, with a rendition of "Asleep in the Deep" playing in the background, Romano was lowered into the cell, which was ringed by stagehands armed with axes to smash the glass in case something went wrong.

Before his head went under the water, Romano glanced over at Roxanne. There was a worried look on her face, different from the overly dramatic one she usually gave him for the benefit of the audience. This one was genuine.

"I'll be all—" he began to say, but just then his words were cut off by the cold bite of the water against his skin.

Silence.

A curtain was raised around the tank.

Darkness.

Romano began his escape procedure, slipping out of the straitjacket with relative ease, as the lubricating effect of the water made the task easier to accomplish than on dry land. Then it was onto the stocks around his feet. Normally it was just a simple matter of twisting his foot and sliding his ankle through the stocks, but this time he felt there was something different about the setup, something wrong. He could feel his ankles pressing hard against the stocks, as if they were tighter than usual.

He looked up through his goggles, through the water, and saw that the lid had not been closed properly. The holes for his feet were slightly overlapped, causing them to be considerably smaller than normal and making it almost impossible for him to complete the escape as planned.

Romano twisted and pulled at his feet, feeling the first aches beginning to stab at his oxygen-starved lungs. Soon his body would start to weaken, then grow numb. Of course, he could use his magick to get himself out of this predicament, but he dared not — not this early in the show, and certainly not with a Technomancer in the audience, front-row center.

With his lungs screaming for air, he curled himself up and began pulling on his ankles in earnest. Closing his mind off to the pain, he jerked his foot roughly through the shackle, scraping it badly.

One leg free.

Blood flowed from the torn skin around his ankle and on top of his foot, clouding the water like smoke.

Ignoring the pain, he grabbed hold of his other ankle and pulled on it hard, tearing the skin from his heel.

The water grew darker, but he was free.

Quickly, he turned himself around in the cell, opened the lid and popped his head above the water.

Air had never tasted so sweet.

After a few quick gasps he crawled out of the cell, hearing the frantic calls of Roxy, who'd been timing the escape for the audience.

"Four and a half minutes!" she cried. "It's too long! Get him out!"

Romano hobbled downstage and off behind a curtain. From where he was backstage, he could hear the shrieks from the crowd as they lowered the curtain around the tank, only to discover it empty save for the bloody water.

He limped onto the stage again, waving to the crowd, doing his best to smile.

The crowd was stunned into silence, then broke into roaring applause.

"Are you all right?" Roxanne asked as she neared him on the stage.

"I'm fine," he said.

Then she noticed the blood flowing freely from the gash on his ankle.

"Draw the curtains!" she called. "Somebody help me get him to the dressing room!"

Romano felt hands on him, his body being lifted, carried away. As the curtains drew close, he caught a glimpse of the man in the dark suit in the front row.

He seemed to be smiling.

And Romano realized that the improperly closed lid had been no accident.

It had been a coincidence.

■ ■ ■

"How are they?" asked Roxanne.

Romano stopped to light another cigarette, then finished cleaning up his torn feet. The skin had been badly scraped across the top of his right foot, while the left foot had a deep, long gash around the heel. It would require stitches... after the show.

"It's a little sore, but I'll be all right."

Roxanne knelt down for a closer look. "A little sore? You need to see a doctor, Roman."

Ignoring her, Romano began wrapping his feet with gauze. "I promise I'll have it looked at by a doctor."

"When?"

"After the show."

Roxanne just looked at him, the disappointment on her face unmistakable. "You want to finish the show, right?"

"I have to."

"Don't tell me, your Ascension."

Romano nodded, binding his gauze-covered feet in tape. "I can still do all the second-half tricks, except for the metamorphosis. We'll cut that one and do the rest."

"What about the finale? Your ankles will be cuffed."

"We'll do it without the leg irons."

"What about the man in the front row, the Technomancer?" She paused a moment, as if coming to a realization. "Maybe he had something to do with the lid closing wrong. Maybe he's trying to kill you…. Maybe—"

"It was an accident," Romano said calmly, almost believing the lie himself. Although the lid had never closed wrong in over 500 shows and probably never would again in 500 more, he was convinced the near-fatal gaff had been the work of the Technomancer. But no matter how sure he was of it, he'd never let Roxanne know. Her assistance was crucial for the completion of the show. If she refused to go out with him for the second half, she'd effectively be shutting down the performance and allowing the Technomancer to claim a victory. And he wasn't about to let that happen.

"Roxy," he said, looking at her with his piercing brown eyes, almost able to feel the shroud of fear around her melting away like wax from a flame, "do you think I wouldn't be able to tell if another mage was trying to kill me?"

She looked at him for several long moments, her conviction draining away with each passing second. "All right, then," she said at last. "But promise me you'll be careful."

"Of course I will."

She looked at him skeptically, pointing a playfully admonishing finger at him. "You better be."

There was a knock on the door, and a second later the theater manager came into the room, accompanied by Romano's road manager, Arthur Gardner. "You're five minutes late already," said the theater manager. "The crowd's getting restless. You going back on or what?"

"I'm going on," said Romano. "Just give me a couple more minutes."

"I told you he'd be back," said the road manager. "Nothing'll stop this kid from putting on a show. Nothing."

"Artie!" Romano said as the two men were heading out the door. "Forget the metamorphosis, and lose the leg irons on the finale, okay?"

The road manager looked at Romano for a few seconds, no doubt realizing that he'd actually been injured doing the last escape. "You got it, pal," he said. "Break a leg, huh?"

■ ■ ■

Romano took the stage for the second half of the show wearing a pair of black socks over his heavily bandaged feet, and with a noticeable limp added to his step. He was twenty minutes late, but the crowd nevertheless gave him an enthusiastic round of applause.

After acknowledging the crowd with a polite bow, he began the performance by pulling a rabbit out of a hat — an age-old trick, but one that is incredibly difficult to perform well.

With that first demanding trick under his belt, Romano settled into the rhythm of the act, performing the classic levitation and Queen of the Air card tricks with his usual style and flare.

When it came time to saw Roxanne in half, Romano unconsciously glanced at the man in the dark suit, hesitating a moment before bringing the whirling buzz-saw down onto her torso. There was no reason why the Technocracy would want to hurt his acolyte, he thought. He was the one they were after... right?

He slowly drew the blade through Roxanne's midsection. She screamed, as she always did, but tonight's cry seemed sharper somehow, more terror-stricken than usual. Romano pulled back the blade for a moment, doubting himself and checking to see if everything was all right. When he realized that the problem was all inside his head, he quickly finished the trick and gladly presented a whole and healthy Roxanne May, absolutely stunning in her blue-sequined gown, to the appreciative crowd.

Romano then filled in the time usually taken up by the metamorphosis by doing some tricks with the Chinese Linking Rings — tricks performed by magicians the world over, but still executed by Romano with enough innovation to make the old standards seem new and exciting.

And then it was time for the finale.

As the escape table and daggers were brought onstage, Roxanne ventured out into the audience to find a couple of willing assistants. Romano watched her walk slowly past the man in the dark suit before quickly sweeping onto the stage with three burly young men in tow.

The three men then worked to secure a pair of thumbcuffs to his thumbs and handcuffs around his wrists. That done, he walked downstage to where the wooden table awaited. Directly above the table hung a chandelier barbed with seven silver daggers, each sharpened to a needle point and honed to razor sharpness. The chandelier was suspended in plain view of the audience by a rope that went through an overhead pulley and down toward the stage.

For a bit of dramatic effect, and to let the audience know there was a real danger in doing the stunt, Roxanne released the chandelier, letting it fall to the table. There was a audible gasp from the crowd as the seven daggers knifed through the air and sliced into the wooden table top. Each one embedded an inch and a half deep into the wood.

Stagehands freed the chandelier and repositioned it above the table. While that was going on, the three men from the audience secured Romano to the table, strapping heavy leather belts around his chest, waist and ankles.

Meanwhile, a baby grand piano was wheeled onstage, adorned by an elaborate candelabra with twenty-one long, white candles. When the candles were lit, the flames would eat through the rope, giving Romano roughly two minutes to get out of the cuffs and restraints and off the table. If he didn't accomplish the escape in time, he'd be impaled by the seven steel daggers.

It was this escape that had made him famous. It was also the one escape he couldn't perform without the help of coincidental magick. Two minutes wasn't really enough time to get out of all the restraints, and he often had to resort to coincidental magick to slow down the flames, make the pulley above him stick, or make any one of the restraints be improperly secured. If none of these worked, he could always slow down time, giving him more than a comfortable safety net to work over.

With the Technomancer in the audience, Romano had a feeling he might be using the last variable for one of the few times in his career.

As a hush fell over the audience, Roxanne walked over to where Romano lay and gave him a long, soulful kiss. "I love you," she said.

He gave her a wink and said, "Let's do it."

Roxanne walked over to the piano and sat down.

Romano nodded to the stagehands, and a white silk curtain rose up around him, concealing him from the audience's view. As he began struggling against the restraints, the twenty-one candles of the candelabra were lit and the clock began ticking.

Then the stage grew dark, and Roxanne began to play the piano — the haunting title tune from Andrew Lloyd Webber's *The Phantom of the Opera*.

He got out of the thumb and handcuffs easily enough, taking up thirty seconds to do so — just over a quarter of his allotted time. He began working himself out of the straps, contracting his muscles in wave-like patterns in order to snake himself free.

Suddenly, Romano froze as a ripple of Quintessence — the spiritual energy radiated by mages — washed over the stage. An instant later, the flames atop the candles burst into bright yellow gouts, slicing at the rope like knives.

The man in the dark suit had played his card, likely using a rote that made use of some paraffin that had been trapped in the candles during the manufacturing process.

Thus, the Technomancer's Pogrom against him had begun.

The crowd gasped at the sight of the flaring candles.

Roxanne played on, but any hint of a melody was lost.

Romano frantically began to invoke a rote on each of the straps, calling for them to be insecurely fastened by the three burly men from the audience.

Nothing happened. He could feel a tingling in the leather bands strapped across his body and realized his rotes had been blocked by the man in the dark suit.

Above him, the chandelier rocked slightly as the flames were no doubt licking their way up toward the pulley, chewing on the rope with fiery teeth.

At last he managed to counter the Technomancer's rote on the strap across his chest. He began to work at the other straps with his free hands, but then he felt the strap across his chest beginning to tighten. He grabbed at it with his hands, but still it pulled tighter against him, cutting off his air, crushing his ribs.

Roxanne had stopped playing.

Continuous loud shouts were coming from the audience now, and he knew he had only seconds to escape with his life.

He invoked his rote over time, his safety net, the vulgar little trump card that would give him all the time in the world to complete the escape.

Nothing happened.

It was as if his rote had come up against some invisible

brick wall, bouncing off it like a ball in a schoolyard.

Above him, the chandelier faltered.

And fell.

Romano saw the daggers glint under the stagelights, looking for all the world like fangs in a hungry maw, and he cast one last, desperate rote.

The daggers sliced through him as if through butter, nailing him down onto the table.

Miraculously missing all of his vital organs.

He let out a shrill cry of agony as blood spurted from his wounds, streaking the white curtain surrounding him with angry red slashes.

The crowd began applauding, probably expecting to see Romano suddenly appear on the stage in one piece, but slowly their cheers died out.

The ensuing silence was replaced by a scream, then another, and another, as individuals in the crowd slowly came to realize what had happened.

Finally Romano recognized Roxy's voice above the din of confusion. "Somebody get a doctor!"

The blood-soaked curtain came down around him, and he became aware of the frantic scene on stage.

Stunned stagehands circled him, wondering how to best get him free.

He twisted his head around and gazed out into the crowd.

As people in the audience rushed forward to the foot of the stage, the man in the dark suit casually got up from his seat in the front row and walked against the flow of the crowd, making his way out of the theater.

Romano closed his eyes, somehow knowing they would meet again.

INTROIT
■■■■■■■■■■■■■

Jackie Cassada

Thou preparest a table before me in the presence of mine enemies..."
   —23rd Psalm

Inside the Mission Street Shelter, the line of street people moved steadily past the tables of hot food and sandwiches. Johanna Talbot looked at her watch and tried to calculate how much longer she would have to offer cheer to people whose lives had little room for optimism. The shelter's doors had opened at sundown, over two hours ago, and Johanna had spent most of that time standing behind the serving table trying to dole out finite portions of hot soup to a seemingly infinite number of hungry people.

"The line's starting to thin out, Sister Jo. Why don't you take a break?" Clarence Dawson left his post behind the sandwiches and moved to stand next to Johanna, resting a large brown hand on her shoulder as he spoke. Johanna smiled at the shelter manager gratefully.

"Thanks, but I'm leaving early tonight. I should be all right for another few minutes."

Clarence shrugged. "Whatever you say, but you look pretty ragged to me. You might want to get home before the storm breaks. The wind might blow you away if you get caught in it." He chuckled as he returned to the sandwich table.

Johanna ladled a large serving of pale-orange soup into a bowl and handed it to a grizzled old man who mumbled something inarticulate before moving on to the nearly depleted array of sandwiches.

"What's this stuff?" An elderly woman in a faded print dress at least two sizes too large for her bony frame peered suspiciously into the soup tureen.

"Shrimp bisque," Johanna answered, offering a bowl to the woman.

"Where are the shrimp? I don't see any shrimp in here."

"Um, I think it's been run through a blender, Ms. Potter." Johanna congratulated herself for remembering the woman's name. She had been working at the Mission Street Shelter for six weeks, long enough to recognize the regulars who came most nights for a hot meal and sometimes a bed. They were street people, homeless and hungry. Once Johanna had dutifully prayed daily for the relief of the "faceless" suffering. Now she gave them food and saw that they had faces — and names.

"Call me Irene," the woman said, finally accepting the soup and moving down the line toward Clarence and the sandwiches.

"What kind?" Johanna heard her ask the manager of the shelter.

The ceiling lights flickered momentarily, followed by a low rumble of distant thunder. It had been raining on and off all weekend, and tonight promised no change in the weather. Visualizing her black umbrella still resting in its stand in her apartment, Johanna hoped the rain would hold off until she got home. One of these days I'll have to replace it with something more colorful, she thought. It was one of the few things she had brought with her from the convent when she came to San Francisco, though, and she hated to part with it.

"Ma'am?" A male voice, hoarse and weary, brought her

back to the present. A young man, not more than thirty and accompanied by two children, shifted uneasily as he waited for her to ladle out three bowls of soup. Johanna tried to smile at him, but a tightness in her throat made the corners of her mouth shake. She gave up and settled for what she hoped was a sympathetic grimace. Sometimes she forgot that homelessness was not restricted to luckless individuals. Whole families were finding themselves suddenly without roots.

Impulsively, Johanna hooked her ladle over the edge of the soup tureen and shoved a hand into the deep sidepocket of her denim vest. "Wait a minute, sir," she said. "I have something for the kids." She concentrated on the packets of candy corn lying on her kitchen table. She had bought them this morning in anticipation of Halloween. Softly she hummed to herself, focusing her thoughts. *All places are one place*, she reminded herself. *My hand is both here in my pocket and there, reaching for the small, tasty treats.* Cellophane crinkled under her touch, and she triumphantly retrieved the candy.

"Here," she said. She held the packets in the flat of her hand for the man's inspection. "I thought I'd brought some with me. For Halloween?" At the man's nod, she offered two packets to each child. It's not enough, she thought. Never enough. She watched the trio as they continued through the food line.

"That was nicely done," she heard. Johanna turned, surprised by the soft, cultured tones that had caught her attention. Out of habit she retrieved her ladle and dipped it in the tureen.

"Not necessary, thank you, I've already supped." The man who had spoken to her looked out of place among the shelter's inhabitants. Johanna judged him to be close to her own age, perhaps even younger. His clean-shaven face and carefully tailored clothing spoke of regular baths and unexpired credit cards. His voice held a trace of an accent, too faint to identify. He stared at her for a long minute, during which Johanna became painfully aware of her own unprepossessing appearance. Her short blond hair and pale blue eyes, together with her small frame, had prompted the sisters at the convent to refer to her as "diminutive." Here, at the shelter, Clarence had once described her as "a scrawny waif."

Johanna forced herself not to flinch from the stranger's arrogant scrutiny. Suddenly, she felt a coldness that had nothing to do with the sudden gusts of wind that blew into the shelter's dining room from the opened door. An almost physical sense of pressure made her stumble backward, and she reached out for the table to steady herself.

"Is anything wrong, Sister Jo?" Johanna nearly gasped with relief at the sound of Clarence's voice. All she had to do was say the word and the stranger would be escorted out to the street. But what word could she say? He had made no overtly threatening advances. He merely stood opposite her and stared intently in her direction.

"Please, don't be hasty." The man's voice rang with urgency, and at first Johanna failed to realize that he had not spoken the words aloud. Her resistence crumpled as she recognized an appeal in his tone that she could not ignore or shunt aside.

"Everything's fine, Clarence," she said, speaking slowly to keep her voice from trembling. "He and I..."

"Gideon," she heard inside her mind.

"Gideon and I know each other." Johanna felt her face flush. Lying had never been her forte.

"That's right," Gideon said, proffering a hand in Clarence's direction. "Jo and I go back a ways." As the two men shook hands warily, Johanna felt Gideon's presence leave her mind.

"Well, in that case, I'll butt out," Clarence said, stepping backward and looking about the room. "We seem to have run out of takers, Sister Jo," he said.

Johanna wrenched her eyes from Gideon's face and saw that the food line had dissipated. The shelter manager smiled warmly at her. "Why don't you go on home before the rain catches up with us?"

It took Johanna less than a minute to retrieve her jacket from the back room where the shelter's staff stored their things. As she straightened her collar, reluctant to return to the outer room, her hands fingered a thin, gold chain around her neck. Reaching inside her cotton shirt, she pulled out the stylized sun pendant that hung from the chain and brought it to her lips in a gesture that kindled a spark of memory within her...

Her lips brushed the back of the Mother Superior's hand.

"You have doubts, my child?" The older nun stood motionless as the black-clad young postulant knelt before her.

"I hear voices... a voice... in my mind, Mother Superior," Sister Johanna whispered. *"The thoughts that come to me lately are not my own. I'm frightened."*

"Are you overtired? There is such a thing as too much devotion and too little sleep."

"I think I may be going mad."

"Not every inner voice is the voice of insanity, Sister Johanna." The Mother Superior of the Convent of the Heavenly Spirit extended both hands for Johanna to take. "The Maid of Orleans heard voices. So did Bernadette." Johanna felt herself lifted to her feet by surprisingly strong hands. The Mother Superior was smiling.

"I think that you are not insane, daughter. I think you are beginning to Awaken."

Johanna's pulse quickened at the sound of the unfamiliar term.

"Awaken?"

"Behind all religions, even this one which we claim to be the one true faith, is a truth greater than any single body of beliefs.

When we stand on the verge of discovering that greater truth, something within us emerges — or Awakens — to guide us into the fullness of our knowledge." The Mother Superior's face seemed to glow as she spoke. "Come," she said to Johanna. "I will show you a mystery…"

Still clutching the symbol of the Celestial Chorus, the order of mages into which she had been initiated at the convent, Johanna sought inside herself for some direction. She had volunteered to come to San Francisco, where the Chorus had only a nominal presence. Her instructions were to make herself useful and wait. She had done both those things. And now Gideon had walked into the shelter and spoken directly to her mind.

"Is this why I was sent here?" she asked, seeking an answer from within.

"If not this, then what?" Johanna recognized the voice that sounded from within her. It belonged to that fragment of divinity inside her which made it possible for her to alter reality in ways that could only be described as magick. She had learned that the Awakened spirit within her was called an Avatar, but in her own mind she envisioned a creature of fire and light and painful beauty, not unlike the descriptions of angels in the holy texts of many religions. Though it had been a long time since she had heard its celestial melody, her being resonated in tune with its harmonies. She tucked the pendant and chain securely into her shirt again and went to meet Gideon, uncertainty and anticipation rising in antiphonal measures within her.

He was waiting for her by the outer door, his aristocratic features bearing no evidence of impatience. As she said good night to Clarence, who was busily restocking the food counter for the latecomers, Gideon took her arm. The gesture bore all the markings of an old-fashioned courtesy, but the firmness of his grip hinted at something more custodial. Once again, Johanna fought down the urge to panic.

"There's really nothing to fear," he said to her as they put the shelter behind them and headed north, toward Union Square. It wasn't until they had walked several blocks that Johanna remembered that she had intended to go home, and that home lay in the other direction.

"What do you want?" she said, finally voicing the thought that had been in her mind since Gideon had made his appearance.

"I need your help," he said simply. Johanna glanced at him out of the corner of her eye. She revised her earlier estimation of his age, placing him now at that indeterminate thirty-something. Under the glare of the streetlights which illuminated the darkness, he looked more vulnerable than he had inside the shelter. It was that unshakeable self-confidence he had projected, and had since dropped, which had made him seem younger. Uncertainty had left its mark on her own face, she knew.

"How do you know I can help you?" she asked.

"Because you're a mage," he answered in a voice purged of all pretense. He waited for a break in traffic, then steered her quickly across Mission Street. As they paused on the other side, Johanna looked carefully at him.

"So are you," she said. He nodded, once.

"Do you know this city?" he asked.

"Sort of," Johanna replied. After she had left the convent, she had spent her first two weeks in the city wandering around, gawking at the overwhelming mix of sights and sounds which contrasted so radically with the sheltered peace within the cloister.

"Then take me somewhere where there's a crowd, where we can both get lost."

Johanna thought of The Lost Chord, a club near Union Square. She had visited it more than once, attracted to it first by the name and later drawn back by the quality of the bands that played there. Initially, she had felt awkward —

and a little guilty — at entering an establishment so far removed from the life of prayer and devotion she had known at the convent, but the vibrant music that filled the club spoke to her of a different way of praying, a raucous paean in celebration of life that was no less meaningful for its lack of reverence than the solemn choruses in which she had once participated. She had come to San Francisco to taste of the city, to sample the world in its fullest before deciding whether or not to put it behind her and take up the life of a nun once more. Her guilt had soon faded.

"I think I know a place like that," she said. She pried her arm from Gideon's grasp and set off in the direction of Geary Street.

Gideon hurried to catch up with her. "Take a roundabout way," he said, looking around him nervously.

"Don't you ever say please?" Johanna asked as she kept walking, turning down a side street without breaking her pace.

Two blocks from the club, a disheveled teenager in ragged jeans and bare feet accosted them. "Spare some change?" His speech was slurred. Johanna recoiled from the odor of cheap wine and pot that wafted from his direction. She tried to push past him, but he blocked her path. Johanna had just noticed that his left eye was completely red when Gideon interposed himself between her and the panhandler.

"Bugger off," he snapped at the youth. As if someone had punched him in the stomach, the man staggered backward and tripped on the curb.

Time seemed to warp around Johanna as Gideon took her arm once more and pulled her past the fallen figure. Backlash, she thought, moving in slow motion past an endless building. She had always been careful not to work obvious magick in front of anyone not already aware of its existence, and so she had never directly experienced the phenomenon known as Paradox Backlash, when the laws of reality struggle to reassert themselves in the face of blatant violations. Gideon had not made physical contact with the red-eyed man, but had used his power as a battering ram. She glanced at Gideon, and noticing his apparent unconcern, forced herself to remain calm. By the time the club was in sight, her temporal sense had returned to normal. Gideon let go of her arm and looked apologetic.

"I saw one of those red-eyed people earlier this evening," he said. "It unnerved me then, too."

Johanna nodded. "There was a wrongness about him. I couldn't put my finger on it, but I just wanted to get away from him."

A few more hasty steps brought them to the door of the The Lost Chord. Gideon paused to look around, then motioned to Johanna. "Let's go inside, quickly," he said. He let Johanna lead the way.

Inside the club, both Johanna and Gideon scanned the crowd. A few people were dancing to the hypnotic music emanating from the stage. All the tables were filled with the usual mix of drinkers, talkers and listeners. Johanna fastened on the music, picking out phrases of Gregorian chant and Eastern harmonics amid the pulsating throb of electric guitars. She recognized the band, a group called Mantra, from earlier visits. Despite the gothic look the band members affected — all black clothing and white makeup — their sound spoke to her of a spirituality their image denied.

Gideon grabbed her hand and pulled her through the crowd to a table that had suddenly emptied. They sat while a waitress removed glasses and bottles. Gideon ordered beers for both of them. Neither spoke until their drinks arrived.

"Lucky for us those people were leaving," Johanna said to break the silence. "I was beginning to think we'd have to go somewhere else."

Gideon raised an eyebrow. "It wasn't luck," he said quietly. "I believe the people who were sitting here suffered a sudden attack of uneasiness and had to leave. It's amazing how effective a simple tweak to the human nervous system can be."

"Oh." Johanna felt her face harden with disapproval.

"Don't be so quick to pass judgment on me," Gideon said. "We needed this space and we have fewer options than most. We need to talk." As he spoke, he glanced about the room, nervously searching the club's interior.

"You said you needed my help," Johanna said. "Why?"

Gideon took a long pull from his glass.

"I'm on the run," he said.

"From whom?" Johanna asked. "And why?"

Gideon leaned back in his chair until his head rested against the wall. Only the slight drumming of his fingers on the table top betrayed his uneasiness.

"You've heard of the Men in Black, haven't you? Superiors? HIT Marks?" he said.

"The Technocracy," Johanna said, whispering the words even though she knew that her speech was unlikely to be overheard. The terms were familiar to her, the strike forces of the confederation of Technomancers who waged unceasing war on mages of her kind.

"Well, the Progenitors, actually," Gideon said. "I wasn't sure how familiar you were with the ins and outs of the enemy."

"I know the Technocracy owns San Francisco," Johanna replied. "And I've heard of the Progenitors — they're the bio-scientists, aren't they?"

Gideon nodded. "Among other things."

"It won't be easy to hide yourself from them for long," Johanna said, "at least not in the city."

"I hadn't a hell of a lot of choices," Gideon said.

"Why are they after you?" Johanna asked, beginning to search the crowd for clues that she and Gideon were being watched, realizing as she did so that she had no idea what she was looking for. She knew that the Men in Black were just that — but half the city wore black just to be in fashion.

HIT Marks were supposed to be part machine, which should make them stand out in a crowd, she supposed. She had no idea what distinguished Superiors from other people. She finally settled for trying to identify anyone who seemed to be taking undue notice of herself and Gideon.

"I have something they want," Gideon said.

"What do you want from me?" she asked, suddenly nervous at the prospect of involvement in Gideon's predicament. She forced herself to remain calm, breathing deeply and reciting the beginning of a soothing chant to herself.

"Shelter, for starters," he said, a wry grin toying with the corners of his mouth. "After all, I did find you giving food and shelter to the needy. I happen to be one of the homeless myself, at least for now."

"If a place to sleep is all you need, you could have taken a bed at the mission," Johanna said.

Gideon shook his head. "You felt what happened on the street earlier. I can't afford to surround myself with too many people who are ignorant of the existence of magick. They would seriously hamper anything I might have to do to protect myself if someone tracks me down."

"I wasn't thinking," Johanna murmured, dropping her head as a sudden sting of shame coursed through her. "I should know better than to even consider putting innocent people at risk."

Gideon reached across the table and touched Johanna's chin with his fingertips. She raised her head to look at him.

"Don't bother about it," he said, lowering his hand. "You're obviously not used to this kind of plotting. It wasn't a bad idea, just an unworkable one." Gideon glanced quickly at his watch, then scanned the room once again.

"We can't stay here too much longer," he said. "I do need to find somewhere relatively safe to go." He paused, as if ready to say more, then merely looked at Johanna. This time she could not mistake his intent.

"Does this mean you want to come home with me?" As she spoke the words, Johanna realized that she was enjoying Gideon's company despite — or perhaps because of — the hint of danger that surrounded him.

"Is that so impossible?" Gideon smiled at Johanna, a smile full of innocence. Once again Johanna saw the years drop from his face. "I'm not making improper suggestions or anything. I just want a place to stay for awhile."

Johanna's face reddened. "It's not that," she said. "It's just..."

Gideon straightened in his seat. He leaned forward, his gaze anchored on Johanna.

"The man at the shelter, your coworker, called you Sister Jo," he said. "Are you a nun? Is that why you seem so hesitant?"

Johanna closed her eyes, carefully considering her answer...

"I'm not certain that I belong here, Mother Superior," Johanna said.

Her mentor nodded her head thoughtfully and continued to finger her rosary beads. "The life of a contemplative is not for everyone," she murmured. "Your vows are not yet final."

"It's not that I've lost my faith in... in the One. I just don't know if I can spend the rest of my life here in the convent."

"Perhaps what you need is a change of scene," the old nun said as she kissed the cross that hung from the ritual beads, then turned her full attention to Johanna. "We call our Tradition of magick the Celestial Chorus for a reason, child. Unlike the other orders of mages, who often work individually, our best work is done in a group. But every choir has its soloists, those whose voices are so strong and clear that they demand to be heard without accompaniment. You have a strong voice, Johanna, and whether or not you have been called to sing alone is something you and your Avatar must decide."

"But if I leave the convent..."

"*The convent is not the Chorus. Most of the sisters here are Sleepers, devout women who believe in God and who do much good with their prayers but who are ignorant of the presence of mages within these walls. The Chorus finds the trappings of this place of meditation conducive to its work, and we find no real conflict between this form of faith and our own true purpose. The Church is not perfect, but we work within it for the greater good.*" The Mother Superior paused in her speech.

"*I don't want to hide behind walls, Mother Superior,*" Johanna said.

The Mother Superior chuckled. "*Oh, we don't hide, Johanna. If your destiny lies with us here in the convent, you will see that for yourself. In the meantime, there is work that you can do for us which will take you outside these walls and give you a taste of the world. You will take a leave of absence — a vacation of sorts. The official term, I believe, is 'exclaustration.'*"

"Out of the cloister," Johanna translated.

Her superior nodded. "Literally," she said.

"And what of my vows?" Johanna asked.

"*Your vows — poverty, chastity, and obedience.*" The Mother Superior cupped Johanna's chin in her palm and stared at her with twinkling blue eyes. "*You have not yet made any commitment to the sisterhood that cannot be broken. Until you take your final vows, only you can determine which of them you may keep and which can be put aside due to circumstances. Although you will undoubtedly want to sample that which you must forswear if you return to the convent, I do not expect that you will amass a fortune overnight, nor do I think you will abandon yourself utterly to physical pleasures. And in the end, it is your Avatar who will command obedience.*"

"How long will I have to make my decision?" Johanna asked.

"*Until your work for us in San Francisco is done,*" the

Mother Superior said. "You will always be a member of the Chorus, Johanna. That is not the question. The question is, will you also be a nun?..."

"Is something wrong?" Gideon's voice broke her reverie. Johanna opened her eyes and realized that he was waiting for her reply.

"Am I a nun?" Voicing the question herself brought her no closer to an answer. "I'm not sure. At one time I thought I was."

Gideon arched an eyebrow in puzzlement.

"I've taken a leave of absence from the convent," Johanna replied. "And my name is Johanna."

"That suits you better than Sister Jo," Gideon said. "But it also explains a few things."

"Like my reluctance to take you home?" Johanna asked, beginning to relax.

Gideon nodded. "You're Celestial Chorus, right? The religious mages?"

"Yes," Johanna said, amused in spite of herself at the facile tag Gideon had attached to her. "And you?"

"What do you think?" Gideon's voice sounded almost playful.

Johanna looked him over carefully. "I would guess that you are one of the Order of Hermes," she said finally.

Gideon laughed. "Is it that obvious?"

"It seemed the most likely," Johanna said, "at least judging by appearances."

"Go on," Gideon urged. "I so seldom get a glimpse of myself from the outside."

"You dress conservatively, for one thing," Johanna began, suddenly feeling awkward at trying to attach tangible evidence to an intuitive guess. "If you carry anything that focuses your power, it's relatively easy to conceal — unlike the gadgets and fetishes of some of the other mage Traditions." She shrugged. "I can't pinpoint it any closer than that."

"It's not really that important," Gideon said. "No more so than if we were guessing each other's astrological signs."

"I'm not really familiar with any of the other orders of mages, at least not in San Francisco." Johanna said. "They keep a very low profile so the Technocracy — or anyone else — won't notice them."

"Then I was lucky to find you, wasn't I?"

"As lucky as you were to find this empty table so quickly?" Johanna asked.

Gideon shrugged. "I went looking for a mage," he said, "and shelter. The combination seems to have brought me to you."

"What's that?" Johanna said, catching a sudden movement near the front of the club. Two men in black dusters, their faces shaded by broad-brimmed hats, had just thrown open the door and were arguing with the bouncer.

Gideon jerked to attention.

"We need to leave immediately." He was on his feet by the time he stopped speaking.

Johanna stood up, grateful that her slight frame would help conceal her actions from the figures she sensed were now moving toward them through the crowd.

"Where's the back door?" Gideon asked.

"To your left, past the bathrooms," Johanna said.

"Can you find your way there in the dark?" Gideon asked, his hands feeling along the wall as he spoke.

"I think so," Johanna said. She heard him grunt with satisfaction as he finally located a line of shielded electrical wire.

She reached out to touch Gideon's shoulder, but drew back as she felt a current of power gather about him and heard him mutter something that sounded like a formula — or an equation.

A loud crack of thunder penetrated the din of the club. Almost simultaneously, all the lights went out. "Now, get

us out of here before they get the lights back on," she heard
Gideon say close to her ear. His hand, still faintly tingling,
grasped her shoulder. Amid the confusion that followed,
Johanna pulled her companion steadily through the milling
crowd. They reached the rear door and tumbled out onto a
small alley just off Maiden Lane.

Once outside the club, Johanna looked up at the sky.
Heavy cloud cover obscured the stars, but the rain had not
yet begun. She caught a look of amusement on Gideon's face.

"I suppose the blackout was just another stroke of luck?"
Johanna commented, her voice heavy with sarcasm. "Happy
coincidence?"

"There are certain advantages brought about by
threatening weather," he said. The smile faded. "Let's get
as far away from this place as possible."

Hand in hand, they made their way past the boutiques
that lined Maiden Lane. A few of the shops were still open,
taking advantage of the Halloween weekend crowd.

Johanna pulled Gideon inside an all-night bookstore. An
old man in tinted-green spectacles looked up momentarily
as they hurried to lose themselves among the shelves.
Leaning back against a wall of used books, Johanna inhaled
the musty odor of old paper and worn leather. Except for
the shop owner, she and Gideon seemed to be the only
patrons.

"How did they find us?" Johanna whispered.

Gideon shook his head. "Who knows? They're mages,
too, and even though they use the trappings of science, what
they do — and how they do it — is still magick."

"What will they do if they catch us?" Johanna asked,
trying to remember everything she had heard about the
Technocracy, until tonight no more than a label for
everything the Chorus opposed. In theological terms, they
would be the legions of Mammon, dedicated to divesting the
world of its spiritual connections. But apart from associating
them with rampant technology and passionless science, she

had no clear picture of these people who were pursuing Gideon so fiercely.

"I don't really want to find out," Gideon said.

Johanna heard a scuffling sound on the other side of the shelves. She tensed, bringing her hand to her throat and touching the gold chain to make contact with the focus medallion underneath her shirt. A quick look behind her told her that Gideon, too, was on the alert. His eyes narrowed in concentration as he pulled something from an inside pocket of his jacket — some sort of power focus, she supposed. With his other hand, he gestured for Johanna to take a look beyond the shelves that blocked their view.

As quietly as she could, Johanna began a chant which would allow her to see past the barrier of books. Her vision blurred, and then she was looking not at the shelves which surrounded her, but through them, along the narrow, book-lined aisles.

Scuffling as he dragged his feet, the store's owner came into view. The old man stopped in front of a row of matching leather-bound volumes and removed one of the titles, then made his way back toward the front of the room.

Johanna slumped against the wall, suddenly weak from relief as she slowly eased away from the power she had tapped. "It was just the old man," she whispered to Gideon, who relaxed his stance as she spoke. Johanna folded her arms in front of her to hide the trembling in her hands.

"We can't stay here," Gideon said. "If I were trying to track us down, I'd check all the places that stayed open 'round the clock. We need to keep moving."

"I know," Johanna agreed. "I just needed a few minutes to think."

"That won't be necessary," a low-pitched voice rasped harshly as a pair of figures in black coats suddenly rounded the corner and came toward them down the aisle of books. Johanna saw the flash of metal as their arms reached underneath their coats. Instinctively, she reached once more for her medallion, wondering if there were seconds enough for her to transport herself and Gideon away from their attackers.

"Don't bother, Jo," Gideon said from behind her, his voice dull and without hope. "It's all over."

Before she could answer him, he grabbed her by the arm and pulled her backward, placing himself between her and the black-coated men.

Johanna fell, slamming her head sharply against a wall of books. She had time to see Gideon leap forward, arms outstretched to grab both men. She heard a dull boom as all three men vanished. The words "air displacement" swam into her mind as she lost consciousness.

The stinging aroma of something acrid and unpleasant woke her. She lay amid a pile of toppled books. The old man from the bookstore knelt over her, waving a dark glass bottle under her nose. She coughed once and tried to sit up, then gasped as the movement precipitated a stabbing pain in her head.

"Take it easy, missy," the old man said. "You had a nasty fall there."

More cautiously, Johanna tried once again to raise herself to a sitting position. This time, she succeeded.

The old man hovered over her. "Should I call 911?" he asked.

"No!" Johanna said sharply. "No, I just lost my balance for a moment."

The old man nodded. "I thought I felt the place shake a little. I guess the quake last night still hasn't settled down."

Johanna looked at him carefully. Apart from the obvious concern on his face, he looked unperturbed. She accepted his offer of a hand and carefully pulled herself to her feet.

"You didn't see anything — unusual — did you?" she asked.

"I saw you come in," he said. "And I noticed it was a mite foggy outside — but that's not what I'd call unusual."

"And the young man who was with me?"

"What young man?" The old man looked puzzled. "Are you sure you don't want me to call someone — your doctor?"

"No, please," Johanna said forcefully. "I'll be all right."

"Can I get you anything? I have some tea in the back."

Johanna started to refuse his offer, then realized that she was no longer in any hurry. The hopelessness in Gideon's voice had made it abundantly clear that he did not expect her to pursue the matter. She let the old man lead her to a cluttered office at the rear of the shop. She perched on a rickety wooden chair while the store owner retrieved a tea bag from a desk drawer, filled a styrofoam cup with hot water from a pot that rested on a portable electric burner, and finally offered her a cup of spicy herbal tea.

Once he had done so, he left her alone and began to retrieve the books she had dislodged in her fall. Johanna sipped the hot liquid slowly and tried to collect her thoughts. In the short time she had been in San Francisco, she had had little contact with the other mages in the city. Once or twice someone she thought might be one of the self-taught mages known as Orphans had drifted into the shelter, seeking a free meal, but Johanna had never had the courage to attempt an approach. She knew that there was probably a sizable contingent of Cult of Ecstasy mages, but she suspected that those devotees of magick-as-hedonism would want little to do with someone from the Celestial Chorus. She had been truthful when she told Gideon that all she knew of the Order of Hermes was that it existed. Gideon's entry into her life had been the first real connection she had made with mages outside her own Tradition. His sudden absence left her feeling curiously empty.

The shop's clock chimed the hour. Johanna held her breath and counted. Ten o'clock. Under normal circumstances, she would be on her way home from the shelter. Tonight, with her plans to leave early, she should have already been ensconced in her apartment, alone with her meditations. But this was not a normal night.

"Would you like another cup of tea?" The old man was back, and Johanna realized that whatever she decided to do, she needed to do it somewhere else.

"No, thanks," she said. "If I could impose long enough to call a cab, I'll be on my way." She gave the man the sort of smile that she usually reserved for the shelter's clients, a smile carefully constructed to cover unwanted emotion.

As she wandered impatiently through the shop waiting for her ride, Johanna spied a book of poems by Francis Thompson. She brought it up to the counter and reached in her jacket pocket for her change purse.

"Don't feel like you have to buy something," the old man remarked as she handed him a combination of bills and loose change.

"I want to," she said, remembering how the poet's tortured search for spiritual meaning had given her comfort during her early struggle to come to terms with the reality of her own Awakened power.

"Not many people read his stuff anymore," the old man volunteered as Johanna began to flip through the slender volume, searching for "The Hound of Heaven," Thompson's best — and most famous — poem.

Johanna nodded her agreement. She stationed herself near the door and let her eyes drift over the pages of poems. *I fled Him, down the nights and down the days*; she read. *I fled Him, down the arches of the years; I fled Him through the labyrinthine ways of my own mind…* Between verses, she watched the traffic pass by outside.

The storm that had been threatening all evening finally emptied itself in sheets of rain as the cab pulled up in front of the shop. Johanna called out her thanks to the bookstore owner as she dashed across the sidewalk for the taxi's open door.

On the way to her apartment, she allowed her thoughts to roam, watching the city slip by through the cab's rain-spattered windows. She had blurted out her address to the cabbie instinctively, without consciously realizing that she was planning on going home, and then realized that her tiny walk-up was, in fact, the only real haven she had at the moment. Once she was safe, she concluded, she would again take stock of the evening's events and decide if there were anything she could do for Gideon.

In the privacy of her own apartment, away from outside observation, she could begin to search for him. She sifted through her memories of the last few hours, calling to mind everything she could remember about Gideon, building within herself an image of him which would serve as a focus for her divinations. If she could discover where he had been taken, she would have some idea of how to help him — or if he could be helped.

A feeling of remorse washed through her. If she had not been so reluctant to take him home with her, if she had simply shifted the two them to her apartment from within the convenient darkness of the club, they might both be safe. Instead, he had given himself up to his pursuers, sacrificing himself to protect her. He had placed his trust in her, and she had failed him. Even though she had only known him for a few hours, Johanna knew she had to do something to make up for what must have seemed to him to be a betrayal of that trust.

The taxi stopped in front of an aging Victorian house on the edge of San Francisco's once-infamous Tenderloin district. She located her keys, paid the cab driver, and quickly made her way to the back of the house, where an external staircase led to her attic apartment. Nearly blinded by the pouring rain, she fumbled with the door key. Wishing she had remembered to leave the outer light on, she finally felt the lock give way.

As she reached for the light switch, the realization hit her. The light had been on when she left the apartment this afternoon. She turned, still halfway in the door, and felt a hand grab her wrist. Johanna tried to scream, but panic froze the sounds that rose in her throat. She tried to jerk her arm away, but she was caught in a vise-like grip which pulled her inside the darkened kitchen. Still struggling to free herself and fighting to find the breath to scream, she heard the door slam shut behind her.

"I told you it was all over, Johanna," a familiar voice said, as another hand moved past her in the dark and flicked on the light.

Gideon was seated comfortably in one of her two kitchen chairs, an empty coffee cup on the table beside him. In his hand, he held a gun. One of the black-coated men stood with his back to the apartment door, his hand still poised near the light switch. The other man held her by the arm.

Gideon kicked the second chair away from the table and motioned for Johanna to sit. Stunned into complacency, Johanna allowed herself to be guided into the chair.

"First things first," Gideon said. He leaned toward Johanna, carefully keeping his gun hand away from her and, with his free hand, lifted her pendant from her neck and dropped it into the empty cup. "I suppose I don't have to warn you not to start singing or chanting or whatever it is you do." His voice was gently soothing, deliberately so. "I'd hate to have to gag you, since that would make conversation difficult."

Gideon nodded to the man holding her arm, who released his grip and stepped backward to stand against the wall with his companion.

"How did you know to come here?" Johanna asked, making her voice as flat and uninflected as possible.

"It wasn't difficult," Gideon said, a trace of amusement in his voice. "Clarence assured me that you had nowhere else to go. I was prepared to wait all night for you to come home."

"Clarence?" Johanna felt a surge of panic rise. "What have you done to him?"

Gideon laughed. "Clarence is fine. He's been working for us for some time now. We're not as heartless as you make us out to be, Johanna. It's in our interest to care for the masses, too, you know."

Johanna closed her eyes as the truth resounded in her head like a bell. She opened her eyes again and chose her next words carefully.

"You're not what you said you were," she said.

"I never said," Gideon replied. "You guessed that I was Order of Hermes. I simply neglected to otherwise inform you."

"So this whole evening has been a ruse? You weren't running from the Men in Black?"

Gideon shook his head. "No, I wasn't running, Johanna. You were. It was you we wanted."

"Me?" she asked, still not comprehending. "But why?"

"Because you're new to the city," Gideon said. "Clarence has been watching you for us since you showed up at the shelter. He didn't think you'd had time to make any connections, and your actions tonight confirmed his assessment."

"I'm alone here," Johanna said. "I can't lead you to anyone, if that's what you want." The thought of Clarence's betrayal stung.

"It's not that at all," Gideon said quietly. "I'm glad you haven't had the chance to talk to any of the Tradition folks here. They would have gotten you involved in one of their conspiracies against us. As you said, the Technocracy owns San Francisco. We don't intend for that to change. We can't afford to." Gideon stared thoughtfully at his pistol for a few seconds, then tucked it out of sight inside his jacket. He moved forward in his chair until his knees almost touched Johanna's.

"You need to know the truth about this city." he said. "You need to know in case you've come here thinking you can bring about changes we don't want."

"I won't be a Judas." Johanna's voice sounded strident in the small kitchen. Remembering Gideon's warning, she tried to dampen the indignation that colored her words. "I didn't come here to fight anybody," she said softly, "but I won't betray anyone to you." Thinking of her own admission of isolation, she added, "I can't."

"No one's asking for that," Gideon said. "I don't expect you to betray anybody." He let the words hang in the air and watched Johanna's face intently.

Johanna felt the blood rush to her cheeks. Less than an hour ago she had berated herself for not acting to prevent Gideon's capture.

Johanna looked around the room, then back at Gideon. He regarded her calmly.

"What's next?" she asked.

Gideon's eyes took on a distant look. His face was a mask of seriousness.

"I'm afraid you'll have to submit to what I hope will be the only unpleasantness of the evening."

Johanna's temples throbbed as a current of fear coursed through her. "What do you mean?" she asked, suspecting that she already knew the answer.

"I removed your obvious power focus," he said, tapping the coffee cup which now contained her gold medallion. "I need to be certain that you aren't concealing anything else you might use to harness your powers."

"Please don't do this," Johanna said, her lips barely forming the words.

"It has to be done," Gideon said. "We can do it here, if you'd like, in front of these very unmatronly gentlemen," he remarked, allowing his mouth to soften, "or we can go into another room so you won't feel quite so..."

"Quite so naked?" Johanna said bitterly. "What do you think you'll find, some sort of sub-dermal implant? A symbol tattooed on my chest?" Her voice rose despite her efforts to control her tone. "You've already taken my focus. I have nothing else that could be of any use to me," she said.

Gideon shrugged. "I have to make sure. I promise I won't compromise you."

Johanna nearly laughed in spite of herself. "It's a little late for that promise. You've already compromised me just by being here. I'm sure you've already conducted a thorough search of my home."

The look on Gideon's face confirmed her statement. "I'm afraid you have little choice in the matter," he said. "Your options are limited to your choice of location. I can search you here or in your room."

Johanna felt the walls close in around her. Abruptly, she rose from the table. One of the guards moved toward her, then halted as Gideon motioned him back with his hand. He looked up at Johanna expectantly.

"Can we just get this over with?" Her voice was dull, each syllable an effort of will. "You probably know where my bedroom is," she said. "That's as good a place as any."

Gideon trailed behind her as she made her way through the apartment and into her bedroom. Once inside the room, he closed the door behind them and stood silently as she removed her clothes. Johanna felt a surge of anger as she noticed that someone — Gideon probably — had already laid a change of clothing out on the bed. Neither the denim skirt nor the lightweight blouse he had selected for her had pockets. A pair of sandals rested on the floor at the foot of the bed. He was obviously taking no chances that she would be able to secrete anything about her person after his search was completed.

Gideon's inspection was thorough and professional. Johanna found that if she closed her eyes, she could almost imagine that she was undergoing a routine physical. She steeled herself as his hands made contact with her flesh. The coolness of his hands surprised her a little, and she opened her eyes. Gideon's face registered no emotion; his eyes focused impersonally on her body as if he were examining a piece of machinery for flaws in its construction. She forced herself to remain aware, fighting the urge to disassociate herself from what was happening to her. As his fingers continued their inexorable probing, she sought within herself for a means of quelling the anger and humiliation that continued to build inside her.

"*I am light clothed in flesh, incorruptible spirit encased in corruptible matter,*" she recited to herself, remembering a fragment from a book of meditations she had studied during her first year at the convent. She took some comfort from the words, finally understanding their full import. Her body became a protective barrier, shielding her true self from invasion. Instead of feeling violated by Gideon's intimacies, she experienced an odd sensation of pride. The power that dwelt within her rested in a place he could not reach. Despite his attempts to impress upon her the helplessness of her position, she was, ultimately, inviolate. The realization overwhelmed her, and she caught her breath.

Gideon finally stepped back from her and broke the silence. "You can get dressed," he said, turning his back to her and giving her back her privacy.

Afterward, when she finished dressing, he opened the door and escorted her into the small living room, where a tray of cold cuts and a bottle of soda rested on the coffee table.

"I thought you might not have eaten anything," Gideon said.

Johanna realized that she was, in fact, hungry. She sat in the chair he held out for her and began to nibble at the food.

"I hope you can forgive me," he said.

Johanna steadied her voice and said, "For what? Deceiving me when I trusted you? Subjecting me to a search that you knew would turn up nothing?" A shadow of what might have been guilt passed across Gideon's face. "There's nothing to forgive," she said dismissively.

Gideon crossed the living room and disappeared into Johanna's kitchen. She heard muffled voices, followed by the opening and shutting of the outside door. A few seconds later, Gideon re-entered the room and took a seat on the sofa across from her chair.

"I sent the others outside. They've done their part," he said. "They won't be far, but you won't have to worry about them hanging around like a pair of guard dogs."

Gideon helped himself to a slice of rolled turkey. "I think it's time for us to talk — for you to tell me why the Celestial Chorus has sent an agent to San Francisco."

"There's nothing I can tell you," Johanna said quietly. "I live in this apartment and I work at the shelter — and I go to mass sometimes. I'm not here in any official capacity."

"You came here for a reason," Gideon persisted. "I want to know what that reason is — what your agenda in the city is."

"I have no agenda," Johanna replied.

"Why San Francisco?" She was elated at the thought of visiting the city on the bay, of seeing the Golden Gate Bridge and wandering through the picturesque neighborhoods.

"I was born there, too many years ago," the Mother Superior said. "I will always have a certain fondness for the city for that reason alone." Her keen eyes studied Johanna's face. She smiled. "But I can see that you aren't satisfied with the thought of indulging an old woman's vicarious pleasure."

Johanna looked stricken for a moment, then relaxed as she saw the crinkles at the corner of her mentor's thin lips. The Mother Superior allowed herself the ghost of a laugh before she once again grew serious.

"I had a dream — or a vision, if you like. Call it a message from within. Sending you to San Francisco has to do with that dream."

"But why?" Johanna persisted. "Is there something I need to do there?"

There is always something to do wherever you are, Johanna," the Mother Superior said. "The opportunities for good works are boundless in a city like San Francisco. I'm sure you'll have no trouble finding a worthy cause to devote your energies to."

Johanna stopped herself before she blurted out, "But I meant something important!" Once before, she had made the mistake of devaluing the Chorus's efforts to care for the material needs of the Sleepers in their midst. Her knees ached for weeks afterward from the time she spent scrubbing floors in the soup kitchen operated by the convent. She kept silent.

"I don't know what awaits you in San Francisco," the old nun said. "But whatever it is, it will find you."

"Are there others I should seek out when I get there?" Johanna asked.

The Mother Superior shook her head.

"There are a few members of the Celestial Chorus in the city," she said, "and a few other Traditions have a presence there, but I don't think your destiny lies with any of them. You expressed a desire to test your vocation, to see if the life of a community is what you want. I think you will find a singular path to follow during your stay in San Francisco. I suppose you could think of this as a mandate for a solo performance." The Mother Superior chuckled dryly.

The opening words of the Latin mass sprung to Johanna's mind and she spoke them without thinking.

"Introibo ad altare Dei," she murmered, quoting from the Introit which began the almost-extinct Latin mass.

"I will go to the altar of God," the Mother Superior repeated, nodding. "Perhaps San Francisco is your altar, the place where you will perform a miracle...."

"Johanna? Are you all right?" There was a note of concern in Gideon's voice.

"Yes," Johanna said. "I was just thinking."

"I would appreciate it if you would share your thoughts

with me." Though couched in courtesy, Johanna could hear the implicit command in Gideon's words.

"I came here to make myself useful," she said.

He raised an eyebrow.

"You wanted to know what my agenda was," she continued. "If you're looking for a conspiracy of some sort, you won't find it in me."

Gideon sighed.

"I was hoping you would give me a place to start based on your intended purpose here. Since you claim not to have one, I'll just plunge into the heart of the matter."

"I'm listening," Johanna said.

"Earlier tonight, in the club, you told me that the Technocracy controls San Francisco. Obviously, I'm already aware of that." Gideon permitted himself a deprecating smile. "What you may not be aware of, however, is why we consider this place so important, what we're doing here." He paused.

"I hadn't given it much thought," Johanna replied. She toyed halfheartedly with the food in front of her. Her thoughts were racing. All the old signals were becoming confused. She was, in a manner of speaking, in the hands of the Technocracy. She had been violated, her privacy invaded. She should be feeling afraid, but fear had no part in her current emotional stew. She was still angry — at Gideon, at Clarence, and at herself. But she was also curious.

"You told him you were listening." Her Avatar, more active tonight than since she had first Awakened, filled her mind. *"Do so."*

"I assumed this was just another stronghold for you, like so many other places are."

Gideon looked pained.

"Regardless of what you've been taught, we're not monsters." He leaned forward, coming as close to her as he could without leaving his seat. "We have a mission in this city — several missions, actually — but our primary purpose here is to keep this place from falling apart, literally. If we fail, thousands of helpless people will die. This is something you Tradition mages can't seem to understand. The more you try to meddle with reality — particularly in a city like this one, which needs our framework to maintain its solidity — the more you threaten to unleash forces which your weird sciences or mystical unities or entropic balances can't hope to control. It's more than luck that keeps San Francisco from being ripped apart by earthquakes. The Technocracy is all that holds this city together."

Johanna felt an almost physical force powering his words. As he spoke, Johanna observed him carefully, trying to pick up some clues from the subtle movements of his body, the sound of his voice, the expression on his face. She recognized the passion that surrounded him, and saw in him a devotion that was akin to her own. It was a revelation, and the beginning of a purpose made itself known within her.

"We have a vision," Gideon continued, "and it has nothing to do with some distant Awakening of humanity. We see the achievable creation of a better world — through concrete advances in knowledge. For the first time in history, we stand a chance of meeting the universe on our own terms, not bowing before it and praying for survival. We can't allow that opportunity to go to waste."

He paused, momentarily exhausted.

Outside, the rain continued to fall steadily, its lulling rhythm reminding Johanna of the lateness of the hour. She felt suddenly tired.

"What's going to happen now?" she asked.

"That's entirely up to you," Gideon replied. "Tonight we gave you a small demonstration of how easily we can control your experience of reality. You reacted quite predictably to the stimuli we provided."

Johanna felt her face grow hot.

"I really thought you were in trouble," she said. "I don't like being played with just to prove a point."

"No one does," Gideon said. "But there are some things you will just have to accept, if you choose to remain here."

"Do I *have* a choice?" Johanna asked, and this time she could not keep the bitterness from welling up inside her.

"You have many choices." Gideon stood and walked over to the window, where he parted the curtains and peered outside before once again turning his attention toward Johanna. "You can leave the city and go back to your convent — or to some other city, where you'll be someone else's problem. Or you can stay here — and behave yourself."

"What do you mean?" Johanna raised her head to meet Gideon's gaze as she spoke, realizing as she did so that by standing and distancing himself from her, he had cast her in the role of supplicant.

"You can remain at the shelter, continue your charitable works there under Clarence's watchful eye, and stay away from anyone who wants to enlist you in the battle against the 'evil forces' that control the city."

"That's all?" she said.

Gideon nodded. "For now, that's all I ask. I wouldn't consider trying to hide from us," he added. "I have your pattern now and I can locate you whenever I want. Besides, you might have trouble finding another apartment as nice as this — or any apartment, for that matter. It would be best if you were to remain accessible."

Johanna shook her head. "I won't become a traitor to my cause," she said. "I have a vision, too, and I can't deny it any more than you can yours. I didn't come here to fight the Technocracy. I came here to make myself useful, to serve the greater good."

"Then work with us, Johanna, and you will be serving that good far better than you are at the moment."

"You told me I could stay or leave," Johanna said. "What if I stay and don't cooperate with you? What then?"

Gideon's face became a mask of hard lines. "Then we will do what is necessary to see that you don't get in our way."

He left the window and resumed his seat on the sofa. "We don't have to be enemies, Johanna," he said, more gently. "When I leave here tonight, you can retrieve your focus, your holy symbol — that is what you call it?

"Yes," Johanna said.

"It will be almost as if none of this had ever happened," he said. "But I do need an answer from you — tonight."

The finality of his words resounded in the silence that followed. Johanna closed her eyes to focus more clearly on the inner vision which was beginning to form in her thoughts. The moment of decision had come, she realized, and there was no one to help her make it.

"No one?" her Avatar whispered. *"Think again. Even alone, you are part of the One."*

So are we all, Johanna thought, even the Technocracy, even Gideon. Her vision clarified. The image of a bridge filled her mind, a vast span linking two alien countries to one another. She was the bridge, a miracle of architecture and faith. She knew that she would not be the first one to try to heal the gap between magick and science, Tradition and Technocracy. Others had tried and, she suspected, failed. There would be some who would see her coming actions as treason, and herself as a betrayer. If so, and if she could be the one to succeed where others had faltered, the sacrifice would be worth it.

"I will go to the altar of God," Johanna murmured, her decision made.

"What was that?" Gideon asked.

"I'll do what you want," she said. Deliberately, she stood up and crossed the room to sit next to Gideon. Only a little space now separated them, a few inches of emptiness that contained both her destiny and his.

Gideon let his arms drop to his side. His fingertips brushed her skirt, closing the gap between them. His face relaxed into a smile.

"Then we have an understanding," he said.

"Yes," she replied. Careful to maintain the tentative physical connection between herself and Gideon, Johanna wrapped her mind around the image of her pendant, coiled inside the cup on the table in the next room. His hands, which had recently become so familiar to her, had touched the chain. Johanna fought to establish a link between the symbol of her power and the agent of her powerlessness. Warmth flooded through her as she felt the circle close. Quickly, before Gideon could respond, Johanna slipped inside his mind. The changes she wanted to make were subtle ones, intended to prepare the way for the vision that had awakened inside her. The beginnings of receptivity were already there, she realized, waiting for the touch which would quicken them, the touch she now provided. As softly as she had entered his thoughts, Johanna withdrew.

"I thought you'd see reason." Gideon said, looking at his watch. "It's late, though, and, unless you want me to stay here, I'll leave you alone for now."

Johanna shook her head. "I need some time to myself," she said quietly.

Gideon rose from his seat and smiled down at Johanna. She studied his face for a moment, searching for signs of her handiwork. Then she returned his smile, satisfied with what she saw.

Johanna walked with him into the kitchen and watched silently as he retrieved her pendant from the table and handed it back to her.

"A gesture of good faith?" she asked, bringing the medallion to her lips before replacing the chain around her neck. She left it hanging outside her blouse.

He shrugged. "I don't think you can harm me," he said. He paused at the door. "I'll look in on you from time to time. I think it's important that we keep in touch."

"You know where I live," Johanna said, "and where I work. The shelter can always use volunteers — especially tomorrow night. Holidays always bring a crowd."

Gideon hesitated for a moment, as if surprised by her sudden forwardness. Then he smiled, accepting her invitation as a natural outcome of their new understanding.

"Tomorrow night, then," he said.

Johanna waited until he had gone before she returned to her bedroom. She retrieved her watch from the pile of discarded clothing that still littered the floor. It was past midnight. Tomorrow, she would have to remember to bring the Halloween treats she had bought to the shelter. She looked forward to seeing Clarence, wondering if he would be able to sense a difference about her. Along with Gideon, Clarence was also a part of the purpose she had created for herself. She was not certain if she could walk the perilous path she had chosen without stumbling, but she felt a glimmer of approval from the portion of the One that dwelt within her.

"Is this what you would have me do?" she asked her Avatar. Instead of an answer, she felt within her a raging tumult of sounds warring for prominence, an orchestra of clashing timbres without form or direction. As her soul listened, the fragmented pieces of noise resolved themselves into a glorious cacophony of dissonant harmony, a chorus of light and dark that lacked only a melody to give substance and form to the whole — a soloist's voice. It was the music of the city she heard, the brittle song of the Technocracy waiting for the infusion of spirit she intended to offer it.

She would remain in San Francisco, in this city of the adversary, where technology threatened to bleed away the magick that struggled to survive here. Gideon thought he had won her cooperation, her agreement not to try to undermine the technomantic power structure that, in his words, held the city together. He was not yet aware of what she had won from him. He would provide the cornerstone for the bridge of her vision.

"Long ago, all magick — including the magick of science — was one," she heard from deep within herself. *"It can be so*

again."

Outside, the rain had stopped. Johanna walked to the window of her bedroom and peered past her reflection into the rain-streaked darkness beyond. The convent which had sheltered and guided her magick was behind her now, in a past that would forever remain part of her but would no longer serve as refuge. She was striking out into unknown territory, with only her inner voice to guide her. There was terror in that knowledge, and beauty in the terror.

Chanting softly to herself, Johanna marveled at the mystery her future had become.

WHEN THE MOON
■ ■ ■ ■ ■ ■ ■ ■ ■ ■ ■ ■ ■

James S. Dorr

Eddie Marsdon was just coming up from a drug induced dream when the earthquake hit. He felt the floor shifting under his bed. He passed out a second time, dreaming of the eyes of the punk kid who'd sold him the Horse — no fancy designer stuff for Eddie Marsdon, who blew cornet in a back-to-roots jazz group — a waif-like woman he'd run into on Kearny Street. Then of the cats — their wailing outside his apartment window that Friday afternoon after he'd shot up. The preternatural brightness he'd seen outside. Then of his girl, Ann.

He woke again, screaming. Another rumbling, the first of the aftershocks, shook his building, and this time he knew enough to pull his pants on, dive for a pair of shoes, a shirt and jacket, and push his way out through the spilled books and music, through trembling hallways and falling mortar, until he was out in the open-air courtyard behind his building. The sun was just rising.

He needed a drink. A fix. Something to calm him. The rush from the heroin still made his head ache. That and something else — it wasn't just H, but something else the kid might have added. He knew about heroin from two years back before he'd kicked the habit at Ann's insistence, or so he had thought. He *shouldn't* want Horse now.

Except Ann had left him.

Except that the streets of San Francisco were still mean and dirty, and all the worse now from the note she had left him that Friday morning, when all he had done was stay out all night arranging a gig, an outdoor concert, for Saturday evening, the night before Halloween.

That was *this* evening. And. . . .

Where was his cornet?

He'd gone on running, instinctively ducking the showers of brick dust, plunging down the steps on Vallejo Street until he reached Mason, then — God, he hadn't the slightest idea why — dodging south toward the brooding, ruined mansions that climbed up Nob Hill like so much rotting ivy. And now he realized, he'd left his cornet behind. He'd had it Thursday night on a club gig with part of his band, Buddy Ferrin on trombone, Cruse on the drums, Ken Genovese playing piano and others they'd picked up, then brought it back with him Friday morning. He'd placed it on the table by his bed, then, finding Ann's note, Ann the straight-arrow who'd said in the note she could no longer take his chaotic habits even when he was clean and sober, he'd left it behind him to wander the sidewalks. He'd seen the punk first on Grant, just above Chinatown, then seen her later on Kearny Street dealing. Saenz Red. Blue Something. Pills and nose candy. She asked him his pleasure.

He didn't know why — chalk it up to old habits. "You got the Big-H?" he asked.

"Sure," she'd answered. "Say, don't I know you?"

And then the cats wailing. Four-legged cats, that is. He'd shot it up then and there on the sidewalk and, shambling back to his Russian Hill digs, he remembered something about how animals sometimes knew hen there'd be an earthquake.

And now he needed to climb back up Russian Hill to

his apartment, skirting cars that were crushed beneath fallen stone. Skirting bodies. And street people — *creatures* — that scuttled from shattered, darkened doorways, attacking the corpses.

He realized then fog had come — fog mixed with grime from burst open buildings. He'd thought it was morning, just after sunrise, but now he realized it must be past noon. He heard shots in the distance.

Something was wrong with time.

He saw a group of men striding down Jones Street, briefcased and dark suited, two of whom had — he blinked and looked again — almost glowing, completely red left eyes.

He heard a cable car bell ring on Hyde Street, but when he got up there he saw it was empty.

And then he heard a scream. Rag-covered street people coursed out around him, streaming along the track with its stopped cable and, caught up among them, he swept north with them past Green and Union, breathing their stench of beer and stale urine. And something else also. Of blood and. . . .

Of dead flesh.

He heard the scream again and elbowed through them, to where they had stopped, surrounding a body. A body still moving.

He recognized it — the North Beach punk he'd met on Kearny, her frightened, black eyes peering up at him through circles of dark rouge that stained bone-white cheekbones. Her hair cut short and black, black as the night sky, black as the clothes she wore. And one of the street people, hauling a knife out, switching it open, starting to slash at her leather jacket, paused and stared up at him through a red left eye.

That was enough for him. "No!" he shouted.

He charged, his fists swinging, scattering her assailants

around him. He kicked and gouged. He even bit one of them, spitting the foul taste out of his mouth, trembling in anger. Anger and —   *Crashing down.*

— anger and fear as well, swinging at air as the rag-creatures faded off into a fog that reached even *this* high up the twin peak of Russian Hill. Until, panting, he finally sank down exhausted.

■ ■ ■

"You need a fix, Eddie?"

He sat up, startled. Had he been dreaming? The woman, the punk, was sitting next to him.

He shook his head. "Yes." Then he looked at her thin, yet clearly   female form leaning against him. "No," he said this time, attempting to clear his thoughts. "I don't know. I. . . ."

She smiled and waited, a sexy smile, somehow, despite her emaciated condition.

"How do you know my name?" he finally asked.

"Eddie Marsdon? I heard you play Thursday. The best cornetist this side of New Orleans."

"Including New Orleans," he growled, half thinking he must still be dreaming.

She went on, ignoring him. "Like Uncle Louis, back in the 'twenties. Hot. Traditional. Backed by Kid Ory, before he came west. And Johnny Dodds and Lillian Hardin. Johnny St. Cyr."

"You know Louis Armstrong?"

She nodded. "You think I dig metal, maybe? Because of the way I'm dressed? I knew the Kid when he played trombone at the Club Hangover downtown on Bush Street. And after him, Turk Murphy and Lu Watters." She smiled, then laughed out loud. "You did too, Eddie. And you know them now as well. You know what day this is?"

"Saturday afternoon." He shook his head again. "Who *are* you anyway?"

"They call me lots of things, but you can call me Sparrow," she said, getting to her feet, reaching down to help him up with her. "Today's the day before Halloween. Tonight, after midnight, the people I've mentioned — their ghosts come out with all the others."

Eddie's mind went back to Thursday night, to Friday morning, to an elderly black man who'd sat at his table after they'd finished and set up their gig for an outdoor concert in Washington Square. For the night before Halloween. He remembered the man's dark glasses, how he'd been unable to make out his face. How he'd received half the money up front, and taken his share home to tell Ann the good news.

"*Jesus!*" he said. "Sparrow, you've got to help me. The cops'll have cordoned off my building — the place was practically collapsing when I left it. But I've got to get there to get my instrument."

■ ■ ■

More street people. The fog was beginning to clear at least, but it was already late afternoon and they had to hurry. They dodged them as best they could, going blocks out of their way when they had to. They came across others, men and woman wearing more respectable clothing but, nevertheless, looting stores and apartments while what police they saw seemed content to just look on and take notes on their wristpads. They saw one woman, blonde and glossy, looking a bit like Ann, gnawing on something that looked like a human arm. While, over everything, even though most of the fog had blown away that high up Russian Hill, smoke from burning buildings hovered, acrid and gritty, coating the streets with a uniform cover of murky gray.

They ducked through alleys where buildings leaned one against the other, roofing them over as if they now scurried through vast, surreal tunnels, and dodged chunks of mortar that crumbled around them. And they saw the sky brighten just as they came out to Eddie's courtyard.

As he'd predicted, the cops were waiting.

"Just hold it there, you two," one of them growled. Eddie looked up at a tall, thin man, dressed in black from his boots to his helmet. He saw the policeman take something from his belt, speaking into it as his partner grabbed Sparrow's shoulder.

"What is it, Officer?" Eddie said. He tried to be polite, even as the policeman glared at him. "This is my building — we're not looters, honest. I just have to get something, then I'll be right out." He gestured at Sparrow. "And this is my girlfriend."

The cop shook his head. He held the speaker-phone up to his ear — an ear that seemed half made of metal as well — then took it again to his mouth and spoke into it. "Eddie Marsdon," he said in a flat voice. "And that's not your girlfriend. Your girlfriend's Ann Paxley. She's blonde and she's got a better figure. She left you, Marsdon, and do you know why?"

"We broke up," Eddie said. "That's all, we may get together later. But in the meantime I left my cornet in my apartment after the quake hit. I've got to get it to play a gig."

"She left you for the same reason you're not getting in your apartment. You've got to grow up, Marsdon. Get a steady job, working with real people" — he turned toward Sparrow — "and not with punks like *her*. I've heard your music. Me and my partner, some nights we draw duty down in the places guys like you play at, and I think it stinks, Marsdon. Noisy and blaring, nothing but chaos. Unable to keep a tune. Even unable to keep a steady beat like the metal they play in the punk joints, but starting something, then drifting around it, getting farther and farther away from what the guys who wrote it intended it to be. It's what's wrong with the world today, Marsdon — like you without a job, not even able to hold onto a steady girlfriend. What do you call it?"

"Improvisation. And it keeps the tune and it keeps the beat too. It just augments it. But officer, look, I don't really have time to discuss the meaning of jazz right now. Just let me get inside, to get my cornet. And let Sparrow go and. . . ."

The policeman cut him off. "So get a trumpet. There's plenty of pawn shops that're filled with trumpets from guys like you when they run out of money. What's the difference?"

"The *sound* is different." He was beginning to get angry now, in spite of himself. "It's mellower. Fuller." He twisted around to the other policeman, still holding Sparrow. "And you let go of her."

"No, Eddie, it's okay," Sparrow said, glancing up above them. Her eyes flashed in a peculiar way, reflecting the sky that was brightening even more as she looked at it. A cat screamed, suddenly. Then he heard dogs barking.

"*Earthquake?*" he whispered.

"Aftershock, Eddie. A big one's coming." She twisted, suddenly, out of the cop's grasp. "You see it in the sky. Hear it in animals when they cry out, because they see it too."

Then he heard another, more distant sound, like rumbling thunder, and smelled a sharp odor of methane and sulfur. He ducked past the first cop, already joining with his partner to flee to their car, then turned back to

Sparrow.

"I can't go in with you," she shouted. "But thank you. For saving me from the ghouls. And watch yourself, Eddie, once you're inside there. Mind what you see and remember, always, what you went back for."

And then she was gone. Just like that. She wasn't there. Out in the street, beyond the alley, he saw people running, one with a red eye.

He looked at the sky and the sky was bright yellow.

He ducked beneath the tape of the police cordon and went inside, feeling the building shake as he climbed up the stairs. Any moment he knew it could fall in, trapping him under tons of rubble, but it didn't matter. He lurched his way down the hall, grabbing the walls as the floor shifted under him. Reaching the door of his walk-up apartment, he half fell through it into his bedroom.

Jesus, he thought, *he needed a fix now*.

No! He shook his head.

Out of the corner of his eye he thought he saw spiders. The web of a spider.

He shook his head violently, reaching forward, reaching to grasp the cornet in its case where he'd left it, untouched, on his bedroom table.

Then looked up to see Ann.

■ ■ ■

"You bastard," she whispered, after they'd stared at each other for minutes, his hand still outstretched to take the instrument. Minutes that seemed like hours. "Don't you get it, Eddie Marsdon? I heard the policeman through the window, talking to you in the courtyard down below. Don't you understand what he was saying? You took drugs, didn't you, after you found me gone, not even stopping to wonder why. Still not realizing even now how drugs — and the chaos they cause in your mind — are only reflections of your unstructured life. And of your music."

He felt himself ache to hold her, and yet he still reached his hand out to the cornet, a yard, a foot from him. The floor was knee deep in broken plaster with more raining down from the ceiling above him. He felt himself being trapped.

And yet he loved her.

And yet, the cornet. The part of him she so clearly hated. . . ."No!" he shouted. "It's you who don't understand. Jazz isn't unstructured, Ann. Not the way you think. Help me get out of here, then come and listen."

Ann shook her head, her features seeming to shift for a moment into another's that he remembered. A woman who'd died from drugs, crying and vomiting while he'd held her, trying to help her. But then Ann lunged forward, grabbing the cornet case just before he could.

"Bastard," she said again, backing away from him. "This night of all nights. Tonight and tomorrow. There are things that are happening outside of us, Eddie, that are bigger than either of us can understand. But, if you'd listened, you might have had me back."

Then she turned and pushed her way past him with a strength he didn't remember her ever having. She knocked him backwards, just as the room shook, shifting the plaster around his legs enough for him to pull free.

He followed her out the door, down the swaying steps just as the hallway collapsed behind them. He plunged outside, inches away from her fleeing back. Running behind her down streets and alleys, not knowing where, while the pavement beneath their feet heaved and groaned. And then, again, silence.

The aftershock over.

He looked up to glaring lights, reds and harsh purples, while around them costumed people — people with parties to go to this Saturday just before Halloween — bobbed and whirled as they might in New Orleans the evening of Mardi gras, except in blacks and grays, stark whites and blood crimson. Some with red eyes shining. And just ahead, still, Ann, cradling his instrument. Always just out of reach.

He chased her down Sacramento Street, farther south and east than he'd realized, then north on Stockton — the heart of Chinatown. And, as she glanced back, he saw not Ann, but Vanya, the woman he'd loved before her, who'd died of an overdose in his arms. Then he saw Charlee, the woman before that, yet all in Ann's body, legs pumping while he pursued.

Almost reaching her.

Then across Broadway, street people pursuing too, into North Beach where the punkers held sway, turning back west to Russian Hill, then arcing north again, keeping the ancient mass of Telegraph Hill to their right side. Always just inches from his outstretched fingers.

Then they reached Green Street, veering to straddle the slot of the Powell-Mason Line cable, rust-specked and fraying, then Union and Filbert, when he saw just ahead, under a street lamp, a thin, waif-like figure, with hair bobbed and black as night.

"Sparrow!" he called out. He saw her turn from the man she was talking to. He heard dogs barking.

"Sparrow," he called again. This time she saw him and, smiling, she nodded.

The sky flashed yellow.

The aftershock this time was tiny, but was just enough to cause Ann to stumble. She staggered to her left, fighting to keep her feet, twisting away onto Columbus Avenue just where it crossed Mason at an angle, when —

"No!" he screamed. He lunged to grab her. His hand caught the cornet just as she twisted, once more, away from him —

When hands grasped his shoulders, strong, masculine hands, and pulled him backward just as the cable car crashed on Columbus. Driverless, brakemanless, empty just like the car he'd seen earlier back on Hyde Street. Freewheeling down the hill. Leaping the slot where the tracks made their sharp bend.

Where Ann — the thing that was Ann — had been standing.

He looked up, crying, openly crying, and gazed at the man he'd seen talking to Sparrow, Ken Genovese. Behind him he saw Cruse, and then Bill Taylor, his clarinetist. And Carl Santiago, who played guitar with them.

"Hey man," Genovese said, "let it go, okay? You tried to save her, but it happened too fast. And anyhow. . . ."

Santiago broke in then. "We been looking for you."

Eddie nodded, still not sure what he felt. There in his hands — the cornet case. He fumbled it open and took out the instrument.

Sparrow caught up to them then and he saw she was holding a package, wrapped in brown paper. "I got your fix, Eddie," she said. "Remember? Just like you asked me for."

"Yeah," he answered. He started to reach for it, then looked down at the instrument in his hands. What was it she'd said, later on with the cops? After they'd left? Always remember what you went back for?

He smiled and shook his head. "Yeah," he said again. "Thanks anyhow, Sparrow, but I won't need it."

And later after he'd started playing, his sidemen around

him, Eddie Marsdon realized he wouldn't need drugs again ever. He surveyed the crowd and thought he saw Sparrow, but it didn't matter. He knew she was out there. What mattered now was the jazz. The music.

He had the band rip into "Muskrat Ramble" and, pulling the microphone close to his horn's bell, he wailed along with them, improvising an octave higher, then dropping back down to play chase with the trombone. He had them play blues tunes, "Wang Wang" and "Limehouse," spilling his sorrow for Ann and what happened, that she would no longer be able to hear him. Or Vanya. Or Charlee. He had them play ragtime.

He had them play roots-music, back to the birth of jazz in New Orleans. And he wailed with them, exuberating in improvisation, the freedom of chaos but — as Ann had never been willing to recognize — still bound to order. The order of harmony and rhythm, despite what the cop had said. Not the lock step beat of heavy metal, but freedom in ebullience, augmenting melody. Yet still, always, ever in balance.

The stuff of the universe, music that made the spheres spin on its razor's edge, bobbing, yes, to and fro, yet always not straying quite from their orbits. And midnight came — and with it Halloween morning — and Bill and Ken and Buddy and Cruse and Carl understood too as he had them play "The Saints" for their first encore. He had the crowd sing with them, growling the words in the mike so they'd know what to sing while the group played.

And he saw others pick up their instruments, shadowy figures that stood behind the crowd as it pressed forward. He saw that Sparrow was right about Halloween, as Uncle Louis himself led the first chorus. Satchmo himself — *"When the saints, when the saints, when the saints go marchin'"* — then Turk and the Kid and Lu Watters and Lillian, Miss Lil Hardin all classy and sleek in her fringe-skirted chemise and feathered boas, who'd married the master, and even the moderns like Brubeck and Coltrane.

Second verse. Chorus. And Art Blakey dueling with Cruse on percussion. The sun "ceased to shine" and yet, in the morning, the music in balance, the sun *would* still be there.

And then the third — *"Oh when the moon, when the moon"* — he sang the first part, then picked up his cornet and jammed with Louis —

"the moon turns into blood" — with Louis's spirit, the shade of Louis, and Eddie Marsdon and his own jazz band shrieking the chorus. Watching the moon rise, hanging, the night's eye, red through the smoke from fire and earthquake.

"I want to be in that number when. . . ."

And it didn't matter.

THAT WHICH IS GIVEN
■■■■■■■■■■■■■

Don Bassingthwaite

"Ms. Sanders? Ms. Sanders! Hold the elevator!"

Christopher Kent sprinted the last few yards to the elevator and joined the stiffly dressed, blond-haired woman already in it. He smiled at her, nodded his thanks, and jabbed the button for the underground parking garage before she could press it herself. There was an uncomfortable silence in the elevator as it began to move, then Christopher coughed and said casually, "That was an excellent debate."

"I'm surprised you would want to share an elevator with the woman who defeated you and crushed your motion."

Christopher's smile faltered momentarily. "It's irrational to hold a grudge. I try not to. Besides, in the end it was the judgment of the Symposium that your motion was the better of the two."

"It's not every day that the Technocracy uncovers Tradition plans to activate a dormant Node of magickal power in a nightclub, Mr. Kent." Ms. Sanders kept her gaze fixed on the flashing numbers over the elevator door. "It only makes sense to monitor the site for further activity and then move against the Tradition mages when the time is right. The suggestion of Iteration X that the club be destroyed out of hand is inefficient."

"Whoa there!" Christopher held up a hand. "You don't have to go through your whole case again. I see your point. You've convinced me!"

She finally glanced at him out of the corner of her eye. He knew what she saw — an attractive man around her own thirty or so years, with short brown hair and wearing a tailored suit. It was an image he had cultivated carefully. He flashed her a grin. "By the way, you don't have to call me 'Mr. Kent.' My name is Christopher."

"Kate," she said simply.

Silence re-established itself as the elevator dropped past the sixth floor, and Christopher waited for Kate to say something else. She just stared at the back of the elevator door as if he were not even present. Christopher let out a slow, quietly whistling breath and looked up at the ceiling. The Technocracy was an organization dedicated to controlling and improving the world through its science-based magick. It placed great importance on the values associated with science, such as rationality, logic, and cool detachment — unlike its opposition, the Traditions, with their hodge-podge emphasis on mysticism and mumbo-jumbo. Christopher glanced at Kate. Both of them were Technomancers, mages working for the Technocracy, but there was still a world of difference between them. Around the second floor, he ventured, "So what does the New World Order have planned next?"

"We'll be installing monitoring cameras around the Node site at the club. I dispatched a work crew immediately after the Symposium announced its decision. The cameras will be in place and operational in a matter of hours."

"Today? Work crews on a Sunday?" Christopher joked. "And on Halloween to boot? Won't that look a little suspicious?"

Kate gave him a cold look. "No more suspicious than a meeting in an empty corporate office on a Sunday. The Technocracy doesn't take holidays."

The elevator doors slid open on a dim and dirty underground parking garage. Christopher made an exaggerated grimace at the smell of car exhaust. "Phew! They need a better ventilation system in here!" He followed

Kate from the elevator, stretching his arms and shoulders as he moved. "What a day! Can I walk you to your car?"

"That's not necessary." She pointed at a car about thirty feet away. "I'm just over there."

"What a coincidence, then." Christopher smiled. "I'm parked right beside you."

"Coincidence?"

"Believe it or not." He pointed at his car with his right hand. There was a slight whoop as the alarm deactivated, a chorus of clicks as the doors unlocked, and a quiet purr as the engine turned over.

Kate's surprise was betrayed only by a slightly raised eyebrow. "An interesting effect."

"Iteration X technomagick." Christopher patted his right arm. Iteration X was the branch, or Convention, of the Technocracy to which he belonged, just as Kate belonged to the New World Order. Each Convention had its own duties and areas of technomagickal expertise. "Cybernetic. The remote controls are built-in."

"Fascinating." She deactivated her car's alarm with a more standard key-chain unit and unlocked the doors with ordinary keys.

"Kate..." Christopher shrugged off his suit jacket and leaned against her car. "I actually enjoyed the debate today. That's not something I can usually say. You were a real challenge."

"Thank you, Christopher."

"I'd like to talk sometime. Maybe we could get together. I could show you some more Iteration X magick."

"Thank you, but really, I'm very satisfied with the New World Order's magick." Kate opened the door and got into her car. Christopher caught the door with his cybernetic hand before she could close it.

"So cold, Kate?" he said engagingly. "It makes you sound so much like the perfect Technomancer. Unfeeling, rational.... You need to let your hair down. I've seen the ads for that club where the Traditions are putting their

Node. What's it called? *Pan's*? Those ads make it look like it's going to be a pretty hot place. Maybe we could go...."

Kate's face settled into a blank, expressionless mask. "Mr. Kent," she said icily, "I am interested in the mages behind Pan's. I am not interested in the club itself. I am not interested in the advertisements for the club. I am not interested in letting my hair down or in Iteration X cybernetic magick. I sound like the perfect Technomancer because I am a Technomancer, and I, at least, know how a Technomancer should behave." She paused, letting her words burn Christopher's ears. "Please let my car door go."

Christopher gave her a good-natured, playful smile. "What if I don't want to?"

He felt the subtle shifting of reality that marked the working of magick before the words had even cleared his lips. A fraction of a second later, a police car came sliding around a corner of the parking garage, pausing nearby. A window rolled smoothly down, and a fresh-faced police officer stuck his head out. "Is everything all right, miss?" he called.

Kate glanced at Christopher. He nodded, conceding to her, and released his grip on the car door. Kate turned to look back at the police officer. "Yes, thank you. Just wrapping up a meeting." She slammed the door on Christopher, then, under the protective eyes of the police officer and his partner, backed out of the parking space and drove away. The police car followed her, the officers inside watching Christopher intently as they drove by. Christopher waved at them jauntily.

When both cars were out of sight, he hurled his jacket against a nearby wall in frustration. It landed in a patch of oil. Christopher swore. He left it lying there as he wrenched open the door of his own car and thrust himself into the driver's seat.

How dare she?

"Eblis!" he snapped.

Here. The voice that whispered in his left ear might have

come out of thin air. In reality, it was generated by a simple bone-conducting amplifier implanted against his jawbone and connected to an innocent-looking computer chip in his arm. Still, the voice had a dark, smoky quality that lent an eerie depth to its words. It could have almost come from something alive.

"I'm going to open a connection to the San Francisco police computer system." Christopher felt the faint vibration in his right arm as the cellular phone link there came to life and dialed at his will. "I want you to enter the system. Locate car number..." He concentrated, trying to remember the number of the car that had responded to Kate's magick. "...334 and access the on-board computer."

It was the work of a moment. *Done.*

"Link with the other computer circuits in the car."

I have access to braking and steering, Eblis said, *as well as climate control, system monitors...*

"Current speed?"

Forty-five miles an hour.

"Turn the car ninety degrees and lock the brakes."

This time it took a little longer for Eblis to return a report. *I can no longer make contact with the on-board computer of police cruiser 334, Christopher.* There was a note of satisfaction in Eblis' voice. *I suspect it has been damaged beyond repair.*

"Well done."

I could do the same thing to Kate Sanders' car.

"No. She's a Technomancer. She would notice your presence." Christopher touched his cybernetic arm as though he were petting a dog. In a way, he was. Eblis was his familiar, though he certainly wouldn't have used that term to describe the artificial intelligence that lived on a chip in his forearm to another Technomancer. Most Technomancers didn't take familiars, but then, he was hardly most Technomancers. Nor was Eblis quite like most familiars. Or even most artificial intelligences. Christopher had originally summoned Eblis as a spirit before placing his familiar's essence on a chip. Eblis was his advisor and his aide, with a few magickal skills of his own. As a computer-based entity, Eblis was able to perform certain tasks with an ease that would have attracted considerable Paradox, the force that attacked mages and Technomancers who bent reality too far with their magick, to Christopher had he attempted to duplicate them. The familiar's aid was invaluable. And Eblis was part of a bargain that Christopher had once struck.

Christopher shook his head. "I will deal with Ms. Sanders myself."

How?

"That's my concern. Sleep, Eblis."

The familiar's silence was proof enough that he had returned himself to a dormant state, awaiting his next summons. Christopher sat back for a moment, relishing his revenge against the young police officer Kate had summoned to her aid. The thrill of revenge was mild, though. The police officer was nothing, a pawn. He wished that he could do the same thing to Kate herself. Eblis had been remarkably perceptive, however, when he had asked how Christopher planned to take his revenge against the New World Order Technomancer. Any magickal attacks he made against her were sure to be traced back to him by the other Technomancers of San Francisco. And he couldn't afford that kind of suspicious scrutiny.

Christopher slammed his organic fist into the steering wheel. Damn the woman! Until she and the New World Order had interfered, the Node that was hidden amid the renovations at Pan's had been his! An Iteration X agent in the city's planning department had discovered the first signs of Tradition activity at the club — magickal elements built into the refurbished architecture which were clearly detailed in the blueprints for those who knew what to look for. Christopher himself had been the first to realize the true purpose of the intricate patterns of wires, support beams, and colored floor tiles. It all pointed to plans to activate a dormant Node of magickal power. The higher ranks of

Iteration X had handed responsibility for the destruction of the club and its nascent Node over to him. Then the New World Order had learned of the secret behind Pan's.

He had been so close! Not that he had really wanted to see the Node destroyed, of course. As long as the Technocracy had thought the Node was gone, it would have been happy. The Traditions would have fled the scene. And he would have had sole access to the Node and the Quintessence it would eventually produce for his own use. Thanks to Kate Sanders, though, Pan's was now under the unblinking eye of the New World Order. There was no way he was going to be able to get close to either the club or the Node without being watched.

He wanted revenge on Kate Sanders. The Node he could live without. Its loss was a bitter pill, but it wasn't going to destroy him. Kate needed to be taught to mind her own business. Unfortunately, she was proof against all of the dirty tricks he might normally have used against Sleepers or enemy mages. He couldn't jeopardize his own position by being caught attacking a fellow Technomancer. His attempt at seduction had been more reflexive than planned, a very mundane attempt to bring her under his sway in some way. Too bad that New World Order Technomancers, of all of the servants of the Technocracy, had to be so bloody cold and emotionlessly disciplined!

Christopher's fingers, both cybernetic and flesh, drummed against the rim of the steering wheel. He needed a more structured, plotted course of attack. A plan. Something that would humiliate Kate Sanders — if not destroy her outright. Something that wasn't directly magickal. Something that couldn't be traced back to him. Preferably, something that might even leave him smelling like a rose and back in control of the Node at Pan's. Something...

His fingers stopped, then tightened about the steering wheel. He reached down and shifted the car into reverse, backing out of his parking space. He smiled as a plan came together like pieces of a puzzle dropping into place. He shifted up again, into drive. The car surged forward with a growl like a hungry cat. "Wake up, Eblis."

Yes?

"We need to find a mage of the Traditions."

■ ■ ■

The police cruiser that had arrived in response to Kate's magick pulled up beside her car as they drove out of the parking garage. The officer at the wheel gave her a quick smile, then accelerated past her and drove off south, down Montgomery Street and into the evening gloom.

The Technocracy had chosen to hold the Symposium deciding the fate of Pan's in a boardroom in one of the office buildings clustered in San Francisco's financial district. The area was more or less neutral for both the New World Order and Iteration X, as the financial world belonged to the Convention called the Syndicate more than it did to any other branch of the Technocracy. Kate always felt at home in the cold austerity of corporate office buildings, though. They reminded her of New World Order regional headquarters. Except that Iteration X Technomancers were a good deal better behaved when they entered New World Order territory.

Christopher Kent was pathetic. She had seen through his charade of seduction in an instant — his pitiful small talk, his ostentatious display of magick, his attempt at intimidation. Cybernetics, indeed. He should have known that that would do nothing to impress her. The New World Order was more interested in the magick of the mind than in the magick of the body.

On the other hand, he should also have known that no New World Order Technomancer would have allowed herself to respond emotionally in any case. Christopher's own emotional involvement with the matter of Pan's had cost him and Iteration X victory in the debate. He was too caught up in the issue. Kate had simply presented her facts calmly and rationally....

Three cars ahead of her, the police cruiser made a sudden, sharp turn, stopping broadside to the oncoming traffic. Brakes squealed as other drivers tried to bring their cars under control. It was too late, though. Everybody drove a little fast here. The impacts were shattering. The officers in the cruiser never had a chance.

Kate was busy herself, coolly dodging the cars around her and carefully applying the brakes. Fortunately, she was an excellent driver, and her car had been modified to include Technocracy-created advanced braking and steering controls. She came through the scene of the accident without even touching another car. Three other cars, plus the police cruiser, were not so lucky. One had a buckled fender; two others, crumpled front ends. The police cruiser had been totaled, hit from two directions at once. It was difficult to believe that the cruiser had not been slammed into four or even five times, so massive was the damage. So difficult, in fact...

Kate stepped out of her car and walked up to the cruiser. Other motorists had stopped, and some men were working on getting the officers' mangled bodies out of the tangled steel. One man tried to turn her away, as though the sight might be too much for a woman. She pushed him aside. There was no point in trying to help the officers. They were dead. It was sad and tragic, but there was no reason to be overly sensitive about it. There was something else about the crash that she wanted to investigate, a theory that tickled at her brain. She brought a tiny device resembling a thick pen out of her purse, turned it on, and surreptitiously pointed it at the wrecked car.

A red light in the handle of the device began to blink slowly on and off. The car had been under the influence of magick. The crash might even have been initiated with magick.

Kate frowned. It was possible that the device, a product

of New World Order technomagick, could be picking up the remnants of the magick that she had used to bring the cruiser to her. That seemed unlikely, though. The residue that magick left in the fabric of reality was extremely volatile. Her magick should have faded by now.

She walked forward, casually running her device over the cruiser. The light in the device's handle began to flash more quickly when she brought the device near the wheels — especially the front wheels. Ignoring the stares of the Sleepers, the mundane humans who might never Awake to their magickal potential, she reached into the twisted mess of the cab and touched the device to the steering wheel. The light began to flash as regularly as a ticking clock. She ran the device around the wheel, watching as the flashing grew faster and faster. It was at its quickest when it was on the far side of the wheel, next to the blood-splattered remains of the car's on-board computer terminal. On a hunch, Kate brought the device into contact with the computer. The light began to flash so quickly that it just seemed to flicker. She bit her lip. Her magick would not have manifested itself through the computer.

"Excuse me, miss." One of the Sleepers, a big man in a plaid shirt and blue jeans, touched her on the shoulder. "What are..."

"FBI," she told him perfunctorily. The lie came easily. She showed him the madly blinking light. Almost unconsciously, he took a step back. "Stay away from the wreck until emergency crews arrive."

Kate didn't have to elaborate or use magick to make him obey her. The red light and the apparent involvement of the FBI were enough to convince him to follow her instructions. The man didn't even try to stop her as she walked back to her own car and drove away.

The magick that had brought on the crash had been worked through the computer. One group of the Traditions, the Virtual Adepts, used computers to generate their magick. The crash could have been an attack by a Virtual Adept, but why? And why when she had been so close by? Could it have been coincidence? Kate had lost her belief in simple coincidence shortly after she Awakened. Could the magick have been an off-target attack on her? Not likely. Magick seldom missed its intended target.

But Virtual Adepts weren't the only ones who worked magick through computers and machines. Iteration X used computers extensively as well. And surely it was no coincidence that the dead police officers had helped her fend off an Iteration X Technomancer.

Christopher Kent.

Evidently he had taken his defeat and her rejection of his advances harder than he had let on. The destruction of the cruiser was apparently meant as a warning to her. Kate turned, heading toward New World Order regional headquarters. It wasn't unusual for Technomancers to compete among themselves, but the competition was seldom deadly. She would need more solid evidence of an intent to kill before she could report Christopher to her superiors and have them take her seriously. In the meantime, she intended to learn whatever she could about him — before he attacked her again.

■ ■ ■

Christopher had hoped that he might find a Verbena, one of the witch-mages of the Traditions, in the Presidio, out celebrating a wild ritual under the full moon that sailed the velvet Halloween sky. Instead, all he found were cars full of Sleepers clogging Doyle Drive and Park Presidio Boulevard for miles. Eblis connected to the police communications network and reported that heavy fog had closed down the Golden Gate Bridge. The cars on the freeways wouldn't be going anywhere until the fog lifted and traffic could move again.

Stalled traffic wasn't much of a barrier to a Technomancer, however. Christopher had Eblis analyze the city and state road construction plans for maintenance access points. As coincidence would have it, there was one up the shoulder of the road not ten yards away. Shortly, they were driving south again, back into the city. The traffic jam had cost them time, though. Halloween celebrations were moving into full swing. Traffic everywhere in the city was beginning to slow down as people surged into the streets.

Christopher clenched his fists in frustration. They had been driving around San Francisco for hours looking for a Traditions mage. First North Beach, then the Marina district, Russian Hill, and the Presidio. Christopher hadn't caught a sign of a single mage in that time, only Sleepers, more and more of them milling around as the night grew darker and Halloween's madness settled over San Francisco. On this night, of any during the year, Christopher would have expected mages to be out in the city and working magick. That was what he was looking for — just a hint of active magick. Where there was magick, there was bound to be a mage.

Perhaps, suggested Eblis, *it would be helpful to search Iteration X's files on known and suspected mage activity. It might provide a starting point.*

"No. I need a single mage. If we follow the files, we're more likely to find a group of mages."

Why a single mage? Do you intend to overpower him? Eblis sounded as eager for blood as a hungry wolf.

Christopher couldn't suppress a laugh. "No. I'm going to convince him that I want to defect to his Tradition."

Eblis' own laughter was rich, deep, and rolling, like thunderclouds boiling on the horizon. *Oh, that would be too funny. A mage who is a Technomancer who is a—*

"Don't say it."

A riddle wrapped in a mystery inside an enigma.

"I'm not actually going to defect, I just want to make it look that way." He drove into the Haight-Ashbury district. "Could you infiltrate a New World Order monitoring camera and alter the information it was sending back to the New

World Order? Could you jam the picture?"

It would be difficult, but not impossible.

"I presume you have a digitized record of Kate Sanders' voice."

Suddenly Kate's voice whispered in his ear instead of Eblis'. *Of course. But why do you need it?*

"Let's just say that while the mage will be talking to me, with your help, the camera will be transmitting a jammed picture with the voice of Kate Sanders talking to a mage about defecting to the Traditions."

Where do you intend to find a monitoring camera?

Christopher grinned triumphantly. "Pan's. Kate said they'd be up and operating tonight."

Eblis laughed again, resuming his own voice. *You are devious. The New World Order will assume that it was Kate's intent all along to preserve the Node under Pan's so that she could protect it for her Tradition allies.*

"Exactly. While they're investigating her, I can step in, raze Pan's, and hide the Node away for myself."

Are you sure you don't want to try this with a group? A group of mages is better than no mages at all. The Waydown is nearby, and the files show it is a common gathering place for mages. Eblis took control of Christopher's arm for just a moment, pointing out of the car window. *Perhaps...*

"No." Christopher glanced toward the gothic nightclub, housed in a half-burned church, that Eblis indicated. "One mage. Alone. One mage will be easier to deal with afterward. We don't want the New World to get its hands on him and drag out the truth about what happened. Our mage is going to have to disappear after our charade is finished." He turned off onto one of the quieter, residential streets in the area.

Why did you do that?

"We can move faster this way. Cover more ground."

Since when did mages grow from the ground?

"What's that supposed to mean?"

Mages are people. Doesn't it make sense to look for them where there are the most people?

And the most people were on the busy streets he had just left. It was a good idea. Sometimes even Christopher was surprised by his familiar. He returned to the traffic, letting his mind wander through the crowds, hunting for mages and signs of magick. Whenever he approached an intersection, he turned in the direction that the traffic and the crowds seemed heaviest. If there were a mage out there, he would find him.

On Post Street, just west of Polk, he found one. Or rather, he found traces of magick.

A man lay on the sidewalk, his body twisting and spasming violently. Sleepers walked around him, avoiding him and his thrashing touch. Christopher, however, could sense something different about the man, the subtle twisting of reality that meant magick had been used here. And not very long ago.

A pale girl with teased black hair squatted on a doorstep nearby, listening to a Walkman and watching the man's seizure with a distant indifference. Christopher pulled over to the curb near her. "Hey!" he yelled from the car. "Hey! Do you know what happened to him?"

She shrugged. "Man came by and touched him."

"Which way did the man go?" Christopher asked. The girl pointed. "What did he look like?"

"Dunno."

"But you saw him?"

"Yeah."

Christopher ground his teeth. "Eblis," he whispered under his breath, "jump to her Walkman. Make her cooperate."

Eblis didn't acknowledge his command, but sudden shock washed over the girl's face. Her mouth fell open and her eyes went wide. The little color that was in her face drained away. She rose and walked over to stand beside the car. "Now," asked Christopher a second time, "what did the man look like?"

"He was wearing black. And he was singing. He went

that way." Her hand, the one holding the Walkman, came up and pointed west.

"Is that all?"

A shudder passed through her body. "Yes."

"Leave her, Eblis."

The girl collapsed suddenly, falling to her knees as though in prayer. A trickle of blood ran out from under her earphones and dripped down the white line of her jaw. Her eyes stayed wide, staring into the night. *Her taste in music is atrocious*, observed Eblis in a detached tone as Christopher drove away.

"What did you do to her?"

Not much. She hears different music now. And she doesn't need a Walkman to hear it.

"You're evil, Eblis," Christopher commented with a smile.

Of course.

■ ■ ■

Kate frowned slightly as she stared at the monitor of her computer terminal. Christopher Kent had a record as clean and ideal as the record of a Technomancer could be. From his Awakening to this afternoon's debate, it would appear that he had never made a mistake worth recording.

It had been a fairly simple matter for her to tap into the Iteration X databases. Iteration X maintained a high level of electronic security around its files, but the New World Order was, after all, the master of information. All Kate had needed was some time, patience, and the aid of a few New World Order technomagickal computer utilities. Now that she had obtained access to Christopher's files, though, she was disappointed. His service record was sterling, the commendations from his superiors were golden, and his attitude, in general, was exemplary.

To judge from his behavior in the parking garage, she would have expected at least some marks against him, but there were none. Kate could see about three possible explanations for the discrepancy. One, she was dealing with someone who had experienced a burst of truly erratic behavior. That seemed unlikely. Two, she was dealing with someone who was such an adept actor that he could effectively lead a double life. Given the blatancy of Christopher's attempt at seduction and his intense emotional involvement in the debate over the Node at Pan's, that seemed unlikely as well. She didn't think he would be able to pull it off. Three, she was dealing with someone whose files had been altered. That appeared to be the most likely of the three alternatives — except that she could find no indication that the files had been tampered with. But no one could possibly have such a perfect record! Not even her own files were this spotless!

Frustrated, Kate expanded the scope of her search, hunting for any indication that Christopher might be less-than-perfect or that his files had been changed. She poured over his service records again (nothing new). She looked for any personal files on the system (there were none). She checked his most recent system activities (he had looked up information regarding locations of mage activity in San Francisco). She dipped into his medical records, and discovered that even his health was perfect. Finally, Kate was left staring blankly at the schematics for Christopher's cybernetic arm as she massaged her aching temples with her fingertips. The arm was a marvel of technomagick, even though most of the intricacies of its design were lost on her. Something though... something about it tugged at her. Something was ever-so-slightly wrong.

The design was for a cybernetic *left* arm.

Yet she clearly remembered Christopher indicating his right arm as he bragged about Iteration X's magick.

Instantly, Kate was digging deeper into Christopher's medical file. She was met by the same facade of perfection as before: The surgery had been flawless, and Christopher's recovery time remarkably short. Someone different must have been responsible for altering this file, however. The cover-up was far from perfect. Preliminary reports referred to Christopher's left arm as being selected for cybernetic replacement, but the reports from during and after the procedure referred to his right arm. Design reports for the arm, on the other hand, consistently specified that it was the left.

Kate pulled up the files on the medical team, all Technomancers, who had performed the replacement surgery. Although most of the cybernetic surgical procedure was done by robotic, computer-controlled equipment and nanotech machines, a few real people were still necessary. Of the five humans who had been on the medical team that operated on Christopher Kent, four, she discovered, were now dead.

Two had been killed a year after the operation in an attack on the medical station by the unholy Nephandi, mages who had sold their souls to dark and malignant powers. A third, the chief surgeon, had later been executed as *barabbi*, a traitor who had joined the Nephandi. He had gone to his death screaming his innocence. The fourth victim had died in a car accident. The fifth member of the medical team had been transferred away from San Francisco to a very high-security Iteration X operation in Japan. Just six months ago, she had been found in her quarters, screaming like a madwoman as she hacked at her right arm with a scalpel. She was now confined to a Technocracy-run mental institution.

On an impulse, Kate returned to Christopher's service record. He had been to the Iteration X operation in Japan briefly, to consult with the Technomancers there. The visit had been a special honor for someone from outside the operation. It had only lasted three days — and it had taken place six months ago.

Kate sat back in her chair, the pale light of the terminal flickering over her face. She had found what she was looking for, there was no doubt about it. Here was information on Christopher Kent. Here was information about someone who would alter his own files to present a glowing, perfect image. Here was someone who would kill two innocent police officers out of hand, either as a warning to her or, the thought struck her suddenly, as pure revenge. Here was someone who might want revenge against her as well.

She began the process of downloading the information that would damn Christopher. Her superiors would want to see it, as would Christopher's superiors in Iteration X. They would deal with him.

Her computer terminal signaled that one of the files she was downloading had a related record, a working document that had somehow never been erased; did she want to download that as well? Kate brought the document up onto her screen before replying.

It was a copy of the surgeon's notes made in the operating room. Everything had apparently gone according to plan until Doctor Sahgal, the woman who had later gone mad in Japan, had put the robotic amputation module into place. The device, a stainless steel framework that covered the whole body, had malfunctioned, severing Christopher's right arm instead of his left. It turned out that the anesthetic had malfunctioned as well. Christopher was still awake and screaming inside the metal womb of the amputation module. It had been sheer luck (coincidence, Kate thought, always coincidence) that Christopher had been experimenting on a prototype cybernetic right arm himself. The prototype was quickly brought to the operating room and successfully attached. The incident had been covered up by the surgeons to protect their reputations.

Kate bit her lip. Had Christopher been so vengeful before the accident, or had the error of the medical team made him that way?

The answer was worse than she could have guessed, and lay hidden in several digital pictures that were electronically linked to the forgotten file. They showed Christopher's prototype arm before it had been attached to him, a naked skeleton of gleaming metal and computer chips. There was something etched on one of the chips. Kate enlarged that section of the photograph, then cross-referenced the etching with the New World Order's database of magickal symbols. The surgeons, concerned with the events in the operating room, had probably never really examined the symbol.

She found a match. The etching showed a narrow triangle, pointing up, with some kind of almost-human creature contorted, head down, within. The symbol was used by the Nephandi.

■ ■ ■

Christopher had never really realized before how many people wore black in San Francisco. Especially on Halloween.

The crowds grew thicker as he drove west. It must have been around midnight. He scanned the sidewalks, looking for any of the black-clad multitudes who might be singing. Eventually, he was forced to park and continue his search on foot when the crowds became too heavy. Frustrated, Christopher took a package of cigarettes from his pocket and shook one out. Cupping his cybernetic hand, he activated the lighter that was built into his palm and lit the cigarette. Blue smoke writhed around his head as he walked. He should have gotten a more complete description of the mage out of the girl. Wearing black and singing were just too vague. The search was next to impossible!

Fortunately, coincidence was on his side. As Christopher stepped off Post Street into Union Square, he almost ran into a woman dressed in a slinky vampire costume. She took no notice of him at all. Her gaze was fixed on a bare brick wall. Her arms were outstretched, and she was praying loudly. There was a strange brightness in her eyes, a kind of ecstasy Christopher had seen only on those caught up in religious trances. She was smiling. Every few seconds, she would slap her hands into the wall. Her palms were already bleeding. Magick surrounded her as it had the shaking man, but much more strongly.

Christopher turned to look into the heart of Union Square. Night lent the benches and palm trees an air of unfamiliar strangeness that they lacked in daylight. The pigeons that thronged in the park during the day had left for some nocturnal roosting place. Most of the homeless people who, like the pigeons, spent their days in the park, had also departed, leaving the dark square to the costumed legions of Halloween. Among those legions, beneath the column in the square's central, brick-paved courtyard, stood a figure in black, arms raised and mouth open as if in song.

"We've found him, Eblis," Christopher whispered.

The familiar was silent for a moment, then replied quietly, *I don't like it. Something is wrong.*

"What?"

I don't know. Why has he done this to these people? Why has he been so open with his magick?

"He hasn't been that open. Sleepers will think the man is an epileptic. They'll think the woman is on drugs."

Perhaps, ventured Eblis, *we should look for another mage.*

Christopher shook his head. "No. We're going through with this tonight." He felt the muscles of his stomach tightening in anticipation. "I want my revenge on Kate Sanders now."

Christopher...

"What can he do to us, Eblis? There's one of him and two of us." Flicking his half-smoked cigarette away, he stepped into the courtyard. He was probably still fifty feet away when he first heard the mage's song over the noise of the crowd. It was wordless, but so full of force and passion that Christopher hesitated for a moment.

There's still time to get out of here, Eblis advised him.

"No." Still, Christopher made his way around to the far side of the courtyard so that he could at least get a good look at the Traditions mage before approaching him. Most of Union Square was in shadow, the lights either burned out or deliberately broken. The people in the square tended to avoid what pools of illumination there were and stick to the darkness. The mage, however, stood directly beneath one of the few functioning lights.

The first things that struck Christopher were the mage's eyes and face. If the praying woman's eyes had been bright, the mage's eyes were radiant. His face was also alight with joyful transport, as if he could see something that no one else could, something wonderful. Only slowly did the rest of him come into focus: black clothes as the girl with the Walkman had said, fair skin, very tall, and very thin, with black hair combed back and a black goatee framing a mouth that was open in song. He looked like he had stepped out of a painting by El Greco, elongated and illuminated by an ethereal light. He was also surprisingly young, perhaps in his mid-twenties. It was difficult to tell.

Christopher hesitated again, trying to decide how best to handle the mage. He had hoped that he might be able to establish the mage's Tradition before speaking with him, but the man was like a combination of several Traditions, all of which had very different beliefs and could require very different approaches. To judge by his enraptured expression, the mage belonged to the Cult of Ecstasy. His youth and dress suggested that he was one of the Hollow Ones. His heavenly singing indicated membership in the Celestial Chorus.

He would have to wing it, Christopher decided, basing his tactics on the mage's responses. He settled a neutral, but serious, expression on his face and walked toward the column.

The mage's song stopped instantly, as though someone had turned it off. Christopher noticed that the mage's eyes were as black as his clothes. "The path you follow," the mage said tranquilly, "is broad and smooth, with meat and wine at hand and deep shadows to shield you from the light."

Christopher froze.

He knows, said Eblis in a soft, dangerous hiss. *Be careful!* Christopher didn't need his familiar's smoky voice to make him realize this. But the mage's words could be interpreted in two ways. Christopher chose to interpret them in the way that was most likely.

"The path I follow is smooth," he replied confidently, as though no other answer were possible, "because the Technocracy has made it that way." He let his face fall a little bit. "But that's not why I'm here. I need to talk to you. My name is Christopher." He extended his hand.

The mage stared at it as though it were something unclean and profane. His eyes returned to Christopher's face. His deep, luminous gaze was like a weight. Christopher let his hand drop. The mage was silent a moment longer before responding, "I am Rafael. The healer."

"A healer! This couldn't better!" Excitement rose in Christopher's voice, exactly as though that were really the case, and he beamed brightly at Rafael. Meanwhile, he searched his memory frantically, trying to remember all he could about the Traditions. Was "healer" some kind of special rank among them?

Eblis must have anticipated his need. *The database compiled by Iteration X contains no mention of* healer *as a position or honorific used by the Traditions in a regular way.* He hesitated. *In Christian iconography, however,* Raphael *is the name of an archangel associated with healing.*

Christopher twitched his thumb, acknowledging Eblis' report. Perhaps Rafael was a member of the Celestial Chorus after all. He bowed his head. "I need healing, Rafael. The Technocracy has done terrible things to me." He paused, a little dramatically, then held up his right arm. "They stole my arm." He could almost feel genuine tears on his cheeks. Soon, Ms. Sanders, he thought confidently, soon...

"That which is given cannot be called stolen."

Christopher's head came up with a snap. He could sense Eblis' shocked silence. His masters had lightly demanded his right arm as part of the cost of his Rebirth — his right arm, when all of the arrangements had already been made to have the replacement performed on his left. He had had no choice but to obey and create a new plan on very short order, making the sudden amputation of his right arm look like an accident. But how could Rafael have know that? "I didn't..."

Rafael was halfway across Union Square, walking south with a graceful, measured stride. Christopher had to sprint to catch up with him. "I didn't know what I was doing!" he insisted defiantly. He spun out a lie desperately. "I was newly Awakened. The Technocracy offered me guidance! You know what Awakening is like."

Rafael paused in mid-stride. "I have never Slept."

Behind them, on the spot where Rafael had sung to the column, a man yelled with joy and threw his arms around a woman. Rafael looked back at them. "After six years of trying, she's pregnant."

Christopher blinked. "Did you do that?"

"Yes."

"And the man and the woman on Post Street?" Rafael's "healing" seemed rather erratic.

"Who?" Rafael turned his gaze to the sky. "There are so many who require healing in this world. I lay my touch wherever there is need." He sighed, a deep, gentle, weary sigh. "I cannot heal your arm, Christopher. It is gone forever."

"I don't want my arm back." Christopher drew a deep breath, ready to make his move. "Rafael, I want to leave the Technocracy. I want to join you."

Rafael looked at him again. "Is it so easy to put oaths and allegiances behind you?"

This time, Christopher barely even heard Eblis' warnings. The skin on the back of his neck was crawling and his hands itched unpleasantly with the urge to destroy the person who seemed to know so many of his secrets. "I beg your pardon?" he forced himself to ask calmly.

"Is it so easy to let go of old allegiances?" Rafael's face was serenely peaceful. "Can you truly put your past behind you?"

His words were simple, without malice or device. There

was nothing duplicitous about them. Rafael really was far too innocent for his own good. As Eblis waited anxiously, Christopher relaxed. A smile spread across his face. "No, it isn't easy to let go. But I can do it if I have to. Heal me."

An answering smile spread across Rafael's face. "Then you are welcome among us." He reached to take Christopher's hand.

Christopher stepped away. "No. I need to talk with you more first." He looked around at the crowds in Union Square. "Not here. I know a place where we can talk without being interrupted. Come with me." Gesturing for the mage in black to follow, Christopher set off across Union Square, heading into San Francisco's South of Market district. He glanced back to see Rafael gliding like a priest in his wake.

I hope, said Eblis earnestly, *that you're going to kill him. He knows far too much about you — your arm, your allegiances.*

"I don't think he does," Christopher whispered under his breath. "He's not all there, if you know what I mean. I suspect he Awoke as a child, and his mind snapped under the strain. Some of what he's saying might be dead-on, but I don't think he understands it. He's perfect!"

What?

"I lure him to Pan's, we act out Kate's defection for the cameras, and then..." Christopher glanced back at Rafael. The mage was still there, following him like a shadow. He nodded and Rafael nodded back. Christopher looked forward again and his grin turned feral. "Then we kill him and no one will notice he's gone."

I still don't like it, Eblis muttered. *We should get rid of him now. How far is Pan's?*

"Not far."

"Christopher," said Rafael abruptly. Suddenly the mage was walking right beside him. "A devil sits on your left shoulder, and you talk to him."

"He torments me, Rafael," Christopher replied blithely. "When I join you, will you do battle with him?"

"Of course."

"I knew you would."

■ ■ ■

Kate stood before the desk of her immediate supervisor, a cold woman with a scar on her face and hair that had been pulled back in a tight bun. The woman looked up from her computer and the information that Kate had brought her.

"You think that Christopher Kent may have joined the Nephandi?"

Kate nodded slightly. "All of the information points to it, Julia. It is the rational conclusion."

"I concur." Julia sat back, folding her hands in her lap. "Unfortunately, there is nothing I can do about it until I consult with Iteration X. Do you know where Mr. Kent is now?"

"No. I think he may be plotting against me, however."

"Why?"

"This afternoon I defeated him in the debate over the Node at Pan's." She hesitated, then added, "I believe that he may have had ulterior motives in arguing that the site should be destroyed. I think he may have wanted to hand the Node over to the Nephandi."

Julia raised one eyebrow. "Do you have evidence to support this?"

"Only suspicions. But it's a possibility, isn't it?"

"I can't act on suspicions." She frowned. "However, I can see that he might attempt to attack the Node, anyway, as a simple act of revenge. We should try to stop him." Julia glanced up at Kate. "Take a squad of Men in Black to Pan's. Maintain a watch for Mr. Kent. If he does attack Pan's, you are authorized to use deadly force to stop him."

"What would constitute an attack?" inquired Kate seriously.

"Given the evidence against him?" Julia leaned forward. "I think his slightest appearance could pose a threat."

■ ■ ■

"...and I have six brothers, Christopher. Though they may not know it."

"Michael, Gabriel, and..." Christopher paused as Eblis fed him a third name. "Uriel?"

"There are others," said Rafael happily.

You're right, commented Eblis. *He is crazy.*

Christopher nodded and murmured sourly, "Pan's isn't far now. Then—"

"You talk to the devil again, Christopher." Rafael reached for his shoulder. "What do you say to him?"

"I say that our destination is not far." Christopher stepped away from Rafael's fingers. "And that once we're there, I will be able to rid myself of the burden that tortures me."

"Ah." Rafael let his hand drop. "Did I tell you that I have followers, Christopher? The legions who have felt my healing touch?"

"You might have mentioned it."

"There are more, though. So many more..."

If Rafael's pattering monologue had not already driven him to the depths of frustrated distraction, Christopher might have noticed the ambush before it happened. As it was, however, all he heard was a sudden rush of bodies from out of the shadows, and then there was a knife against his throat and the sharp point of another pricking into his side.

"Don't move!" snapped a rough voice in his ear. "Don't even breathe!"

On top of everything else tonight, he was being mugged. Christopher almost pitied the would-be thieves. Out of the corner of his eye, he could see Rafael, the knives of three punks touching the pale skin of his neck. The mage was smiling beatifically at them. "Eblis," Christopher whispered, "how many—"

"No talking!" The knife at his throat pressed a little closer. Christopher decided that the punk holding that knife was going to die a little more slowly than the rest.

Eight, Eblis reported. *All with knives, two with guns.*

Not bad odds — provided Rafael wasn't too squeamish and didn't do anything stupid. But he needed a little breathing space. "My money is in my pocket."

"We don't want your money." One of the punks, a flannel shirt tied around his waist, stepped around where Christopher could see him. On his chest, blood was soaking through his T-shirt. "This isn't a trick-or-treat. You have no idea what kind of night we've had. We just want a little fun."

"Look—" Christopher began, but Rafael interrupted him.

"You're wounded," the mage observed.

Eblis groaned. *Oh no.*

The punk with the flannel shirt gave a short, bitter laugh. "Like I said, you don't know what kind of night we've had! We pick this little group as a mark, figuring they won't be a problem. What happens? They whip out these big fucking knives and go nuts!" He pulled up his T-shirt, exposing nasty, shallow, raking cuts. Christopher could barely suppress a snicker. The punks had badly underestimated their marks twice in one night.

"I don't think one of us got away without some bloody souvenir," the punk leader continued. "And all we wanted to do was have a little fun on Halloween." He smiled viciously at Rafael. "You wouldn't want to deny a bunch of kids their Halloween fun, would you?"

"Let me heal you," said Rafael dreamily, as if he had heard nothing the leader of the punks had said. He reached out and put his hand gently against the chest of one of the punks holding him. There was a sudden, tiny flash of white light.

The young man shrieked as a tremor ran through his body. His knife clattered to the ground as he staggered back, clutching at his leg.

"Jesus Christ!" yelped another of the punks. Rafael touched him before he could move away, and there was another flicker of light. He went down to the ground in a shaking heap. Rafael turned his serene gaze on a third punk as he lowered his knife hesitantly. The punk had a two-inch long gash on his face, running along his cheekbone. Rafael moved his hand up and ran one finger along the cut. The punk's eyes went wide, and his mouth opened as if he were ready to scream, but no sound came out. Rafael's finger left a bright smudge behind as it moved, and when the light faded, the cut had healed. When he took his hand away, the punk slipped to the ground, unconscious.

Rafael smiled at the punk leader.

The man with the flannel shirt pulled out a pistol and pointed it at him, at the same time gesturing with his free hand at the punks holding Christopher. "Do him!" he ordered. He fired three quick shots at Rafael.

The bullets turned into blazing white streaks in mid-air, vanishing before they reached the mage.

The punk with his knife at Christopher's ribs backed away at the sight. The punk holding his knife against the Technomancer's throat was either more disbelieving or just plain stupid. He didn't move. Christopher's cybernetic arm pistoned up and his hand clamped onto the punk's forearm, plucking it away as though it were a child's arm. The punk screamed in pain. Christopher thrust him back, the strength of the arm easily throwing him twenty feet.

All thoughts of how the punk would die were gone out of his mind. Rafael's magick was tearing viciously into the fabric of reality. The mage was making no attempt to disguise his actions as coincidence. Rafael was using vulgar magick, magick that was sure to attract Paradox, in the most casual manner Christopher had ever seen. "He's crazier than I thought."

Christopher! Eblis began urgently, *I think—*

"Eblis, where's the one with the other gun?"

Gone. They're running. Christopher, I—

He ignored his familiar's voice. "Rafael! Stop!"

The mage in black was walking slowly toward the leader of the punks. For his part, the leader was pumping bullets at the smiling figure. Just as with the first three, though, every shot vanished in a streak of light before it could hit its target. The punk emptied the clip in his pistol, shooting point-blank at Rafael's chest. When the gun clicked emptily, Rafael laid one hand against the punk's blood-soaked T-shirt and brushed the other against his forehead.

"Your body isn't the only thing that's wounded," he whispered. White light flared again, and the punk's eyes rolled back in their sockets. Rafael held him for a moment, kissed him on both cheeks, then lowered him gently to the ground.

Christopher stormed up to the mage in a towering rage. Except for the unconscious punks, they were alone on the street. "You idiot!" he screamed. He leaned across the body of the punk leader, and his organic hand lashed out, slapping Rafael sharply. "Haven't you ever heard of Paradox? You could have killed yourself, and I need you alive, damn it!" He struck the mage again. "You could have killed both of us!"

Rafael just kept smiling. "I was never in danger from Paradox."

"You were throwing enough vulgar magick around to bring down a horde of Paradox spirits!" If Rafael destroyed himself now, where would he find another mage to take to Pan's? Christopher raised his arm again — but this time it was his cybernetic arm that came up. Shocked, he froze it in mid-swing and forced it down. "Eblis? What are you doing?"

Kill him now! shouted the familiar in a voice like howling winds. *Kill him! You can't see it, can you? He's—*

Rafael reached out and touched Christopher's jaw, just below his left ear. The flash of light cast strange, unearthly shadows across his face. Christopher felt a wave of nausea pass through him, and a strange pinching sensation in his jaw, as though Rafael were squeezing a very large pimple. Christopher clamped his lips shut against a howl. When Rafael's hand came away, he was holding a tiny device of steel and plastic, with a very fine wire trailing from it. It was his link with Eblis.

"What have you done?" he breathed.

"I have taken the devil from your shoulder. I have begun your healing."

Christopher took a slow, deep breath and stepped back from the mage. "Damn you," he hissed. "Damn you." Then in a roar, *"Damn you!* I don't care if I have to search for a decade to find another mage and take my revenge on Kate Sanders, I'm going to have my revenge on *you* right now!" He raised his cybernetic arm, pointing his palm at Rafael, and triggered the same lighter he had used to ignite a cigarette earlier that evening.

Now a screaming gout of flame gushed out to engulf the mage. Rafael didn't even have a chance to move.

Christopher lowered his arm, cradling it. "I'll get you reconnected, Eblis. Just be patient."

Fool... Eblis' voice was as distant and weak as thin smoke, but distinct, and inside his mind instead of humming through his bones.

The pillar of flame that was Rafael sighed. Christopher looked up.

The mage was regenerating as quickly as the fire could burn him; his skin, hair, and clothes reconstituting themselves from ashes in a massive display of the most vulgar kind of magick. The flames around Rafael began to change color as well, slowly shifting from orange to blinding white. In the middle of the inferno, Rafael looked at him and said, "When you have walked in the fires of heaven, the flames of Earth hold no heat."

"No!" Christopher jumped back as Rafael walked, still burning, toward him. This was impossible! So much vulgar magick — surely the mage should have been writhing in the throes of Paradox!

Fool, whispered Eblis again.

Christopher gritted his teeth. "I am not a fool!" He straightened his back.

Rafael glided forward. "Let me heal you, Christopher."

Christopher spat at him. His spittle sizzled in the flames. "No mage of the Traditions is going to lay so much as a finger on me!"

Rafael paused, cocking his head, then laughed, a musical sound against the crackling fire. "How long have you thought that I belonged to the Traditions?"

"About as long as you thought that I belonged to the Technocracy!" he shot back. Christopher reached for the corruption deep inside himself, the corruption that had been cultivated by his Nephandi masters. He spat at Rafael again, but this time his spittle was black and putrid-looking. It didn't evaporate in the flames, but passed through them, splattering against Rafael's cheek. Christopher sneered at the mage. The spittle would consume him slowly, eating away at his substance.

Rafael wiped it off, leaving only an ugly acid burn behind. He looked at Christopher sadly. "The things of Entropy and the Nephandi-Lords have little power over me, *barabbi*."

Christopher stared at him, open-mouthed in shock. And the significance of Rafael's words finally sank into his brain. *How long have you thought that I belonged to the Traditions?* He resisted the darkness of the Nephandi. He was immune to Paradox. Rafael wasn't a Traditions mage. He was something else, something totally insane, something whose nature defied the laws of Paradox. Rafael was a Marauder, a mage consumed by madness!

But the madness of a Marauder also granted power greater than that of the Technocracy or even the Nephandi. Marauders were dangerous! And he had been walking and talking with one! Christopher spun, ready to flee, only to find himself against a blank wall. He turned back to Rafael. How was it possible? How could he not have recognized the mage for what he was? The very presence of a Marauder was supposed to warp reality!

"Ah," said Rafael, as though he were reading his

thoughts. Christopher slammed a mental shield down around his mind, but Rafael didn't seem to notice. "What makes you think reality *hasn't* been warped? I am the healer — perhaps I am only replacing things in their proper order."

Grabbing desperately at his magick, Christopher hurled himself through space. He had no particular destination in mind. Any destination would do, as long as it was away from Rafael.

His magickal journey came to an abrupt, stomach-wrenching stop. He had moved about six feet from his starting position. Rafael was pointing at him, immobilizing him with countermagick. "You need to be healed. You must be healed!" The Marauder reached for him.

"No!"

Although he couldn't use magick to move himself away from Rafael, there was nothing wrong with his legs. He ran.

"The corruption inside you is part of the plague on the world. You know yourself that you need healing, Christopher!" Rafael called after him. "Why else do you think that you found me? Coincidence?"

Christopher turned a corner, putting the Marauder behind him. He tried dialing the cellular phone in his arm as he ran, calling Iteration X for back up, knowing they would help him. All he got was a busy signal. He used magick to reach out with his mind to any other Technomancers or mages nearby. And got a headache. Rafael was still blocking his magick!

"Eblis!" he shrieked. "Eblis!" There was no reply.

It was Kate Sanders' fault! All of it! If she hadn't beaten him at the debate, none of this would have happened! Damn...

Wait! Pan's was only a block or so away now! Rafael couldn't possibly know about the New World Order cameras there! He couldn't block them! Tears began to stream down Christopher's face. The New World Order monitors would see him on the cameras and send help to him! He sprinted down the sidewalk and around another corner. Pan's was so close...

Rafael erupted out of the air in front of him, the white fire spreading behind him like huge wings. The blast threw Christopher back against a wall, stunning him. His vision went dim. Rafael almost seemed to be drifting toward him, his feet not touching the ground.

"I have a world to heal, Christopher," he was saying gently. "There are so many people that need my touch. Many find it hard to accept, and this causes them pain. Some, like the woman in Union Square or the young men back there, need healing of the body. Others need healing of the mind." He paused, kneeling in front of the Technomancer. "You need healing of the soul. Accept my touch, Christopher."

"No!" Christopher thrashed helplessly, trying to find some way around the angelic Marauder. "I won't!"

"But you already have." Rafael smiled at him. "*I need healing*, you said, and *heal me*. Haven't you already given your assent?"

"Eblis!" Christopher screamed one last time. "Do something! I know you're still there! Stop him!"

No. Eblis' voice echoed in his head again, stronger this time, like thunder in his mind. *You wouldn't listen to me. I tried to tell you.*

"Eblis! We had a bargain!"

You are a fool.

There was a sudden, horrible pain in his shoulder. A cold, sharp pain. A pain Christopher remembered from the day that his arm had been replaced, and he had had to stay alert enough to sabotage the amputation module with magick and cut off his own arm. The pain of knives cutting into his flesh — but this time from the inside.

Rafael laid a hand on his head as though blessing him. White fire lashed through him, fighting the dark corruption in his belly, burning it away. Burning everything away.

"Careful," Kate told the Man in Black, "he may still be awake."

The Man, one of seven she had brought with her to Pan's, nodded and reached slowly for Christopher Kent's body. His six comrades, two standing protectively beside Kate, had their pistols trained on the Nephandi. Kate held a pistol as well, though her concentration was focused mostly on keeping watch for signs of magick. Christopher seemed comatose, his eyes wide and staring, but there was every chance that he was very much alert and waiting for an opportunity to strike.

Kate and the Men in Black had arrived at Pan's only about fifteen minutes ago. Ten minutes later, one of the Men in Black had discovered the unconscious Christopher here in the shadows, almost within sight of the club. Christopher lay slumped on his side, eyes open, a pool of blood spreading out from under his body. Aside from the unseen wound, there wasn't a mark on him. It seemed as though a fire might have raged around him, however. The sidewalk and the wall behind his body were scorched and dusted with dark ash in a three foot radius. Christopher must have been leaning against the wall — when he had fallen over, he had wiped some of the ash off the wall. The bricks underneath were as clean as if they had been freshly sandblasted.

Kate held her breath as the Man in Black touched Christopher's body, fully expecting something horrible to happen. Nothing did. The Man in Black touched the body again, then struck it firmly with his fist. The body shook with the impact, but that was all. Kate exhaled, relieved, and put away her gun. Under the watchful eyes of the Men in Black, she moved closer to Christopher and put a hand on his neck. His skin was still warm, though perhaps slightly cooler than normal, and his pulse was weak but regular. He was still alive. Kate bit her lip in thought, then took a small electronic device from her pocket. She pressed it to Christopher's temple and touched a button on its side. A liquid crystal readout came to life on the device. It showed absolutely nothing.

With a sigh, Kate deactivated the device and put it away. She stood, unclipping a cellular phone from her belt and dialing it without looking. Julia answered.

"We found him," reported Kate. "He's... not a problem."

"Are you sure?"

"He's catatonic." Kate glanced at the ash and scorch marks around Christopher's body. "It may have been a Paradox Backlash of some kind. He must have been using vulgar magick." She took a deep breath. "It burned out his mind, Julia."

"Can we reconstruct it? We may be able to extract some valuable information on the Nephandi."

"No. It's gone completely. There's no higher neural activity at all."

"Too bad," Julia said coolly, "but at least his own stupidity saved us the trouble of destroying him. I was able to contact Iteration X. They support our actions fully and congratulate you for uncovering the *barabbi*. Well done, Kate."

Kate looked down at Christopher's face. His expression had been fixed in a terrible, silent scream. "Thank you, Julia." She hesitated for a moment, then asked, "What would you like me to do with the body? He's still more-or-less alive."

"Iteration X doesn't want it back, and we don't have any use for it. It may be tainted. Have the Men in Black dispose of it."

"Yes, Julia." Kate hung up. She stared at Christopher's face a moment longer, then turned her back on the Nephandi. "Get rid of the body," she instructed the nearest Man. "File the usual report." She walked away, returning to the dead-black Cadillacs of the New World Order that were parked in front of Pan's.

The other Men in Black followed her. The Man Kate had assigned to clean up Christopher Kent's remains squatted by the body and rolled it over. The movement released a fresh spray of blood from Christopher's right shoulder. His right arm was missing. The Man in Black didn't give it a second thought. He just hoisted the dead weight of the body over his shoulder and followed the other Men, already mentally preparing the disposal report. Another report to be lost in the massive, endless files of the New World Order.

■ ■ ■

Eblis crawled through the shadows, dragging himself along by his fingertips. He was effectively blind. Christopher had never seen a need to build visual sensors into his arm, only contact sensors so that he could feel through it and audio sensors so Eblis could hear him. Eblis was limited to the senses of touch and hearing, with a small ability to sense the minds around him through magick.

And he sensed a mind now, a crazed, jumbled mind. Why hadn't he thought to scan that mind before? He would have recognized the mind of a Marauder instantly!

"Going somewhere?" asked Rafael.

Begone, Eblis broadcast using Mind magick. *There's nothing you can do to heal me.*

"I'm so sorry."

Eblis laughed bitterly. *I imagine you actually are sorry that I'm beyond your influence.* If he could have spit, he would have. *I know about you now though, Rafael. When I am able to contact other Nephandi again, we will hunt you down and destroy you.*

"*When* you are able contact other Nephandi again — so it seems Christopher wasn't the only one to give something away." Rafael ran his hand along Eblis' "back." "Christopher gave himself to the Technocracy... and then to the Nephandi... and then to my healing. What did you give up?"

Nothing. I am Nephandi. I do not give — I take!

"Then why can't you contact other Nephandi?" Rafael waited for an answer. "You're trapped, aren't you? You gave yourself to Christopher and allowed yourself to be trapped in there. Like a genie in a bottle."

Eblis curled suddenly, lashing forward with his shoulder joint like a scorpion striking with its tail. A circle of blades bristled there, scoured clean of Christopher's blood by the Marauder's healing fire. The blades had been part of the arm's design from the very beginning, originally designed by Christopher so that he could remove the arm quickly if Eblis ever turned against him. He had never realized that Eblis knew they were there.

Now though, the knives met with nothing but empty air. Rafael was gone.

Eblis settled back down to the ground and resumed pulling himself along. After a little while, he began calling out with his Mind magick. Eventually someone would hear his call, someone like Christopher. A young mage or Technomancer, newly Awakened but weak and greedy and desperate for the power that the Nephandi could offer. *Come, Eblis whispered. Come and give yourself to me...*

WAITING FOR YESTERDAY
■■■■■■■■■■■■■

Brett Brooks

The man sitting at the table looked down at his watch, across the room, and back at his watch. The time was still the same: 9:45. He picked up his glass and took a small sip. He could feel the waiter moving toward him, though he didn't need to turn around to see it actually happen.

"Do you wish to order anything, sir?" The question was more of a reminder than a request.

"No thank you," he told the waiter. "I'm still waiting for someone."

The waiter nodded, turned, and walked away. The man picked up his glass of water and took another drink. He looked at his watch. It was 9:47 now. He had lost another minute. What had happened to 9:46? He realized that time wouldn't wait for him any longer.

Some might have argued that time had been remarkably kind to this particular man. The old saying that age makes a man grow more distinguished was very true in his case. As he had aged, his hair had turned gray, and his body had become a bit less defined, but overall, his physical appearance had improved. He was attracting the attention of more women now than he ever had as a youth — though he was now only marginally interested in the opposite sex.

It used to be that he was able to keep track of every second of his life. He made a point to know where time was and how he could best put it to use. He even joked about being the master of time to his peers — when they would listen to him. Now he was lucky to remember all the things he wanted to do in a day, let alone do them with remarkable timing and precision. He would lose a minute here, or an hour there, and never find out what had happened to them. The hands of the clock kept moving, and his comrades moved on with them.

He sat thinking of people in the past, wanting to cling to the moments that he had spent with each one. Although time wanted to take even this little comfort away, he found that memories can live forever with a little effort. The friends of today meant even more to him, mostly because there was only one left. The two of them weren't very close, but their relationship was very dear to him — and to her, he thought. He would cling to that for as long as he could.

He looked at his watch. It was 9:56. Time had stolen from him once again, and disappeared without a trace. He was still alone at the table.

"Excuse me. Is anyone sitting here?" The woman was tall and beautiful. She was wearing a bone-colored dress that was cut high on the collar, with long sleeves and a tight-fitting skirt. A string of pearls was wrapped several times around her left wrist, and a small brooch of something that resembled an abstract gear was perched on her right breast. She had auburn hair that was pulled up on top of her head with only a pair of wispy strands left to frame her face.

"I'm sorry, but yes," he replied, "that seat is occupied."

"By whom?"

He found it hard to tell her that there was someone already there when the table setting was obviously untouched. The napkin, glass and other utensils were all in their properly appointed spots, just as though they had been placed there only moments ago. "Actually," he said, "I'm waiting for someone to arrive."

"Your wife?"

"No."

"Girlfriend?"

"Um… no, actually. Just a friend."

"Well, let me keep you company until they arrive."

He was hesitant to make a move. His life was his own, and he did not willingly share it with strangers. Instinct told him to trust this woman, however.

He stood up and walked to the other side of the table, pulled out the chair, and let the woman take the seat across from him. The setting was a luxurious display. Each table of the restaurant was unique, an intimate setting. A person did not come to this establishment for a casual meal, but rather for an experience to remember. The chairs were plush red velveteen, with high backs and deep cushions. The table was adorned in the Victorian style, with elaborate woodwork and lead crystal to complement the intricacy of the design. The man could pay no attention to the table, though, for he was still fascinated with the woman who had come to meet him. His eyes lingered on her features, trying to memorize them for some future task. He spotted a small scar on the top of her forehead and smiled easily. The man took his seat across from the woman, and rested there comfortably.

"Thank you," she said, adjusting in the chair as he returned to his.

"You're welcome. Pardon my asking, but what brought you to my table?"

"Well, I saw you sitting here, and I was about to be seated myself. I thought that maybe we could enjoy each other's company."

Before he was able to reply to her statement, the waiter returned to the table. "Can I get you anything to drink?" he asked in rehearsed fashion.

"Yes, please," she replied. "I believe I'll have a fruit manhattan."

The waiter turned to the man, who said, "Just the water, thank you."

The waiter smiled and walked off.

"Just water?" she asked. "Don't you like the drinks here?"

"It's for health reasons. I don't believe we've introduced ourselves. I'm Peter Thomas."

"I'm Elizabeth Montgomery."

Peter winced at the name and extended his hand to clasp hers.

"I hope it doesn't seem like I'm prying, but who have you been waiting for?"

"How long do you think I've been waiting?"

"Over an hour, I know. I was sort of stood up myself tonight."

"That's hard to believe."

"Thank you. I didn't really know him that well, and I guess I should have chosen a slightly less-expensive place to eat. Maybe I scared him off."

"Oh." Peter slowly picked up his water and took a sip.

"I take it you don't want to answer the question?" she asked.

Peter set the drink down and stared back at her. "It's not that, really. I guess I'm just not sure how to answer the question. I was waiting for a friend — or at least someone who I thought was a friend. Her name is Leda Evincia. We've been meeting here every Halloween for the past six years. I've come to cherish these set dates and wouldn't let anything stand in the way of being here. Apparently, she doesn't feel the same way."

"Why do you say that?" she asked, the tone in her voice softer than before.

"Because the friend I knew wouldn't come into a restaurant an hour and a half late looking like someone less than half her age and lying about her real name."

The woman's mouth dropped. She threw herself back in the chair and let her hands land firmly on either arm. "How did you know? When did you figure it out?"

Peter was laughing lightly as she questioned him. His

demeanor had already changed dramatically, and his face lit up the table. "I figured it out just after you sat down, though I suspected it when you walked up."

"But how did you figure it out?"

"Well, you were doing your best to disguise your voice, but you didn't even try to hide your speech pattern. There's also the matter of the scar on your forehead. The average person might not see it, but I know you too well to miss something like that."

"Damn!" she said softly.

"Plus... Elizabeth Montgomery? The woman from *Bewitched*? That was the best you could come up with?"

"I'm sorry it isn't up to your standards," she replied sarcastically, echoing Peter's laughter. "With all the time I had, I should have come up with something better. I'm sorry I'm so late, there was this horrible fog over the bridge, and—"

"Don't worry about it. But," Peter pointed toward Leda, motioning up and down the length of her body, "what happened to you?"

"What? This little thing?" Leda sat up in her chair like a proud schoolgirl, displaying the youthful body in question. "Do you like it?"

"You didn't come up with some crazy machine to do this, did you?"

"No, no." She smiled. "Guess what happened."

"I don't want to play this game, Leda."

"Oh, come on. Please?"

Despite everything else, she was still a beautiful woman, and Peter was more than slightly influenced by this fact. "Well, last time I checked you were still happy with the... eccentricity, shall we say, of the Sons of the Ether. Working with those magickal machines was your life. So I'm guessing that you're still a member of that order."

"Right."

"Though I must admit, you never have struck me as the

'mad scientist' type that they try to give off as an image."

"Don't push it. Go on."

"Well, you seem to be breathing and everything, so no vampires were involved."

"Right again."

"So what happened?" Peter said, trying desperately to get out of the guessing cycle.

"I met someone." Leda fell out of the game willingly.

"What do you mean, 'you met someone'?'"

"I mean that I met someone."

"Oh, so you've suddenly lost forty years off your life because you met some guy? Pardon me for thinking this, but I believe that you've left some details out of that statement."

Leda laughed just as the waiter arrived with her drink. He placed the drink carefully in front of her and began to go through his speech about the evening's menu. Somewhere around the grilled sea bass, Peter lost track of what he was saying. He was paying close attention to the woman across the table from him. When he had seen her last year, she had been a sixty-plus-year-old woman who hadn't aged as gracefully as he. That hadn't really mattered to him, though, because Leda Evincia was the type of friend he had always needed. She respected him for who he was, she was someone who could understand the art he practiced, and she didn't care about politics — not the politics of state, but the politics of magick, which prevented far too many people from becoming friends because of something as simple as the way they worked. Now he was sitting across from a woman who was trying to flirt with him, entice him, and... what else? He was trying to see past her physical appearance, into another world where visuals don't matter as much as essence. He wanted to see what she looked like now.

"Well, I think that the duck sounds great." Leda brought him back to the table. The waiter was walking away.

"I'm sorry," he said. "I was miles away."

"Yeah, I could tell. That's not very polite. Especially with an old friend."

"That's just it, Leda. You're not an old friend anymore. You're young. I'm worried about you. That's part of being a friend."

"I know. You don't need to be worried about me, Peter. I'm a big girl — maybe not as big as I used to be, but still old enough to take care of myself. I want you to be happy for me, not worried."

"I'd like to, but there's still a lot that I don't understand. There's a lot that you haven't told me. Who is this person you met? What did he do? How did he do it? Just what exactly happened to you?"

"In all the years I've known you, that is the one thing that I think is most annoying about you," Leda said abruptly.

"What?"

"The way that you try to center everything around yourself."

"What do you mean? I was asking about you."

"Oh no. Don't try to make it out like you were being some glorious savior, trying to play the knight in shining armor come to my rescue. In case you haven't noticed, I don't need to be rescued. I took my own experience and put it to my own good use. You were trying to direct the conversation the way you wanted, so that you could ferret out all the information you thought I wanted to hide from you 'because it might hurt me.' You think that you have to know everything. Isn't it good enough that I'm happy?"

"No, it's not!" Peter sat quiet for a moment before continuing. "You're acting strange, Leda. I don't know exactly what happened, but this change is more than just physical."

No one seemed anxious to break the definite air of tension that had arisen across the table.

"Look, Leda… I'm sorry. I guess I do get a little carried away sometimes. As long as you're safe and happy, then I should be happy for you, too."

"Thanks. I appreciate that."

"Still," he said in contrast, "suddenly getting forty years younger is a big deal. I really do want to know what happened. Why won't you tell me?"

"Because."

"Good reason."

"Because I promised that I wouldn't. Not even with you. I'm sorry."

"You promised this new man in your life. I'm jealous." Peter was only half-joking.

"Yes, I did. I'm sorry."

"It's okay. I take it you told him about me."

"Well… sort of. I told him that I was meeting an old friend tonight, and that I really wanted you to meet him, but I didn't tell him anything about you, or how we met, or, well, much of anything, really."

"Good. At least you are trying your best to keep both of us in the dark about each other."

The couple stopped their conversation as the waiter arrived at the table to take their orders. Peter once again lost himself in observing the woman sitting across from him. He studied her features closely. They were very similar to those of the woman he knew, but altered in such a way that she wasn't quite the same. With the return of her youth, it seemed that she had lost some of her life. She sat there mindlessly chatting with the waiter, a big difference from her normally aloof behavior. Their distance in time was suddenly putting a distance in their relationship. In mere minutes, a friendship that had built itself on trust and honesty was seeing deceit and uncertainty work their way in with little effort. He wondered if the youth inspired her attitude, or if it simply allowed him to see something that he wouldn't notice before — perhaps out of the fear that he would suddenly feel older. In either case, he couldn't deny the youth in her face and features.

Her suddenly flawless face and features.

"And you, sir?" the waiter asked.

"I think what she ordered sounds wonderful. I'll take that, too," he said, hiding his lack of knowledge about the menu.

"Very good. Your salads will be out momentarily," the waiter said before walking away.

"Well, that's surprising," Leda said. "I didn't think that you liked fish."

He didn't, but he wouldn't drop his bluff now. "I thought you wanted the duck? Doesn't matter. I'm entitled to a change. Besides, I do like it occasionally. Just not often." Peter reached inside his jacket to find his note pad and pen.

"What are you doing?" Leda asked.

"Oh, just jotting down some notes. You know me, once I get an idea, I've got to start getting something down right away," Peter answered in a calm and level voice.

"Right now?"

"Yes. Don't worry about it. I'm not going to drift off on you."

"Peter, of course you are, but I've gotten used to that."

"Anyway," Peter said while scribbling some figures on the pad, "tell me about this guy. Where did you meet? Did you find him at a meeting, or through that magazine of yours, or what? I mean, I know you don't get out much."

"Well, for one thing, Paradigma isn't a magazine, it's a journal for members of the Ether, so there aren't any classifieds in it. Can you imagine if there were? 'Lonely female soul seeks quiet, scientific partner to explore the limits of a joint reality. Must have long extension cord.'"

Leda started laughing before she finished her own joke. Peter laughed along with her, taking only a moment to glance from his notebook to her face and back again.

"Hey, maybe we've got something there," Leda said. "We can start up a private singles magazine. We could call it *Magemaker: For That Magickal Match*."

"You're avoiding the subject again, Leda."

"Fine. Pardon me for wanting to lighten the mood."

"If you want a light mood, just tell me about Mr. Wonderful."

"Well, to start off with, his name isn't 'wonderful,' it's Smith. Benjamin Smith."

Peter looked up from his writing, pensively.

"I've heard that name before," he said, "or at least I think I have."

"Well, that is possible. He is into the arts. The magickal type, not opera or the theater. Well, not really, anyway."

"How did you meet?" Peter asked, returning to his notebook, turning to a new page and starting again.

"It was kind of strange, actually. I met him at the grocery store. At the time, neither one of us had any idea about the other one — in a magkical sense, I mean. I rarely show much of an aura, and neither does he. I guess we both carry the same paranoia about being revealed.

"I've always hated the fact that mages aren't accepted in society. The fact that people who are able to perform these feats — tap into powers that most overlook — cannot freely enter into society as beneficial members is ludicrous. Do you realize all of the good that we could do if everyone could just accept that magick and science can both exist? Why, some of the machines I've created myself could help cure many of the world's ills, but I can't use them openly. No, that would be "vulgar." Magick so blatant that it breaks the world's illusion of normalcy — whatever that is — creating such a disturbance that... I'm rambling, aren't I?"

Peter chuckled politely.

"Anyway, I had been running into Benjamin at the grocery store for the past few months, and—"

"The past few months?" Peter interrupted. "How long have you been with this guy?"

"About three weeks."

"He did all this in just three weeks?"

"I thought we weren't talking about that."

"Sorry," Peter said, returning again to his notes.

"Anyway, we had been seeing each other at the store for a while, and we got to the point where we recognized each other walking down the aisles. We stopped and talked, and then went on about our shopping. Eventually, we just kept talking more and more, and, well, ended up seeing each other away from the store."

"Uh-huh. How old is this young man?"

"He's thirty-three."

"And you didn't see anything wrong with a man half your age asking you out?"

"It so happens that he likes older women."

"Then why did he make you young? It was him, right?" Peter looked up from his pad to confront Leda's scowling face.

"You're doing it again," she said.

"What?"

"Trying to control the situation. You're trying to manipulate me into telling you about what happened. I already told you that I promised not to talk about it. If you want, you can ask Ben when he gets here."

"Wait a second. He's coming here?"

"Didn't I mention that? He's going to join us in an hour or so. He had some things to take care of, and he wanted to let me have this evening to myself, so he won't be coming by until later. He didn't want to come at all, but I really want you two to meet."

"I'm rather looking forward to it myself, I think."

"I think you'll like him. He's such a sensible man, and knowing you, I think you'll see eye-to-eye."

"Uh-huh. So, what order is this young man with?"

"Well, I guess I'll let you ask him about that." Leda looked past Peter to the approaching waiter. "Here are our salads."

Peter quickly closed his notebook and moved it to the side, placing his pen across the top to secure the pad. The pen was cobalt blue, with elaborate runes etched into its surface. To the naked eye it was a plain pen, with no extraordinary aspects to it beyond a superficial beauty, but the pen was enchanted so that Peter — and perhaps the few colleagues he had whose power surpassed his own — was the only person who could lift or move it in any way. Peter realized that many people would not appreciate this function, but when one is guarding secrets, then security measures are always near the top of the priority list. No one could look in that pad while the pen rested on its surface. That pen had become one of Peter's most valuable tools. It was quiet simplicity, and it suited him perfectly.

The waiter delivered the salads, made sure that nothing else was needed, and left. Almost as soon as he had left, Peter returned to his notebook.

"What are you scribbling down?"

"Just some notes. I told you."

"Well, yes, but we only see each other one night a year. I would think that you might want to spend some of that time with me."

"I know. I will. I mean it, but I've got to finish this first."

"Finish your notes?"

"Yeah."

"Right."

Peter didn't pay much attention to anything else that was happening. He had almost completed the conjuration in his book. With the formula ready, he could proceed with the spell. Words are a means of power, as Peter knew, and names are among the most powerful of all words.

"You know," Leda said, wiping the corners of her mouth, "you're missing a great salad."

"I know. I've had them before."

There was a brief silence before Peter spoke again. "So, outside of your friend, this… what was his name again?"

"Benjamin Smith."

"Yes," Peter spoke while writing in his booklet, "Ben. So,

outside of meeting him, what have you done in the past year?"

"Well, I did complete my study into the relationship between the circuit and the soul. I published the paper in Paradigma, but you probably never saw it."

"No. Sorry, but they haven't included me on the subscription list. Did you have any trouble? That still sounds like a risky experiment to undertake."

Peter was working through the formula now. The B and the S were the keys to the knowledge. They belonged in their places at the beginnings of the names. The rest of the letters were wrong, but bordered on the truth.

"Well, I did have a couple of rather difficult moments. For a while I was actually considering using the marrow of a human skeleton to work into some circuitry to try and tap into the netherworld as a power source. I'm sure the level of necromantic energy would be considerable, and almost limitless. I mean, can you imagine the power that must be derived from death? If we could tap into these levels, find the very source of death, I'm sure we could obtain results that have never even been dreamt of before. The council voted against the proposal though. I can't say that I blame them. After all, we don't want to cause any unnatural disturbances — or anger the Euthanatos. They're a little too obsessive with the idea that they are the only order capable of dealing with death. I was really more concerned with the unnatural disturbance idea, though I've already had enough of those for one lifetime."

"Enough? Enough what? What are you talking about?" The T and the S were correct, even if the word was wrong. The length was right, but the order was wrong. Position was everything.

"Well..." Leda began, "I had a problem a few years ago. Before I met you. I didn't listen to some advice, and I took things a little bit beyond where they were supposed to be at the time. I was still young and foolish, but I guess I learned my lesson. I'll never do anything like that again."

"What did you do?" He saw the problem. Inversion.

"Well, I'd rather not say."

"My, it must be very personal, then." Everything was taking form. Now it was just a process of elimination. Insert the right letter, remove the wrong one.

"Everything is personal, Peter. You know that."

Peter sat straight up in his chair. "Brandon Smitts."

"What?" Leda looked very confused.

"I'm an idiot. I'm a complete idiot."

"No, you're not. I don't know what you're talking about, but I've known you for too long to think that you're an idiot."

"No. I am. I never thought to check before. Fell for an illusion."

"What are you talking about?"

Peter looked at Leda across the table. Her face was shining with innocence. He couldn't tell her. Not yet, anyway. "You've never heard of Brandon Smitts, I take it?" he asked slowly.

"No, I haven't."

"That's no surprise. Most people haven't. It's sort of a secret."

"Well, who is he?"

"Somebody I'm hoping can help me with a problem." Peter took a drink from his glass. "So, this Benjamin of yours will be joining us?"

Leda looked at him piercingly. "What are you up to, Peter?"

Peter hesitated for only a moment before answering. "Trust me, Leda. I'm not up to anything. I really want to meet him. For your sake."

"You're making it very hard for me to trust you right now."

"Do it anyway."

Peter could feel Leda looking at him, trying to see past

the veil of his smile. As always, he was the perfect gentleman and the perfect companion.

"Okay," she smiled back, "but only because we're such old friends."

The waiter came and took the salads from the table. One plate was full, the other empty. He promised that the entrees would be brought out soon, smiled and left.

The table was suspiciously quiet after the waiter left. Peter felt uncomfortable, not knowing what to say or how to say it. He knew he needed to get more information before the night was over, but when might prove to be just as much a problem as how. He looked down at his scrying pad, with his pen laid across its cover. He moved the pen off the book slowly, opening to a new page. The weight of the pen was suddenly very obvious to him.

"What are you doing now?" Leda asked.

"I've got something else I have to work out. I'm sorry to be doing this on our night, Leda, but it has to be done. It has to be done right away. It's important to me."

"Well, I'm not happy, but I do understand."

"Thanks." Peter opened his book and began inscribing symbols along one edge to prepare the paper. He was finished in under a minute. He thought briefly about how he had transferred the symbols to the page with such speed. When he had begun his studies so many years ago, it had taken Peter almost an hour to complete the same simple preparation. Now he was well past that, and moving toward the end of his life and his career. He had... what? Maybe ten years left in him? Twenty if he succeeded in hiding from his enemies for long. Of all his regrets, and there were more than he could properly remember, never finding the time to make peace with his enemies rested on the top of his list. And he was thinking of making a new enemy tonight. Tonight of all nights.

"Hello?" Leda said in a sing-song voice.

"Hi," Peter answered. " I guess I drifted off again, eh?"

"That I'm used to. I'm not used to you being so distant. Normally when you drift away, you take me with you. I still remember two years ago when you started telling me about that time you spent in Death Valley. I would never have thought that anyone could make that place sound beautiful, but there I was, listening to you describe this place like it was the temple of your soul, and you made me feel like I had missed out by never having been there. I'll never forget that."

"I remember that night, too. I remember the Valley."

"Maybe, but I'm not sure. You might remember being there, and you might remember telling me about it, but you don't remember what those events meant to either one of us. What's wrong, Peter? Is my change that difficult for you to handle?"

"Lord, no. It's not the change itself that bothers me, it's just..."

"What?"

Peter looked Leda squarely in the eyes. "Why didn't you ever tell me about the Paradox, Leda? That is what it was, right? You got a little carried away with your magick, and it caught up to you. The spell backfired, and you took the brunt of the damage. The magick came back, and... and it aged you. You lied to me."

Leda shifted uncomfortably in her chair, glancing away from Peter's eyes for a brief second. "How did you know? Is that what you were working on?"

"No. Honestly, it wasn't. But it did get me thinking about what must have happened."

"Well, I guess there really is no way to keep a secret from you guys, is there?"

"Nope. We know everything."

Peter smiled, and Leda smiled back, but neither smile was natural.

"How old are you? Really?" Peter asked.

"I'm twenty-six."

'Twenty-six? But that would mean that you were only..."

"Eighteen. I was eighteen when it happened."

"You're just a child."

"A child!" Leda rose in her seat. "I've been coming here for the past six years of my life, meeting with you over dinner so that we could have a friendly, non-competitive conversation and because I enjoyed your company. I never once heard you call me a child in that time, and I don't appreciate you doing it now."

"Let me ask you something," Peter countered. "Did you enjoy fooling with me all those years? Was it some sort of kick for you to play with the old man?"

Leda's jaw dropped. "I never thought that."

She sat a moment longer, and then pushed her chair backward and stood up. "I think that I had better leave."

Peter jumped from his chair and moved to her side. "No. You can't"

"Watch me."

Peter grabbed her arm as she started to walk past. "No, Leda. Don't. We need... we have to wait for your friend to show up."

"What? Benjamin? Why?"

Peter broke. "Because his name isn't Benjamin. It's Brandon. Brandon Smitts. You've really never heard of him, then?"

"No. What do you mean? And why are you telling me his name isn't Benjamin? You've never even met the man."

"Sit down."

Peter helped Leda back into her chair, and then returned to his own. "Leda," Peter began, "did Brandon... Benjamin help you to restore your youth? Answer honestly, please."

"Well, yes. But it was perfectly natural. He'll explain it all once he—"

"He's a Paradox thief."

"A what?"

"A Paradox thief. In fact, he's the only one we've ever

been able to prove exists. They're a rare form of artist, Leda. They can manipulate Paradox like it was magick. They drain it off and use it for… something. We don't really know what. Since he began doing this a couple of centuries ago—"

"A couple of centuries? That's not possible."

"Let me finish, please," Peter continued once Leda agreed with a nod. "He preys on the innocent. The naive. He seduces them, either through love or friendship, and exploits their conditions. He's posed as members of all the studies, from a variety of Chantries — every magickal house in the world, almost. He always finds those who are afflicted with a serious Paradox condition, one that will probably never clear itself. Like your aging. I think he drained off the harmful magick that reflected back onto you somehow. He gave you what you wanted by taking what he wanted. He promises hope and then he delivers it. But it's not real, Leda. It can't be."

"What do you mean?"

"What do I mean? You're the scientific one, just think about it. We both view magick as a force of nature, right?"

"Yes."

"Then it has to abide by the forces of nature, right?"

"Yes."

"That would include a Paradox, Leda. Don't you see?"

"No."

"Okay. Look at it this way: Nature abhors a vacuum. If you take something away, then something else is going to fill it right back up again."

"Yes."

"That works for the Paradox, too. Somehow, just somehow, this man is able to take the Paradox away from others. He takes this massive, powerful harmful force — the Paradox — and moves it to some other place where it doesn't exist like we know it — at least that's the theory."

"What for?"

"We don't know. The common suspicion is that he's

somehow using the Paradox as a battery of sorts, tapping into it as a means of drawing out more power. We do know that he has been able to create magickal effects beyond anything we ever thought possible. The rumor of the Paradox thief goes back for as long as we can find written records on magick. Nobody knows how they came about, or where they come from. Until your... friend came along, we weren't even able to prove that they were real. These people bring a whole new meaning to the word secret, and have apparently been performing miracles for mages for a very long time. They can do amazing things, Leda. Look at you — he restored your youth. This man is able to take away a force that positively frightens most beings and play with it like a child with a toy. But the important thing for you is that once the Paradox has been taken from someone, then something has to replace it. Something that can replace Paradox."

"What's that?"

Peter saw the fear in her eyes. "More Paradox. Usually worse."

"What do you mean?"

"I mean that Paradox doesn't like to be played with, and since it apparently can't find Smitts — the thief it wants most of all — it goes after the person who had it to begin with — with a vengeance."

"You make it sound sentient."

"Some say that it is."

"So, what happened to me?"

"Well, he took away your Paradox. That made you young again, but another Paradox replaced it."

"Another Paradox? What do mean? I didn't notice anything."

"No, you didn't. You're going to be a little numb for a while. You probably can't detect any magick on you right now."

"Well, what is it?"

Peter shifted in his seat. "When did you get that scar on

your forehead?"

"This?" she asked, bringing her hand to her forehead. "In the accident. When I was eighteen."

"It's gone."

"What?" Leda grabbed her purse and shuffled through it until she brought out a small mirror. She looked at her reflection, pawing at the spot on her forehead where a scar had once been. "Oh no. Oh no. Oh no," she mumbled repeatedly.

"You're getting younger, Leda. The scar disappeared tonight. You've changed tonight."

Leda sat quietly as she realized the meaning of Peter's words.

"How long have I got?"

"I don't know. Not yet."

"But... but... what are we going to do?"

"We're going to wait and see if 'Benjamin' shows up."

"What if he doesn't?"

The waiter arrived at the table and presented two gloriously prepared pieces of fish. The smell of the sea, combined with capers and a hint of citrus, swam around them. Peter hated the smell of the fish. He hated everything about the sea. The waiter asked if he could do anything. The couple shook their heads, never taking their eyes off each other as the waiter walked away.

Peter looked down at his food. He picked up his fork and carefully removed a piece of the meat, raised it to his mouth, and began to eat. He could barely taste the food, almost didn't even notice the texture, and raised another bite to his mouth. He looked up at Leda and smiled. She was probing the fish delicately with her fork.

Peter picked up his pen, opened the pad once more, and began to run through some calculations. He was taking time out to eat some of the fish now and then.

"This isn't too bad," Peter said.

"What?" Leda replied desperately.

"The fish, Leda."

"Oh."

Peter saw Leda staring nervously at his hand, trying to catch a glimpse of what he was writing. Even if she could see it clearly, it wouldn't make sense to her. The order was very diligent about making sure that no one knew their languages. They even went so far as to change them every few months to make sure that no one could decipher them.

"Have I ever told you about the wonder of numbers, Leda?" Peter asked, trying to change the subject.

"No. Not really."

"Everything in the world — or even near the world, or related to the world in the most casual of manners — can be explained by numbers. If you take the time to become one with them, to learn what they do, and how you can use their own special magick for yourself, then you suddenly feel like the most powerful person alive."

"Can you help me?"

Peter stopped writing and looked up at her. She was so young. He heard it in her voice, like a frightened child calling to her parents. If he listened back, remembering her voice all the other times they had talked, he could always hear the child in her voice. When they first met, when they finally got to know each other, in the times when they were at each other's throats, she was still the child, reaching out to a parent. What had he seen before that had deluded him? He didn't know, because he couldn't remember. The woman he knew was completely gone. Time had taken something very precious from him.

"Tell me, Leda," Peter began, "what was it like? Being the wrong age, I mean."

"Why do you care?" Leda asked, still pushing the food around her plate solemnly.

"Because I want to know. I find out that there are aspects of you which I never knew existed, and you expect me to just sit here and wonder about them? I know you too well, and I would like to know you better."

Leda looked straight into Peter's eyes. Peter left his eyes with hers as his hand drifted across the paper.

"I don't know," she answered. "When I was old, it seemed natural, even though it wasn't. The only place that it ever affected me was in my head. I was perfectly healthy. I still had my experiments to keep me occupied, but I... I was older. It's hard to explain, I guess."

Peter smiled at her. "Do you want to know what it was like being twenty-six?" He didn't wait for an answer. "When I was your age, I was living in the Midwest. Indiana of all places. In the '50s everybody thought that they wanted to be a rebel. You lived by your own code — or at least they portrayed us that way in the movies. You would be surprised how little change has come over the country in the past four decades. Sure, there have been a lot of superficial ornaments hung on the problems we faced. Yes, the world has become a bit more cynical, but nothing has really changed. We thought that the world was on the brink of destruction then, the same way that people do now. If you don't believe me, then just check out the other films of the time. Nuclear annihilation was on every marquee. Horrible monsters were destroying the planet, and the stars were our only hope. The funny thing is, once they made it into space in those movies, they found that there were monsters out there, too.

"Now, with all that going on, try to imagine becoming a mage. Choosing to follow a Tradition that dated back so far that no one could remember exactly when it started. We could have been the first people to ever tap into magickal energy, you know? The Order of Hermes, that is; it is a very powerful society of mages that has existed longer than most would even admit. In any case, there I was, a man who was torn between the utter destruction of mankind and false rebellion that surrounded me — and I chose to take the path less traveled. At least I think that's the quote.

"I don't think that I realized at the time just how much

work I was getting involved into. I was blinded by the glory of the magick. Don't tell anybody I said that, we're supposed to be beyond those things, you know. I would spend hours slaving over calculations that my instructors could do in their heads. That made me so angry. I never let on, of course. I was the quiet, diligent student, willing to learn all that they would teach me. I've never been patient, though. I wanted to learn everything right away. They knew better. They probably even knew I was faking being patient, come to think of it, but they never let on. They let me grow into my own power. They let me make my own mistakes. They let me become my own person.

"I still have some regrets. I don't like that I never found time for a personal life. I guess the best I've done is to know you for the past few years. I also regret breaking from the Chantry. The Order of Hermes took me in and really taught me everything I know. It's a house of True Magick, not just of spells. The people in that one house became my parents, and then eventually my peers, and shaped my life as much as anything that I've done myself. You should never abandon your peers, Leda — even if they are the most obstinate, short-sighted people you've ever met. Especially if that's the case. If I had stayed, maybe I could have helped them, and I wouldn't be carrying around all this guilt right now. Now, I'll never go back. Maybe that's for the better, anyway. Who knows?"

"I thought you knew everything?"

"Shhh. You'll ruin my image."

Leda chuckled. A genuine laugh that made Peter smile. "Well, I have to admit, that sounded suspiciously familiar," Leda said.

"How so?" Peter asked, still working in his pad. Moving numbers and using forces.

"Well, we've all been there, haven't we?"

"No, Leda. You're there right now."

Leda stopped for a moment. She silently stared forward.

The waiter came and removed the plate from in front of her, and then moved over to Peter, who indicated that he was finished, and took his plate as well.

"Would either of you care for coffee?" the waiter asked.

Peter nodded for the both of them. The waiter smiled and walked away.

Peter looked at the figures he had reached on his pad. He tried to show no expression.

"Well?" Leda asked.

"What?"

"How long have I got? That is what you were working on, right?"

"Let's just say that it's not over yet."

"In my case, maybe that should be, 'it hasn't begun yet.'"

"Whatever."

"Tell me something, Peter. If you were in my position, what would you do?"

"Do you really want to know?"

"Of course I do. Please?"

"I'd make the most of my time."

"Then why aren't you?"

"What?"

"Why aren't you making the most of your time? I mean, you're great at speeches and everything, but you aren't doing anything. When is the last time you went out with someone besides me?"

"I like going out with you."

"But once a year?! Please, Peter, I think everybody should always listen to their own advice. I think you need to start making the most of your life. Go see your brethren. See if they'll speak with you. Work things out. Get on with your life."

Peter smiled, remembering the enthusiasm that accompanies youth — and maybe even feeling some of it return. "I think maybe I will. Maybe we both will."

Leda looked at Peter, and then moved her eyes around

the room. "Benjamin's not coming, is he?"

"You don't know that."

"No, but... what am I going to do if he doesn't show up?"

"We will worry about that when the time comes, and it hasn't. Not yet."

The waiter came up and poured coffee into Leda's cup. He then moved over to Peter's and filled it. "Would either of you be interested in seeing the dessert cart?"

The couple looked at each other. "Yes, I think we would," Peter said. "Oh, and bring a bottle of champagne. Your choice."

"Very well." The waiter walked away.

"What was that for? You don't drink."

"You never know when you'll have something to celebrate."

They both smiled. "How long should we wait?" Leda asked.

"Where else do you have to go?" Peter answered.

"Questions to answer questions. You'll never change, you know that?"

Peter raised his coffee cup up, and moved it halfway across the table. "Here's to tomorrow," he said.

"Here's to yesterday," she said. They touched cups and then drank deeply.

CANDLEDARK
■■■■■■■■■■■■■

Thomas S. Roche

The news came like a nightmare amid whines and screams and popping noises over the ancient radio in the stolen car. The broadcaster at KKBA said the bridge was all but impassable, the cotton fog of San Francisco had blanketed the Bay in white. Paragon glanced at Christian, shaking his head slowly. Christian only frowned and took a puff of his Camel. Things were totally fucked up.

"He'll kill us," said Paragon, as if it were a simple fact of life and not a very important one. His voice, even so, was a rough growl, a low-intensity monosyllabic threat.

Christian shrugged, flicking the cigarette butt out the window of the speeding car. "And what if he does?" he growled in an identical voice, also without emotion. "He's the one who came up with us in the first place, right?"

Paragon looked for a moment too long at Christian, regarding with just a bit too much emotion the beautiful lustrous olive flesh of his face, the strong cut of his jaw with its five o'clock shadow, the muscular build of his body beneath the bulky, black wool car coat. Paragon's eyes, crystal blue, flickered over his partner. His tongue slid out to lick light pink lips. Paragon's eyes and lips were identical to Christian's.

Their eyes met, and both sets of eyes seemed to open up brightly.

"Just keep moving," said Christian. There was a new softness in his voice, but Paragon knew it would be fleeting.

In response, Paragon turned on the wipers.

The fog came down like a vengeance.

■ ■ ■

Nurse Jacobs was at her wit's end. This weird, punk rocker Hackensack girl creeped her out. She'd been working the private home for three years, with five at General before that. She seemed to have a talent for dealing with extremely disturbed types. But Caroline Hackensack defied all attempts to communicate or understand.

Jacobs would have to have a chat with Dr. Halloran in the morning. The girl was getting worse. Dr. Halloran had prescribed new drugs after the girl's little "episode," but still Ms. Hackensack continued her alternating symptoms of agitation, anxiety and depression, the Thorazine shuffle being merely the latest variation in her doomed, ghostlike idiom. And Ms. Hackensack's psychotic breaks continued to increase in frequency. Sometimes her delusions had an eerie reality to them. She always talked about machines and wizards and the Mob, and occasionally vampires and werewolves. She spoke softly of death and whimpered when she considered the night.

Sometimes Ms. Hackensack insisted on being called Candle, the name that was tattooed inside a haphazard line drawing of a black rose above the girl's slight left breast. Halloran had told Jacobs off-line that "Candle" had been Caroline Hackensack's street name back when she'd turned tricks. Jacobs shuddered. The girl had been fifteen. That was too young to be doing those things, too young to be a runaway. But then again, seventeen was too young to be locked up in an insane asylum and stark raving mad.

Jacobs prided herself in being able to speak to crazy people. She knew how to understand them and to make them understand. She could breach their seemingly infinite walls of psychosis and help them open up. She could bring a touch of healing to their broken lives, even if it was only a little touch. It was a talent, a gift from God, she thought, crossing herself haphazardly, and she had an obligation to use it. But Jesus fuck a duck, this girl, this cracked flunkie from the MTV VJ academy, was going to drive Nurse Jacobs insane.

It was sad. Caroline was a pretty girl, and no doubt perfectly smart and sweet somewhere under that cracked exterior. The girl's long brown hair was really quite beautiful, though it had been dyed a mangy black when Caroline had arrived at Holy Ground. (Back then the girl had also had a nose ring, a nipple ring, a stud in the middle of her lower lip and six silver hoops in each ear, but Jacobs didn't like to think about those things, and in fact felt vaguely queasy whenever she did.) Despite Caroline's, er, unconventional preferences when it came to her appearance, she was a fine young woman.

The thing was, Jacobs sometimes felt for the girl. Jacobs could tell that Caroline really cared about her art, and that meant something. Caroline Hackensack, alias Candle, would sit in front of the easel in her private room and paint for hours, painting crazy shapes and dangerous things, abstract oils that spoke of machines and faceless, doomed illusions. Jacobs didn't like the idea of a psychotic using oil paints, but the girl's rich family, managing her private care in *absentia*, had insisted. Jacobs was convinced that the painting contributed to Ms. Hackensack's condition, but Halloran, that USC prick, told her not to worry about it, it couldn't do any harm. And what the hell, he told her, the girl seemed to have talent, even if she did have a "condition."

Jacobs sometimes stood in the doorway, watching the girl paint. Caroline would sit there, almost motionless, lost in the texture and grain of the canvas, lost in the painting and creating its abstract shapes, layer upon layer of oil paint being slathered on day after day. The girl's lustrous hair cascaded over her shoulders and seemed, despite all of Jacobs' better judgement, to move faintly in the shadows of the room as if blown by an unseen wind. Caroline would lose herself so completely in the painting that she wouldn't be aware of Jacobs standing there, staring into the rich textures, into the *reality* of the painting, for what seemed like hours.

Caroline had been working on the same painting for a week now: sn ancient fire-scarred church. But as the work neared completion, it seemed somehow unlike a painting; it was shimmering, alive. Caroline Hackensack had talent, that was for sure — the painting was incredible. What really irritated Jacobs was that she couldn't remember where she'd seen the church before, and that disturbed her. It was probably nothing. She'd probably seen it on a postcard somewhere.

Jacobs had agreed to work Halloween because all the parties she'd been invited to would be full of sleazy guys, and besides, she hadn't been able to think of a costume so she'd be too embarrassed to show up at any of the parties.

At first, Jacobs thought maybe it was just because it was Halloween that Caroline's painting was especially disturbing her. She stood behind Caroline, watching the girl paint as she had done many times before. Jacobs discovered her mind slipping. She seemed to be losing herself into the brilliant representation of the blackened old church. Jacobs felt like the painting was real.

"Caroline, your painting's going well," Jacobs said finally, tearing her attention away from the picture. She spoke hoarsely, nervously, trying (unsuccessfully) not to be patronizing. "But it's time for lights-out."

"My name's Candle," said the girl. She continued to paint. Half a minute later, Jacobs heard the sound of weeping. "They're coming to get me."

Jacobs started forward, reaching out to touch the girl's shoulder.

"Who's coming to get you, Caroline?" Jacobs was very patronizing now, the condescension flowing more freely, making it easier to disregard the girl's madness.

A wave of terror crossed the girl's face. "Them," the girl whispered, pulling away from Jacobs, her chest exploding in a sob. "The 'Mancers, Technocrats, Technomancers. They're the government, and the Army, and the Mob. They've sent creatures after me. They've sent their servants. They've sent their *things*." Caroline shuddered and buried her head in her hands. *"They're coming for me!"* she wailed and dissolved into sobs.

Caroline would say no more, and Jacobs put the oils away as Caroline moved to the edge of the bed, sobbing. Nurse Jacobs helped the girl into her gown and then put her to bed.

It seemed to Nurse Jacobs that she and Caroline Hackensack had gone through this ritual a thousand times. But Jacobs knew damn well it couldn't have been more than twenty.

■ ■ ■

Fog like this hadn't come in over the bay in all the broadcaster's years in San Francisco, and he continued in that vein, driveling on about fog and the bridge. Christian snorted in vague disgust. Without really caring, he turned off the radio.

Paragon, not missing a beat, took the West Grand exit, then left on Cypress, passing the area where the bridge had come down in the last big quake. Christian recalled vaguely that the carnage had been a motherfucker. Thousands had died, or a couple hundred anyway.

Paragon and Christian had all relevant data about the region downloaded into their brains through cybernetic link.

Christian felt the knowledge bubbling up into his brain as
he looked around at the landscape. In his mind's eye,
Christian saw the photos on the news, heard the
broadcasters on TV and radio. There was something about
a chainsaw and the paramedics having to cut some poor
chick in half to get to her seven year old son or something.
"Man, oh, man," muttered Christian in a vaguely
disinterested fashion. "That would suck."

The projects seemed to go on for miles, enormous
salmon-colored Towers of Babel. Guys in sweats and Raiders
caps mingled around, watching the car go by, aware of its
silent menace. All the liquor stores were huge concrete
blocks, like Algerian fortresses, with only a tiny door and a
couple of barred windows, each a foot square. Christian
thought, *They're like pillboxes*.

Paragon went a couple of times around the parking lot
of the train station, checking to make sure the transit police
weren't in view. The car was pretty much untraceable, but
Paragon didn't want to take any chances when it came to
transit police. Regular cops were one thing, but those
fuckers were scary.

As Paragon checked out the scene, Christian slipped a
cellular phone out of the pocket of his coat. He dialed a
long-distance number in an area code that didn't exist, spoke
a few phrases in a low voice. He shut the phone down and
replaced it in his pocket.

"It'll be waiting," he said flatly.

Paragon parked the car. There was no need to wipe for
prints, since Paragon and Christian didn't have any. They
left the doors open.

Panhandlers sitting at the entrance to the station looked
the other way as the two men passed. The station agent
stared in confusion as the two near-identical figures stood
at the ticket machine. Big black coats, uniform-style, well-
tailored. White shirts bulging with muscle, identical
burgundy ties, black engineer boots, dark hats pulled low.

Paragon's hair hung straight and slick past his shoulders in corn-husk yellow; Christian's was equally long, but black. Other than that, the two men were identical.

Paragon went through his pockets unsuccessfully. He took out a cigarette and lit it. "You got a dollar-fifty-five, Christian?"

Christian laughed grimly, shaking his head. "Nothing but twenties."

"Damn."

■ ■ ■

Candle supposed it wasn't a bad place as insane asylums went. Only ten other residents, and the staff was reasonably pleasant. Skylights and big windows, even if they were bolted shut and covered in thick iron bars and grating.

But Candle didn't care if she was staying in the Taj Mahal. She still had to get out or she would be a very snuffed Candle before long. Security was tight, and Candle knew she couldn't escape before they came to get her. Her family would never understand the danger she was in. Or *maybe they're even behind it*, thought Candle sadly.

Candle faded in and out of a Thorazine daze, staring at the ceiling, her slender bony arm drifting across her eyes, trying to blot out the light from the barred skylight. As Candle dozed, she was tormented by the visions that had come to her so frequently. And when she slipped into waking, she found her body racked by choking sobs.

She knew they were coming for her. No matter how many times Dr. Halloran tried to convince her that they were a delusion, Candle *knew* the things would be here. Since the earthquake, she had known it would be soon.

When Candle woke up for the tenth time that night, she was bathed in sweat. She stared at the ceiling, suddenly aware. The psychotropic daze had left her. Her eyes were wide. She felt suddenly lucid, alive, as if she were free of the thick layer of drugs which had been heaped upon her. She could still feel the effects of the Thorazine, but they were vague, distant, beneath this new artistic clarity. She had to finish the painting. Her pulse raced. They were coming. It would be tonight. They would murder her on Halloween.

Candle slipped out of bed, cautious of the creaking floorboards. She put on her slippers and robe. The light came slanting obliquely through the skylight. She would have to work in the dark. They would be here well before dawn. The painting must be finished.

That damn nurse had already put away the paints. No matter. She eased the chair into its position in front of the easel. Furtively, Candle slipped the safety pin out of its hiding place under her hospital gown. Just as she had done so many times in the last week, she pricked her fingers and squeezed until the blood flowed. She let the thick drops fall into the oils and mixed the paints up quickly, not sure and not caring if she had the proper texture. Over the past week, she had no idea why she did these things. It was just a sort of instinct. The psychiatric drugs had blotted out any real artistic knowledge she had ever had. Now, though, her art was coming back to her. Now she *knew* what she was doing.

Closing her eyes, Candle began to work.

She couldn't have seen a thing in the dark, but it didn't matter. Candle painted with feeling.

■ ■ ■

As the two men walked toward the escalator, a little guy with an entirely red left eye almost bumped into Christian. Christian looked at Paragon, who had seen the eye as well.

Christian stepped onto the escalator.

The BART station was full of derelicts, persons society considered wasted husks. Junkies and homeless and whores and poor guys from the projects and electronics salesmen were all fond of eyeballing Paragon and Christian. But a single glare from either of the men would invariably make the offender turn away. The two men waited at the end of the station, in the shadows where the rats lived.

A girl in a red latex miniskirt looked them up and down, unable to believe what she saw. Christian grinned at her dangerously. The woman backed away, her white, acne-scarred face a mask of nothing. She turned and started walking toward the middle of the station.

Christian and Paragon stood there, hands in pockets, watching the tracks. After a time, Paragon turned and regarded Christian for a long time before turning away again.

Then, Christian, too, turned his head and looked at his identical partner. His lips parted slightly. He looked back down at the train tracks.

SAN FRANCISCO/DALY CITY

The sign flashed violently in red bulbs, half of them burnt out.

BOARD CENTER 4 CAR TRAIN

Paragon and Christian turned, as the wind from the approaching train lifted their hair. They stared at each other, their eyes full of longing. In the explosion of wind, the two men grasped each other, embracing suddenly. Their lips met in a fiery kiss.

SAN FRANCISCO/DALY CITY
BOARD CENTER 4 CAR TRAIN
BOARD CENTER 4 CAR TRAIN
BOARD CENTER 4 CAR TRAIN

The train screamed into the station, rats howling beneath. Christian and Paragon parted and slipped noiselessly onto the train.

■ ■ ■

Paragon and Christian were two beings cut from the same cloth, their genetic material taken from the pancreas of a specimen the Company scientists considered genetically flawless. The clones had been vat-grown in a top-secret Company laboratory in Basel. They had undergone a computer-controlled accelerated aging process while years' worth of experiences had been downloaded to their brains through 19,200-baud cybernetic brainlink. Twenty-five years of intense schooling had been poured into the clones' brains as well as artificial memories of a childhood that some would have considered harsh. Company psychologists had designed the construct of childhood to create a pair of killers.

And Paragon and Christian had been programmed as lovers. It was the opinion of Company psychologists that the ideal partners for killing operations would owe their allegiance, sexual and otherwise, only to the Company and to each other. Years' worth of computer analogs had shown this to be true. But Paragon and Christian were the height of real-world proof. They were highly-trained assassins who had killed many times on Company orders. And they felt nothing. Except for each other.

■ ■ ■

The two men disembarked at 24th, walked down Mission for a couple of blocks, turned right toward Twin Peaks and found the metered public lot. The car was waiting, a big American late-model. The keypad next to the door handle opened the locked door with Christian and Paragon's birthdate, and the keys were under the front seat.

Christian drove this time. Paragon stared at him longingly as they cut back up 26th to Valencia and headed north toward Market. At Market, Christian made an illegal turn. The car moved effortlessly through traffic, past the Castro, onto the road that led up to the mansion homes of the Peaks.

■ ■ ■

Candle wept as she painted. The oilwork had taken on an entirely new form, filled with beauty and terror. She knew she would never finish in time. She cased her brush in intricate traceries around the painting, her tears staining her nightgown and mixing with the oil paints and blood.

■ ■ ■

Christian found the proper street and parked the car. Holy Ground was in a renovated house with bars on the windows.

The security guard had recently decided to take his coffee break on the back side of the house, away from the girl's room.

The police, who generally executed an hourly drive-by of this area, had been bribed by the clones' employer to forget about this particular hour and to, instead, get some donuts on the other side of the beat.

The alarm system of the hospital had also been arranged for. The guard had short-circuited the alarm system just before taking his break.

There was only one nurse on duty. Pushover. The other nurses had, of course, wanted the night off because it was Halloween. Everything had been arranged by Paragon and Christian's employer.

The two men approached the house silently. Paragon slipped a flat black box out of his pocket and pressed it against the deadbolt of the front door. He gave the device a whispered voice command, and the lock opened with only the faintest sound. The two men went inside.

Paragon glanced back at Christian, who moved to the front, blending in with the darkness. Christian withdrew a 9mm Uzi without a stock, rigged for full auto and registered to some poor sap in Denmark, from his jacket. Paragon carried an identical weapon, registered to a randomly selected South African nun. The two men moved up the stairs, cautious, despite the fact that the security guard was out of the way.

The nurse, however, should be at her station, away from the girl's room. They would have time to do the job and get out before the nurse made it to the top of the stairs, thus they would be free from the obligation to waste her.

Christian moved into a crouch as he reached the top of the stairs and saw the neat, white cap on the woman's head. Christian's lips moved in a silent curse as he realized that the nurse had taken this inopportune moment to make her rounds. That totally fucked things up.

But there was no time to waste. "Time to move," Christian whispered to Paragon. "Try not to take out the nurse. But don't try too hard."

■ ■ ■

Candle's eyes went wide as she heard the door opening. Nurse Jacobs shrieked in dismay, "Caroline, what have I told you about getting up after lights-out! I thought the sedative would eliminate this sort of behavior —'"

"Oh shit," muttered Candle through her tears as the two dark figures appeared behind Nurse Jacobs.

Candle's mouth opened in a silent scream. She turned to face the painting in the split-second after she recognized the two forms from her nightmares. They were the two clones, and she knew they had been sent by the 'Mancers that Giancarlo had told her about.

Candle stared at her painting, trying hard to blot out

everything else in the world. She had known this feeling
for so long. She felt the pulse of the universe coursing
through her veins, felt the blood of salvation inside of her.
She could see the beauty in her work and in the architecture
of the old church, the delicious mystery that was art. For a
moment, she could hear the screams of Nurse Jacobs and
the clacking sound as the two men cocked their weapons,
but all was nothingness in a split-second as Candle slipped
into the painting. Her whole being was consumed.

She had begun to Awake two years ago. She had begun
the process of Ascension without knowing it. That was what
led her away from home, onto the street. She had lost
herself, learning her tricks and trade without pattern or form,
guessing at some things, groping for others, her instincts
guiding her. She had made friends on the street, dangerous
friends who had begun to teach her and promised to protect
her. She had learned to love them, Giancarlo best of all.
But the trauma of her childhood made Candle's learning
slow, even though Giancarlo told her she had quite a
formidable talent. Candle had learned a few of the words,
though her Ascension was nowhere near complete.

She had learned as best she could until her father,
employing his own private security force, had tracked her
down and placed her in the hospital, locked away where she
couldn't embarrass her family any longer. The psychiatric
drugs had blotted out her powers, stopped her Ascension,
preventing any further Awakening. Candle had died, and
only Caroline Hackensack remained: blocked, angry,
psychotic, abandoned.

It was only sometimes, in her dreams, that she
remembered any of the things she'd learned on the street,
words like *Verbena*, or any of the things she'd done. The
things she had done: the rituals, guided by her instinct, her
need to drink magick from the chalice of Life with her many
tricks, in a dark and perverted version of the magick that
was the Ascension. The carnal rites she enacted had

afforded her only the tiniest fragments of true experience.

Even dimmer still were the memories of her previous life with her family. Her sonofabitch father. How, guided strictly by dark instinct, she had slit her wrists (not enough to kill herself, just enough to get the right amount of blood), smeared a painting of her desire across the big white wall in her bedroom, and then vanished into it as her mother appeared in the doorway behind her and screamed in terror. The painting of her desire had taken Candle to a place of her dreams: San Francisco, where she'd learned to make her living while enacting the carnal rites of those Giancarlo called the Verbena.

Candle had remembered all these things in occasional bits and pieces while she was in the hospital. But most of the time, she hadn't remembered anything, until she'd been assaulted by the dreams.

At that point, Candle knew that the powerful forces would finally come for her. She wasn't sure exactly why, but she knew, from bits and pieces of memories that she received from her dreams, that it involved a wealthy Swiss man in his early twenties who had been a frequent client of hers. Hans was his name. Candle could remember the texture of his limousine's seats. Hans told her that his father was a very powerful man. Hans knew many secrets, and he told a few of them to Candle. The last night Hans had picked Candle up in his limousine, he'd told her that his father was really mad, something about a brain-scan and some sort of company secrets that Hans had told Candle. She didn't really remember, since she rarely paid much attention to what Hans said. But Has made Candle promise never, never to tell anyone. Candle agreed, figuring she couldn't very well tell someone something she didn't remember.

That had been the last time Candle had seen Hans. Standing in front of an electronics store, she saw a news story about his disappearance. She was vaguely concerned, but within a few days she'd had her own troubles: her father's men had found her and put her in the hospital.

■ ■ ■

Candle blinked and looked around. There were the sounds and smells of a Halloween party going on around her. Ghouls, vampires and wizards stalked past on the sidewalk. The clones had vanished. Candle felt her freedom course through her system like blood from the chalice.

Candle's feet, still clad in hospital slippers, stood within a ghost-image of the wooden frame of the painting she had drawn in the asylum. Deftly, she stepped forward, and the frame dissolved into sparkles and then disappeared amid wisps of vapor.

■ ■ ■

Christian got his arm around Nurse Jacob's throat, pulling her back and kneeing her in the back before turning to face the open door. Paragon had already started blazing. The Uzi lit up in a fire of damnation.

Jacobs fell with a clunk on the threadbare carpet, her head spinning as the sounds exploded all around her.

Splinters of wood and medical plastic filled the room as bullets tore into everything in sight. Christian put up his hand, and both of the clones stopped firing.

Christian shook his head sadly. "The death-rocker got away."

"God damn it!"

The two men raced into the room, toppling the bullet-riddled easel, upending the bed, kicking their way through splintered wood and shattered plastic. The girl was nowhere to be found.

Christian and Paragon slammed fresh magazines into their guns. The two men stood over the bullet-riddled painting. Their eyes flickered as their brains accessed the information which had been downloaded into their biological brains through cybernetic implant. The two of them recognized the church at exactly the same time and looked at each other pointedly.

"Time to vacate," said Christian, and the two men disappeared into the darkness. Their booted feet made rhythmic sounds going down the stairs.

Sobbing, Nurse Jacobs pulled herself to her knees and peered around the doorjamb into the room. Candle was indeed gone. Nurse Jacobs shook her head, trying to banish the explosive ringing from her head.

■ ■ ■

Paragon slipped into the driver's seat and gunned the motor, warming up in the dense midnight fog so that clouds of exhaust blew back over the car. "We're fucked," he said. "We've got to find that death-rock bitch."

Christian lit a cigarette, shrugged. Casually, he slammed another magazine into his Uzi.

"We're going to church," he said flatly. "After all, it's Sunday."

Paragon floored it, and rubber burned as they pulled onto the street.

■ ■ ■

Candle looked around, blending into the darkness. She half-expected to see the clones following her through the painting. But in actuality, she doubted that the two boneheads were that smart. Instead, Candle stood in the middle of the street and regarded the burned-out front of the church. The statues of St. Francis and the animals in front had almost been destroyed by age, but still lent a haunting religious air to the entrance. Someone had put jack-o-lanterns on what used to be the heads of the animals surrounding St. Francis. The heavy beat of Goth-industrial music throbbed into Candle's breastbone, and she *sensed*, rather than heard, the ritual poem being recited beneath the music.

Candle heard screeching tires and realized that she was still standing in the middle of the street. She jumped onto the sidewalk as a speeding hearse came tearing around the corner, windows rolled down, brutal death-metal blaring from the stereo. Candle slipped and almost smashed into a telephone pole covered in what appeared to be rock flyers drawn by Edward Gorey. She stepped back, dazed. She had almost lost her hospital slippers.

She felt highly self-conscious as Goths moved about the entrance to the club, partaking of the celebratory ritual of the Haloween party. She wasn't, she told herself, exactly dressed for the scene. Then she laughed suddenly. She realized that her outfit was the perfect twisted Halloween costume. Candle, still wearing her hospital robe, was dressed for a highly Gothic Halloween. She even noted a couple of black-lace ghoul girls eyeing her jealously, as if they were wishing they'd thought of the hospital gown as a costume.

Smiling to herself, Candle slipped into the crowd.

■ ■ ■

Nurse Jacobs, still shaking from fear as she stood in the room waiting for the police to show up, stared down at the tattered canvas, the only thing that Caroline Hackensack had left behind her when she had disappeared. But Nurse Jacobs was fairly convinced by now that she was the one who had gone insane. Something about the painting upset her, seemed entirely *wrong*....

She picked up the canvas in its balsa-wood frame. Jacobs could remember, clearly, the picutre that she had seen Caroline Hackensack painting hours ago. This picture, while clearly rendered in Candle's (Caroline's) hand (a *very* realistic hand) seemed like it was a living, breathing entity. As if Jacobs could step into it. With a wave of inspiration, Jacobs realized what church it was.

"My God," she whispered. "The girl painted it from memory. . ."

The lights in the painting seemed to flicker.

Jacobs put the painting down, spooked. She heard the sirens outside, heard the voice of the security guard as he greeted the cops at the door.

■ ■ ■

The Waydown, in Ashbury Heights uphill from the Haight, was the Goth club where Candle had first met Giancarlo Giovanni, back when she'd been turning tricks in the Tenderloin, only vaguely aware that her tricks were part of a Verbena ritual she enacted subconsciously.

Candle wasn't sure how the club owners had gotten their hands on a burned-out old church, but it was sure the perfect setting for the particular kind of Goth-fetish indulged in by its rather pretentious, if perhaps somewhat naive, clientele. Still, these people were just like Candle's few friends back East, only infinitely cooler. Candle began to feel very much at home in the Waydown.

She managed to slip past the doorman and was wandering around inside the club, enjoying the feel of the dark music. A pair of Goth-girls, replete with facial piercings and tattooed crosses and black lace spiderweb eroticism, passed before her. One of them soundlessly placed her fingertips on Candle's forehead and smeared it with aromatic chrism. *Someone's raided a church supply shop*, Candle thought to herself. The two girls then drifted off, holding hands, while a skinny guy in stretch jeans, a raincoat and a "CHOOSE DEATH" T-shirt ambled by. Candle smiled, vaguely pleased.

As she slipped deeper into the crowd, Candle felt her

fear returning, her initial exultation at being free fading with the bad hangover of psychiatric drugs. She knew the clones would be after her.

Behind her, she heard a resonant voice with a heavy Italian accent: "Candle?"

Candle tuned, suddenly afraid....

"Giancarlo!"

She threw her arms around Giancarlo, hugging him tightly, much to his gentleman's surprise, and pressed her cheek against the lustrous fabric of his Armani suit.

"My dear! We were a little short on beautiful women, but now that you have graced us...and what a fetching costume! Delightfully imaginative!"

Candle kissed Giancarlo on the check, her eyes filling with tears. "I thought I would never see you again."

Concern furrowed his brow. "My child, why are you so upset? Your trip down South went badly?"

She had begun to sob, "They're after me, Giancarlo. I knew only you could save me."

His eyes darkened. He glanced around to make sure no one could hear him over the music.

"Who's after you?"

"The ones you warned me about. The 'Mancers."

"The Technocracy?"

"Right. My parents had me picked up at the Greyhound station. They were private dicks, in more ways than one. They put me in a home."

Giancarlo looked very dismayed. "How could I let this happen?" He put his arm around Candle and guided her to his table. "My dear, you must tell me everything that has happened, and I shall put myself at your eternal service in an attempt to rectify things. I can't believe I was so careless with you. Please, my dear, sit, and tell me everything."

She hesitated. "What about them, Giancarlo? The 'Mancers?"

"Do you think they'll follow you here?" He was very

calm.

Candle looked down, embarrassed at Giancarlo's confidence in the face of her terror. "They'll follow me. There's two of them, clones. Identical, except one of them's dyed his hair black. The other is blond. They've got machine guns and big black overcoats. Oh, and they have cleft chins."

Giancarlo nodde,considering the problem. "This could be a dangerous situation. It's very tricky to work in crowds like this. Very dangerous. Especially with creatures like these...."

Candle felt a wave of fear. She looked toward the entrance and then toward the back door.

"Wouldn't it be better to run?"

"It is better to confront them in a place of our power, a place made for ritual, such as this. And to join forces." Giancarlo's smile broadened. "And besides, my dear, it would be rude to leave the party. It is Haloween!"

■ ■ ■

The black car screeched to a halt in the street outside the Waydown. Paragon double-parked and slipped the keys in his pocket, leaving the hazard-lights on. The two clones rounded the car, slipping into the crowd.

Children rubbed elbows with ghosts. There was the scent of sweat and blood and smart-drug B.O. The two clones, as one, felt the sensuous shape of their Uzis under the thick wool overcoats. As one, they grinned.

Paragon and Christian were armed to the teeth. Besides the machine pistols, they wore .357 magnum revolvers in shoulder holsters and knives in belt-sheaths. They had been created to be the ultimate killers, and both men knew they were very close to the kill. It was as if they could smell the death-rocker's blood.

Christian frowned. Something seemed wrong.

He spotted the death-rocker across the dance floor. She was running as best she could in the thick crowd. She slipped behind a big guy in head-to-toe leather. Christian motioned to Paragon, and the two men started elbowing their way across the crowded dance floor. The death-rocker ducked down into the crowd, and they lost sight of her.

■ ■ ■

"I found them!" Candle panted to Giancarlo. Her face was a mask of terror. "They're on their way across the dance floor."

"You must present a target," he said, holding her arm, "but one they will not be able to attack immediately." Giancarlo glanced toward the cage suspended from the second floor balcony. There danced a skinny, pale, young man with fangs wearing PVC jeans and a chainmail bra. The club usually paid go-go dancers, male or female, to grace the cage for a couple of hours a night. This gave the other dancers something to aspire to and look at if they got bored. It was a very hip thing in San Francisco, and being a go-go dancer was a very fashionable way to see and be seen.

Candle's eyes were wide. "They....they can see me there! They'll just shoot me!"

Giancarlo shook his head and spoke soothingly, "Candle, listen to me. They can't be *that* obvious. They will try to get you out of the cage. That means they'll have to take the back way up the stairs. Trust me. And take this."

Giancarlo was familiar with the techniques of Candle's magic. He slipped his pocketknife out of the pocket of his suit coat. Gently, he pressed it into her hand.

Candle's eyes were filling with tears, but she managed to take the knife and nod. "I trust you, Giancarlo." Her voice was shaking.

She turned and ran for the stairs to the loft.

■ ■ ■

"We lost her!" Paragon had to shout above the noise of the club.

"Not for long," said his clone-brother. Christian tightened his grip on the Uzi, but kept it down under his coat. "She'll head for the back exit, but she'll have to make it across the bar. Not a chance." The bar was a Halloween zoo, with vampires, ghosts, and psycho killers screaming desperately for Guinness and Bloody Marys.

Suddenly Christian started to laugh.

He nudged Paragon and pointed toward the cage hanging over the dance floor, suspended from the choir loft. Candle had elbowed the latex-boy out of the cage and was dancing to the Goth-industrial beat, her hospital gown flailing wildly.

"She thinks she can hide in the open," said Christian. "Smart chick. We've got to get her down from there and then take care of business. Up the stairs." Paragon followed Christian as he started for the loft, roughly elbowing Goth-kids and darkwave losers out of the way.

To both of the clones, the air in the club seemed to shimmer and dissolve. Paragon glanced around nervously, looking at Christian. Christian looked up, his eyes wide. And then he screamed.

The Uzi had turned into a writhing mass of snakes, tiny snakes the size of garters. Christian pulled his hand back as two of the snakes dug their fangs into his hand, drawing blood. Christian danced through the crowd, knocking people over, ripping the snakes out of his flesh and smashing the remaining snakes on the floor where they dissolved into a mass of tiny rats and went scattering across the ancient church floor.

Meanwhile, Paragon had similarly screamed as his Uzi dissolved into a giant rat squirming and trying to get its teeth into Paragon's flesh. He threw the offending rodent violently against the leather-jacketed back of a six and a half foot tall biker with a dripping red "Satan Lives" painted across his leathers. The biker turned and regarded Paragon, disgruntled, as the Uzi dissolved into a tiny fanged gnome that danced over and sank his teeth into Paragon's ankle.

The biker grinned wolfishly, showing his fangs, and slowly began to grow and change. His flesh became translucent, melting into fetid rot, as he grew larger; his ample flesh stretched paperlike, revealing his skeleton. His eyes bulged. The biker had grown into an enormous skeletal apparition. Paragon backed off, unbelieving.

Christian was a step behind Paragon, the two staring together in disbelief. The Goth-children and punk rockers and costumed weirdos of the club had begun to glow and change, and it seemed as if the whole mass of them was evaporating. Suddenly, the entire group of children had become ghosts.

Christian moaned in terror. Paragon whimpered.

The many ghosts of the club, their bones showing through their translucent flesh, reached for the two clones, with nightmare grins across their white faces.

"Fuck this!" shouted Christian. "It's a trick! Get up the damn stairs!" His voice shook with fear. Paragon and Christian clung to each other, fighting their horror. Viciously, the two men sidestepped the demon-biker, pushing skeletal wraith children out of the way. The clones ran for the choir loft stairs and disappeared into the darkness at the back of the church, their screams of fear wrestling in their throats.

The biker shook his head, his four-inch lip beard waggling curiously. He slipped off his tiny round mirrorshades and put his arm around the slender waist of the pierced and tattooed woman at his side. "Bad fuckin' drugs, Pixie." He licked the woman's throat and laughed. "Watch the fuck out what you buy on the street, baby, or you end up like those two psychos."

■ ■ ■

One by one, the Goth-children who filled the club began to look up toward the choir loft cage. A girl dressed up like a mental patient had just elbowed the latex-clad Goth-boy out of the way. He hissed a catty, *"Bitch!"* and disappeared down the stairs.

There were a few scattered cheers as people saw Candle's costume and showed their approval. Meanwhile, Candle began to dance.

She drew herself into the music and felt the overwhelming heartbeat taking her over, the drum machines and machine-gun synth rhythms throbbing into her. She started slowly at first, humming along with the music. The DJ was still playing something with some sort of ritual lyric. Candle couldn't tell what sort of ritual yet, but she took hold of that sound and let herself go.

Her dance increased in its intensity, and her hospital gown flapped wildly. Candle had begun to recite her spell along with the music, drawn more by instinct than knowledge. The many sounds of the music seemed to take over her whole body as she slipped out Giancarlo's knife.

The ritual poem embedded in the music was one of an erotic nature. Candle used that lyric to increase her own concentration.

There was a chorus of shouting just below her. She heard everything with increased clarity, as if she were newly alive. She could feel the magick of the club flowing through her body. Candle heard the screams. It was Giancarlo's distraction; she didn't have long now. Candle tugged the hospital gown over her shoulder.

Candle drew the knife-blade across her arm, avoiding the artery. People underneath her watched, rapt, enveloped by this piece of performance art. The blood beaded on Candle's flesh. She drew her hand across the cut and smeared the blood over her fingers.

The blood seemed to thin and multiply, running down over Candle's shoulders and face.

There was a moan of approval from the crowd.

Slowly, Candle leaned down and drew a line of blood across the entrance to the cage with her finger. She stood up, her hands and forearms already sticky with the drying blood. She continued the recitation. As her magick reached its peak, the clones reached the choir loft. The scent of Candle's blood and magick had begun to waft through the club.

The club-goers saw the two big guys grabbing for the girl. Club security, probably. They were just mad because she'd pissed off the regular go-go dancer, but this girl's performance was infinitely cooler. There was a chorus of disapproving groans from the crowd.

The men got hold of Candle, and the three of them disappeared into the darkness of the choir loft. Suddenly, the cage was empty, and the music stopped in a heartbeat. The club exploded in applause and screams of approval.

Paragon and Christian, having broken the protective screen formed by Candle's blood, fell into the blackness and began to scream.

■ ■ ■

Candle found herself suffused with magick, overwhelmed with power, as she stood over the two men. She could feel her heart pounding as the blood continued to flow from the long, thin cut on her arm. But the cut had begun to glow and smoke, and the blood on Candle's hands radiated a terrible power. The two clones cowered on a cold marble floor, looking around desperately, trying to figure out where they were.

They seemed to be on an endless plain of black marble. Pentagrams were drawn on the floor in red, each a foot across. The symbols stretched as far as the eye could see.

"Where the fuck are we?" muttered Paragon.

"I was hoping you could tell me," said Christian hoarsely. He drew his .357 and leveled it at Candle. Paragon did the same.

Candle stood before them as a vision of holy vengeance. Her hospital gown had disappeared; she was naked, but swathed in translucent fire and light. Flames rose from the circle drawn around her and began to wrap protectively around her body. Candle laughed, cruelly, evilly, bringing the fires up like a cloak as she regarded the twin muzzles of the revolvers. She was a vision of the holy Goddess, screaming her rage as the clones dropped their weapons, which had burst into flame.

Christian, cursing, shook his blistered hand. He went for his dagger and tried to get to his feet. He screamed as his hand came out of his coat. The dagger was caked with blood, and the blood had begun to squirm with maggots that burrowed into his flesh. Christian threw the knife down, howling.

"Where the fuck are we?" repeated Paragon, more hopelessly this time.

Candle's laugh echoed like a cold wind across the marble plain. She had disappeared, but the flames still rose around the place she had been. "You're in my world, friends. And there's no escape."

Paragon and Christian, hearing that, screamed.

The marble plain went black. Everything was silent.

Paragon and Christian groped around in the blackness, trying to find each other. They clung together and kissed desperately in the darkness.

A flickering light, candlelight, came into being all around them, though there were no candles in sight. The clones discovered that they were in a very different place than they had been. The marble floor had transformed itself into a vast field of lush red silk strewn with black velvet pillows. Paragon and Christian looked around, dazed, as human forms came into being all around them. The figures seemed to coalesce from the very substance of the candlelight.

"Impossible," said Paragon vaguely.

"Unlikely," muttered Christian in response.

The two clones were regarding duplicates of themselves. Dozens — no, hundreds — of them. An infinite plain of Paragons and Christians, dressed identically, stretching as far as any of them could see, all standing on red silk. The center of the plain had vanished, any point being identical to any other.

"Oh, yes," said the many clones as one and moved toward convergence.

An entire world of clones descended upon itself, and the ritual of the flesh began.

■ ■ ■

Candle smoothed her hospital gown over the places where the blood had soaked it. The bleeding had long since stopped, and Giancarlo had helped her clean the cut. She would have to rest soon, but she wanted to sit for a moment with Giancarlo. Numerous Goths had already come up and congratulated her, telling her how incredible the performance was.

"You're fabulous," whispered a girl dressed in a cheesy vampire costume. "It was a work of genius, and it seemed so spontaneous! You summed up all the anguish of being a psychiatric patient.... It really spoke to me."

"Thanks," said Candle nervously. "Thanks a lot." The vampire girl drifted away.

"It really was a wonderful performance," said Giancarlo. "Unbelievable, in fact. Executed with style and diplomacy. Defeating your enemies by giving them exactly what they desired most — that was sheer genius, Candle."

"Thank you, Giancarlo. I couldn't have done it without

you."

"Don't mention it, my dear." He smiled at her. "It was the least I could do. Simply think of it as a favor for an up-and-coming mage, even if you are destined to be Verbena. That is the best thing about being a free agent. You can perform favors for everyone."

"You saved my life, Giancarlo."

"You saved your *own* life, Candle. Never forget that. 'Teach someone to fish...' How does that go?"

Candle laughed, "I could never forget you, Giancarlo!" she threw her arms around the Italian again, kissing him on the cheek. "Let me repay the favor some day. Anything I can do — anything!"

"Please, Candle," he smiled suavely.

"Sorry!" Candle laughed. Then she whispered, "It's in my blood."

Candle lifted a golden chalice to her lips, spilling blue-flaming punch on the table. She could feel the psychiatric drugs fading away. The presence of magick all around her helped. She could feel the magick seeping into her blood through her skin, coursing through her, cleansing her mind of the madness injected into her through the doctor's needle.

Giancarlo smiled at her. He spoke to her in a gentle, soothing voice, "I assure you, your troubles shall cease, my dear, or at least they shall ameliorate...."

Candle smiled and felt Awakened.

■ ■ ■

Paragon stared up into the trees, his eyes glazed. He was naked, and his body was covered in dirt. All around him swirled the cold morning fog. Not far away from him lay Christian in a similar condition. Christian still wore his jockey shorts, but they were on his head.

They seemed to be in Golden Gate Park somewhere — Paragon thought he recognized those windmills. Paragon couldn't for the life of him remember what had happened the night before, except for the episode with the biker, and that weird shit in the club, and something about a room full of Paragons and Christians locked in an unholy ritual of desire on an endless silken plain....

"Oh, yeah," Paragon muttered to himself. "Whoa."

Paragon crawled over to Christian, overwhelmed with sudden concern. If *anyone* had hurt Christian, things were *really* going to get totally fucked up.

Paragon cradled Christian's head in his lap. Christian's eyes opened, and he looked up, fully understanding, at his brother-clone. Paragon gave a sigh of relief and kissed him, running his fingers through Christian's jet black hair.

MAKE 'EM LAUGH
■ ■ ■ ■ ■ ■ ■ ■ ■ ■ ■ ■ ■

James Lowder

The leading man danced across the screen. Singing self-reflectively about the joys of song, he twirled his umbrella and splashed through a puddle on a backlot street slick with machine-blown rain. The camera danced along with him, swooping in to frame his face. The captured smile illuminated the dark theater like a sunbolt. His song resumed a moment later, synchronized sound tailored to soothe a troubled soul, Prozac in stereo.

In the projection booth overlooking the empty Oasis Theater, Miranda Peake felt her spirits lift for the first time since being tossed out of Professor Summerlee's lecture two nights ago. The official notification of censure had arrived from the Sons of Ether earlier that afternoon. It should have reached her sooner, but the earthquake had made it difficult for even Doctor Armstrong's cleverly disguised cybernaut courier to be timely in its appointed rounds.

She had carried the note about with her for the past three hours, neurotically reading and rereading it. Now, finally, Miranda tossed the letter onto the mountain of paper atop her desk. The pile shifted, then avalanched onto the floor. Sheaves of bills stamped *Past Due*, the pages of an unpublished article, and assorted movie stills from B-pictures too obscure even for late-night cable slid across the floor with a disgusted sigh, as if they shared the annoyance of

Miranda's creditors at her slovenly bookkeeping.

Miranda didn't notice. She was busy soaking in the film's message: true love fulfilled and perseverance rewarded. *Cheer up*, the movie seemed to say. *Sure, the Oasis's box office is dwindling with each passing week and your membership in the Sons is threatened, but you can dance through those grim raindrops. Let me show you how...*

Miranda heeded that advice and shrugged off the cloak of despair, at least a little. *People are still interested in happy films*, she decided, her gaze transfixed by the dancer on the screen. *The Sleepers are staying away because of the neighborhood.*

She couldn't really fault anyone for avoiding her squalid little corner of San Francisco, especially the Sleepers. They were blind to the presence of magick, so the Oasis was just another theater to them, one with a bleak and dangerous location. The pot-holed and glass-strewn streets, the crack heads and the hookers, the ever-present possibility of errant gang gunfire bursting through your windshield or blasting open your date's chest — why brave all that for a double feature when you could stop at the local strip mall and stroll through an orderly, aseptic, mega-chain video store? For a couple of bucks and a flash of a laminated membership card, the acne-scarred clerks would give anyone the ability to conjure Pickford or Bogart or Karloff right into her own living room for a two-evening command performance.

Of course that conjuring was only technological sleight-of-hand, not the sort of True Magick Miranda attempted at the Oasis. The most advanced home theater speakers and a bowl of low-fat microwave popcorn could never weave the same spell as the ancient, hissing sound system of an inner-city movie palace or the cholesterol bombs masquerading as popcorn in the lobby. They were part of the incantation, right along with the torn seats and the sticky floors and the overloaded trashcan vomiting up crumpled candy wrappers by the exit.

"Someday the Sleepers will understand," Miranda said forcefully, defiantly. "I'll open their eyes to the possibility of magick, audience by audience, one packed house after another. Then those doddering old skeptics at the Sons Chantry will have to make me a full Fellow of the cabal."

She gave the etheric movie projector humming at her side a light-fingered caress. The contraption resembled something from the set of *Frankenstein*, all blinking lights and arcing Jacob's ladders, a mass of old tubes and thick black cabling. Like the other mages who identified themselves as Sons of Ether, Miranda wrought magick through a weird combination of science and arcane rite. In recent months, she'd transformed the theater's clattering old projector into a Talisman, an object of no small worth that could utilize the magickal Quintessence holding the universe together. But that success paled beside her greater goal.

With the twist of a dial, the unique and potent projector went to work. Through sorcery and technology, the Talisman strengthened the images that flickered across the screen. Suddenly the silver-white sheet became a window, a gate between two worlds. The leading man danced right through the two-story tall casement. He stepped gracefully from the dream realm he inhabited into the gloomy theater, as if the move had been choreographed into his dance all along.

Miranda adjusted two switches on the etheric projector, banishing the picture and silencing the soundtrack. As the mute celluloid continued to spool onto a take-up reel, the mage dashed from the projection booth. She nearly stumbled over a box heaped with tools and unused electronics. Overdue bills swirled about the room like dead leaves in her wake.

At the padded double-door entrance to the balcony, Miranda drew a deep breath, then pushed through. The theater seemed wrapped in a cemetery stillness, but she knew better. The gate was still open. The dancer and a few others of his kind lingered on this side. She could feel them, like the power infusing the air before a thunderstorm. To see them, to hear them, she merely had to focus her mind...

"I'm singin' in the rain, just singin' in the rain..."

"Remember, you're fighting for this woman's honor, which is probably more than she ever did..."

"I always say a kiss on the hand might feel very good, but a diamond tiara lasts forever."

A host of dim, wavering phantoms filled the air — Kelly and Groucho and Monroe. Miranda recognized them all. No matter how many times their costumes or their ghostly faces melted and re-formed, they remained familiar. Most often, their hollow, whispering voices repeated snatches of dialogue recorded years, even decades, past. But the spirits were not anchored to static reality by a strip of celluloid. They sometimes moved in ways unrehearsed before any camera and spoke words not found in any script.

The monolithic studios of Hollywood's golden age had unwittingly created these weird umbroods, along with the dream realm they inhabited. Yet, unlike the fleeting, transient realms wrought by one person's fancy, Filmland — as Miranda had come to call it — seemed permanent. A pristine, comforting place, it drew strength from everyone across the globe who'd ever seen *Gone With the Wind* or *Duck Soup*, *The Maltese Falcon* or *Casablanca*.

Bela Lugosi, cold and proper in his guise as the Count, materialized at Miranda's side. An eerie half-smile quirked his black lips. *"Listen to them... children of the screen! What music they make!"*

She did not reply. Experience had taught her that the phantoms were not interested in conversation. They crossed into the mundane world for as long as the etheric projector would allow, darting about like children on a playground. Some, like Lugosi, tantalized her with brief, whispered comments. Most remained playfully aloof, entertaining her by noisily donning and shucking the cheerful facades they'd created for directors long-moldering in overpriced graves down the coast in Los Angeles. And though they were personable enough, the umbroods were adamant in their refusal to converse, as if they so loved their respite on this side of the screen that they dared not waste a moment of it.

Miranda hoped some fine-tuning of the etheric projector would solve that problem. Even after drawing the potent Quintessence from a Hollywood gem like *Singin' in the Rain*, the machine only gave the umbroods a few fleeting moments of freedom. The Talisman could open the gate, but for some reason it couldn't draw the spirits fully into static reality.

If she could offer the umbroods more time, they might cooperate with her plans. They could be useful, these familiar phantoms. If a Sleeper came to the Oasis to see a wholesome, reassuring picture, the gentle specters might step out of the film to speak with him, to coax his mind to a more agile state wherein he might find magick more acceptable. And to provide the unenlightened this escape from the profane, all Miranda need do was lure them into the dark. They would enter the old movie palace utterly asleep. After two hours, complete with cartoon and coming attraction, they would rouse and exit as potential acolytes of the Ascension.

For now, though, Miranda could only use the etheric projector to shuttle the phantoms into the Oasis for the briefest of stays, then watch helplessly as they dissipated.

The last of the current mob of specters had just vanished, melting into a puddle of mist like Margaret Hamilton at the end of *The Wizard of Oz*, when the door to the theater's lower level creaked open. The old hinges were desperately in need of oil.

"Another packed house at the Oasis." The words echoed up from the dim, empty lower level. A pitying sigh followed the sarcastic comment, which only made it that much more offensive.

Miranda muttered a mild curse, something you might hear from the lips of Frankie and Annette, or maybe Andy

Hardy. She recognized the man's voice and briefly considered ducking down in the seats until he left, but her anger got the best of her. "It's a meeting of your fan club, Murnau. Looks like you're the only member."

"Ah, but you're here, too," the man said as he strolled out from beneath the balcony. "That must make you president."

Erich Murnau, junkie-thin and clad in black leather, paused in the center of the aisle. The footlights at the end of each row of seats revealed his mocking smile. "I came here to see if the place was still standing." He brushed a rope of long, stringy hair from his ice-blue eyes and looked around.

"We weathered the quake rather well. There are a few more cracks in the ceiling plaster. One of the Buddhas in the lobby fell off its perch, and the popcorn machine spewed kernels all over the concession stand. That was the worst of it." Miranda turned away. "I have to get ready for the five o'clock show, so if that's all you came to find out—"

"Actually," Erich interrupted, "I came to ask a question. Have you told that mob of drooling old conjurers at the Sons cabal to sod off yet?"

The question spun Miranda around, and a look of shocked annoyance crossed her pretty countenance. Her discomfort only widened Erich's smile.

"News of the censure is all over the street," he noted. "I've got a copy of the letter here somewhere. It's amazing how fast these things circulate."

He patted his pockets distractedly. Finally Erich unzipped his jacket and produced a folded piece of paper from the shadowed lining. He held it up with overblown theatricality, as if it were a rabbit he'd yanked out of a silk top hat.

"Disrupting an important lecture," he read, scanning the page. "Insulting a Fellow… Behavior unbecoming a Disciple *and* a young lady." Erich clicked his tongue disapprovingly. "This isn't like you at all, Mira."

"Summerlee used his standing in the Sons to have an

article of mine dropped from *Paradigma*," Miranda snapped. "They'd already accepted the piece, and he had it killed!"

Again Erich Murnau reached inside his scuffed leather jacket. This time he produced a packet of two dozen pages, typeset just as they would have appeared in the Sons' scientific journal. "*The Awakening at Twenty-four Frames per Second*. Nice title. Clever." He thumbed through the unpublished article. "So what was Summerlee's objection?"

"As senior Fellow of the Chantry, he claimed the right to see anything I put forth for publication. 'Not enough proof to support this,' he said after he read the article. 'Needs further study.'"

"Yeah, he'll study it further all right — to see if there's any ideas worth stealing." Erich held up the letter in one hand, the article in the other. "Here's what I did when Summerlee gave me a notice of censure." Twin gouts of flame devoured the pages. Chuckling, Erich brushed his hands together to rid them of ashes. "Too bad he was still writing the note when it went up. Two years, and I hear his eyebrows still haven't grown back."

The thin young man didn't wait for a reply. As casually as he had entered the theater, he strolled up the air itself to the balcony. The magick-wrought stairs he trod upon were invisible, but his footfalls resounded as if his boots were scuffing stone. "You need to break away from those ether-sniffers. Go freelance."

"Oh, the life of a rogue is obviously preferable to that of a Tradition," Miranda spat.

"Being a mercenary has its benefits," he replied. "And not belonging to a single Tradition is the biggest. You're learning now what being shackled to a cabal like the Sons means, all the restrictions and the political in-fighting. The others are no better — Euthanatos, the Cult of Ecstasy, the Virtual Adepts. They've all got blinders. Being a rogue means I can pick my battles — and my beliefs — more carefully."

"And you can use vulgar magick all day long without caring how much Paradox you create."

Hands clasped behind his back, Erich stepped nonchalantly over the railing. He perched atop one seatback and put his booted feet up on another. "Paradox?" he repeated, then dismissed the word with the wave of one stick-fingered hand. "To create an anomaly you've got to use magick in front of a Sleeper. You believe in magick, don't you, little girl?"

"Not the kind you practice." She jerked a thumb over her shoulder. "If you're such an expert on living a mercenary's life, you'll want to loiter in front of the theater after nightfall. Some desperate young ladies work from this block. You could probably teach them a thing or two about getting the best financial return for services rendered."

Erich chuckled basely. "Money's part of the world, too, sweetheart. So are a lot of things you and the Sons don't want to admit exist. Hatred and rage and lust—" He reached out to stroke her face, but she swatted his hand away. "The Sleepers may not understand the Ascension, but they see their own pathetic part of the universe pretty clearly. To them, reality — the whole Tapestry — is a nightmare. You'll never open one pair of eyes to the bigger picture until you recognize that truth yourself."

Cobra-quick, Murnau leapt to his feet and grabbed Miranda. She struggled against him, but he was much stronger than his bony, scarecrow frame suggested. "Look," he said, "I read your article. If these smiling, little film umbroods of yours are going to help anyone along the path to enlightenment, you've gotta provide them with an audience — one that has all kinds of warm, fuzzy thoughts about dead millionaire stars and the pabulum they churned out under contract for their billionaire bosses."

"I have regular patrons, people who want to see the kind of pictures that generate the phantoms."

Erich snorted. "I don't see anyone here but us."

"There was an earthquake last night," Miranda said, but any anger that might have given her reply an edge was undercut by the self-doubt welling up in her heart. The theater had been just as empty in the days before the quake as it was now.

She lowered her eyes. "People are digging themselves out."

"You know why you can't draw a crowd?" Erich demanded as he spun her to face the rows of empty seats arrayed before the screen. "'Cause you show crap that the Sleepers can't understand. Musicals and beach party flicks without a single naked chick, and bloodless, so-called horror movies with genteel mad scientists and vampires in tuxedos and top hats. The films are irrelevant antiques — like the creaky old chairs you find in your great-aunt's sitting room. They're nice enough to look at, if you find dusty chairs intrinsically enthralling, but pretty friggin' useless when you want someplace to park your ass."

Erich shoved her away. "It's Halloween tomorrow. What've you got scheduled?"

Scowling, Miranda rubbed her arm; a bruise was already purpling there from the man's brutal grip. "A Lugosi double feature: *Ghost of Frankenstein* and *Mark of the Vampire*."

"Pathetic," Erich spat. "Like Bauhaus says: 'Bela Lugosi's dead.' Let me pick some real Halloween flicks to show. I'll have the Sleepers lined up six deep in the lobby. They'll be knifing each other for seats."

"I keep that sort of riff-raff out of here," Miranda sniffed.

"Hardly the egalitarian attitude I would expect from a Son. Gang-bangers and addicts and low-lifes are entitled to Ascension just as much as eggheads and mystics, right?"

"Since when do Sleepers matter so much to you?" Miranda said, more loudly than she would have liked. "Why do you care who I let in?"

"It's not the Sleepers I'm concerned about, it's you." Erich's kind words were tainted by his annoying, pitying tone. The condescension made Miranda stammer with suppressed fury, but Erich continued, unfazed by her obvious anger. "I hate to admit this, but Summerlee's right: You've got no test results to back up your claims about the film umbroods. You'll never get those results, either. The experiment's a wash."

Miranda lashed out. The blow's suddenness and strength surprised Erich, and in his haste to avoid a second slap he tumbled backward over a row of seats. When he climbed warily to his feet, his pale cheek throbbed crimson. "Attacking me only proves how right I am."

"Hardly," Miranda said. "It only proves you're an annoying bastard."

"I'm willing to wager on it. On whether or not my flicks will draw a bigger crowd, that is — not on what you said about me being a bastard." Erich smirked. "I'm afraid I'll have to plead *nolo contendere* to that charge."

"Forget it. I don't want you showing trash on my projector. You can just—"

Erich held up a restraining hand. "Your precious magickal View Master will remain virginal. I'll provide a projector and suitable security for the place, along with at least a half-dozen prime flicks. You don't normally advertise, so I won't either. Just word of mouth.

"And if I pack the house — something you've never done in the short time you've run this place, if I'm not mistaken — you will admit that the Sleepers are a bunch of disillusioned brutes, and the Tapestry is a lot darker than you've allowed yourself to see. If that wises you up enough to break with the Sons, so much the better."

"And if you can't fill the theater?"

Erich paused, tapping his chin as he pondered a suitable payment. "If there's a single seat left unsold when the first flick rolls, or if there's a single seat empty when the last flick's over, I'll admit you're right to put your faith in the Sleepers. In fact, I'll immediately petition the Sons for readmittance. I think that's more than fair, considering I'm only asking you to *consider* your allegiance to the ether-sniffers."

"You wouldn't offer to rejoin the Chantry unless you'd stacked the deck."

Erich pulled back his jacket and made the sign of the cross over the breast of his ragged Thrill Kill Kult concert shirt. "Scout's honor," he mocked. Then his cynical sneer vanished as swiftly and completely as one of the film umbroods. "Honestly, Mira, I haven't set you up. My confidence comes from knowing my view of the Tapestry is a thousand times more accurate than yours."

Miranda's intellect told her to reject the wager outright, but her heart labeled any such prudence as nothing less than cowardice. "All right. We'll open the doors at seven."

"Agreed," Erich said. He held his hand out to seal the bargain, but Miranda had already turned away.

"If the theater is damaged in any way, you're paying for the repairs," she said over her shoulder as she stalked toward the exit. "And be here at least two hours before show time. I'll have some sort of oath devised by then, some way to test you. I want to be certain you haven't paid a crowd or something like that."

"That's awfully cynical of you," Erich called after her. "Good. You're starting to smarten up already."

Miranda pushed through the padded doors to the hallway, leaving Erich alone in the theater. When he was certain she'd gone, the mage leapt up onto the metal railing. Arms straight out at his sides, head thrown back, he drew a deep, open-mouthed breath.

There was some inherent power in the place. Nothing staggering, but enough to make his fingers itch and his scrotum tighten. Maybe the Oasis housed some minor well of Quintessence. He'd have to ask Miranda about that, if she came around to his way of thinking.

Shaking his head, Erich walked lightly down the

conjured and still-invisible steps to the theater's lower level. No, Miranda could never be stripped of her hope for universal Ascension. She was too stupidly certain that something pure and sacred dwelt beneath the filth encrusting San Francisco and its scabrous citizens. Losing the wager would shake her confidence, maybe even force her to go Rogue. But she would never give herself over completely to the darkness. Not like Erich had.

He knew there was no sacred heart beneath the city's blighted facade. It was corrupt right to the core.

As a rogue, unhindered by the blinders the Traditions forced upon their Disciples and Apprentices, he'd discovered that the entire Tapestry of existence was woven upon a loom of pain, its threads spun from suffering and spite. Better to unravel it, to allow Entropy to swallow it all back up, than to allow the imagination-dead Sleepers and the idiot mages to continue blindly, foolishly pursuing an Ascension that would never come. And if Miranda couldn't be made to see that, she would have to be destroyed.

Her death would be something of a loss to Erich. He'd always fancied Miranda. She had some skill in magick. And even if she hadn't, he found her pretty enough to satisfy other, purely physical needs.

But then, Erich reminded himself, *there's nothing to prevent me from forcing her to satisfy those needs after I've broken her will — or even after I've killed her.*

Erich Murnau knew the notion should have revolted him. It would have once, before he'd bargained his soul away. Now he was a Nephandus, an agent of Entropy, a general in the legion of darkness. And the fact that he felt no disgust only galvanized his resolve to cripple Miranda's spirit before she could spread her message of hope.

And all he needed to accomplish that was a few bad films.

The nameless zombie shuffled across the screen. Moaning with the agony of the damned, the thing threw itself against the unlocked door. The woman in the room beyond squealed and braced her back against the wood. As the door slammed shut, it captured the corpse's fingertips. The bits of flesh dropped to the floor like bloody hailstones.

But the zombie was not so easily denied.

Fiercely, methodically, it set to work battering the wooden barricade to splinters. Soon the hole was large enough for the decaying hands to reach inside, to grope and claw at the woman's breasts. Rotting stumps of fingers twined in her hair. Maggot-gnawed muscles contracted, pulling her toward the spikes of shattered wood standing erect around the breach. The camera zoomed in to frame her face, and the image illuminated the dark theater in spurts of light like bursts of automatic gunfire. The woman's screams resumed a moment later. Then, with a sickening, liquid squelch, the largest splinter pierced her right eye and lodged itself in the blind, bloody socket.

A bespectacled old man in the back of the moviehouse sent up a triumphant cheer. Someone else shouted a foolish joke about safety goggles and woodworking. No one groaned in disgust at the impaling's realism. No one shrieked in horror at the bloodshed. They'd all witnessed worse carnage before — on the screen, in the streets, in their homes. A few had orchestrated more terrible real-life scenarios themselves.

In the projection booth overlooking the packed Oasis Theater, Miranda Peake covered her tearing eyes with her hands. It was just as Erich had predicted. The Sleepers were six deep in the lobby. Not a ticket remained unsold, not a seat stood empty. Never mind that it was Sunday night and Halloween, never mind the neighborhood's usual dangers and the chaos caused by Friday's earthquake, the crowd had come. Not even the strange fog that had settled over the Golden Gate Bridge, paralyzing traffic throughout the city, could keep them away. They'd abandoned their cars and walked, rather than miss the festival of cinematic slaughter and degradation.

Erich hadn't paid them. He hadn't compelled them magickally. The test Miranda had forced upon the mage had proved the truth of that. A vague promise of blood and sex and chaos had lured the crowd to the Oasis, and now it kept them anchored to their seats like so many quadriplegics.

To Miranda's horror, she'd recognized some of her regular patrons in the mob. The trendy men in their overpriced Irish wool sweaters and the women in their gaudy Home Shopping Club jewelry howled right along with the rowdy gangsters. She'd seen these staid suburbanites weep for Shirley Temple and root for John Wayne. But it was clear now that they craved blood as much as the inner-city kids girded for Halloween with child-sized hockey masks and toy chain saws and gloves tipped with plastic finger-knives.

A rap on the projection booth door drew Miranda's attention away from the audience. Happy for the distraction, she turned to see Erich duck his head inside the noisy little room. "You busy?" he asked, but shoved the door fully open before she could speak. "There's somebody here who wants to talk to you."

A moment later, a policeman pushed past Erich. He was short, but brutishly muscled. The hard line of his mouth and the sharp crease in his trousers bespoke an unforgiving personal discipline. "Ms. Peake?"

"Yes. I-Is there a problem?" Miranda wiped the tears from her eyes and stepped away from the ancient, clattering projector Erich had provided for the evening. Unconsciously, she positioned herself between the cop and the large box that hid her own etheric contraption.

"This is my beat." The officer surveyed the slovenly booth with an appraising eye, then turned his gaze on Miranda. His disapproval of her untidy dress manifested as a slight sneer. "I've never had reason to come in until tonight," he began. "Your friend here says that you're going to be showing these sorts of films regularly now."

"Seems likely," Erich chimed from the doorway.

The cop waited for Miranda to confirm this, but she remained silent. After an uncomfortably long pause, he nodded at her, then held something out in his left hand. Miranda stared at the rectangular, plastic box as if it were alive.

"I couldn't get a theatrical print," he said. "Usually I can. It depends on what the vice squad confiscates, of course. This was just a slow week."

Miranda finally took the box. It was a black video-cassette case, a title printed on its spine in Japanese.

"Your friend says you might be able to use this anyway," the cop continued. "Consider it a get-acquainted gift. We can discuss my usual rates next time."

With military precision, the policeman turned and marched from the booth. Erich waved to him as he went by, but the stone-faced cop ignored the young man.

"He insisted on handing the print over to 'the proprietor,'" Erich noted once the officer had gone. In response to Miranda's puzzled stare he added, "I put out word that we were looking for some special movies, ones even I couldn't locate. I didn't even dare to hope someone would scare up that little treasure you're holding. It's a Japanese 'pink' flick, hard core S & M, real rough stuff. I'm surprised Joe Friday didn't keep the tape for home use. Must mean he's already duped a copy."

Erich gestured at the cassette. "Think you might be persuaded to burn a little Juice to fix the flick's format?" He shrugged and untangled an arcane-looking circuit tester from a box of junk electronics. "If magick's out, maybe you can jury-rig something to convert it the old-fashioned way. Looks like you've got enough hardware in here to do it... Damn!"

Smiling broadly, the mage drew a pair of plastic glasses from the box. "If I'd known you had some of these, I would have brought *3-D House of Slave Chicks*." He held the colored lenses up to his eyes, then set the glasses on Miranda's desk. "So you think you can have the pink film ready to run after *Faces of Death*? It'll be 2 a.m. by then, and most of the younger tykes will have scampered off to roll closing-time drunks."

"Fine," Miranda said flatly. Any chore that might take her mind off the revolting films and the even more revolting spectators was welcome.

Erich left without another word, without even a victorious grin. He didn't need to bring up the wager. The dispirited look in Miranda's face and the defeated slouch of her shoulders revealed her imminent surrender just as surely as if she'd been tying a white cloth to a stick. The Sleepers wanted trash, not magick. The gibbering, lunatic mob filling the Oasis was proof enough of that, even for a romantic like herself.

At first, Miranda refused to waste one scintilla of Quintessence transferring the tape to celluloid. She set about gutting an old VCR and an editing machine to gather a few essentials for this new piece of hardware. But she gave up quickly. The dingy cerements wrapped around her spirit had dampened even her love of tinkering.

Instead, she broke open the cassette and began to thread the tape through the pinched thumb and forefinger of her left hand. Digging deep within herself for the energy, she transmuted the tape inch by horrible inch into a 70-millimeter print, complete with THX soundtrack. She refused to look at a single frame, afraid of what she might find there.

It was tedious work, and her fingers throbbed painfully before she'd transformed half the movie's length. As she toiled, her mind wandered from the terrible reality around her to the clean and genial streets of the Filmland dream realm. Naturally, then, she dismissed the faint song echoing through the booth as nothing more than a happy memory welling up to soothe her troubled soul.

"*I'm singin' in the rain, just singin' in the rain…*"

But the song only grew louder. As other voices picked up the familiar tune, Miranda paused to listen more closely. To her astonishment, she realized that the music originated not in her memory, but in the theater itself.

Miranda dashed from the projection booth before another word was chorused. As she ran, she prayed desperately that her umbroods had returned to lead the Sleepers out of this self-inflicted nightmare. A small part of her spirit rallied at the thought; here, finally, was proof that the Tapestry was forged of light, not darkness.

That hopeful spark died in Miranda the moment she burst through the balcony's padded double-doors.

Faces of Death had concluded, and the movie screen hung blank. A haze of anarchy loomed over the place. Vicious fights raged in a dozen places, with fists and bludgeons and knives landing blow after blow. In the back stalls, couples copulated like crazed beasts. Spilled beer and blood and semen swirled together on the floor in foul rivulets. The air was thick with screams and groans, but the eerie, keening sound of the show tune lilted over the cacophony.

The white-jumpsuited leader of the chorus frolicked across the stage at the theater's head. He was busy re-enacting a scene from his favorite film, if his carefully patterned Halloween garb was any indication of his interests. In time with the tune, he bowed, tipped his bowler appreciatively — and planted a jackboot in the face of the man lying before him. To his right, illuminated by the light from a burning trashcan, his three *droogs* tore the clothes off a struggling woman in preparation for a little of the old "in-out, in-out." Her shrieks made one thing clear: She wasn't a willing part of the stage show.

"Stop it!" Miranda screamed. Her outburst only brought laughter from the seats nearest her and a slick-fingered hand groping up her skirt from behind. She sprinted forward a half-dozen steps to escape the assault.

Almost unconsciously, the mage reached out with her power for the theater's sound system. The wires crossed and recrossed, until they could pick up and transmit only one specific sound: her voice. "I said stop it!" she boomed in rumbling stereo, the command loud enough to draw trickles of blood from the ears of those closest to the speakers. "All of you! Get out of here!"

The scenario from A *Clockwork Orange* playing out on the stage ended; the woman snatched up the tattered remnants of her clothing and fled. An incomplete, wavering hush descended upon the other patrons, the same sort of half-quiet that settles over a theater in that instant after the lights go down. Miranda walked to the edge of the balcony.

Just before she spoke, she regained wits enough to cup a hand before her mouth and pretend to be speaking into a microphone. No use encouraging Paradox with a blatant use of vulgar magick before such a Tapestry-blind throng. "The projector is broken," she began, only slightly more calm. "We won't be able to fix it tonight, so you all might as well go home."

A hand clamped down on her shoulder and turned her around. "Are you insane?" Erich hissed. "They'll riot!"

As if one cue, the fights on the lower floor resumed. Angry shouts came from all quarters. Somewhere, metal whined in protest as a seat was ripped from the concrete floor. A woman leapt onto the stage and kicked the burning trashcan into the mob. Flaming debris rained over the first four rows.

"You've won, Erich," Miranda said. When she heard her own bitter words echo back at her from the speakers, she dropped her control of the sound system. "I concede. They're animals. They've got the world they deserve. Get them out of here before they destroy the place!"

Erich put two fingers to his lips and whistled. The sound was answered by identical shrills from all around the theater.

For an instant, the chaos gripping the crowd intensified. Then it became clear that some organized force was breaking up the mob and herding each separate cluster toward a different exit.

Hulking thugs made up the majority of Erich's brute squad. And from her vantage point, Miranda thought she saw the flash of large, bloodstained blades — and not any stage props, either — in the hands of the bouncers who took it upon themselves to handle the most violent men and women in the mob.

Sometime during the scuffle, Miranda collapsed into an empty seat. For a time she was vaguely aware of Erich standing over her, barking orders. Then she was alone. The mob had gone, and the machete-wielding brutes with it. Even Erich had vanished.

Numbly, Miranda stood and surveyed the ruins of the night. The first few rows of seats were a smoking wreck, patterned black and white with ash and fire retardant. The discarded extinguishers littered the sooty floor before the screen like spent shells. Blocks of seats had been torn out or toppled in other parts of the theater. Ropes of synthetic padding bulged like spilled intestines from slashed and savaged cushions. Someone had started to spray-paint the symbol for anarchy on the movie screen, but the graffiti remained incomplete; Erich's goons or the crush of the crowd had swept the tagger away before he could finish

Miranda stared at that symbol for a time, futilely attempting to conjure memories of the beautiful people and the breathtaking vistas it had supplanted. Finally, her eyes began to play tricks on her. The ragged, dripping lines appeared to shiver. She started to turn away, but a glimpse of movement from the stage froze her in place.

The painted lines — or, more precisely, the screen beneath them — were bulging. The silver-white sheet stretched outward, like a barricade of translucent rubber. Slowly, the amorphous bulge became the imprint of a hand, each finger the height of a man. Other hands pressed against the screen, and torsos, and faces caught in silent, open-mouthed screams.

A cold finger of fear traced a line up Miranda's spine, settling at the nape of her neck. She shuddered.

Yes, she had definitely heard it.

Beneath the seeming silence in the Oasis hissed a low, slithering murmur of voices. Their words worked into her ears like tiny insects; by the time she'd realized they were there, it was too late to stop them from burrowing into her mind.

"*Do you know why the pathetic umbroods you conjured wouldn't talk to you?*" a smooth, cultured voice asked. "*They were afraid you would discover the truth about our happy little home.*"

Miranda gripped the balcony rail. "The truth?"

"*Yes,*" the voice lulled. "*But we aren't afraid of the truth. If you want, we can show you the dream realm's true face. We can take you behind the facade.*"

"Show me," Miranda said.

"*There's a price,*" cautioned the voice. "*There's always a price for knowledge.*"

"Show me."

The screen burst open. Through the gap Miranda saw a familiar, rain-slicked city street, with its cozy brownstones and smiling, singing passers-by. As the pedestrians rushed along in the perfectly orchestrated downpour, the buildings collapsed one by one. They were nothing more than flats, useless as shelter from the storm, but heavy enough to crush the happy citizens just the same.

Miranda didn't scream when she saw what lay behind those facades, or even when the gray-fleshed arms reached out from the shattered screen and tangled their rotting finger-stumps in her hair.

"Show me everything," she whispered as they drew her

face toward the jagged, silver-white splinters spiking up around the breach.

■ ■ ■

Erich Murnau returned to the Oasis Theater at dawn. He'd spent the last few hours watching an enjoyable show put on by the gangsters he'd hired as security. The young toughs had chased the worst rioters out of the movie palace and herded a dozen or so into an abandoned warehouse for a deadly game of cat and mouse. But the sunrise had signaled the game's end, and sent the thugs hurrying off to other, less strenuous pastimes.

Now Erich stood on the theater's balcony, surveying the destruction. The place was an utter shambles. Only the screen had been spared. Somehow, the monolithic silver-white sheet stood unblemished. It reminded him of a photograph he'd seen of St. Paul's during the Blitz: The cathedral's dome rose defiantly above a sea of black smoke as London, reduced to glorious, flaming rubble by the Luftwaffe, burned around it. Only after a moment did the mage realize the comparison made him vaguely uncomfortable.

"I have something for you... *sweetheart*."

Erich turned to find a pale face framed in the small projection window overlooking the theater. "Mira? I pounded on the door to the booth and shouted for you. Didn't you hear me?"

She giggled vapidly. "I was working on your present."

Miranda's voice was softer, seductive. In fact, her whole demeanor had changed. The uncomfortable feeling in Erich's gut transformed into a full-fledged gnawing dread. His stomach twinged unpleasantly. "Er, what happened to you?" He pointed to the bloody bandage wrapped around her head and the right side of her face.

"I got something in my eye," Miranda said, then giggled again. "It hurt... a lot." She disappeared from the window for a moment. The house lights went down, and a projector whirred to life.

"Sit down, Erich," Miranda said through the speaker system. "I spliced together a loop from the flicks you left — those and a few other bits of film I got from some new friends of mine. Maybe we can use it between features, once we get the Oasis cleaned up and running again. Anyway, I think it shows how much my experience tonight changed the way I see things."

There was no title, only a short leader that counted down to the first grotesque image. Erich had no trouble recognizing the earliest clips:

Heads exploded in Technicolor splendor, then melted into anatomical close-ups of porn stars rutting disinterestedly. Documentary footage of pathetic "real-life" cannibals merged with scenes of greasepaint zombies — blind Templars in moth-eaten robes — pursuing bikini-girls around a phantom galleon. A young Japanese man convinced that he was part machine writhed in pain as he shoved a length of metal pipe into the open, gaping wound in his thigh. A woman stared wide-eyed as someone sliced her cornea with a straight-razor, a sacrifice to the cause of Art.

In the balcony, Erich stifled a yawn and considered leaving, or at least going back to the projection booth to talk to Miranda. She'd obviously suffered a breakdown. The only question he had now was how completely she'd snapped.

But the next scene to play across the pristine screen riveted Erich in place. It was footage the Nephandus had heard about, but never actually seen:

The veteran actor slogged across the soundstage rice paddy, an Amer-Asian child tucked under each arm. He was only pretending to be in a war zone. The malfunctioning helicopter that crashed down on him in a blaze of killing shrapnel proved him wrong...

The Brat Pack leading man hammed it up for the camera, in a bedroom scene not so unlike others he'd done in countless teen exploitation flicks. Only this time it was for real, and the girl in his embrace wasn't old enough to drive...

The perfectly pumped action star burst through the door, ready to do battle with a gang of stunt thugs. The role might have been his ticket to the big time — a superhero for Generation X, a dead man fighting for the living in a lurid nightmare city. Sadly, the guns weren't harmless props that day, and the young actor hadn't the supernatural powers to return from the grave to avenge himself against the key grip and his union flunkies...

Erich slid forward to the edge of his seat, trying to discern the real blood from the corn syrup and food coloring spattering the actors. He didn't dare take his eyes off the screen for fear of missing some marvelous new atrocity. "Christ, Miranda!" the mage shouted. "Where did you get this footage?"

"I told you, from some friends," Miranda cooed in Erich's ear. "This isn't even a fraction of the things they showed me."

Murnau gave her the briefest of glances as she stepped over the row of seats to take the spot next to him. "How much did this stuff cost you?"

"Nothing," she giggled. "And everything. I promised to let them spend some time in the Oasis now and then. They're all here, waiting to meet you," Miranda added. She ran an ice-cold finger from his jawline up to his eye, then pointed toward the darkened lower level. "Down there. You were too busy watching the flick to notice them come in."

The movie's first half concluded, and the screen blared white with pure, uninterrupted light. "Go on and say hello," Miranda prompted. "This is the intermission. You've got a minute before the big finale."

Squinting against the glare, Erich stood and peered over the balcony railing. The seats below were crowded with monstrosities. Children gutted in snuff films huddled next to straitjacketed psychotics. Perfectly tanned men and women with unwavering smiles and grotesquely huge genitals stroked the chitinous shells of drooling, multi-jawed aliens. As if they could feel Erich's eyes upon them, the silent, infernal creatures turned as one and met his gaze. They regarded the mage for a moment. Then the nightmare mob donned 3-D glasses and turned back toward the blank screen.

"Silly me," Miranda said airily. "I forgot to give you your glasses. You'll need them for the next part of the production." She held out a pair of cheap, plastic 3-D glasses. Wires snaked along the frames, and five or six small antennae bristled up from the bridge. "The modifications help them to work with my etheric projector."

Erich slapped her hand away. "I don't think so," he said darkly. "Not until you explain what the hell's going on here."

"Movie magick," Miranda said, her voice suddenly edged with steel. "The stuff you tried to take away from me."

Rough hands grabbed Erich from behind and slammed him into a seat. He tried to muster a defense, something to drive the swarming, pummeling fists away, but it was no use. The blows landed too fast. Any thoughts of resistance or magick were knocked out of his head almost as soon as they blossomed there.

Quickly, the glasses were crammed onto the mage's face. The bases of the antennae wires dug bloody furrows as they slid up the bridge of his nose. Pins on the inside of the lenses pricked his eyes and his eyelids, making it impossible for him to blink. Two decaying hands clamped to either side of his face and twisted his head so he would face the screen. The violence of the movement cracked Erich's neck. Showers of maggots rained from his assailant's decaying wrists.

A barrage of images flashed across the movie screen. At

first, Erich thought himself safe from whatever weird assault Miranda had planned, since the scenes were passing too swiftly for him to comprehend. But his mind could register the images much faster than it could unpack that information. After a moment, the compressed scenes began to play out in the mage's head, slowly, so he could savor every sight.

The world was all smiles and laughter. A nutty professor with buck teeth and a mixing-bowl haircut transformed himself into a smarmy lounge singer. As a rubber-faced lunatic in a tutu searched for lost pets, a crowd of equally manic men and women tore up a park, looking for the treasure buried under "the big W." Stooges smashed each other with mallets, and fifty people packed themselves into a stateroom barely large enough for two. Nothing was too dark, too grim to be mocked, as hick cowboys rode falling atomic bombs like broncos and the dreaded SS danced and sang for a groovy, beatnik Hitler.

"Enjoying the show?" Miranda asked coldly. "The glasses really make it special. They help the film phantoms get a better foothold in static reality — well, actually only the cheerful ones need the assistance." She shook her head sadly. "Even the plain old projector you brought in last night was enough to open a gate for the corrupted umbroods. Their part of the dream realm is so perfect a reflection of our world that they're equally at home in either place. And if I use the etheric projector on them, they're just as solid as you and me — as you can tell by those hands holding you down."

Erich's mind reeled as the phantoms happily dismissed broken limbs and lampooned unspeakable horrors. "Stop the projector!" he shouted. "No more."

"Wherever you say, sweetheart," Miranda cooed in her best Melanie Griffith voice. She gestured toward the projection booth. The camera went dark, and the house lights came up just a little. At the same time, the foul fingers clutching Erich loosened their grip.

The Nephandus shot to his feet, the glasses already crushed in one hand. The zombie standing right behind him — and the half-dozen more stationed on the balcony — burst into flame. Groaning, the umbroods melted down into puddles of stinking, bubbling film stock. "Now," Erich growled, leveling a finger at Miranda. "You're going to—"

The threat died in his throat. He blinked, then held a hand up to his eyes. The host of specters dancing before him didn't vanish, didn't dim. "No," he hissed. "They're inside my head."

Dapper and debonair and smiling ear-to-ear, they filled his vision. There were leading men clad impeccably in top hats and stylish white tails, and cloyingly cute little girls toting striped lollipops, and fat men bumbling after their rail-thin compatriots. And to Erich's horror, every last one of them was recounting some inspiring fable about the power of virtue and the triumph of hope.

"We poisoned Filmland years ago," Miranda said. "Snuff films and kiddie porn and the other trash we put on celluloid darkens both sides of the screen. But we haven't destroyed the possibility of happiness in either realm. Not yet."

Erich lashed out blindly with his power, trying to banish the phantoms and quiet the voices inside his head. Each blow he struck did more damage to himself than to the umbroods. For every specter he destroyed, a dozen more sprang to ghostly life.

"We were both wrong about the Tapestry," Miranda continued. Her hand drifted up to the bandages that covered the blackened, empty socket that had held her right eye. "But I can see things clearly now — the dark and the light. The umbroods helped me to recognize how I was overestimating the Sleepers, and how easy it must have been for the Nephandi to dupe you. You certainly weren't much of a challenge for me. A few dead comedians, and you're down for the count." She chuckled. "Shirley Temple kicked your ass."

But Erich wasn't listening. He shrieked and clawed at his face, tearing bloody runnels into his cheeks. His pupils vanished. The color drained from his irises and trickled down his face like ice-blue tears, leaving his eyes glassy white marbles. Finally, he collapsed into a seat. His colorless eyes stared straight ahead at the empty movie screen, and a thin line of spittle worked slowly down his chin.

Miranda lifted one of Erich's arms and let it drop limply into his lap. She made her way through the padded double doors, and down to the lower level, where the mob waited patiently in the whispering dimness. "He's all yours," she said softly. A few of the more agile monstrosities had already scaled the walls or leapt up to the balcony by the time she'd finished that simple utterance.

The mage despised the monstrous umbroods, and pitied them, but she would not be fool enough to ignore them ever again. They were a reality, a part of the Tapestry. They might even be useful. Some Sleepers were obviously going to need rougher guides to enlightenment than Gene Kelly or Vivian Leigh.

A smile crept across Miranda's lips. An evening with the infernal specters might be just the thing to convince Professor Summerlee how wrong he'd been to have her article killed. She'd have to set up a private double feature for him as soon as possible.

Blood spattering down from the balcony drew Miranda's attention. She glanced up to find Erich's head, attached to his neck by only a few hardy sinews, dangling over the railing. It hung there for a moment before a taloned hand drew it back into the mob of umbroods. Miranda didn't dodge the shower of crimson. Instead, she held one palm up, as if testing for rain, then broke into song and cheerfully set to work cleaning the ruined theater.

Before too long, the zombies were whistling the familiar show tune right along with her.

A BLOCK OF TIME

■ ■ ■ ■ ■ ■ ■ ■ ■ ■ ■ ■ ■

Jane M. Lindskold

"Come and dance, China Doll. The day is night and the moon is right... for love."

Even if the invitation had not been leered from a dark street in one of San Francisco's shabbier neighborhoods, Tieh still would have been disinclined to accept. The speaker was a solidly built Anglo clad in torn jeans and an even more disreputable tuxedo shirt. His features were concealed behind a rubber caricature mask of a long forgotten politician.

, Tieh glanced from the open switchblade in the man's hand to the half-dozen similarly clad youths who backed him.

"Pardon, sir, but day can hardly be night and the fog is so heavy that one cannot see the Bridge, much less the moon."

"Don't like my verse, China Doll?" He paused as if searching for a rhyme.

Tieh took a step back towards the shadowed alley-way behind her, her breathing was slow and even, her eyes steady, giving away nothing.

"No, Rubberhead, I don't mind your verse, but I don't like you!" While he hunted for a clever retort to silence the mocking giggles of his band, she attacked.

Never would she have used a kick above waist high with

a real fighter, but this was just a street thug. She easily struck the knife from his loose grip and if she intensified gravity just a bit so that it fell point down and plunged through his canvas sneaker, who was to know?

"My foot!" he screamed.

When all eyes flickered to him, she stepped back into the narrow alley. Reaching for the fire-escape above, she swung up and crouched silently, brushing rust and particles of black paint from her palms. She waited motionless until the last of Rubberhead's gang had stumbled off, searching for one who was right in front (and slightly above) them.

"How typical of Sleepers, ah, Tieh?" came a voice, dulcet and feminine, yet with a distinct acerbic bite.

Tieh looked about, her hands in a defensive stance. Her eyes widened as she saw that the busted window beside her had metamorphosed into an enormous grandfather clock, the gilded face benignly marking off the hour, the brass pendulum swinging with majestic regularity in the case below.

The clock's glass door stood open and standing in it was a shapely woman with eyes of blue ice and a fall of white hair that touched all the way to her bare feet. Her robe was silk, patterned with a dizzying multiplicity of Daliesque clocks. She held a large brass key in one hand.

"Hello, Serena," Tieh said, lowering her hands.

"Out 'Trick or Treating' rather late, aren't you?"

"Nonsense. I despise Halloween. It has become a time for children, vandals, and fools. What do you want, Timekeeper?"

"Would you believe that I merely sought to see if you required assistance?"

"No."

Serena chuckled, "I had to try. Come into my studio, Butterfly. No matter how you feel about Halloween, there is power tonight and omens say that great things may be done."

"I have no interest in great things," Tieh replied, knowing that she was being stubborn, "Only in the Way."

"You may not care, Tieh, but others do." Serena's expression hardened, "Or have you forgotten the Pogrom - Yueh Ch'iu, Hung Po, Master Shan?"

"I have not forgotten. I will never forget, but one cannot change the Past."

"Perhaps not, but there is the pleasure of crippling an enemy." Serena turned as if to depart, "And those who do not learn from the Past are condemned to repeat it. Will you turn away from great things?"

"I have no interest in great things," Tieh repeated, "but I do have an interest in revenge."

"Follow then," Serena said. "Mind the pendulum and the weights."

"I learned to fight blindfolded in the Cavern of Clashing Winds," Tieh said, lightly dodging the swinging round of brass. "These slow things are nothing."

"Pride," said a new voice among the ticking of clocks, "or merely youth which masks uncertainty with arrogance. Welcome, Butterfly."

The speaker was a black man so knotted and gnarled that his body seemed an animated bundle of sticks topped by a husked coconut. He wore a long stripped robe of rough cotton and leaned on a staff as knotted as himself. In his free hand, he held a long pipe and the air about him was wreathed in smoke rings that kept their shape even as they wove themselves into ropes and distorted faces.

"Abraham." Tieh folded her hands and bowed, concealing a fond smile.

"Let me see you, girl. You don't visit as often as you might," the shaman said.

Tieh spun slowly on one kung-fu slippered toe, aware that her dark green cotton trousers and matching watered-silk, mandarin-collared shirt were lightly flecked with black paint from the fire escape. Her long hair remained neatly contained in its butterfly clasp and trailed her like ink from a writing brush.

When she stopped, she included Serena in her smile.

"I have always enjoyed visiting the Timekeeper's studio," she admitted. "Forgive my earlier rudeness. You surprised me."

Serena glanced with pardonable pride at the hosts of clocks in different shapes, sizes, and styles. There were several towering grandfather clocks, each proud wooden case subtly different from the next. There were digital clocks, some with red LED displays, others with plastic flaps that clicked as they marked the minutes. There were ceramic clocks, wooden clocks, plastic clocks, cuckoo clocks, clocks with second hands, clocks with faces for every time zone, and Braille clocks. Tieh's favorite was a black plastic cat clock liberally sprinkled with rhinestones whose eyes and tail moved back and forth to mark the passing seconds.

Remarkably, not one of these clocks was set to the same time, and so the studio was continually filled with the buzzes, chimes, whistles, and tweets that announced the hour, half-hour, and quarter hour all over-laying the continuous ticking. Tieh had once asked Serena why she didn't set her clocks to the right time and the Timekeeper had replied, "Somewhere it is always the right time."

Now, watching the cat's tail switch its rhythm, Tieh wondered just how much the white-maned mage knew of that Sphere which her own teachers had claimed was but illusion, but which, illusion or not, generated the most dangerous of Paradox spirits.

"Well, I won't flatter myself and believe that you just wanted to see how I'm growing up," Tieh said." Serena mentioned the Pogroms — and revenge."

Abraham patted the floor beside him, "Sit with me, Tieh. You know that I am a Spirit Talker — a Dreamspeaker. I am very old and perhaps because of my age Mother Earth talks to me a bit like a friend. Lately, she's been complaining about an ache that's paining her. I felt sorry for her and started checking with spirit after spirit down to the early days of the city until I learned where the hurt came from. Then I came to Lady Timekeeper here and asked what we might do."

"Time, Tieh, is fluid," Serena explained, "like a river that flows in one direction while we ride with the current. As with a river, one may ride with the current or attempt to swim against it . In moving against it one can move into the Past."

"Wait," Tieh said. "Does this also mean that one can also move into the Future?"

"Well," Serena hesitated. "Yes and no. We believe that this is possible but — to extend my analogy to the point of clumsiness — downstream the river breaks into a delta with many small channels. Until events deepen one channel into what will be, the water of the future is too shallow to travel upon."

"Going into the Past is easier?" Tieh asked.

Serena grimaced, "Somewhat, but there is a problem— rather the inverse of the problem of going into the Future In the Near Past, the channels that Time runs through are narrow and shallow. Going back through them is rather like canoeing rapids in reverse."

"Without a paddle," Abraham added with a contented pull on his pipe.

"Yes." Serena continued, "so Near Past and Future are both difficult to access, but the Further Past is more accessible. I have developed a ritual by which I believe I can send someone not only to the Past, but to a precise point in the Past."

"And you want to send someone to learn what is 'paining' Mother Earth," Tieh said, "How is this revenge for the Pogroms?"

"For this, you need to know a bit of what the spirits taught me," Abraham replied. "You ever hear of a placed called the Montgomery Block?"

"Sure," Tieh said. "It was one of the oldest buildings in the city, but didn't it get wrecked back in the mid-sixties?"

"That's right. They built the Transamerican Pyramid in its place," Serena said, "and if you think that was a coincidence..."

"I never thought that the Pyramid was there by chance," Tieh said, "Tell me, what's so important about the old Block?"

Abraham blew a thoughtful smoke ring. "The Block was nearly as old as San Francisco; it was finished on December 23, 1853. Captain Henry Wagner Halleck was the Block's designer, financier, and one of its first tenants. He served in the government when California was but a territory. He mined and farmed, and later would serve as a general in Lincoln's Union Army. Spirits hint that Halleck was also in the service of the Technocracy."

"I think he probably was originally of the Order of Hermes," Serena added, "because one of Halleck's reasons for building the Block was to provide a fireproof, water-proof, earthquake proof repository for his library. He was a lawyer, too, you see, and so had justification for owning many old and rare books."

"Lawyer!" Tieh spat, "Laws have become the chains by which the Technocracy binds reality into the shape of its choice."

"This was even the case in Halleck's time," Serena agreed. "Many an Indian or Spaniard was defrauded of family holdings by interpretations of the law. But that is too vast a thing for us to change. Our goal is smaller, but still important. When Halleck built his Block, he did something to protect it from the forces of Dynamism — the Wyld. This, not his engineering talents, is why the Block survived fire, flood, and quake without much harm. The Pyramid magnifies this stabilizing force, assisting the Technocracy in maintaining San Francisco within their version of reality."

"Wait!" Tieh raised her hand in protest, "I've heard that the Montgomery Block was once a haven for artists, poets, and painters — people like Jack London, Robert Louis Stevenson, and Ambrose Bierce. I can't see the man who wrote Call of the Wild thriving in the locus of a Technocracy stronghold."

"I asked the spirits the same question," Abraham said, "and learned that the Wyld tried destroying the Block with water, quake, and fire, but what Halleck had done was too strong. The Dynamic force found its ally in the very redwood foundation on which the Block was built. Redwood is exceptionally prone to dry rot and the parts that were kept free of water began to deteriorate."

Tieh clapped, "Kept from water, the wood rotted. It sounds like a Zen koan."

"Indeed. When the foundation was weakened, enough of the Wyld found entry to make the Block hospitable to the bohemian elements you mentioned, but," Abraham's wrinkled face saddened, "in time the foundation's weakness was discovered. The redwood was replaced by poured concrete, and stagnation again took hold. San Francisco never lost its reputation as a cradle of bohemian culture, but the Technocracy grows strong just the same."

Tieh shuddered, "What do you need me for, Serena? I don't understand what a young Akashic can do that either of you cannot."

Abraham grunted, "Maybe, but the omens say that you are the best choice for this task."

"What?" Tieh stared at the gnarled Dreamspeaker. "Abraham, I respect you deeply, but your riddles are no help."

"Simply then, Tieh. Your name 'Tieh' means Butterfly," the Abraham said, "and the Chinese character for your name is made up of three symbols — a three part compound ideogram. You are 'butterfly,' but you are also 'leaf', 'generations', and 'worm'. Perhaps your name is simply 'the worm that generates a flying leaf,' but a Dreamspeaker can see that this may also mean a force that will generate a new leaf from the Wyrm of Entropy or make the Wyrm turn over a new leaf — make it change."

"And no matter what the Technocracy says," Serena added, "their efforts to keep reality in one shape has contributed to the imbalance of Entropy, Stasis, and Dynamism, leaving Gaia open to the raw corruption of those who seek to command the Wyrm and are in turn commanded by it."

"The Nephandi," Tieh whispered. "The Technocracy I despise. The Nephandi I fear."

"You are wise, Butterfly," Serena said softly, "for as the Technocracy seeks control, the Nephandi seeks decay."

Abraham's expression was pleading, "I believe that you are the observer we need to send back to the time when the Montgomery Block was built. Our investigations tell us that the central point for Halleck's magic must be in the foundation. Serena will send you within a few hours of Halleck's sorcery to observe what is done."

"When do we start?" Tieh asked.

Serena glanced at a crystal pendulum grandfather clock as if it held the true time. "I will begin my ritual now. It is long and the night is passing quickly. Be on guard. Other Mages may sense my workings and neither the Technocracy nor the Nephandi will respect the politenesses set by the Council of Nine Traditions. The Technocracy will surely attack."

Abraham pulled a burlap sack from behind a stately Tiffany pedestal clock and tossed Tieh a bundle.

"Clothes for the time period to which you are going. While you dress, I am going to bind a spirit to you. His name is Lung Lei and he knows the building site for the Block well. He died of malnutrition and fatigue the day before we plan to have you arrive."

"Lung Lei, the Thunder Dragon," Tieh translated. "I am impressed. That is a powerful name."

"He is an interesting spirit," Abraham replied, pulling from his burlap sack a shallow clay bowl painted in bright geometrics, several packets, and a mortar and pestle. Singing a wailing, atonal chant, he began to blend his ingredients.

Across the room, between two of the grandfather clocks, Serena spread uncut amethysts and lapis lazuli on the floor in a careful pattern. When she finished, she rose and drew from her pocket a braided silver chain with a polished chunk of hematite at the end. Swinging this over the pattern on the floor, she used her free hand to scatter tiny numerals and clock hands into the air. Her incanted "Tick-tock, tick-tock" worked a counterpoint against Abraham's wailing and the constant soundings of her many clocks.

Tieh's Tradition scorned many of the outer trappings of magic, but she felt her Avatar tremble in response to the power the other two were focusing. While she reached behind to braid her hair into a long queue, she focused her mind on creating a male image for herself. Starting at the feet, she gave herself a new walk, bending the knees and slouching the shoulders from bearing burdens. She reminded her eyes of the downward cast that a servant holds in the presence of his masters and edited the grace of a martial artist from her posture.

A loud pounding jolted her from her meditations.

"Uh, oh, trouble with the Technocracy's taste!" Abraham said, hauling himself to his feet with his staff. "Serena, are you finished?"

The white-haired Timekeeper continued her ritual without reply, but the desperate expression in her ice-blue eyes was answer enough. Swinging the hematite pendant clockwise, she intensified the pace of her chant. As if in response, her long hair began to sweep in a slow counterclockwise in odd congruence.

"The gates of Time are opening," Tieh said, "but the door

into this studio will fall first."

"Perhaps." Abraham gestured as if throwing something with both hands. "Lung Lei is with you. Stand ready for Serena's command."

"No," Tieh protested. "You two will need my help. Neither of you are fighters!"

"Your talents are needed in the Past," Abraham said, hurrying to where the studio's door was buckling inward. "Lung Lei, prevent her from being foolish."

Cool, solid hands grasped Tieh's shoulders. She snapped back her arm in a blow that should have sent whoever was behind her gasping to the floor, but her elbow passed through nothing. Stumbling to regain her balance, she cried out warning as the door burst open.

"Abraham!"

Skeletal executives in ragged suits, all with the skulls of horses for heads, crowded outside the broken door. They swung leather briefcases and deadly sheafs of legal paper. The Dreamspeaker thumped his staff thrice on the floor.

"Douglass! Carver! Malcom X.! Booker T.! Spirits of my ancestors, build a ward for me!"

A mahogany fog immediately billowed from all sides and solidly filled the studio doorway, barring the Technocracy's sendings from entry. The harsh clatter of their teeth rattled through the fog.

"Should have horse's asses not heads," Abraham muttered, glancing worriedly at Serena.

Tieh struggled against the hands that still held her, "Abraham, tell your creature to release me!"

"Your creature, your guide, your countryman," Abraham replied without looking away from the doorway. "No one but you will see him, hear him, feel him."

Tieh's retort was cut off as Serena shrieked and dropped her conjuring tools. Her face was as pale as her hair and her eyes were drained of color. The pattern of amethysts and lapis lazuli the floor had become a purple-blue swirling of numbers. With apparent effort, Serena stooped, grasped the pattern by its edges, then peeled it from the floor.

It hung limply from her hand for a moment, the magic in it so potent that the numbest Sleeper would have sensed its power. Then Serena flung the pattern at the grandfather clock with the crystal pendulum. It vanished, but the clock flared with a violet and azure light, the hands on its painted face whirling wildly backwards.

"Go, Tieh! The door to the Past is open!"

"But Abraham's ward won't hold!" Tieh protested, pointing to where bony hands were shredding the Dreamspeaker's ward.

"I will help him!" Serena said weakly. "Go!"

Tieh frowned, turned, and wrenched the glass door open. The brass key fell from the lock and rattled across the floor.

"Behind the pendulum," a male voice said in musically perfect Mandarin. "Quickly!"

Tieh dove behind the heavy crystal pendulum, braced despite herself to thud into the clock's wooden back. There was a sensation of being wafted a great distance, then she was rolling to a stop in a dusky, crowded room, rank with the odors of human sweat, rice, and stale spices. Recumbent heaps marked sleeping bodies. Here and there someone hunched over a writing tablet or game board. A dull "plong-plong" sounded from a badly out-of-tune musical instrument.

"Lie still," the male voice commanded, "and all will believe you to be asleep. Many here are strangers to each other still and too many die as I did to make seeking friends a rewarding task."

"Lung Lei?" she whispered.

"Who else?" Tieh could almost hear the spirit's shrug. "I sense the Dawn. Soon the bosses will come and awaken the 'coolies.' When they do, rise quickly and do not refuse the breakfast rice — you will be hungry later."

Tieh nodded, numbly aware that she was suddenly afraid. To distract herself, she peeked through her lashes and studied her guide. He was a handsome young man, not much older than herself, clad in the cap and robe of a student. He seemed calm as he gazed out over the sleeping men, but there was sorrow in the slump of his shoulders, sorrow and homesickness.

"Lung Lei," she said softly, "Do you have any idea how I'm supposed to get back to my own time?"

"No." He looked apologetic. "I believe that Serena would have told you had you not been interrupted by the Technocracy's sendings."

"Then I have to figure it out for myself or I'm stranded."

"That is how I see it, Mage."

A rhythmic banging on a brass gong forestalled any further conversation and jarred the laborers from their sleep. A few didn't rise and as Tieh shuffled with the majority to where sticky rice was being ladled into cheap wooden bowls, she saw a couple of gang bosses go and shake the laggards. Two were kicked to their feet, three more pronounced genuinely ill and assigned to light duty. A final one was prodded and then gingerly dragged out.

"Dead," Lung Lei said, his laconic manner not enough to hide his pain, "As I was yesterday. I came to San Francisco after failing my exams for mandarin. I was told I would be given a post for an educated man — a bookkeeper or a purser — but I was thrown in as slave labor like all the rest. The skilled jobs won't exist until the Block is completed. Halleck's great project will be built by Chinese labor, decorated by Chinese artists, and staffed by Chinese servants."

Tieh mutely accepted a bowl of rice and a cup of weak green tea from an ill-looking man and then sat against a wall to force the stuff down. She ate with her fingers — apparently chopsticks were not provided.

"The lucky ill ones are given simple jobs," Lung Lei said. "They prepare and serve the food, sweep the barracks, and tend those who are too ill or injured to work. Some recover.

Some pass on their sickness with the food and nursing. I wonder that any of us survived."

Tieh shuddered, "I don't dare miss whatever it is that Halleck is going to do. Do you remember anything that might be helpful?"

"I was already dead," Lung Lei said, "and did not care. You are a Mage — surely you must have ways to learn what you need."

Tieh scowled at him. Pretending to drowse over her rice, she sent her spirit away from her body. Lung Lei's droning voice became an anchor as she quested outside of the barracks. A group of Anglos were just arriving in carriages and on horseback.

She recognized Halleck immediately, stiff in his bearing, round-faced and already double-chinned although he was not more than thirty-five. His air of authority set him apart from the others, that and an aura of magic that surrounded him with rare force. Another in the group, a bow-legged, bristle-bearded man with coal dark eyes, also showed evidence of being Awakened. His buckskin shirt and trousers were less elegant than the outfits worn by the rest of Halleck's comrades, but he had an aura of tough self-reliance the rest lacked.

With two unknown Mages present, she dared not try anything further and withdrew into her body. Lung Lei had stopped speaking and squatted next to her, a quizzical expression on his broad features.

"Finish your rice," he hissed. "They will be sending out the work gangs any moment now."

"What do the work gangs do?" she whispered around a mouthful of cold rice.

"Dig or carry dirt away in baskets. Sometimes we carry away mud. Halleck's Folly is being built on land reclaimed from the sea."

"Does Halleck often come to the diggings?"

"Sometimes, in the afternoons, to supervise and set right

things that have been done incorrectly."

"Then, if he's here already, is that odd?"

"Very."

The shouting of the gang bosses ended further conversation. Tieh hurried, imitating the rushed but not eager pace of those around her. Among these men of the Past, she was tall and in her dirty work clothes not terribly feminine. She found the observation rather depressing.

Outside, the day was already muggy. Halleck and his cronies were a distance away inspecting an already completed portion of the foundation hole. Enhancing her hearing, Tieh shamelessly eavesdropped on their conversation.

"... start laying the raft here today. The timber has been floated from across the Bay. Tell the coolie boss to get a crew of strong men over here. We don't need many for starters."

Excited, Tieh worked her way through the milling laborers until she was near the boss making the selections. It was child's play to shape a charm so that she would be certain to be chosen.

"Now," she muttered to Lung Lei as they were marched over to their work site, "I'd better hope that Serena sent me to the right time and that Halleck plans to enchant the Block's foundation today. Where has he gotten to?"

"Keep your head down!" Lung Lei scolded, "You can't risk being noticed. Let me tell you what I see."

Tieh dutifully lowered her head, dismissing the idea of conjuring magical second sight. Lung Lei was right. Being noticed would be dangerous and Halleck was certain to be jumpy on such an important day.

"Halleck and his men are walking to inspect the redwood. There are wagons laden with winches and runners and wedges and great quantities of rope."

"Guess I know what we'll be doing," Tieh said between clenched teeth.

Tieh "gloved" her hands by concentrating on toughening the skin. Kung-fu didn't exactly prepare one for hauling ropes and timbers. For the next several hours, she strained at the ropes with the rest of the Chinese, while Halleck's group shouted instructions.

From what she could tell, as the foundation digging was completed more and more labor was diverted to setting the redwood timbers into interlocking tiers. Tired and sore as she was, she had energy enough to worry that she might find herself too far from Halleck at the key moment. Then, a few minutes before high noon, the gong sounded.

"Lunch?" she hopefully asked Lung Lei.

"Odd, again," he replied, "They've never given a general break before. Usually they let people rest in shifts."

"Halleck's going to do it!" Tieh said. "He wants to do it at high noon — under the watchful eye of the sun and all that! I bet he is of the Order of Hermes, like Serena thought."

Fortunately, the redwood floored pit offered ample hiding places behind gear and unset wood. Taking cover, she composed herself to resist any urge to interfere. Lung Lei hovered at her shoulder, whispering guidance as she crept after Halleck and the young man with the bristling beard and coal-dark eyes. They strode purposefully to a section of the foundation that Halleck selected with the aid of compass and sun dial.

"Here we are," Halleck said, removing from his jacket pocket a small, symbol encrusted vial. "Hold this, Ned."

The buckskin clad frontiersman carefully cradled the vial in his calloused hands while Halleck waved his hands over it and muttered a few words. Then Halleck took the vial back and knelt to pour the liquid over a section of the redwood. After a hiss and a puff of pungent smoke, a hole about eight inches in diameter and about the same depth appeared in the wood.

While Ned suspiciously scanned the edges of the

foundation hole for spies, Halleck removed a gold band about an inch thick and twisted into a circlet about six inches in diameter from his pocket. Tieh enhanced her vision and saw that the band was etched with symbols representing each of the four elements, runes for Dynamism and Stasis, and the mathematical symbol for infinity.

Halleck muttered a few Latin sounding words over the Talisman and then set it into the hole. Ned helped him seal the hole with a "knot" swiftly carved from a scrap of redwood and another muttered ritual. While they worked, Tieh reached out with her Mage's sense for power.

"Halleck's power is much diminished!" she muttered to Lung Lei. "He is barely stronger than his apprentice."

The spirit squeezed her shoulder. "Could he have invested too much of his potential in trinkets like that ring Talisman or in various incantations?"

Tieh nodded, "Even I could have sealed that hole better and I am a novice in the Sphere of Matter."

Halleck and Ned completed their ritual a few minutes after noon and strode from the foundation pit, chatting about having lunch and a drink at the Graham House.

When they had left, Tieh and Lung Lei crept away to a storage area where the spirit said they would probably not be disturbed. Tieh slumped against a heap of bricks, her muscles protesting their morning's work, her throat dry, and her stomach rumbling with vague hunger. She banished these annoyances with practiced discipline.

"Now," she said, almost as much to herself as to the spirit, "We need to find our way back to my Present. How do we get back?"

The spirit shrugged, "I do not know, Mage. As a man buried without rites, far from the lands of my ancestors, all places are alike to me in that none will bring offerings to my spirit. You are my anchor within Time, because Abraham has bound me to you. I perceive a Present and a Past and Future relative to that Present because you are in it, not because Time has any control over me."

Tieh scowled, "I know where the Talisman is, but that won't do Serena and Abraham any good if I remain trapped here. I suppose that I could take a few decades and study, but I doubt that a Chinese woman would find much sympathy or many teachers."

"You are a Mage," Lung Lei said, "The Talisman will remain where it is until you get to another Time and remove it."

"Will it?" Tieh said, suddenly remembering what Serena and Abraham had told her. "Didn't the others say something about the foundation getting dry rot? What if it was moved then?"

"Then it won't be where you think it is when you return to your Present and all of this will have been wasted effort."

"Has anyone told you that you're a damn cheerful companion, Lung Lei?"

Tiredly, Tieh buried her face in her hands and reviewed everything that she knew about the nature of Time. After a long while an idea occurred to her. Excitedly, she began to whisper to Lung Lei.

"Serena explained Time to me as a river. She was very convincing, but earlier teachers taught me that Time was an illusion, governed by our own subjective measurements."

Lung Lei smiled, "The summer days that each last a lifetime, until the week before school when they fly past. The eternity of the hour before a beloved arrives versus the brevity of a fortnight's holiday. Yes, I remember. Continue."

"In college physics, I learned that Time is relative — a function of velocity through space." Tieh etched a wiggly line in the brick dust on the floor, "Each of these views is convincing and I am convinced that each is right — even when they contradict each other."

"So, Mage, continue. I admit, you've made me curious."

"So, none of it is what I need to get where I need to go," she grinned, "All I need is me and you. You said that spirits are not limited by Time as the living are, but that you lack points of reference for guidance."

"Yes, that is true — at least in my case."

"Very well, I will fix my Mind on that section of the Block which holds the Talisman. Then you will take us through Time, while I provide us with directions."

"Rather like the blind carrying the lame," Lung Lei said doubtfully. "I don't know where to go, but I can move through Time. You know where to go, but can't get there."

"Are you willing to try?"

Lung Lei extended his hand, "Tell me what to do."

"Just move towards the Present — I mean away from Now into What is Then. I'll tell when to slow down or turn if I feel my awareness of Halleck's Talisman fading."

"Don't we need to go somewhere special — like that strange clock the white-haired Mage turned into a door?"

"No," Tieh focused her mind until she could feel the Talisman and the redwood surrounding it. "No, all of that is unimportant. I have our anchor. Walk and I will follow."

Lung Lei hesitated and Tieh realized that he was afraid of failing her. She squeezed his hand and he smiled at her.

"Very well, Tieh. I think I will find it easier to take you out of the Present and into the stream of Time if you close your eyes and keep a tight grasp of my hand."

Tieh obeyed.

"Walk with me now, Tieh," Lung Lei said. "We will move at a brisk pace until you tell me we have gone astray. Then we may slow while I find the path you want us to follow."

They walked this way, hand in hand, for what seemed like hours to Tieh. Sometimes, Tieh would tell Lung Lei to adjust their course right or left. Occasionally, they back-tracked and picked up the course from a new angle.

As they grew comfortable with their odd method of progress, they talked, at first about what they might find when they reached their destination, later about more personal matters. Lung Lei told Tieh about his home in

China, especially about his early years in school when learning was a delight and he didn't doubt that he would pass his examinations.

Tieh told him about her early years in her parent's kung-fu and tai chi studio, how she had excelled early and later disappointed them by turning away from solely Chinese traditions to see what other cultures held. She was just beginning to tell him about her joyful discovery of the underlying Way that connected all practices when the trace by which she had been guiding them vanished.

"Stop, Lung Lei, I've lost it. Let's retrace our steps carefully. When are we?"

"I have difficulty with this barbarian calendar, especially this far beyond when I lived. I would estimate that we are sometime between 1920 and 1940."

"Good enough," Tieh said, resisting an impulse to open her eyes. "I think we've found the time period when the dry rot in the foundation was discovered. Walk back along the way we just came while I sense."

"Very well. What do you feel?"

"Nothing... Nothing. Wait! Keep going. Yes! There it is again. I can even feel the damage in the redwood now that I'm trying."

"Do you wish for us to step back into this moment?"

"Hold on. Tell me what you see. Are we near the Block?"

"Of course. It is quite impressive still, though the balconies and sculptures are gone and the entire structure has a slight list that is especially evident along the front."

"Balconies and sculptures? Never mind. That tilt must be the result of the Dynamic force attacking the structure damage. Are we alone?"

"You mean would we be alone if I brought us out into this Time? No, there is a small gathering, but I cannot understand its purpose. My English is poor and, for this time period, archaic. Can you do anything, Mage?"

"'Mage' — Is that a reminder, Lung Lei?" she smiled. "I may be able to manage something. Take us out into a place we won't be noticed and I'll work something. Don't be worried if I seem to vanish or you can't find me."

"I will always be able to find you," Lung Lei said, slightly haughtily. "The Dreamspeaker bound me to you."

"Very well, whenever you are ready."

She felt a gentle shove and found herself standing in an doorway, shielded from the street by a pile of cartons set out for the trash pick-up. Bending the light rays so the she would be invisible was fairly simple; she had a bit more difficulty in composing herself enough to become the Watchful Self, passive, only observing, and thus unnoticeable, even to a telepath.

Stepping around the cartons, Lung Lei beside her, she joined the small group of people standing in front of the Block. Most carried note-pads and one or two had cards that said "Press" stuck in their hat-bands. As she was registering this, a man in his late forties emerged from the Block and said, "Follow me, please."

Confident that she was in the right place and Time, Tieh trailed along. Their guide lead them directly to a musty, subterranean area. As they walked, the guide answered questions from the reporters.

"Why are there so many rooms down here?" said a man with an lilting Welsh accent, "It looks like a dungeon."

"Well, Idwal, originally the Montgomery Block was constructed with twenty-eight basement rooms. These frequently served as vaults. During the history of the Block, wine, rare books, even gold have been stored here. Henry Halleck was a smart man. San Francisco was even more vulnerable to fire in 1853 than it is today. He promised fireproof, earthquakeproof storage and he kept his word. Even the great fire of 1906 didn't get the Block."

"Is it true that the Block is collapsing?" Idwal asked.

"No, but Halleck's genius has proven to be this old

building's undoing..."

Tieh stopped listening. While the guide had been answering questions, she had been lazily scanning the group of reporters, wondering if any of them was the Mage come to relocate the Talisman. A few seemed promising, then a trim, grey-haired old man in a tidy linen suit had looked up from his clipboard to laugh at one of the guide's quips and she had seen his eyes —dark, coal-black eyes. A thrill went through her as she recognized him as the young frontiersman who had been Halleck's aide when the Talisman was placed.

He looked a healthy seventy or so, far younger than he should be, but many Mages learned to control the aging process. Tieh had little time to consider the implications of his presence for the guide was directing their attention to where a section of redwood was being drawn forth.

"This beam shows an example of the damage that dry rot has done to the seemingly indestructible foundation of the Block..."

Tieh tuned out the tour guide, risking detection to examine the log more closely.

Lung Lei whispered in her ear, "Certainly that is the very log in which we saw Halleck place the Talisman. This is too much of a coincidence!"

"Not where magic is concerned," Tieh replied.

She schooled herself to exquisite passivity, remaining in the room when the guide led the reporters out. Moments later, a chic blonde reporter returned. Without even mussing her fingernails, she removed the patch from the redwood log and pulled forth the heavy Talisman. She was placing it in her bag, when a voice from the doorway halted her.

"Give the Talisman here, Mabel," came the gravelly voice of the frontiersman, "or I'll have to take it from you."

"You're a foolish old man, Ned," Mabel remarked in a voice as crisp as her suit. "All I need to do is scream — your reputation won't handle much more controversy and the Technocracy is tired of covering for you."

"Scream," Ned suggested dryly. "The Sleepers won't hear. I've deadened the air between us and them. They won't miss us either. I played on your pretty fib about a headache and said that I'd just go and see if you were fit to get home."

"Why do you want Halleck's Talisman? It belongs to the City. I'm going to re-set it after the repairs have been completed so that it can continue to ward the city."

"Maybe I don't believe anymore that the city deserves such constant guardianship. Maybe it's been better off when the changes came more easily."

"Ned! I though you were in agreement with us. You were Halleck's own student!"

Tieh stood mute, her fingers biting her palms as Mabel reached the same conclusion she already had.

"Ned, you're not —"

"The enemy? One of the Nephandi?" Ned's grin was ugly. "Why not? Because of Halleck? Hell, that old coot was half gone to the Wyrm himself, always going down to his quicksilver mine and listening to the mutterings while growing rich off of the poison they mined there for explosives. Some have been telling me that he did go over in his later years . Lots of folk blamed him for the screw-ups in Union tactics, y'know, and he changed an awful lot after his return from D.C. He didn't visit nearly so much with the old crowd then, but you wouldn't remember that. You're just a young tool, a young fool, like I was then."

Mabel did scream then and lashed out with raw blue lightnings that spoke as much of her panic as it did the strength of her Avatar. Ned retaliated with a shower of silver rain drops that scattered the lightning into stone fireflies.

With Halleck's Talisman hanging from her wrist, Mabel shaped myriad forces against Ned. The frontiersman was less adept at manipulating raw energies, but he was hung with discretely concealed charms that diverted most of Mabel's attacks.

Ever aware of the threat of paradox, Tieh could only watch as the Mages dueled. At last, the exchange of attacks came to a halt. Ned dipped his hand into his coat pocket and came out with a revolver.

"I didn't want to resort to this, Mabel," he said, "but I can't let you walk out of here — not with that and not with what you know about me."

Mabel's vaguely triumphant expression changed to one of fear as she realized that her skill as a Mage had condemned her to death. Ned's coal-dark eyes narrowed to a feral glitter and his finger began to tighten on the trigger.

As she had with the switchblade on that far to come Halloween night, Tieh altered gravity, centering her area of influence on the revolver so that it became of fifty pound weight in the old man's hand.

The gun tore from his fingers and Mabel sprang forward, swinging the arm wearing the heavy gold Talisman into Ned's gut. He doubled forward and collapsed. With much enthusiasm but little finesse, Mabel knocked him unconscious. Then, panting, she stepped to the doorway and listened. Satisfied that no one was likely to interrupt her, she waved her hands over Ned. His breathing slowed and regularized. After another listen at the doorway, Mabel quickly studied the room.

Tieh could almost hear her internal monologue. The foundation would not be secure until the concrete was poured, but with the Nephandi seeking the Talisman, she could not delay reinstalling it.

Moving decisively, Mabel loosened the mortar around a brick a few rows from the floor and then dug a shallow wall safe. The gold Talisman went into its new hiding place followed by a muttered rote of concealment. Once the brick was back in place, Mabel shaped mortar and sealed Halleck's Talisman into its new resting place. A quick rote and a handful of dirt made the new mortar match the old.

Shaking her outfit into place, Mabel took off her jacket

and bent over the recumbent Ned.

"It's a shame that you dropped your gun that way, but old boys shouldn't play with guns," her expression was analytical. "You shouldn't have interfered with me."

She laid her folded jacket over Ned's mouth and nose. Gradually, his breathing slowed, then stopped. Mabel rose, inspected her jacket for damages, and without a backward look departed the basement room.

Tieh spared no concern on Ned, moving instead to inspect the Talisman's new cache. The concealment spell nearly masked its signature, but she had not trailed it through Time to lose it now.

"I've got it," she told Lung Lei, "Can you get me to the Present?"

Lung Lei bowed, "But you interfered, Tieh. You took a terrible risk."

"There were no Sleepers present," she said, "and I was very, very careful."

"So I saw," he replied. "I believe that I can take you directly to Abraham. I borrowed your trick and I believe that I have found his signature."

"That would be wonderful," Tieh said, holding out her hand to him. "Lead on."

Serena's studio bore little resemblance to the tranquil shrine to Time that they had departed. Although apparently only minutes had passed, the crystal pendulum grandfather clock had been thrown on its side, its glass shattered. Other clocks had been flung to the floor or hung crooked on the walls.

Abraham and Serena stood side by side in the center of the room, encircled by the Technocracy's horse-skulled servitors. The battle was much less flamboyant than the one Tieh had just observed in the Block's cellar, the Mages hobbled by their desire to avoid attracting Sleepers and thus create paradox.

From the ruins of the grandfather clock, Lung Lei pushed

Tieh into the Present. After the forced non-interference of her quest through Time she felt delightfully free at the prospect of an honest brawl. Noting that at least one of the servitors had a shattered arm — probably from a Abraham's staffshe concluded that the Technocracy had constructed them to resist magical rather than physical force.

Testing her theory with a well-place kick, she was satisfied to feel the brittle bones shatter. She had destroyed two of the servitors by the time Serena and Abraham followed her example. Only a few moments after her re-emergence into the Present, Tieh spun to a halt beside the last crumpling servitor. She couldn't resist a saucy bow at the expressions of amused astonishment on the elder's faces.

"Tieh! We told you to go!" Abraham scolded. "Now Serena's studio is ruined for nothing!"

"I've been," she said.

"But how did you find your way back?" Serena asked, "I didn't have a chance to show you the way or give you the amulet that I had prepared."

Tieh straightened, remembering Lung Lei's jibes.

"I am a Mage," she said, unable to give the words the frosty tone that she had intended, "and Abraham found me a fine guide. Together we found our way."

"And did you find what Halleck had done?" Serena said eagerly.

"Yes, you were right. He was Technocracy — and maybe Nephandi. He had planted a stasis Talisman," Tieh said, "It was moved when the foundation rotted, but we traced it to its new resting place. It's still in the Block — that is, in the basement of the Pyramid."

Serena looked around her ruined studio, "The Technocracy may send other forces here. Tieh, I know you must be tired, but can you go and retrieve the Talisman? Abraham and I will remain to guard your back and distract any attention you might draw."

"I'll go," Tieh said, glancing at Lung Lei who stood beside

her his hand still holding her own. "Both of us can go."

Abraham looked puzzled, but Serena immediately began sketching the shape of a doorway on the wall against which the grandfather clock had stood.

"As Time and Space are merely aspects of each other, I will create a short-term portal to take you directly to the basement of the Block. This way you do not need to risk being intercepted on the streets," she frowned thoughtfully. "Focus on the Talisman's signature and the portal will carry you to it."

"Ready, Lung Lei?" Tieh asked, when Serena's portal glowed pink and gold.

"Of course," the spirit said, squeezing her hand, "Let us be gone."

As they emerged in a small storage room, Tieh felt the Talisman's presence at once.

"It's right over there," she said, "I can feel the old brick behind the plaster."

The plaster broke away easily. Mabel's mortar was a bit more of a challenge, but Tieh manipulated Matter until it crumbled. She had just drawn the Talisman from its concealment when Lung Lei cried warning.

"Tieh, someone is coming!"

She had barely a moment to realize that the room had no other exit when the door was flung open by a husky Hispanic woman in a police officer's uniform.

"Hold it right there, thief! Police!"

The woman strode in, leveling her police special. Two male officers followed her in, a powerfully built African-American and a blond straight from a Nazi recruiting poster. All three of them had their guns leveled at her and Tieh felt sure that even if she went invisible that they would shoot.

"We've got her, Detective," the woman called.

"Very good, now just keep her from going anywhere," said a familiar, gravelly voice.

A shrivelled old man entered the chamber. Despite what nearly half a century more had done to him, Tieh knew Ned at once. The coal-black eyes had not lost their spark, nor had he lost any of his force of personality.

"So there it is," Ned rasped, his attention for the Talisman as much as for Tieh. "That bitch Mabel hid it while I was out cold. Then she thought she'd murdered me. I'd some tricks she didn't know, but by the time I'd recovered and come back to search it had vanished. I guessed that she'd left it here, but I could never discover where she'd put it. But I felt it when you brought it forth. I don't know how you found it, missy, but I'm much obliged."

The police officers listened unblinking to this incredible speech and Tieh realized that either Ned or the Technocracy had bound their minds that they would only notice what would be of use to their masters.

"I rather suspect you won't much like the reward I have in mind for you," Ned continued, "but another vandal shot by the police on Halloween night won't raise a stir."

"Officers..." he was beginning when the air in the small room became clotted with insubstantial forms.

They seeped in through the floors, through the walls, and dripped from the ceilings, each solidifying into form recognizable as Chinese laborers in the garb of over a century before, garb similar to that which Tieh still wore. Other figures were better dressed: servants, waiters, launderers. One even bore a pyrotechnics kit.

Not all of the spirits were Chinese. Some were Anglo or Hispanic. Tieh thought that she recognized a few artists and authors who in life had been significantly associated with the Block.

The spirits ranked themselves between Ned and Tieh and at their head was Lung Lei.

"When I saw the Ancient returning," Lung Lei said, "I took a leaf from Abraham's book and aroused some of the spirits who were tied to the Block. They are eager for revenge against those who used them so cruelly in the past."

Tieh smiled, "Well, Ancient, your three living against my many dead. Will you at least negotiate for my freedom?"

Ned made a quick gesture and the three police officers dropped off to sleep, still standing with their guns pointed at Tieh.

"Well, missy..." Ned began.

Lung Lei interrupted, "Tieh, a spirit I did not plan to bring forth demands to speak with Ned."

Tieh gasped as Halleck's spirit stepped to the fore. He glanced arrogantly at her.

"I will have business with you in a moment, Akashic, but first..." he turned to Ned, "You have delayed settling accounts with your masters for long enough. Nor can you convince me that you wished to acquire my Talisman for the good of any but yourself."

"No, Henry, you have me all wrong," Ned babbled, his confidence shattered.

Halleck tossed open his hands, "Entropy take you."

With a thin wail, Ned grasped his temples and crumpled to the floor. As his spirit separated from his shrivelled body, Halleck stopped him from departing.

"Wait, Ned," Halleck turned his cold gaze on Tieh, "Those law officers will shoot you if Ned commands them. If you surrender the Talisman to me, I will have him order them to depart and forget all they have seen. If not, you will die and another tool will hand it over."

"Why do you want it?" Tieh said, aware that the restless milling of spirits around her would have little power over Halleck.

"When I made it, I desired the preservation of San Francisco. Now I serve another cause. I wrought too well, however, and my creation has been enhanced by the Pyramid so that it blocks Entropy as well as the Dynamic force I sought to contain. I will take it away and destroy it so that its powers may be rechanneled more appropriately."

Tieh looked from Halleck to the quivering Ned to the dead-eyed police officers then finally to Lung Lei.

The spirit looked at her intently, "Remember, you are a Mage, but you are also Tieh — Butterfly."

The emphasis of Lung Lei's words reminded her of Abraham's prophesy that she was the butterfly who would force the Wyrm to turn over a new leaf. Perhaps Halleck would destroy the Talisman, perhaps he would not, but if the Dreamspeaker was to be believed, her actions would force the Wyrm to change. Certainly, any change at all would be for the better. Heartened, she showed the Talisman to Halleck.

"Tell Ned to call off his police officers and then I'll let you have this thing, for all the good it may do you."

Halleck did not pause, "Ned, do as she says."

When the three officers had departed, Tieh extended the Talisman to Halleck. She felt a shock of cold as their hands met across the golden ring. Then Halleck, the Talisman, and all of the spirits — except one — were gone.

Tieh threw her arms around Lung Lei and hugged him.

"Thank you! I didn't know that spirits could summon other spirits like that."

"Most cannot. I never did get to tell you why I failed my exams. I had other distractions. You see," he smiled down at her and stroked her hair, "I am also a Mage. Farewell, Tieh. Do not forget me."

"Never," she promised, feeling her eyes grow hot with tears, "I will bring your spirit offerings on all the feast days and set a cenotaph in your honor."

"Death, like Time, may be just an illusion," Lung Lei replied. "Perhaps we shall meet again."

He faded, leaving her holding the empty air. Wiping away a tear, she was glad that there was no one left to see, Tieh found her way out of the Pyramid, hurrying away from the Block which echoed after her with all the voices of its Past.

THE JUDAS TREE
■ ■ ■ ■ ■ ■ ■ ■ ■ ■ ■ ■ ■

Richard Lee Byers

I found Tom Baxter in a smoky North Beach bar, a joint with autographed pictures of jazz artists hanging on the walls, and a scratchy Louis Armstrong record playing on the jukebox. I'd studied with Tom for seven years. During that time, he'd told me stories about Aaron Burr and Kit Carson, so I knew he was old, even by mage standards. But until tonight, I'd never seen him look old. It wasn't like his unkempt chestnut hair had turned gray or anything like that; it was the way his shoulders slumped.

The pane of glass on the front of the cigarette machine bulged into the shape of a face — my face. "Go to him," he urged. Nobody else noticed the iridescent mask. I wondered if my new master was really talking to me, or if I was in Quiet again, hallucinating as I had been off and on for the past few days. Not that it mattered. Either way, I already knew what I had to do. I started across the room.

Tom finished his whiskey, then looked around. The bartender was busy chatting to a petite woman with spiky magenta hair. Tom stared at his glass until suddenly it was full of brown liquid again. Down the length of the bar, water rings bubbled and steamed.

For a moment, I froze, waiting to see if something else, something dangerous, was going to happen. It didn't, so I moved on, albeit even more reluctantly than before.

Even drunk, Tom sensed before I spoke. Swaying, he twisted on his stool. His bloodshot eyes blinked. "Jacobi." He never called me by my first name, Francis. He said it didn't suit me.

"Hello, Mentor." Up close, he smelled of booze and sweat.

He snorted, "I'm not your Mentor. Not since you left the Order Come to think of it, I'm not anybody's Mentor anymore. What are you doing here? Did somebody call you?"

"No. I saw you in the cards. I saw Penny's death. I'm sorry."

"You always were good with the Tarot. Too bad it didn't tell you I want to be alone. But since you're here, have a drink." With a pop of displaced air, a glass of whiskey appeared on the bar. The bottles on the shelves rattled. The people around the bar gasped, and innocently babbled about the aftershocks.

I tensed, but once again, his luck held. "Jesus," I said. "Aren't you the same guy who taught me never to work overt magick in front of mundanes?"

"No." He gulped down half his drink. His Adam's apple bobbed. "We buried that fool on Monday, along with his wife. Can't say as I miss him either."

"I imagine your friends do. Look, I came back to Frisco to help you."

"Lucky me. I loved Penny for a century and a half. She died for nothing. Nothing." He took a swig of his drink. "Her car swerved out of control in the Goddamn quake, but I'm sure that after I listen to you little pep talk, I'm going to feel just fine."

"I'm not here to hold your hand." I took another sip of my drink. "With your assistance, I'm going to bring her back to life."

He goggled at me, "What?"

"We shouldn't talk about it here. Can we go to the chantry?"

"We could, but —"

"Then come on." As we headed for the door, I noticed a half-opened purple-red flower, lying on a table near the tiny, vacant stage.

The vision of it lingered briefly in my mind, but it soon drifted off.

■ ■ ■

Tom's home, the Order of Hermes school and stronghold, was one of the brightly painted Victorian mansions near Alamo Square. Though I'd lived there for five years, when I saw its moonlit oriels and gables again, I had the unpleasant feeling that I was barging into a place where my presence wouldn't be tolerated. Maybe Tom was too drunk and grief-stricken to detect what had happened to me, but surely one of his students or acolytes would.

So inwardly I cringed when plump, white-haired Katie, the housekeeper, met us on the stoop. But she just shot me a grateful smile, then focused her attention on Tom. She took his arm and helped him over the thresholds. A half dozen people, their faces full of mingled relief and concern, clustered around him.

"Look at you," Kate said. From her scolding tone, you might have thought that Tom was a naughty child, not an Adept. She'd talked to me that same way whenever she thought I was doing something stupid, which had been at least once a day. "I'm taking you straight up to your bed."

"No, you're not," said Tom.

"You need rest, you're —"

"Get away from me!" he snarled. She flinched. I jumped myself. I realized that I'd never heard him raise his voice in anger before. "Jacobi and I are going to talk in the study. The rest of you stay out." He stumbled across the foyer.

His associates looked at me quizzically. Trying to avoid their gazes, I stepped into the house.

Someone touched me on the arm. Turning, I looked into Lois' lustrous lilac eyes. The last time I'd seen her in 1977, but she still appeared so fresh and sweet that I felt foul by comparison.

"Hi," she said softly.

"Hi."

"I always hoped you'd come back. I should have known you would, if Tom needed you. We knew where he was, but we couldn't persuade him to come home. Every time we tried, he started working vulgar magick to drive us away."

He'd been doing it even when they weren't around, playing Russian roulette with Paradox, the natural force that works to suppress sorcery — and sorcerers — but I didn't see any reason to tell her so. I just wanted to get away from her. "I need to stick with him if I'm going to help him any further."

I guess I sounded cold, because she looked hurt, "But we'll talk later?" she said.

"Sure." I turned away from her and shoved my way through the small crowd. To my relief, the rest of them were strangers.

A flood of memories came to me as I recognized the study, dimly lit by the glow of a red, white and green Tiffany lamp. The high oak bookshelves were overloaded as ever. The scent of old paper hung in the air, and framed specimens of intricately drawn pentagrams and magic circles adorned the walls. Tom and I had discussed so much here; the Art and every other subject under the sun. We had plotted a campaign against a particularly vicious band of Marauders, played innumerable games of chess, go, and gin and to my displeasure, I remembered it all as clearly as I did Lois' kisses.

Tom had sprawled in his favorite seat, a brown leather Morris chair. He waved a snifter of brandy. "Have one."

"Only if you let me pour it myself," I lifted the cut-glass decanter off the sideboard.

"Not a huge risk of rousing Paradox with no Sleepers watching what we do. You know that."

"Sure I do." I raised my glass to breathe in the smell of the liquor. "Just like I understand that it's the reason you decided to do your drinking elsewhere."

Tom nodded, "That, and all those idiots fussing over me. Let's dispose of the rather lame deception you used to lure me home, shall we? We both know that you can't bring Penny back. I'm older than you, I've learned more, and I couldn't do it."

I didn't bother to point out that if he'd been certain of what he was saying, he wouldn't have left the bar with me. "It's true. You do know more than me. But it's all Hermetic stuff, whereas I've studied with Dreamspeakers, the Akashic Brotherhood, the Celestial Chorus, and anybody else who'd give me lessons. You'd be surprised what you can do when you mix the Traditions together."

He shook his head, "I do understand the advantages of treading the Orphan's path. That's why I didn't try harder to convince you to stay here, even though you were the best pupil I ever had. I believe that you can do things I can't. But my own Mentor taught me that no one can truly raise the dead."

"Well, mine taught me that nobody knows the limits of magick, so I shouldn't assume that anything is impossible. Or don't you remember that?"

He grimaced, "Of course I do. In theory, it's absolutely correct. But in practice —"

"I started working on resurrection when I was staying with the Verbena in Germany, just for the intellectual challenge. I admit, I've never tested my ideas, but I think

I've cracked the practical objections. Let me show you." I took a sip of fiery brandy, then moved to the worktable, grabbed a pen and a sheet of drawing paper, and started to write. Tom lurched to his feet and staggered over to watch.

The strength of Hermetic magick is that it's rational. Systematized. That meant that by using the proper diagrams and formulae, I could outline an operation for Tom as readily as mathematicians communicate with equations. I sketched a final pentagram, and handed him the page.

He squinted at it for a while, then set it down, pressed his hands to his temples, and murmured. Even though he'd directed his magick inward, for a moment I felt a stray current of power throbbing through the air.

His intoxication vanished. He studied my notes again. I tensed. I could feel my pulse beat in my neck. Finally he said, "By God, you may be on to something here.

A mask of my face swelled out of a wooden beam above us and leered at me. Somehow I managed not to flinch.

"But the number and magnitude of the forces in play…" he continued.

"It's definitely a balancing act," I said. "But human existence is a complex thing. We have to invoke most of the Spheres if we're going to repair Penny's body and reunite it with her soul."

"I don't comprehend a lot of this, except on the most superficial level." He pointed to a line of symbols, "This, for example…"

"It's Verbena and Euthanatos stuff, blended together. I can explain it, but the underlying assumptions are different from what you're used to."

"But you're convinced that they'll work in this context? Keep the powers from surging out of control?"

"'Convinced' is putting it a little strong. Like I said, I never tested this because it's dangerous. We're likely to die if it jumps the track. But I'm willing to run the risk for

Penny's sake. Provided you agree, of course."

He scowled, "Yes, provided I agree. Tell me, Disciple, what did I teach you about death?"

"To mourn and let go; that dying is only the transition from one life to another, and a part of the quest for Ascension."

"I must have sounded like a sanctimonious ass. How did you manage to listen without throwing up?"

Something twisted in my chest, "You sounded pretty smart to me."

"Well, I've learned something. It's easy to tell other people to accept a loss when you're not hurting yourself. But now I feel ruined. Empty. I think about my apprentices, my studies, my duties to the chantry and the Order, and none of it means a damn."

"Maybe it will again, in time."

"And maybe it won't. When a doctor revives a patient whose heart has stopped, nobody claims he's done something evil. How is this any different?"

"Perhaps it isn't."

"Penny had her own projects and responsibilities. She was going to do a lot of good in the world. Why shouldn't she be given time to finish her work?"

"You don't have to persuade me," I said. "I came here to try the spell, remember? I take it that we are going to do this."

"Yes, God help us, we are." Above his head, the mask in the beam crowed silently. Reddish purple flowers erupted from the smooth brown wood on either side. Unlike the flower in the bar, these were in full bloom, the petals plump, with a color so rich they almost seemed to glow.

This time, of course, I understood that they were a manifestation of the Quiet. I wondered briefly why I'd hallucinated a similar image twice. Conceivably, my unconscious was trying to tell me something, but if so, I couldn't imagine what.

■ ■ ■

Something was wrong with the bus. In place of advertisements, it had along the side identical pictures of a man suspended upside down. And, brakes squeaking, it was slowing to a halt directly opposite me, even though there wasn't a bus stop there.

Last night I'd fled the chantry as soon as I could. Tom had urged me to stay, but I'd claimed that I had private preparations to make before the resurrection ceremony: meditations, purification and the like. I was telling the truth, partially. I'd hoped to spend this afternoon in Golden Gate Park, enjoying the greenery, blue sky, and mild November air, distracting myself from what was to come.

But evidently I couldn't. Some aspect of the super natural — either my new associates or the mild,, transient derangement which is an occupational hazard of magery — had caught up with me again. Half alarmed and half exasperated, I waited to see what, if anything, would happen next.

The bus door didn't open. Instead it distend, just as the glass in the vending machine and the surface of the wooden beam had done. A figure stepped down, separating itself from the side of the vehicle. When its substance turned to flesh and clothing, it looked exactly like me.

The bus rolled on down Fulton Street. My twin smiled and walked toward me. I met him halfway, on an expanse of sunlit grass, near some college kids who were playing catch. I could hear the sound of the baseball smacking in their gloves.

"Nice day," said the double, "if you like that kind of thing." Even his breath was like mine. It smelled of the garlicky slice of pizza I'd eaten for lunch.

"I realize that this is a foolish question," I said, "but are you real, a projection —"

"Or just a phantasm generated by your own fevered mind?" He grinned. I hoped that I didn't look that nasty when I smiled. "You ought to realize, it doesn't matter. I don't just live in the Wasteland anymore. I also dwell in the depths of your mind. We're two parts of a greater whole. From now on, your dreams and fantasies are echoes of my voice."

I though to the nightmares I'd had last night. I tried not to shiver. "All right. But why do you have to look like me? It's ...disconcerting."

He started to stroll, toward a rose garden. I fell into step beside him. "You aren't paying attention. I am you. This is my true form. And if I appear o you in one of my other forms, you probably wouldn't retain our conversation afterwards, any more than you remember the, ah, messier moments of your rebirth."

"Okay," I said. A gull swooped over our heads. "What do you want?"

"Tsk, tsk. You're awfully brusque for a man who's communing with his deity."

"What's the big deal?? If we're the same person, then I'm a god, too."

He laughed. "Touché. I'm going to enjoy running you. You did well last night. Not too cocksure, not too pushy. You played him like a master anger."

"My jaw tightened. "Thanks."

"I have to admit, for a while I though you weren't being pushy enough. There was a moment there when it almost seemed as if you were trying to dissuade him."

I felt myself starting to sweat, "You said it yourself. I used a soft sell, and it got results."

Two fat middle-aged women in brightly colored jogging suits puffed toward us. The shorter and rounder of the two pounded straight at my double, and he sidestepped to let her pass.

"I predict a heart attack before she's fifty," said the apparition. "Yes, you landed you fish. But you should have spent the night in the chantry, reminiscing about old items. I'm concerned that your departure aroused suspicion."

"I told Tom I had things to do. I also tried to make him think that being around Lois made me uncomfortable. He bought it."

"Good. But why did you actually leave?"

"Because I was uncomfortable. This is hard. There was a time when Tom meant a lot to me. I wouldn't even be a mage if he hadn't Awakened me. But don't worry. I haven't got cold feet."

"I believe you." The silvery lenses of his sunglasses and the green T-shirt inside his battered motorcycle jacket turned a purplish red — same damn color as the phantom flowers! Once again, I wondered if it meant something, but only for a second. Talking face to face with a god, even if you aren't sure whether, or in what sense, the thing is really there, is nerve-wracking enough to hold you attention. "So what's the point of torturing yourself with all this …nostalgia? Focus on the future."

"Yeah," I remembered what he'd promised me. "All the knowledge and power I could ever want."

■ ■ ■

The sky was clear, and the night seemed simultaneously dark and full of light. The stars and a waning moon shone overhead. Tom's ruby Showstone burned on his breast, and a massive gold Seal of Solomon ring glowed on his right hand. Silvery circles of protection gleamed in the grass at our feet.

Around us, rows of headstones marched away in all directions. A few trees, mausoleums, monuments, statues of weeping angels and the like, towered above the lesser markers. The more distant of these were just vague masses in the gloom.

Yesterday's slovenly drunk was gone. As usual when working complex magick, Tom wore an elegant suit and tie. His polished wingtips reflected the phosphorescence of his pentagram. He was freshly bathed and shaved, and not a chestnut hair was out of place.

His grooming rituals helped him clear his mind for conjuring. I used different mental tricks to accomplish the same thing, so I was my usual sloppy self.

No one else from the chantry had accompanied us to the cemetery. No one else knew what we intended. Tom hadn't wanted them to try to talk him out of it, or to insist on helping. He didn't want anyone else to get caught in the backlash if the experiment went wrong.

Tom raised the Seal and spoke in Latin. The amber light pulsed. I felt my muscles start to tense, and made myself relax, the way he'd taught me to do. When you're nervous, you make mistakes, and a sorcerer working magick can't afford them.

With a rumble, Penny's grave split open, suffusing the air with the rich, damp smell of loam. In the depths, the concrete vault cracked and crunched. The black soil churned a bronze coffin to the surface. The bolts spun open, one at a time. Air hissed as the lid began to rise.

Penny's delicate, heart-shaped face shone like alabaster. She was smiling slightly, as if enjoying a private joke. They'd buried her with her own Showstone amulet, a mate to Tom's. Abruptly the red stone blazed, kindled by the magick in the air.

Tom stared down at her for a long time. Finally he looked at me and said, "Do it."

I took a deep breath and began to chant.

Almost at once I felt the magick rise. Arcane energies

flowered around me. One manifested itself as the smell of burning rubber, another as a feathery tickle on the backs of my hands, and a third as the click of castanets. Others would have been imperceptible to anyone but a sorcerer. The strands of power lurched and squirmed, scraped and clashed together. By the force of my words and will, I braided them into the proper combinations. Tom called and gestured, his skill supporting mine.

My doppelganger's face protruded from a nearby marble headstone. It winked at me. Despite the light emitted by the magick, the night seemed to grow blacker. Vague forms hunkered in the shadows.

I threw out my arms and shouted a command. Penny's Showstone flared so brightly that I had to avert my eyes. A halo of pink light seethed around the corpse.

Tom gasped, faltering in his incantations. He sensed what I had done. The embalmer's handiwork was disappearing from his wife's body. Her veins and arteries filled with blood.

Flowers erupted from the branches of the trees around me. Despite the gloom, I could see that the blooms were reddish purple.

For some reason, the reappearance of the hallucinatory flowers bothered me even more than the presence of my double. But I couldn't stop to fret about it. I had to concentrate on the ritual. Weaving my hands in an intricate pattern, I chanted on, bringing my voice from bass to falsetto, then back.

I felt the deterioration in the dead woman's cells reversing itself. The neural pathways in her damaged brain knitted themselves back together.

Tom watched with a stunned expression on his face, too entranced to keep up his end of the spell-casting. It didn't matter. I was sweaty and panting but I was in control. Everything, including his fascination, was going according to plan.

A breeze blew. Rosy purple petals filled the air around me, almost as if someone had thrown them to attract my attention. I ignored them.

Penny's heart began to thump. A blush washed away her waxy pallor. Tom moaned. His wife's breasts rose as she drew a breath. Her long-lashed eyes fluttered open.

The sight of them jolted me. Perhaps they would have looked lovely and gentle to a Sleeper, just as they always had to me, but now I discerned a gleeful cruelty and a terrible hunger lurking in their depths.

But Tom didn't notice anything wrong. Maybe he wouldn't have noticed even if I hadn't been spinning subtle magick to befuddle him, simply because he wouldn't have wanted to. Weeping, forgetting everything he'd ever know about the Art, he blundered out of his circle.

Smiling, Penny sat up and held out her arms to embrace him. As soon as they touched, my work would be complete.

Suddenly I realized what the picture on the bus had been. The Hang Man trump from the Tarot. And I understood that the purple-red blossoms were the flowers of the Judas tree, the tree that the false Apostle had used to kill himself; a symbol of betrayal and remorse.

Up until that moment, I'd been in an abnormal state of consciousness. I had been pretty much unemotional; schizoid or psychopathic I suppose. I had been regretting what I was doing to Tom, but not much, and I didn't question the necessity.

Suddenly, I could sense my emotions changing. I knew I loved Tom as much as I ever had and was aghast at my own actions. I was terrified for his life.

I pointed at Penny and screamed for fire.

The dead woman's slender form exploded into blue and yellow flames.

Tom recoiled. An instant later he raised the Seal to undo

what I'd done. But it was too late. The reanimated corpse was charred to a shapeless black husk. The hazy snake-headed demon I'd surreptitiously conjured inside it — the spirit which was supposed to possess Tom and turn him into a creature like myself — loomed in the air above it. Hissing, it struck at my Mentor's head.

I called for a second burst of fire. It immediately incinerated the spirit in mid-attack. Penny's corpse crumbled into cinders. The mask on the tombstone and the snowfall of purple petals disappeared. The sickening stink of burned flesh stung my nose.

Tom lurched around to face me. The glow of his ring and amulet guttered out. He was too distraught to keep any magick flowing through them.

"What have you done?" he cried.

I wished I were anywhere else but here. Hell, I wished I were dead. But I wasn't, so I had to tell him the truth. "I'm sorry Tom. But you must know that that thing wasn't Penny. Her spirit was never really here. You were right, nobody can bring back the dead. Or at least, I don't know how to do it."

He stared at me. I could feel the emotion seething inside him. I imagined that when his shock gave way to rage, that he'd blast me to shreds.

"Then what was all this?" he asked.

I glanced to see if the face on the headstone had returned. It hadn't. "Well. You know how eager I always was to learn everybody's secrets. After I left you, I picked up a bad habit. I started pretending to be someone I wasn't. I even started to pretend I believed ideas I hated or thought were stupid, if that's what it took to persuade a particular mage to share his knowledge with me. And it worked, too. That is, until last month, in Mexico City, when I ran into a coven of Nephandi." In other words, devil worshippers, the Traditions' oldest and deadliest enemies.

Tom's eyes widened at their name, "Dear Lord, you didn't."

I shrugged, "I know it sounds reckless, but these guys seemed like penny-ante Nephandi. Not particularly powerful, and not very bright either. I figured I could con them, pick up a few tricks, and then skip out.

"Only it didn't work out that way. They wanted to initiate me. At first the ceremony seemed like a standard Black Mass, but then, with no warning, they threw me into the Umbra, into the grasp of an entity called the Count of the Wasteland, who'd chosen me to be his slave."

My eyes blurred and stung. I wiped them. "I don't remember much of what happened after that. But I came out of the initiation changed. Brainwashed. A genuine Nephandus."

"And so, when your new friends discovered that I was grieving and therefore vulnerable, you were willing to undertake the task of destroying me." His face was expressionless.

I swallowed. "Yeah. The resurrection ritual was just a shell. Camouflage. The real operation was hidden under its surface. I summoned a succubus, and beguiled you in opening your mind and soul to it. If you'd embraced it, it would have possessed you, and then you would have been Nephandus, too."

"But you didn't let that happen."

"No. Evidently there was a part of my unconscious that wasn't reached by the brainwashing. For the last few days, it's been making me hallucinate, sending a signal to the rest of my mind, trying to snap it back to normal. It finally worked. My old self woke up, at least part way, and I couldn't go through with the betrayal."

"What a shame," said a soft, accented voice. I recognized the pleasant tone of Esteban, one of the senior Disciples of the Mexico City coven.

I pivoted. A ring of perhaps a dozen shadows had surrounded us, their forms so indistinct that it was obvious they'd veiled themselves in magick. Even so, I felt the destructive power throbbing in their auras. Combat spells, readied ahead of time, awaited the pulling of the trigger.

"If you'd passed this little test," Esteban continued, "you and you Mentor would have lived long, happy lives as paladins of darkness. Now you're simply going to die. Unless you'd care to surrender."

"I think not," said Tom. His Seal and Showstone shone. Beams of white light blazed from his eyes. Esteban brandished his focus, a cat-o'-nine-tails. The rays veered around him and blasted a tombstone to rubble. Other Nephandi cried unholy names, unleashing their own magick.

The fight was on.

Tom and I stood back to back, countering the spells that pounded at us, striking back with our own sorcery. Soon I realized I was croaking and hissing incantations that I didn't remember learning. In the Dragon's Tongue, the ugly secret language of the Nephandi, Dark energies, like those the enemy wielded, sizzled from my hands. My new capabilities, hidden even from myself, bothered me, but I was grateful for them.

I needed every trick, every advantage I could get because Tom and I were losing. He was far more powerful than any of the Nephandi, and one on one, I probably would have been a match for most of them. But they had us badly outnumbered. They were fresh, and we were tired from the bogus resurrection. It was only a matter of time before one of them slipped in a lucky shot. I didn't see much point in sticking around until that happened.

According to magickal theory, space is an illusion. Or, to put it another way, all places are the same place. A sorcerer who understands the principle can teleport, like a character in a sci-fi novel. I caught hold of Tom's jacket and tried to shift us back to the chantry.

It didn't work. Before announcing their presence, the Nephandi had built a hyperdimensional cage to hold us. Figuratively speaking, I banged my head against it. Half stunned, I barely managed to deflect a rote that would have changed the air in my lungs to acid.

Behind me, Tom grunted and staggered. Recovering his footing, he chanted in Hebrew. His voice was steady, but tinged with pain.

I had to save him, but how? I wracked my brain, and finally came up with another idea.

One of the Nephandi threw a spell at me. Had it hit me, it would have filled me with blind terror. I barely managed to deflect it, then raked my opponents with a barrage of raw entropy. It took them a couple seconds to shield themselves, and that gave me the time I needed to manipulate Correspondence, the magick of spatial distortion, again.

Thanks to the hyperdimensional cage, Tom and I couldn't teleport. Still, since all places were the same place, every other person in the world was right beside us. If I couldn't go to them, or bring them to us, maybe I could at least make it possible for some of them to see us.

When my spell kicked in, the battle stayed in the graveyard. But to a certain extent, it also started happening on Fisherman's Wharf, in front of the Ripley's Believe It Or Not Museum and the eyes of several hundred astonished tourists. The hardest part was making sure that the abnormal perception only worked in one direction. That my fellow mages didn't realize what was going on was crucial to my plan.

One of the enemy struck me with a spell. A ghastly chill raced through my body. By the time I negated that effect, someone else had slipped in an attack. A huge bell started tolling in my head, louder and louder and louder. The pain was excruciating, and more than distracting enough to keep me from working any more magick of my own. The Nephandi had me on the ropes.

Please, I thought, let my plan work. I'm not religious, but I guess I was praying.

And maybe, Somebody heard me. A green hole opened in the black sky, and a number of creatures resembling man-sized wasps swooped out. I thought that, in the chaos of the battle, I was the only one who saw it happen. I was the only one looking for it.

We warlocks had been hurling vulgar magick around with furious abandon. Why not? There hadn't been any Sleepers watching us. But I'd changed that. I'd shown our struggle to hundreds of gawking tourists, flouting their concept of reality. And now Paradox spirits, the reality cops, had come to bust us for it.

I hastily snuffed the currents of power streaming through my chakras. Whirled, clapped one hand over Tom's mouth, and jerked down his Seal-waving arm with the other. "No more magick!" I yelled. "None!"

God knows why he heeded me, considering how I'd sold him out, but he did. His ring and amulet stopped glowing.

"I'm afraid it's too late to surrender," Esteban said. "You killed three of us." Tom must have done it. I was pretty sure I hadn't dropped anyone. "Blood must answer —"

A Paradox spirit plummeted onto his shoulders and knocked him to the ground. A barbed stinger stabbed into his groin. He shrieked.

In a moment, everyone was screaming. Everyone but Tom and me. As I had hoped, with an abundance of sorcerers to pick on, the Paradox spirits had passed over the guys who'd shut down their magick in favor of those who were still abuzz with power.

Mercifully, the gonging in my brain stopped. No doubt the effect had died with its creator. I looked around, making sure that all the giant "hornets" were occupied. I ended the show on Fisherman's Wharf, then felt for the bars of the cage. They were gone, too. I gripped Tom's arm and shifted us back to his study.

As soon as we arrived, my knees went rubbery. I barely managed to stagger to the sofa. I realized that I'd expended the very last of my strength to carry us away. Now I couldn't have conjured a flame onto the tip of a match.

Tom looked battered and exhausted, too. His forehead was bruised, and the back of his hand was bleeding. but apparently he wasn't in as bad a shape as I was. He stayed on his feet long enough to pour us each a brandy, the normal way, before flopping down on the chair across from me.

"Did you make that happen?" he asked.

I nodded, and gulped down some liquor. Its warmth expanded in my stomach, steadying me. I explained what I'd done.

Tom shook his head, "I've watched people do a lot of desperate things in my time, but I never saw a mage deliberately draw down Paradox."

"It worked, didn't it?" I looked him in the eye. "What happens now, Mentor? Do you want to bring me before Tribunal, or just kill me yourself, here and now? Either way I won't resist."

He grimaced, "In a way, I do want to kill you. Do you know what you did to me? What it was like to believe I could get Penny back, and then have her snatched away again."

His face twisted, and I thought he was going to cry. I wanted to comfort him, but I didn't know how, and I supposed that I'd forfeited the right to try.

After a moment, he seemed to regain a measure of control. "But I set myself up to be hurt, didn't I?" he said heavily. "By forgetting my own principles. So what right do I have to punish you?"

"All the right in the world, it seems to me."

"Maybe so, but I've been tearing myself apart over losing my wife. I doubt that losing someone who's been like a son to me would make me feel any better."

I was almost afraid to believe what I was hearing. "Do you mean you forgive me?"

His lips quirked into a crooked smile, "Yeah. What's the problem, do you need it in writing?"

At that moment, he seemed like his old self. I was sure he was still grieving, and would be for years to come, but now I had a feeling he could handle it. Maybe his ordeal with the Nephandi and me had functioned as a kind of shock therapy, not that that bit of serendipity was any excuse for what I'd tried to do.

"Thank you," I said. My throat felt clogged, and my eyes ached. I blinked and looked away so I wouldn't start bawling. "I don't deserve a friend like you. I'll finish my drink and be on my way."

"What are you talking about?"

"The high priest of the coven told me that nobody has ever defected from the Nephandi and lived to brag about it. I don't think they'll decide to let me be the first. More of them will come after me."

"That doesn't mean you have to run. Stay here, and we'll fight the bastards together. I've been doing it quite successfully for almost three hundred years."

I set down my snifter and stood up. I was still weak and shaky, but my legs supported me. "I know. But I have another problem, too. I'm still bound to the Count of the Wasteland. Even though my old personality is in control right now, I can feel that I have a know of corruption growing inside my soul. If I stayed, I might betray you again, bring disaster on everyone in the chantry. I won't risk that."

Tom scowled. "I understand that. But there must be a cure for what ails you."

"I'd like to think so. I mean to look for it."

"How? Where?"

I grinned, "That's what will make it interesting. I don't have the foggiest idea. Say good-bye to Lois for me, will you? Tell her that if I ever can, I'll come back for a real reunion."

He stood up and hugged me. Then I walked out the door.

END RUN
■■■■■■■■■■■■■
Nigel D. Findley

My legs ache like somebody's worked them over with a fucking "Tonya Tapper", and every time I try to breathe, it feels like someone's twisting a knife in my chest. Blood is still pouring from my scalp, thanks to a few wayward chunks of concrete smashed from a building by a near miss. Paradox ripples in my gut, and pounds counterpoint to the hangover throbbing in my temples. I'm way lost, and unless I get smart — or lucky — real fast, I'll be way dead.

Ever have one of those days?

Well, "nights", actually. Halloween night, to be precise, All Hallow's Eve.

And it all started out so well, too. There was a show of performance art at a converted warehouse down toward Third Street, a whole evening of real edgy stuff. Most of the artists/performers were Sleepers, but I'm not a snob about that. It's the dance that matters, not the dancer, right? You can even argue that it's a meaningless distinction anyway. The act of artistic creation, it's juice, pal. It's Quintessence, same thing as the stuff of magick. When performance artists get it right — really right — you can feel the juice coming off them, shimmering in the air around them. I've often thought that the act of artistic creation is the next closest thing to Awakening, just one step short of seeing the

Tellurian as it really is.

Good show. Good evening. I started getting dry about half-way through, but someone found a couple bottles of whiskey left behind after a rave a week ago (stroke of genius, that one, if I do say so myself). Me and some of my nearest and dearest got happily toasted, which only added to the ambiance of the show.

The night was almost over when my special guest arrived. She was drop-dead gorgeous; pure and unadulterated sex in a tight red wrapper. Her name was Lucy and she's a Sleeper. I'd been working on her for a couple of weeks not only for the obvious carnal reasons (more than adequate though they were) but also because I happened to know one of those tight-assed Order of Hermes dorks had a thing for her (probably a little, tiny thing). If I could get into Lucy and jerk around a Latin-droner, so much the better, right?

Lucy had accepted my invitation and finally showed up — granted, a couple of hours late — but it's better to copulate later than never. I took her by the hand, kissed her gently, and led her off into one of the unused offices that had been left unlocked. The evening proceeded to get even better from there, for a good long time.

Much later, in an effort to be gentlemanly, I put her in a taxi that was cruising by. One last kiss, even sweeter than the first, and the cab pulled away. It wasn't even three a.m. yet, so I decided I'd walk home. The warehouse now stood silent, and the street was empty.

No, not quite empty. Under a streetlight, half a block away, I could see a slim, dark figure, standing there looking at me. For a moment, I toyed with the idea of taking a closer look through the Point of Correspondence, but then I discarded it with a nasty grin. Hell, I knew who the figure was, didn't I? Dorian, the pudknocking Hermetic who'd been lusting after Lucy's sweet yams. So he knew I'd already relished the fruits he'd been so hot for. I flipped him a snappy salute — the one-fingered kind — and strolled away. Let him try something if he had the balls, I figured. What's that wimp of a Latin-droner likely to do, anyway? Challenge me to Certámen? Yeah, right. Let him rot, I figured, and if he wanted to risk his tight little ass trying to take me out, more power to him. I was cranked up and out there.

He didn't follow me. He didn't even move as I wandered off into the night. Not that I expected it, of course, but you learn eventually to expect the unexpected if you don't want to be dragged off by some Paradox spirit one dark night. I hied myself off along Third Street, heading for Market. From there I figured I'd cruise up Kearny until I hit Chinatown, then turn down Pine to my apartment building.

It was a nice night for walking. The air was surprisingly, unseasonably warm. Maybe that's the reason for the heavy fog. I'd heard from the blaring radios of passing cars that the fog had shut off all traffic on the Golden Gate for hours. Thin wisps of fog, kind of like spider webs blown on the wind, drifted over the streets at knee level, but the sky was clear. I kept glancing up at the stars as I walked, a few of them bright enough to challenge the light of the city.

I should have realized earlier I was in trouble. Put it down to post-orgasmic lassitude, or distraction, or pure dumb luck. I was almost to Market Street when I realized I hadn't seen anyone on the street for at least a couple of blocks.

No one. Sure, it was after three in the morning, but Christ on a crutch, this was San Francisco, the town that never shuts down. There should be someone on the street: a broken-down whore, an uptown failure looking to score a hit of temporary chemical happiness, a trashbagger looking for bottles to redeem for a refund. No one. I tried to think back. The last person I'd seen was this hard-core rummy crossing Folsom, looking like he was about to woof his midnight snack into the gutter. I'd noticed something strange about the guy, but in my half-cut mental condition I couldn't remember what it was. Then it came back to me. One of his eyes was so bloodshot it looked like a red marble had been jammed into his socket. That's probably what comes of drinking sterno.

I looked ahead toward Market. Nobody on the sidewalks, nothing moving on the streets. I turned back, glancing over my shoulder. Nobody. Nothing. I kept walking, but started getting this real hinky feeling about the whole thing.

And that was when the first of the streetlights died.

No flicker, no sparking, no fading glow. One moment it was on, the next moment it was as dead as the hospitality suite at an undertakers' convention. It was the light at the end of the block behind me, the one on the right side of the road. I stopped dead. All that liquor in my stomach (it had been this nice, warm, comforting glow) turned into a churning pit of acid. Hell, in the grand scheme of things, it was just a streetlight. So why was I suddenly feeling so twitchy?

I hauled out my harp and wailed off a classic blues riff as I played with Forces. Hey, it wasn't that unlikely that a spontaneous short in the circuitry would kick the streetlight back to life.

Nothing. Not even the faintest flicker of light. In fact, the next streetlight, the next one up the staggered sequence of fixtures, died as well.

And then the next one. And the one after that. One after the other, silently. Darkness marched up the street toward me, each dying streetlight another footstep of some massive invisible creature.

Freaky, or what?

Even then, I didn't take it all that seriously. It was magick. That was a no-brainer. Somebody was dicking around with Forces, or maybe with Entropy, in a big way. That didn't make it a threat, though, did it? Hell, somebody might be showing off for me or the events might have dick to do with me. I had to admit, the light-show was a pretty good lead-up to an introduction. For all I knew, I might have wandered into the middle of some apprentice's Initiation test.

Maybe if I'd been sober, I would have reacted differently (maybe if I'd been sober, I wouldn't have been there in the first place). As it was, I stood there on the sidewalk, mouth hanging open, as the streetlights turned themselves off. When the last one had died, I looked at the street behind me.

That's when I saw him. An innocuous-looking little shit, almost a foot shorter than me, maybe five-two tops. He had skinny little hips, wimpy shoulders, dark hair cropped almost military-short, and a big thick soup-strainer of a mustache. Blackframed glasses, sort of like Wayfarers but with clear lenses, encircled his eyes. He was maybe half-way down the block from me, a big shit-eating smile on his face, and he was walking my way.

Even without the Art, I'd have been able to take someone his size two falls out of three. With the Art, he was catfood. He just didn't know it yet. So why did I feel like I'd just had an ice-water enema?

He called out to me, and his voice echoed hollowly off the buildings around us. "Todd Lucas!"

I blinked in surprise, but shot back the lie instantly, "Sorry, buddy, you've got the wrong guy."

"I have a message for Todd Lucas," he said, still striding toward me.

"Yeah? Well, like I said ..."

"Do you want to hear it?"

I shrugged, suddenly very uncomfortable. "If I see him,

I'll pass it on."

The weedy little shit stopped, maybe a hundred feet from me. His smile grew even broader. "The message is, 'Welcome to Hell, Todd Lucas.'"

And he began to change. His glasses winked opaque, the right lens glowing a dim red. A thin line of ruby light, so intense it looked like a solid bar, flicked out from the glowing lens, painting a red dot on the center of my chest. For an instant I was frozen, as the dot climbed up my breastbone, up my throat and onto my face. Red light flared and dazzled me as the targeting dot settled between my eyes. Through the laser-halo, I saw the structure of the figure's shoulders shift, saw an angular metal assembly tear through the back of his coat, cantilevering itself over his right shoulder. I recognized the distinctive electric whine — I've seen Predator enough times — before I caught a clear glimpse of the six rotating barrels like on a Gatling gun.

I made a cogent and pithy comment — something along the lines of "Oh, shit!" — and I threw myself aside, just as the HIT Mark cut loose with its chain-gun. I dropped and I rolled, a move so graceful that it surprised even me. The piece of sidewalk where I'd been standing an instant before exploded, as did the garbage can and a couple of parking meters in the vicinity. The chain-gun's stream of fire tracked my movement, inhumanly fast. Some of the rounds had to be tracers since I could see the fire-stream, a flexible hose of light reaching out toward me. But I was already coming out of my roll onto my feet, hauling major ass toward a narrow walkway between two buildings. As I sprinted, I toyed with the idea of slowing time for the HIT Mark, taking away some of its electronic edge. Those thoughts didn't go anyplace; I'm not that shit-hot at Time in the first place (counter to stereotype and all), and anyway, despite what some of those Akashic Brotherhood grasshoppers might try to tell you, a reaction boost big enough to make a difference isn't something you can put together on the fly, or in my case, on the run. Another burst of chain-gun fire strafed the corner of the building I'd just ducked around. I could hear ricochets wailing and howling off into the night.

The walkway between the buildings was just that, a path just barely wide enough for one person to walk along. As my boots pounded on the concrete underfoot, my elbows and shoulders brushed the walls on both sides. Great, Lucas real swift, I told myself in disgust. Couldn't you have found a place that made it any easier for the HIT Mark to chop you down? Christ, all it had to do was hose down the area, and any bullets that didn't hit me directly would get deflected back on course by the walls. Peachy fuckin keen. I got the nasty, twitchy feeling that somebody had painted a big target, or maybe a "Shoot Me!" sign, between my shoulder blades. I looked back over my shoulder.

The targeting laser came around the corner before the HIT Mark did. A quarter-sized dot of light, it flashed onto the right-hand wall of the walkway, panned quickly toward me as the HIT Mark stepped into the opening. I had maybe a second, at best, before it splattered my gizzard all over the walls. No time for subtlety.

I'd always been something of a paraphobe, going far out of my way not to invite trouble. Tonight, I could almost wish that a Paradox spirit was on my ass, ready to haul me away. At least you've got a chance to make your way back from a Paradox realm. There was no way back from where the HIT Mark wanted to send me. A memory bubbled up from nowhere — an old buddy of my preceptor, the Merlin who'd seen me through my Awakening. That old bastard was so Wyld and fried he wouldn't even have noticed when the chain-gun cut him in two.

Time to do something, anything. All I could think of

on the cusp was magick of the most vulgar kind. I screamed out a line from the chorus of an Enigma song, and I zapped that biomechanical bastard with the nastiest static discharge I could deliver. Something way short of a lightning bolt — hey, I was rushed — but better than the jolt you'd get touching the wrong part of a gutted TV set. I didn't zap the HIT Mark in the chest (my first choice) or in the chain-gun itself (my second). No, I poured the whole wallop into the right lens of its pseudo-Wayfarers.

Like I'd expected, the lens blew up real good and the targeting laser winked out. Iteration X builds HIT Marks out of countermagickal alloys, real expensive shit. I figured they wouldn't lay out the bucks to magick-shield the cyborg's shades. If I'd hit a human with that much energy, his brain would have boiled, and the steam pressure would have turned his skull into a hand-grenade. The HIT Mark just shuddered slightly, like I'd dropped an ice-cube down its collar.

It didn't chew me into hamburger with its chain-gun, though. I couldn't have blinded it (I wasn't that Pollyanna-naive) but I did figure it'd take a few precious seconds for it to switch to a new targeting strategy. Enough seconds for me to get to the end of the walkway, out onto Fourth? We'd see soon enough.

As I sprinted on, I wove another minor working because I remembered how hinky I'd felt about having that thing behind me and not being able to see it. I didn't have to come close to the Point of Correspondence at all (spitting distance, maybe) to give myself nice wrap-around vision. That little bit of magick didn't do anything to protect my back, but I did feel a lot better about seeing whatever it was that would splatter me.

Even with my static discharge, I almost didn't make it. The HIT Mark adapted faster than I'd expected. Before I even reached the end of the walkway, the thing's left lens lit up laser-red, and the chain-gun shifted on its angular mount until the muzzle peeked over the cyborg's left shoulder.

I hit the corner and hung a tight, skidding left — might as well give myself even the slightest benefit from the geometry, I figured — just as the thing cut loose again. Concrete exploded into shrapnel under the jackhammer-impact of Christ-knows-how-many high velocity rounds. I might as well have been raked by a shotgun firing rock-salt. My scalp felt like it had been flayed to the fucking skull. I shrieked a curse to the gods I don't believe in, put my head down, dug in and I ran.

And that's where I am now, an out-of-shape erstwhile musician, Johnny-come- lately mage with Death Incarnate on my heels. Life has the nicest ways of making you feel important. I'm paying the Paradox price for my little display. My heart's racing like a gerbil, and my stomach knots and cramps. I groan with the pain of it, but force myself on.

Fourth is as deserted as Third was, as empty as the walkway that got me here. Whoever's got it in for me cares enough to do it right.

Who? Who hates me this much?

Okay, Lucas, dumb question. It's the Technocracy, Iteration X — nobody else has HIT Marks on staff, do they? But why is It-X after me? Look up "low-profile" in the dictionary, you'll find my picture. I didn't think the greyfaces even knew I existed.

Well, okay, no that's not quite true, is it? There was that difference of opinion I had with the Black-Hats-and-Mirrorshades crowd last year. Some It-X drones wanted to do something hinky with a Node, and a couple of fellow Cultists decided that wasn't cool. I came along on the raid, but …

Hey, it wasn't even my idea! And I've always been pretty sure that the greyfaces never connected me to that little debacle. So up until now, the only people I could think of who knew of my existence or hated me enough to want me whacked, are all mages of the Traditions. Dorian is at the top of the list, after my diversions of earlier, of course. It-X conceivably could hate me enough to want me dead, but they didn't know I existed — or so I'd thought. Time to re-examine that conclusion. Obviously, the greyfaces had gotten some kind of line on me. How? Could Dorian the Latin-droner have ratted me out to the Technocracy just because I played hide-the-salami with his current lust-object? That's starting to be the only reasonable conclusion.

Well, not much I can do about it right now. The HIT Mark comes around the corner; again, laser-light is its harbinger. The murder-machine is strolling casually. I'm hauling butt like my life depends on it (natch). That means I'm opening the gap between us. The difference is basically irrelevant for high-velocity ordinance, but at least I feel safer, and confidence is half the battle in a situation like this.

In my wrap-around view, I see that chain-gun emit an elongated pyramid of fire, a muzzle flare at least two yards long. The first rounds fall short, but I can see the machine walking the burst toward me. For a moment, I play OJ Simpson, brokenfield running, and cut hard left, then jerk back to the right. I hear the rounds whipcrack by — they're that close — but my body remains unventilated. The HIT Mark adjusts its aim, but I've already jinked left again, turning onto Mission, cutting the corner so tight I clip the corner of a building hard enough to damn near throw myself off balance.

I'm still opening the gap. I figure I've got a good ten, fifteen seconds before the HIT Mark's into firing position again.

So I use it. There's the opening of an alley to the right, and I plunge down it before my mind catches up with something my eyes have already noticed. There's traffic on the street behind me with cars and real people (not bloody-minded cyborgs). That means I'm out of the "killing zone". There's nothing to stop the HIT Mark from keeping on my ass, but at least I can expect that the laws of physics haven't been subverted in advance just to fuck me up.

The HIT Mark must have turned the corner onto the occupied street by now. Where are the screams and yells of alarm? Even south of Market Street, it's not every day that you see a guy with a chain-gun sprouting out of his back... No yells, no sounds at all. Obviously, someone's running "magickal overwatch" on the HIT Mark. The damn thing's probably invisible, or looks like a hooker by now.

Power lines — two braces of them — run down the middle of the alley, blacker lines against the blackness of the sky overhead. I'm sprinting along parallel with them, and for a odd moment I feel like I'm a trolley-car running on tracks under the catenary wires that give me power. Then the image is gone. I cut around a reeking dumpster (OJ-time again) and then —

— slam into a yielding body that yelps "Hey!" in a pleasing contralto.

I've just damn near greased a babe and her beau strolling down an alley and remember that there's the new illegal after-hours joint that fronts onto an alley around here. It's a no-brainer that Juliet and her street-corner Romeo just quit that place to find somewhere more private.

Even in the face of death, instinct kicks in and I give her the ocular once-over, top-to-bottom. Good choice. If I'm going to get splattered, I can think of worse things to ogle in my last moments. Her body's sheathed in black

leather that might as well have been sprayed on. The curves
are even more impressive than Lucy's — and that's saying
something — but it's the face that really snags my attention.
Lucy is classically beautiful with a by-the-numbers aesthetic
that sometimes comes across as almost soulless. This one's
face, in a picture, it probably wouldn't do much for me.
Lifeless on a page, I'd notice the flaws. Mouth slightly too
big, nose a touch off center. In person however, the
vibrancy, the energy, the life shines through and jolts me
like a cattle-prod. If I wasn't this close to violent death, I'd
probably run in circles dragging a wing, or some shit.

The impact has knocked her off balance, and if her
Romeo — dressed in the male equivalent of the same black-
leathers — had not been holding her by the arm, she'd be
flat on her shapely ass. She goes "Hey!" again, as Romeo
hauls her back upright.

"Watch where you're going, asshole!" Romeo twists his
weasel face into an approximation of righteous anger.
Doesn't work worth a fuck. If I had a spare moment, I'd be
tempted to push his teeth down his throat.

My lungs are working like bellows, I know my hair is a
fright, and I'm probably dripping with cold sweat. Not the
most impressive look when you're trying to persuade
someone to pay attention to you. But I've got to try it
anyway. "Look," I gasp at them both, "get the hell out of
here now, if you want to live."

Juliet's eyes widen in surprise. Somehow I can sense that
I've got through to her. But Romeo's still running the
bellicose act. "Hey, who the fuck you think you are?" he
demands.

"Someone who doesn't want to see you dead," I tell him.
"Not right now, at least. Just fucking run! You get me?"

Juliet lets go of her beau's arm, and I think she's ready
to follow me hightailing it down the alley, but Romeo hasn't

worked the testosterone out of his system yet. He grabs her by the upper arm, and drags her closer to him. He clenches his free hand into a less-than-impressive fist. "You look," he grates at me. And that's when the red laser dot paints his bellybutton.

I don't know if Juliet sees the targeting laser, or whether I've really got through to her, or what. Anyhow, she jerks herself free of Romeo's grip. I'm already running past them — I've done what I can, for all it's worth — and in my three-sixty vision I see Juliet take her first step after me.

At the mouth of the alley, the HIT Mark's chain-gun cuts loose, and it stitches Romeo from crotch to crown. His body comes apart like a Raggedy-Andy doll tossed into a shredder, and the air's suddenly thick with the smell of blood and shit. Juliet turns to look, her mouth working silently, but I grab her by the arm (it's her night for being dragged around, I guess) and haul her after me. "Come on!" I scream at her. She's not big, but even a small person packs a fair whack of momentum. The mass of her body slows me, and throws me off my stride. Instead of taking off straight down the alley, I do this hinky little side-step — probably Dorian the Latin-droner could explain the mathematical reality of lever-arms and angular momentum and that — and I zig rather than zag, Juliet in tow.

Which takes the two of us into the shelter of the second dumpster just as the HIT Mark cuts loose with another burst. The big rounds slam into the metal, a deafening fusillade. Juliet screams, and I dive to the ground, hugging my head with my arms. Yeah, right, Lucas — like that's going to stop a bullet? I force myself to look up.

The rattle of impacting rounds cuts off. I can see Juliet's mouth moving, but my ears are ringing so badly I can't hear what she's saying. Her eyes are so wide I can see white all the way around her irises. Her face is pale, almost green, and the sweat is standing out in tiny droplets along her hairline.

It's one of the hardest things I've ever done to force myself to crawl to the corner of the dumpster, to look around it out into the alley.

The HIT Mark is standing in the mouth of the alley. I can feel the juice in the air, and I just know that the people passing by on the street beyond are just not happening to look in the right direction. (How do they explain away the sound of gunfire? Serial backfires, for Christ's sake?) The laser from the cyborg's left eye is scanning over the messy remains of Romeo — probably checking to see if it's completed its mission. That gives me another couple of seconds' leeway to see if I can make a difference. I glance up, see the power lines overhead. That's it, right there.

I haul out my harp, put it to my lips.

"Now's a hell of a time for a concert." I can just hear Juliet's voice, shrill through a tight throat, over the titinus in my ears. I shoot her the best reassuring smile I can manage at the moment which probably looks like a corpse's rictus, come to think of it. I riff off something that could be Junior Wells crossed with Orb. The juice flows and shifts within me, as I play with the threads of Power. I look up at the wires running above us.

I can hear the snap as one of them parts, sparking and spitting as the free end falls toward the HIT Mark. Let's see how you handle this, dickwad. In my mind's eye, I imagine the thing with blue light flaring around it, like the Terminator caught in the hydraulic press.

Ah, shit … I can feel it before I can see it, the shift in Quintessence flow that I know means countermagick. As if driven by the actinic flare at its tip — I know better, of course — the falling cable shifts in flight, changing its trajectory. It's whipping straight toward the dumpster —

the big metal dumpster — behind which we're hiding. And I'm on my feet again, digging in and sprinting off, dragging Juliet behind me.

The cable touches the dumpster. Nice pyrotechnics. Mini-lightning bolts strike out, grounding against anything and everything within a couple of yards. One of them lashes over Romeo's body, charring it nicely. We're out of range, but I still feel the heat pulse on the back of my neck, smell the sharp tang of ozone in the air. We're clear of the sparking, crackling dumpster and the HIT Mark sends us another burst of fire to keep us company. Apparently it's distracted and the rounds go wide, spattering and snapping off the building to our right.

Before it can re-acquire us as targets, we're out of the alley, onto — where the hell are we? I'm totally lost.

There's traffic on this street. The pedestrians don't seem to see us as we haul ass around the corner, clearing the free-fire zone. I'm looking for a large group of people — mobile cover at worst, an incentive for the HIT Mark not to follow at best. No luck. There are people in ones and twos, but no sign of the knot of gangers or merrymakers I'm hoping for.

I feel the Quintessence flow again, and once more I know what's coming. Even though I'm looking in the wrong direction, my three-sixty view lets me see the guy driving a pimped-up Mustang twenty yards behind us. His eyes bug out, then he does a face-plant against the steering wheel. The horn sounds — the rutting call of some great beast and the tires chirp as the dead weight of his foot comes down on the gas pedal. The mass of his unconscious arm turns the wheel slightly, and the mustang rockets toward us.

Before I can respond, Juliet's pulled herself free from my grip. "Just wait one fucking minute!" she yells, planting her hands on her hips.

I don't have time to grab her and get us both to safety before the car pulps us against a building. She hasn't seen it yet. Sic transit Juliet, and all that. What a waste. I sprint away.

Now she spots the car, and her mouth opens as she draws breath. She'll probably be dead before she gets the scream out.

And yet again I feel the Quintessence flow — but this time from a new source. As the car hits the curb, the impact jolts the driver. His weight shifts, his arm turns the wheel, and the mustang swerves aside at the last moment. It misses Juliet by inches before smashing in through the front of a tattoo parlor.

I pull up short and stare at Juliet. For that one, telling instant as the car swerved aside, I saw her Avatar flare. I saw her unconsciously reach out and play with Matter, to deflect the car.

She's staring at the wreck, which is already starting to burn. She doesn't know what she's done. She doesn't know she's done anything, she thinks she's been saved by one of those freaked-out quirks of fate you hear about on Oprah.

I realize with a shock that Juliet — or whatever her real name is — is an Orphan; a "sport" some of the hard-core traditionalists label them. She's Awakened, at least partially, without the training that members of the Traditions receive from their masters. Part of her mind understands that the Tellurian isn't immutable, that reality is what we make it. Consciously, she hasn't gotten a grasp on it yet, but her subconscious — her id, or whatever the fuck you want to call it — is starting to weave the threads of the world around her. She's probably most Awake when she's asleep and dreaming, and almost totally Asleep while she's awake, if that makes any sense at all.

And this realization adds just one more hit of complexity

to the situation I'm in. I'm not like many mages. Don't get me wrong. I don't class Sleepers as worse than cattle, one step up the evolutionary scale from amoebas but one step down from opossums. I've never considered them pawns and cannon-fodder. Sure, they're not Awake, but they fear and they hurt just like we do. Still and all, if it ever comes down to a choice between one of them and one of us, a Sleeper or a mage, I know which way I'd choose. Lifeboat time? Over the side you go, Mr. Sleeper, and better luck next reincarnation.

But what about Orphans? Well, that's quite another kettle of worms, or can of fish, or whatever. They know — peripherally, transitorily, incompletely. They've vaulted themselves into a whole new classification, in my mind at least. Christ, it's not as if there's a lot of us mages in the world, not compared to the ranks of the Black Hats and Mirrorshades. We're outnumbered already, and the occasional pogrom cuts our numbers down even more. I hear that some of the greyfaces hunt down Orphans preferentially, trying to get them before they fully Awaken. I guess it's kind of like pre-preemptive pogrom — just on the off-chance that they might eventually join the Traditions. All of which means it's ultimately in my best interest, and in my humble opinion in the best interest of the Tellurian as a whole, to keep sweet Juliet from getting splattered like Romeo. Can we say "shit"?

I've got to know more before I can make a good decision here. Juliet is still gawking at the smoldering car as I haul out my silver hip flask and take a solid hit. It's pure medicinal-quality alcohol, unadulterated 200-proof firewater. It hits the back of my throat and scours it like acid. I swallow, the jolt of booze burns like a comet on the way down, hits my stomach and explodes into fire. I fight back the urge to gag and choke. Blinking back tears, I take another, larger swallow. This time my mucous membranes are so shell-shocked they don't even feel it.

The buzz hits me almost instantly, that familiar light-headed hollow-brained sensation. Measuring by volume of pure alcohol, I've just choked down the equivalent of six or seven shots of Cuervo in two or three seconds. For good measure, I take one more slug. I feel like I'm suddenly floating with my boot-soles a quarter inch above the street. The crackling of the fire sounds distant, remote, as if I'm listening to it echo through a drainpipe. Little points of light — stars out for their evening constitutional — drift and float around the periphery of my visual field. Man, in three or four minutes I am going to be so fucking ripped it's not funny. This kind of thing is always a balancing act: get the rush I need to do what I do, but not get plastered so fast I forget why I'm doing it. I remember one time …

Shit, I'm losing it already. This is not the time for woolgathering. I'm feeling blotto enough that when I reach out to weave patterns of Prime, the threads of Quintessence seem to anticipate my will, to knot themselves correctly before I've even figured out what I have to do. With my new-found, alcohol-fueled vision, I look Juliet over.

Her Avatar, I can see it clearly now, is the brightest I've ever seen in anyone who's not a Master. She seems to be boiling with Quintessence, churning and flashing and sparking with it. If she could just learn how to control it, she'd be one ass-kicker of a mage. I look at the Patterns inside her, trace them out slowly, one by one. It's difficult. Christ is it difficult. I'm not the best at this kind of thing when I'm balancing on the line just right. I've just never been a detail kind of person. When my pulse is hammering in my ears, my nerves are singing with adrenaline, and four-plus ounces of pure joy-juice are starting to have their way with my neurons, it's even harder. The Patterns keep shifting — well, they do that — but my attention keeps wandering. I think I'm getting a good reading on her (a solid, comfortable grounding in Entropy lurked in there) when the Patterns shift again, and I could just as well be staring at a paisley carpet for all the sense I can make of it. Crap!

There's chaos on the street around us. Pedestrians are running and the few motorists are stopping. People are sprinting toward the car buried in the tattoo parlor. And that's when the HIT Mark strolls out of the alley, and the chaos gets worse (how're the newspapers going to write this one up?). Laser light flickers across the gaping faces of the bystanders, gleams off bugged-out eyes. The targeting beam swings toward us, Juliet and me. With a horrible, gut-busting certainty, I know the HIT Mark's going to cut down Juliet first and then move on to me. It feels like I'm moving in slow motion as I launch myself at Juliet, a flying body block, a wild attempt to knock her aside and get her out of the line of fire.

While I'm in the air, I see her Avatar flare again Yes, it's Entropy — she's got Entropy Patterns out the shapely ass. In the instant that the HIT Mark cuts loose, one of the would-be rescuers stumbles on the cracked sidewalk and lurches between us and our would-be killer. The Good Samaritan screams as he's transfixed by a burning stream of tracer rounds. He convulses in death, a marionette with strings pulled by a puppeteer with St. Vitas' dance.

Time snaps back out of slo-mo, and I slam into Juliet, a perfect chop-block across the knees. We both go down hard, rolling together in a tangle of legs and arms. Another burst of chain-gun fire lashes above us, so close I imagine I can feel the heat of the burning phosphorous in the tracer-tips.

We're dead. I know it. Unless …

Entropy.

I can't do it myself, I just don't have enough jam. But maybe with Juliet to back my play ...

I roll, up onto my elbows. I'm lying on top of Juliet — right idea, wrong place and time — and I can see the HIT Mark approaching, slowly now. It knows it's got us, it just wants to make sure. Ruby light dazzles me, the targeting laser settling on the bridge of my nose. Juliet is staring bug-eyed at death as it walks toward us.

"It's a machine," I gasp to her, praying to the non-existent gods that she understands what I'm telling her. "A computer. Computers have bugs, they've got glitches in their programming. Random bugs. Gremlins. Do you get it?"

She blinks wildly. She probably doesn't even hear me, or if she does, the words probably aren't penetrating. I might just as well be yelling "blah blah blah".

No time. No options. I've got to give it all I've got. If she follows my lead, we live. If not ...

I glare at the HIT Mark. The Patterns I weave originate from the big dragon's head ring I wear on my right index finger. They propagate outward, waves and ripples in the fabric of reality. I see the HIT Mark as a sequence of numbers, of ones and zeroes in an ordered sequence, the order containing the meaning, containing everything that is the cyborg's reality. I envision a wave of randomness, of Entropy, lashing through that order, shattering it, breaking it down into chaos.

I can't do it. I don't have the skill, the juice, to punch through the countermagickal alloys that sheath the thing's electronic brain. The order persists, my waves of chaos battering against it but unable to penetrate.

Then I gasp aloud as I feel a sudden flood of Quintessence from Juliet. Her Avatar burns and glows. The chaos waves grow in intensity. I groan as I feel Paradox wash over both of us, a burning, chilling, cramping flux of wrongness. My vision blurs. Juliet whimpers, as she feels it too. The waves of Entropy vanish.

I blink the tears out of my eyes. The HIT Mark's still standing. Its laser still targets my skull. The muzzle of its chain-gun looks like a railroad tunnel. I brace myself for pain and death.

Nothing happens. One second, two. Nothing. The HIT Mark's still standing, but that's all it's doing. It's stopped walking. In mid-stride, it's frozen. As I watch in stunned disbelief, it teeters, off-balance. Then it falls, rigid as a felled tree, to crash to the ground on its side. The laser paints a parked car, then it flicks off.

I force myself to my feet, bend down and offer Juliet my hand. The alcohol's really hitting me now, and I damn near do a face-plant as she hauls herself to her feet.

Her gaze keeps flicking back and forth between me and the crashed HIT Mark. "What ..." she mumbles. "What ...?"

I take her gently by the arm, and I start to lead her away — a fast walk. Paradox knots inside me, and it's all I can do not to barf. But I'm smiling — grinning like a bandit.

"What the fuck's happening?" Juliet is walking beside me, not resisting. She turns those deep eyes on me, and asks again, "What the fuck's happening?"

I feel my grin grow broader. This is continuing to be one hell of an evening. "Later," I tell her, slurring my words horribly. "We've got a lot to talk about."

PUSHING THE RIGHT BUTTONS
■■■■■■■■■■■■■

Doug Murray

Williams reached inside the box and made a tiny adjustment.   "There," he muttered. "That should do it!"

"Do what?"

Williams turned. Carlos Magruder was standing at his cubicle door, smiling wryly at Williams' expression of mild surprise. "Oh. Hi, Carlos."

Magruder stepped in. "Hi, yourself. What is that," he said pointing to the small box , "thing going to do?"

Williams checked that the box was turned 'off' then dropped it into his pocket. "Sorry, Carlos. I can't tell you."

"Can't or won't?"

It was Williams' turn to smile. "Won't. Now, what can I do for you?"

"Actually, it's more a question — Damn!" The cubicle wall moved under his weight as he leaned against it. He stumbled and then caught his balance. "I hate these things! Why can't they give us real walls!"

Williams shrugged. "Too individualistic. Now you were saying?"

Carlos glared at the sagging partition, then shrugged and turned back to Williams, his smile returning. "Yeah, I was about to say that I found this great new club —right up the coast— about half hour or so from here."

Williams turned back to his desk. "You know how the boss feels about clubs."

Carlos moved closer, slipping an arm over Williams' shoulder. "C'mon! It's Halloween! Think of the costumes! Or lack of same..."

Williams glanced at the clock on the wall. It was after hours. "Well..." he said, hesitantly.

"That's the boy! After all, we can't be perfect all the time, can we?"

Williams grabbed his coat. "Iguess not," adding as an afterthought "I hope this isn't a mistake."

■ ■ ■

"I told you this would be a mistake!" Williams peered through the windshield. There was a wall of police cars in front of them, completely blocking the entrance ramps to the Golden Gate. Beyond the Gate was another barrier — a wall of fog.

"Hey," Carlos turned the wheel, guiding the car toward a side road. "I didn't order fog tonight." He spotted a hole in the traffic and gunned through it. "Did you?"

Williams shook his head, eyes peering into the fog. It was amazingly concentrated. "So, obviously the club's out. What do we do now?"

"Well, there is somewhere else we could go..." Carlos looked to the right as he turned down another street.

Williams made a face. "Not another of your clubs!"

"No. Something better. And it's not too far..."

Carlos turned the car onto another street, and Williams could see the bay to his side. Or rather, he could see part of the bay. There was nothing but grey darkness where he knew the bridge had to be.

■ ■ ■

Carlos brought the car to a stop some ten minutes later, waking Williams who had been half-dozing in the passenger seat.

"We're here!"

Williams looked out the windshield. Now here was a dingy brick building. Williams shook his head. No. It was more than that. He had a sudden vision of red haze oozing from the cracks of the building. Angry red haze. He shook his head again. It was gone; there was only an old building in front of him. He turned to Carlos. "Doesn't look like much. What's so special?"

Carlos opened his door and got out. "You'll see, my friend. You'll see."

Williams opened his own door, scanning the area. Nothing. Just the building and a few neighbors — none close enough to be of any concern should there be a loud party or such. His hand went into a pocket, closed around a compact mass of metal and plastic. Lonely could be dangerous.

Ahead of him, Carlos strode to the oak door that dominated the building's front facade.

"Better stay close to me, at least until I introduce you." He reached toward the doorbell. "And, uh, make sure both hands are in sight!"

Williams wondered at that request, but did as he was told. Carlos pushed the button, but Williams couldn't hear anything inside. Out of order? He glanced at the thick door and the even thicker wall beside it. Or maybe soundproof? But why? He glanced at Carlos, who was fidgeting excitedly. It was obvious Carlos had been here before and was looking forward to being back. His hand itched, but Williams kept it out of his pocket.

Seconds passed. Out of the corner of his eye, Williams again saw the red haze oozing out of the house. It had a different tinge now. Not angry; more anguished and worn out. Williams tried to bring the haze into focus, but it stayed just out of his awareness. It was irritating.

The door opened. Williams turned toward it and was met by a rifle barrel — large bore — pointing straight at his face. "It's all right!" He heard Carlos say, but Williams' gaze was locked on the muzzle. "He's one of us!"

"Okay, Carlos." The weapon dipped and Williams found himself looking at a large man dressed in a police uniform, a lieutenant's bar on the collar. The man stared at Williams' face, as if fixing it in memory, then nodded. "You can come in, both of you." He looked at Williams again, then poked a finger toward Carlos. "And you'd better be right about this guy."

"I am, I am!" Carlos danced in through the door, motioning for Williams to follow. "He works with me in research and development."

The policeman closed the door behind them. "All right. You know the routine here. Have a good time." He pointed to Williams as he racked the rifle with several other weapons in the hall. "And keep him out of the way!"

"Absolutely!"

The policeman took one more look at the two of them, then strode off down the hall. Carlos turned to Williams, wiping his brow with comic exaggeration. "Alright! We're in!"

"In what?" Williams was seeing the red haze again, right at the edge of his vision; filling the halls, dripping from the walls.

Carlos grinned, teeth shining in the subdued light. "Come with me. I'll show you!"

Making sure Williams was following, Carlos led the way down the hallway, following the path the Policeman had taken a moment earlier. "I found out about this place by accident — one of the officers in charge is my cousin."

Williams grinned at the incongruity of it. "You have a cousin in the Force?"

Carlos half-turned, his grin widening. "Two, actually.

But the one I'm talking about is in Special Services." He stopped in front of a large double door. The haze was worse here, flowing under and around the door frame, filling Williams' peripheral vision. It was more red, more painful.

Williams shook his head, trying to clear it — and then he heard the sound. It was a low buzzing, mixed with something else, something Williams couldn't identify. He rubbed the back of his hand across his eyes. What was it?...

Carlos opened the door.

Red haze washed over Williams, his vision filled with crimson. After a few seconds it cleared and then he saw —

Everything.

It was a huge room, walls made of thick stone, re-reinforced with soft plastic soundproofing. The soundproofing was to keep people outside from becoming curious — or suspicious — because the room was full of screams.

Williams followed Carlos as he stepped into the room. Everywhere, man-high frames were set up, bolted into the floor. Immovable. On each frame a naked human form was stretched: men, women, and even the occasional figure of a child.

The men in police uniforms were causing the screams. Using electrical prods, scalpels, even old-fashioned whips, the police were torturing the helpless, hanging figures.

"What the hell...!" Williams' mind reeled as he tried to grasp what he was seeing.

"Isn't this great?" Carlos grin had a nasty edge to it now. "They're traditionalists," he said, pointing to the bodies strapped to the frames. "The boys are trying to get information out of them!"

The Lieutenant from the door walked over to Carlos, an electric prod in his hand. "Pretty tough with this bunch." He touched a body next to him, thumbing a stud on the handle of the prod. Williams heard a buzzing sound, then a muffled groan from the figure as it danced against the current. "They're Verbena — they get off on this!"

Williams nodded at all the bodies. "Verbena. They're Mages, then. Aren't they dangerous?"

The Lieutenant shook his head. "Nope. You hear that buzzing?" Williams nodded. The Lieutenant pointed to a series of wires running from the frames to a particularly sensitive part of the body in front of them. "There's a strong electrical charge running through these to a pain centers. It's not enough to kill them, but is sure hurts like hell!" The Lieutenant grinned at Williams. "Makes it impossible for them to concentrate. And if you can't concentrate..."

Williams nodded. He got the picture. "Not bad— but I thought the Old Men wanted them killed on capture."

The Officer grinned. "What the Old Men don't know won't hurt them!" He turned back to the moaning figure on the frame nearest him. "Besides, you'd be surprised at what they tell us!" He reached out with his prod, a sharp crackle filled the room, followed by a shriek of pain. "You just gotta convince them."

Williams gagged a little as a wisp of smoke reached him. It smelled of burning flesh. He moved a little further from the torture rack. The red haze was all around him. He was trying to localize its source when Carlos grabbed him by the arm.

"Verbena! They'll last a long time!" He pulled a whip off a rack as he walked. "C'mon Williams! Let's get a piece of the action!"

Williams stomach was normal again. But the red haze kept blurring things around him. It seemed to be rising around him. He didn't relish the idea of drowning in the stuff. Perhaps if he found where it was coming from...

Then he saw it — the source — at the far side of the room in one of the corners. Williams brushed past Carlos and started moving forward, oblivious to the suffering all around him.

He detoured around several of the frames, not hearing the moans of the captives on them, ignoring the muttered curses of police pushed out of the way. Williams was interested only in the red haze and its source.

He stopped short when he reached it.

She was beautiful. She had dark hair and a face which, even though it was warped with pain, was angelic and fragile. Williams winced as her body jerked, reacting to a series of tiny wires attached to its most delicate areas. There was a policeman standing near the body, a box covered with tiny switches in his hand — a keyboard to orchestrate her agony.

Williams gaze went to him.

"Hey," The policeman said, taking notice of him. "Want to try it? It's the latest thing!"

Williams moved closer.

The policeman pointed to the various keys on the little box. "Each of these keys feeds electricity to one of those leads." His calloused hand pressed down on one of the contacts. The girl's body shuddered again, her mouth open in an endless scream. "We can control the intensity and location of each jolt anywhere we want." He released the pressure. The girl slumped forward, gasping for breath. Another touch, more agonized movement, almost frenzied now. "Eventually, she'll either talk," another touch, another scream, "or die." The policeman shook his head. "Don't much matter which, although the big boys wouldn't mind if she talked." Another muffled scream. "Kinda fun to watch her dance." He grinned.

Williams stood frozen as key after key was pressed, agony after agony endured. Sweat poured off the woman's body. Sweat and red haze. It lapped at Williams' ankles, rising around him.

He came to a decision.

"Hey!" Carlos turned as Williams pushed past him. "Where are you going?"

Williams ignored him, marching through the big main

door, striding into the hallway where the rack of weapons waited. He pulled an assault rifle out and checked the clip. It was fully loaded. Williams pulled three more full clips out of a drawer under the rack, then headed back toward the room of pain.

It was time.

Carlos met him at the door. "Hey, man — what are you doin' with that— "

Williams concentration was total now. He fired toward Carlos, the bullet impacting exactly where he wanted, directly between the eyes. The police in the room turned at the sound of the shot, two of them reaching for sidearms. Williams shot them, firing quickly, but with uncanny accuracy. There were no wasted shots. No near misses. Every round found a target, and every target died.

Firing as he went, Williams marched through the room, heading for the girl, vision crowded by red haze.

There was only one policeman left now— the big man with the control box. He was frantically looking for cover, too panic-stricken to even pull his pistol, when Williams reached him. Williams shot him once, cleanly, through the heart. The officer fell, hands clenching spasmodically. Williams cursed as he saw the right hand clamp down hard on the keyboard. Behind the cop, the woman went into a frenzy of pain, her body fighting the straps that held her in place. Williams leaped forward, kicking the control box out of the dead cop's hand, pumping three rounds into the electrical device, destroying it.

Williams laid the rifle down, carefully. He might need it again. He moved to the girl's side, fingers feeling for a pulse at the throat. She was still alive! He began removing wire leads, amazed at how many there were. She moaned as he removed the more deeply buried ones, but did not regain consciousness.

Williams carefully placed the girl's body in Carlos' car. Making sure that she was still unconscious, he walked back into the house, locking a new magazine into the rifle. He still had a few things to do before he could leave.

■ ■ ■

"Where...where am I."

Williams was surprised. The girl had taken a lot of punishment. He'd expected a longer period ofunconciousness. This was going to make things easier.

"Just relax." He reached down, offering her water, a straw allowing her to sip without sitting up. "You're safe now."

"Safe..." She looked at him, eyes measuring. "I remember..." She stiffened, pain and fear filling her eyes.

Williams shook his head. "That's over. I got you out of there."

"W..who are you?"

He looked down at her. The red haze was at the edges of his vision again. "A friend."

She lapsed back into unconsciousness.

■ ■ ■

Hours passed. Hours in which the girl drifted, going from near-coma to dreamless sleep. All the while Williams watched. Occasionally, he gave her water, or bathed her face with a cool cloth. Her beauty continued to fascinate him, even as her recuperative powers astonished. She was actually healing before his eyes!

Perhaps the Traditionals have something after all, he thought.

Daybreak found her body almost mended, whip marks gone, burns healed over. Her eyes opened.

"What's your name?" she asked sleepily.

Williams looked down at her face. Her mind and soul were firmly in place now. "Williams."

"Williams..." She half-closed her eyes, thinking. "You're not one of us."

"No."

"Then why?"

Williams turned toward the window, drawing the curtains to keep the morning sun out. "I saved you because I could see — feel — your pain."

"Feel my pain?"

He turned back toward her. "I can't explain it. It was like a crimson haze, not liquid, not gaseous, but there — filling me, drowning me."

She looked up at him. "You're a mage."

He nodded. "Yes."

"Which tradition?"

He turned back to the window, idly fingering the cords that controlled the draperies. "No tradition."

Williams heard her tiny gasp, felt her fear. "Technocracy?"

He nodded again.

"But they were the ones who...had me." She caught her lip between her teeth. "Why would you..."

Williams turned back toward her. "I told you. I could feel your pain."

She looked up at him, struggling to see his face in the shadows. "You're a strange man, Mr. Williams."

He turned away again. Stranger than you think.

■ ■ ■

It was three days before she was ready to leave; three days in which she and Williams got to become friends, and more.

"Tell me again how it felt," she panted, body covered in sweat.

Williams stroked that magnificent shape with his hands.

He still couldn't get over how quickly she had healed. She moaned as his fingers touched a particularly sensitive spot. He allowed himself a small smile. "It felt...looked like a red haze..." He moved his hand again, and was rewarded with another moan of pleasure.

"Do you...see anything now?" Her tone had become low, breathy. Williams smiled, allowing his eyes to unfocus. Yes, there was a haze there, but a blue-white one. It was cascading out of her, hovering all around him.

"I see..." she moved under him, causing him to catch his breath for a moment. "Blue. I see blue, " he answered

She smiled widely. "Good, very..." His hand moved on her body again and all rational communication fled.

■ ■ ■

"What about the others?" She asked the question just as he was about to drift off into sleep.

"Others?" He fought for clarity.

"The ones with me, in that place."

He shook his head. "I couldn't save them."

She turned from him. "Oh "

Williams turned to cradle her in his arms, warming her with his body. He felt the pillow under her. It was damp with her tears. "How did you get caught?"

Her speech was muffled by the pillow beneath her. "We had to cross the bridge, and it was closed, blocked. "

Williams nodded. "That fog."

"The police stopped our van and the driver..." She took a deep breath. "He panicked and tried to drive through their roadblock." She turned, eyes dry and cold again. "It was stupid."

Williams nodded in agreement. "What will you do now?"

A slight smile touched her lips. "Well, I could stay with you."

Williams shook his head.

Her smile grew wider. "No, I didn't think that would work, either."

"They're looking for you."

"And you?"

Williams grinned. "They don't even know I'm involved."

"Could you take me across the bridge?"

"Now?"

She laughed, turning toward him, arms reaching out. "No. Not just yet."

■ ■ ■

As usual, Williams marveled at the sight of the Golden Gate as he drove up the access road. And as usual, he felt all the wonder drain out when he finally got onto the bridge itself. He sighed as he watched the crowds on the span: beggars, petty thieves, even the occasional Hollow One. The police should really clean it up— at least get the damned graffiti off! Williams shook his head. That wasn't his problem. He took the off ramp at the far end of the bridge, pulling up the hill onto the 'scenic overview'. It was time to get directions.

She came out of the trunk laughing. "You really ought to get that disinfected!"

He looked down at the old rug she had wrapped herself in. "Yeah. I used to have a dog."

She held her nose. "I know."

He shrugged. "We're through the toll gate. Where do you want to go now."

She turned toward the telephone booths at the end of the small parking area. "Let me just make a phone call. " She looked him in the eye. "Then I'll show you the way."

Williams shrugged and leaned back against the side of the car. "Whatever you say."

■ ■ ■

Twenty-five minutes and three turns later, Williams had
no idea where he was; he had to trust that she did.

"A little further now...okay, turn left at the corner."

Williams did as he was told. They were up along the
North part of the bay now, he could see houseboats to his
right. He looked at his watch. Almost noon.

"Turn right here!" She leaned forward as he
overcompensated, his tires screeching. "Up ahead there —
that red houseboat."

Williams rolled into the little parking area in front of
the houseboat, braking just a few feet from the unvarnished
wooden plank that connected the residence to shore.
"That's it?"

The girl laughed. "Why not? Who'd ever suspect? Beep
your horn twice."

Williams complied.

Two figures appeared on the deck of the houseboat. Both
were carrying shotguns. Williams turned to the girl,
questions in his eyes. She laughed. "Did you really think
I'd trust a Technocrat?" She pulled herself out of the car,
waving the others forward. "After what they did to me and
my friends? You've got to be stupid"

Williams started to get out of the car.

"Don't get out!" She told him, waving the others past
her. "And don't put your hands in your pockets."

Williams shrugged. "Is it okay if I turn the car off?"

"Why not," she laughed. "We might be able to use it!"

Williams reached forward, his hand brushed a tiny box
alongside the steering wheel. He pushed a button. He felt
a soft beep. He stretched a little further forward. "And here
I thought we had something!"

She laughed again. "Fool! We accept the flesh— we
don't live for it!"

Williams' hand came away from the dashboard. There
was a comforting weight in it now. "Too bad."

Suddenly, Williams became a blur of movement, standing straight up in the car seat, pistol suddenly spitting fire left, then right. The two men with shotgun fell, eyes clouding as Williams' bullets found their brains. More men and women poured out of the houseboat, awaken by the sounds of battle. They all began screaming as they were cut down by automatic fire from police cars silently sliding up from both sides of the street.

The girl watched, paralyzed at this unexpected turn of events.

Williams' gun swung toward her. "You can't," she whispered.

Williams nodded, "You're right." He motioned and several police came forward, handcuffs and truncheons ready. "That would be too easy. You still have secrets. They'll take you back to the city."

Her eyes widened. "No. Not that place again!"

He nodded. "Again and again, until you tell us what we want to know."

She started to scream, a cry quickly cut off as a gag was pressed into her mouth. They dragged her past Williams, who stopped them with a motion.

"Too bad it worked out this way." He brushed the side of her face with his fingers. "But maybe I'll stop by and press a few of your buttons."

Her eyes filled with horror as the police dragged her off. Williams leaned against the car door, watching as other police surrounded the houseboat, covering the exits while explosives were planted on the deck and along the water line. A hand fell on his shoulder.

"She'll talk this time."

Williams turned to face his boss. "Perhaps. But I don't think so. She's strong."

The older man shrugged. "Where she's going, strong is not necessarily a good thing."

Williams noted the red haze appearing at the corner of

his vision and nodded. "True enough."

The old man guided Williams toward his waiting limousine. "You did a good job, Williams. Pity about Carlos and the Police at the house."

"They were corrupt. Disobeying orders. Imperfect."

The old man nodded. "You're right, of course. And yet, their little house is a good idea."

Williams nodded. "Yes. And we'll use it, won't we?"

"Of course. Now, come with me. This calls for a celebration."

Williams held the door for the old man. I'll get a promotion out of this he thought. His eyes moved to the girl being lifted into the Police van. Red haze began to lap around him...

The beginning of my ascension...

DREAMSPEAKER
■■■■■■■■■■■■■■

Bill Crider

I am John Killdeer Smith, Dreamspeaker, and I have talked with the spirits of the earth. I know of the Uktena werewolves, and in my dreams I have seen the spirit of Cataclysm guarded by their caern. I know the spirit of Ascension as all Dreamspeakers must, and I know that the Technomancers do not understand that spirit as I do. I believe that their dream is a corrupt one, and I am sworn to oppose it.

You may think that I sound quite pretentious, and I probably do. I may have confused you as well, but at least my little speech explains why I was in San Francisco, a place that I would ordinarily avoid for its being inimical to my magick. It is not easy to remain in contact with the spirits of the earth in a city of solemn stone.

It was raining when I entered the city by way of the Bay Bridge. The rain was cold and dreary, washing over the windshield of my old minibus and streaking the rust on the hood.

I didn't mind the rain. It suited my mood perfectly, since I had come to the city to kill a man. Death and rain, death and rain-soaked darkness have affinities that lie beyond the rational, and that step beyond the rational is one way of opposing the Technocracy's idea of Ascension.

I parked the minibus on the street near Chinatown, hoping that the parking brake would hold it on the steep hill, and walked through the pagoda-like opening guarded by dragons painted gold and green. The street was practically deserted except for a man carrying a plastic shopping bag. His left eye glowed in an opaque shade of deep red, but other than that, he seemed completely ordinary. Halloween was Sunday, the day after tomorrow; maybe he was wearing a mask.

The rain was still coming down hard, sluicing off the brooding buildings and running along the curb. The sky was a hard slate gray, and it was almost dark as night. Lights glowed in shop windows, people moving silently behind them.

I located Frankie Lee's address and went up a narrow flight of stairs between a souvenir shop and a restaurant. The stairs smelled of spices and cabbage rolls.

There were three apartments at the top of the stairs. Frankie Lee's was number 8. I knocked on the door, which was opened almost at once by a thin, golden follower of the Akashic Brotherhood with very black hair and startlingly white teeth.

"I am Frankie Lee," he said. "You must be the assassin."

I thought he was a little incautious, but I didn't comment on it. I went through the door, and he closed it behind me. There was another man in the room, sitting beside a table. He was in a straight wooden chair with his legs in front of him and crossed at the ankles. He was a Hollow One with circles under his eyes that matched the black denim clothing he wore. His hair was long and hung in his face.

"Now we are three," Frankie Lee said, "if you are the one for whom we have been waiting."

"I am John Killdeer Smith."

"Indeed," Lee said. He turned and gestured the man in the chair. "This is Lowell."

He didn't say whether that was a first name or a last, and it didn't really matter. Lowell grunted something that I supposed was a greeting.

I was not at all sure that I trusted either of these men, but we were the ones chosen for the task at hand. The elders of my people had explained that to me, as I am sure others had explained to Lee and Lowell.

"Tell me about Kane," I said.

Lee smiled without showing his teeth. "All business, I see. Very well. Have a seat, and we will tell you."

I took one of the other chairs at the table where Lowell sat, and Lee took another. We were an oddly assorted trio, one that you would hardly expect to find operating in concert toward a mutual goal, but these are strange times.

"Do you mind if I smoke?" Lee asked.

I shrugged. Dreamspeakers have been known to smoke on occasion, though not usually tobacco.

Lowell grunted and pulled out a cigarette of his own. He brushed his hair out of the way and stuck the butt in his mouth, then lit it with a kitchen match.

Lee took a puff and then said, "As you know, the Akashic Brotherhood does not usually engage in activity against the Technocracy."

I nodded. The Akashic Brotherhood didn't usually engage in activity against anyone. They sat in their austere rooms and meditated on the Way, trying to alter their reality through the exercise of their minds. As far as the Ascension was concerned, it wasn't working.

"Some of us, however," Lee went on, "recently decided that the time has come for action." He tapped the ashes off his cigarette into a small brass bowl in the middle of the table. "Lowell can tell you more."

I wasn't even sure Lowell could talk, but it turned out that he could, and very well, too, though his voice sounded more like an animal's growl rather than anything human.

"We don't generally screw around with any of the other mages, either," he said. "They don't like us, and we don't like them."

Another well-known fact. The Hollow Ones were practically outcasts, excluded from the Council of Nine. They didn't meditate; mostly they just brooded.

I, on the other hand, was a Dreamspeaker, one who can sometimes reach the spirit world through his close connection with elemental nature.

"So what are the three of us doing here together?" I asked.

"That's how it has to be," Lowell said. "The Technocracy is strangling San Francisco. Right now, their drive toward Order is suffocating everything that makes this city a place where Ascension could happen. That Weaver they've got isn't entirely free of some Wyld influence, but Kane is going around snuffing every Wylding in the city. He has to be stopped."

Kane was still more or less just a name to me. I needed to know more. "Tell me something about Kane himself."

Lee fielded that one. "He's the head of the Technocracy's secret police. I don't mean the real cops. The Technocracy's men don't operate by any rules, and they get away with murder." He crushed out his cigarette. "Literally."

"And the three of us are supposed to stop him?"

"You should know," Lowell said. "It was your people who had the vision."

He had me there, but I hadn't been told much. One of the elders had come out after a week's stay in the sweat lodge to report that a man named Kane had to be killed. According to his vision, there were to be three men in the team assigned to the job: a Dreamspeaker, a Hollow One and a member of the Akashic Brotherhood. The arrangements were made, and in less than a day I was on my way to San Francisco in the minibus.

"The goal of Ascension has been corrupted," Lee said. "By all of us — the Council of Nine, the Technocracy — there's blame enough to go around. But we have a chance to do something about that."

"By killing someone?" I asked. "That sounds more like something the Marauders would propose. Or even the Nephandi." Both those groups followed a discipline of disorder and used violent means to achieve their purposes.

"Maybe their methods aren't entirely evil," Lowell growled, "but they're too wrapped up in their own ends. We'd be doing this for everyone. Maybe that's why they wanted misfits like us involved. No one would expect this kind of action from any of our groups. They probably wouldn't expect any action at all."

It made a kind of sense if you looked at it that way. "And how will killing Kane help Ascension?"

Lee lit another cigarette and exhaled a thin stream of smoke. "It will feed the Quintessence flux, change the balance of power. This city is in danger of becoming static, frozen with the Technocracy in control. Kane's death will tilt the balance toward the dynamic."

"All right," I said, though I still wasn't sure about it. "How do we find Kane?"

"That," Lee said, "will be the hard part."

It seemed that Kane had his headquarters in the former prison of Alcatraz, impervious to both weapons and magick.

"There's not really even any way to get near it," Lee said. "The only approach is by water. Kane's men strictly control all the boats in the area, and he has riflemen in all the watchtowers. If any boat gets too close, they fire a warning shot; back off, or you're dead."

That didn't sound promising.

"Even if you could somehow get to the island," Lee went on, "you couldn't get inside the walls. Prisons are just as hard to break into as they are to break out of, and you can bet that Kane has had everything beefed up since the prison days."

"Then what are we supposed to do?" I asked.

Lowell grinned thinly. "Like I said, it was your people who had the vision. Maybe you're supposed to tell us."

I didn't know what to say to that. I had been instructed to come to San Francisco, meet with Lee and Lowell, and work out a way to get to Kane. But there didn't appear to be a way.

"What about when he comes and goes from the island?" I asked. "Can we get him then?"

"We might," Lee said. "If he ever left. As far as we know, he hardly ever does, and certainly never according to any kind of schedule. And if he left, he'd be surrounded by bodyguards."

"This is going to take some thought." I was always adept at the act of understatement.

Lee nodded. "Of course."

Lowell wasn't so patient. "We better think fast then. If we don't, it might be too late to tip the balance."

We talked it over for another hour, but we didn't come up with anything. Lee said he'd try to get his hands on some copies of the plans for Kane's island fortress, though he didn't really think it was likely that he could, and we agreed to meet the next day to go over them.

That was the inconclusive and unsatisfactory end of the meeting, and I left wondering why I had been sent in the first place. I believed in visions, of course, but it was possible for a vision to be misleading or ambiguous. I was beginning to think a mistake had been made somewhere.

Lowell left Lee's apartment with me, and we made our way down the street through the rain. It was late afternoon and even darker than before, but I could see the two men watching us from a doorway. The men wore snap brim hats, black suits and ties so thin that they might have been made from shoestrings.

"Kane's," Lowell said when I nudged him.

The two men moved out of the doorway and fell in about half a block behind us. A man with a red left eye passed us going the other way, but he paid no attention to Kane's flunkies. He just kept on walking through the rain.

Another man stepped out of a restaurant just ahead of us. He was carrying a sack of take-out food and didn't notice that anything was going on.

As we passed through the pagoda, Kane's men speeded up. I saw one of them reach under his suit coat, going for a gun or what a Sleeper might call a remote control. I called it a spell transmitter.

One of the dragons above the pagoda began to move. Its green scales shimmered in the rain, and its golden eyes glowed. Spell transmitter.

"Oh, shit," I said.

"Let's haul ass!" Lowell yelled, grabbing my sleeve and pulling me along. I wasn't sure I entirely trusted him, but I didn't have much choice.

The dragon began to slither forward, spreading its wings. Its mouth gaped open, and a stream of orange fire shot out, hissing through the rain and singeing the hairs on the back of my neck. A puff of steam rose from Lowell's shoulder where the flame had burned through his cotton shirt.

The man from the restaurant stared back at us in horror. The sack of take-out lay scattered on the sidewalk.

"Fuck this!" Lowell snarled. "Can't you do something?"

I didn't know what he expected. There in the steel and stone citadel of the Technocracy, my magick would be practically useless.

The dragon flew closer. I could see its glowing eyes through the downpour.

And then I realized that there was at least one elemental spirit that should be easy to reach, even in the city. I put my hand inside my shirt and touched my medicine pouch, muttering a few words that I hoped Lowell would find incomprehensible. I don't like to use magick near someone who might try to steal one of my spells.

Almost before the words were past my lips, the rain increased in intensity. It had been hard to begin with; now it was almost a solid curtain between us and the dragon. There was a flash of lightning and a nearly simultaneous blast of thunder that must have shaken windows for blocks around. The lightning did its work, and the dragon crashed to the pavement, writhing in agony, its scales scraping the sidewalk.

"Let's get out of here," I said, and Lowell and I ran for the minibus. He didn't want to be there anymore than I did.

We were drenched when we got to the 'bus, but we jumped inside without worrying about the seats. The engine started with a sudden roar, and we pulled smoothly away from the curb.

I looked in the rearview mirror and saw Kane's men pounding past the fallen dragon, pulling sidearms from beneath their jackets. If they couldn't get us with magick, they'd go with conventional weapons.

I whipped the minibus around a corner, almost losing it as the rear tires lost their grip on the slick pavement. They grabbed hold, and we were around the turn just as the first shots chipped the bricks of the building on the corner.

"Those guys are seriously pissed," Lowell murmured.

He was right about that, not that I cared whether they were pissed or not. What bothered me was why they were there in the first place. How could they have gotten onto us so soon? I looked at Lowell, thinking about it.

"Which way?" I asked him.

He looked out the rain-streaked window. "You know where the Waydown was?"

"No. What's the Waydown?"

"It's nothing. Not now. It was a nightclub where a lot of us hung out, but the Techno-cops kept raiding the place until it finally closed down. Bunch of Orphans hang out there now."

That was interesting, I suppose, but it didn't tell me what I wanted to know.

"What's that got to do with where we're going?"

"My place is around the block from there. Just keep driving. I'll give you directions."

We drove through the rain-sodden city, with Lowell talking only enough to tell me where to turn. I saw the derelicts sheltered in doorways, the crumbling facades of buildings, the garbage-choked alleys. A rat swam against the current in a swollen gutter, trying to keep its head above the rushing water. Ascension seemed a long way off, and I was glad I didn't spend much time in the city.

We passed the seemingly deserted night club, and Lowell told me to turn right. He directed me to a three story building filled with broken windows and covered with graffiti. It looked more like a deserted warehouse than a place to live.

"Be it ever so humble," Lowell said. He flipped a hand, and a graffiti-splattered door began sliding upward. "You can park inside."

I drove in, parked the minibus in the cavernous garage, and got out. Water squished from my moccasins when I stepped on the floor, which was covered with oil stains and old newspapers. My wet clothes clung to me like a dead man's fingers.

"Where is everyone?" I asked, still not sure I trusted Lowell. My voice echoed from the walls.

"They're upstairs," Lowell said, pointing toward a steel

door covered with peeling gray paint.

We started toward the door and were about halfway there when it crashed open and slammed against the wall. Two men dressed in black suits and thin ties stepped out of the stairwell and began firing nine-millimeter automatics without warning, filling the room with thunder.

I acted without thinking, turning and making a dive for the floor. When I landed, I rolled under the minibus with lead striking sparks from the concrete beside me. Lowell somehow got behind the 'bus, and I could hear the bullets poinging into the sheet metal.

My own weapon was right over my head, but there was no way I could get to it, and I wasn't going to be able to call up any elemental spirits from the hard floor under my cheek.

The firing stopped and I heard the last brass casings strike the floor and bounce musically on the hard concrete. Kane's minions ejected the expended clips from their pistols, slammed in new ones, and I yelled to Lowell, "Your turn, man!"

I had to trust him now. There was no one else to turn to. I didn't even know if he had any magick, but it was time to find out.

I held my breath, waiting for the renewed assault, but it didn't come. Then Lowell was pulling on my foot.

"Let's get out of here," he said.

I rolled out from under the minibus. The shooters were still there, moving as if they were immersed in heavy oil.

"Time distortion spell," Lowell said. "It won't last long. C'mon!"

He was already halfway in the 'bus, and I followed him without hesitation. In seconds we were back in the streets. The rain had stopped, but it had been replaced with a heavy fog. The minibus' headlights gave a ghostly glow to the street ahead of us.

Lowell looked over his shoulder. "Here they come."

I glanced at the shine of headlights in the rearview mirror. Two cars. Maybe three. The Technocops had staked the place out just in case we got away from the gunners inside.

I shoved the accelerator down. The tires spun briefly on the pavement, and then the minibus surged forward. The original engine had been replaced by a far more powerful one, which was fortunate considering the hill that confronted us. The cars behind kept pace easily as we passed street after street of pastel houses crowded together with hardly the space to slip a playing card between them.

"How many of you lived in the warehouse?" I asked Lowell.

"Three," he answered shortly. "Besides me."

He and I knew he wouldn't be seeing the other three again. There were few enough Hollow Ones before. Now there were three fewer.

"Those three were my friends," Lowell said. He tried to keep his voice steady as he looked at the lights behind us, and I felt a surge of sympathy for him. Then he turned back to face the front. "But I guess there's one thing about it that's good."

I couldn't see what that might be, and I told him so.

"The bastards that killed them are scared of us."

"That evens things out then. I'm scared of them."

And I was. The lights behind us were getting closer, and I knew the shooting would start soon. I tried to get more speed out of the 'bus, but it was giving all it had.

Lowell wasn't any happier about the situation than I was. "They've gaining," he said. "You got any plans for how we're going to get out of this mess?"

We crested the hill and started down.

"No," I said, feeling something like panic clutch at my gut. Headed downhill, the minibus was able to go a little faster. "How about you?"

"Hell, no." He glanced up and saw that we were reaching a cross street. "Hang on!" he yelled.

We hit the street nose down. There was a clang when the bumper hit, and sparks flew up in front of us. Then the front of the minibus jumped up and the back bumper scraped across the intersection. We bounced a foot when the tires hit on the downhill side, and I was glad the suspension had been strengthened when I'd had the new engine installed. The cars behind us were going to have an even rougher time than we were, because they were built lower to the ground.

That didn't discourage them, however. They slowed a little as we plunged down the hill, but they kept coming. There was very little traffic, thanks to the fog, so there was no way to lose them.

"Gimme the wheel," Lowell ordered, trying to elbow me aside.

"What?"

"Get out of the way. You don't know where the hell you're going."

He was right about that, so I slipped out of the driver's seat as he slid in under me.

I moved to the back seat and picked up my bow, feeling a tingle of power when my fingers came in contact with the smooth wood. I looked at the arrows in their quiver of soft deerskin.

"Is there a park around here?" I asked. "Somewhere with trees and grass?"

"Golden Gate Park," Lowell said. But he knew what I was thinking and he added, "It's a man-made park, though. Grass and trees didn't grow there on their own."

"It might work."

We were nearing the bay. I could see Ghiradelli Square looming through the fog. I thought I could also make out one of the stanchions of the Golden Gate Bridge far to the left.

"Muir Woods would be better," Lowell said.

Muir Woods was across the Golden Gate in Marin County, and the Golden Gate was a powerful bastion of the Technocracy's magick. I had heard once that there had even been a human sacrifice to bind the final spells.

"Can we get across the bridge?" I asked.

Lowell shrugged. "You got a better idea?"

I didn't, so he twisted the wheel hard to the left. He almost lost it when the back wheels broke loose from the slick street, but he wrenched the wheel and shoved his foot down on the accelerator, and the tires squealed and caught.

One of the cars behind us wasn't so lucky. It went into an uncontrollable skid and smashed sideways into the brick façade of an old building at about fifty miles an hour. I watched as it burst into flames and exploded, sending a fireball into the street. The other two cars didn't even pause. They came right through the fire as if it weren't there.

"One down," Lowell said, brushing his long hair back out of his face with a hand that seemed a little shaky.

We got to the bridge with no further trouble, but I hadn't been worried about getting there. I was worried about getting across it, and I was right to be. The Techno-magick was strong there. We could almost hear it singing in the strands of wire that held the mighty bridge suspended above the bay.

There was a strong breeze blowing in from the Pacific, and the fog was blowing away in gray wisps. To the right I could see the rock that was Alcatraz rising from the water. I wondered if Kane knew what was going on and decided that he probably did.

Traffic was heavier on the bridge than it had been in the city. Lowell swerved in and out of the lanes and actually seemed to be pulling away from our pursuers. But three-quarters of the way across, the minibus began to slow down. It was almost as if something were strangling the engine.

"Shit!" Lowell howled. "Are we running out of gas?"

I looked at the fuel gauge. Fuel wasn't the problem.

"The bridge knows we're in here," I said.

The minibus was slowing even more.

Lowell grimaced. "I was afraid you'd say that. What do we do now?"

"You steer. I'll get out and push."

I swung out the door. By the time I got to the back of the 'bus, it had almost stopped. Horns were honking behind us. There were so many cars that I couldn't distinguish Kane's lackeys from the rest.

Directly behind us was a guy in a big red Dodge Ram. He leaned out the window. "Need a push?" he asked.

"Sure do."

I waved him forward and waited until I could get his bumper lined up with the rear of the 'bus. I gave him the "okay" sign and ran to get back in the 'bus.

"Hey!" Lowell said. "I thought you were gonna push."

"It's taken care of," I replied, and the minibus began to move.

The traffic had cleared in front of us, so we made good time until the truck behind us died.

"Damn," Lowell muttered.

But it was all right. We had enough momentum to coast on off the far end of the bridge. As soon as we crossed onto solid land, the engine caught. Lowell was surprised, but he didn't waste any time thinking about it. He sped away, leaving the Ram stranded on the Golden Gate. I hoped it would delay our pursuers, maybe even through them off our trail.

In only a few minutes, we were on the twisting byway leading to Muir Woods. There were too many turns on the road to suit me. The minibus was fast, but it wasn't built for maneuverability. Sure enough, Kane's enforcers soon showed up behind us.

"How much farther?" I asked.

"Mile or so. The weather's not bad on this side of the bridge. There might be some tourists there."

Sleepers, I thought. They wouldn't know what the hell was going on. Maybe if they stayed out of the way, none of them would get hurt.

When we came in sight of the woods, I could almost feel the power flowing into me. The redwoods were so tall that their tops were nearly lost in the clouds. No one had planted these trees.

The parking lot was far from full and Lowell pulled into a spot not far from the entrance to the woods. I grabbed the bow and arrows and followed him outside.

Lowell looked at my weapon. "Gonna be hard to get permission to carry that in."

I started to tell him that it wouldn't be a problem, but then I saw his thin grin.

"You going to make us invisible, or you want me to do it?" he asked.

"Be my guest," I said, and we went breezing into the woods. None of the Sleepers saw us go, though the magick might not have worked so well against Kane's men, who might have been proof against it.

As we started along the path, Kane's men were piling out of their cars in the parking lot. I stopped long enough to see how many of them there were. Six. Against the two of us. The odds were about right.

We followed the path for only a few yards. Then we turned off and went into the trees. Their tall shadows surrounded us. Water dripped from the leaves, and our feet were cushioned by the mulch that had accumulated over many years. As we went farther into the trees, an almost sepulchral silence gathered around us, broken occasionally by the buzz of an insect or the call of a distant bird. The woods were cool and damp and dark. I could feel the earth through my moccasins, and I felt as if I were home.

We took up our position behind two massive trees. I rested my palm against one and felt the power of the forest spirit flowing into me as I breathed a short prayer. There is a power in wood that persists even after it is separated from the tree in which it grew. This was as good a place to make a stand as we would find, much better than some man-made park. I nocked an arrow and waited.

Lowell wasn't as comfortable as I was. He kept brushing at his face, worrying at the gnats, but at least he was quiet about it. There was no sound except birdsong and the occasional chatter of a squirrel.

Kane's soldiers were even less comfortable than Lowell, as was typical of members of the Technocracy; they weren't happy with nature and understood nothing of the balance of life. I could hear them long before I saw them — the slapping of hands against flesh and clothing as they encountered insects, the curses as they nearly tripped on vines, the crack of a branch as they carelessly shoved it aside.

The first one came into view. There was something that looked like a pocket calculator hanging from a thong around his neck.

"Spell blocker," Lowell muttered. "Damn."

I wasn't worried. I hadn't been planning to use any spells, though maybe Lowell had given it some thought. I stepped out from behind the tree and put an arrow through the man's throat. It punched in almost to the fletching.

The man went down with nothing more than a gurgle, but it was enough to warn the others. They opened fire with their automatic weapons, clipping leaves and shearing off branches. I stepped back behind the tree as slugs slammed into the trunk. I could almost feel the tree groaning.

"Sorry, brother," I whispered.

As suddenly as it had begun, the firing stopped and the sudden silence was almost more intense than the noise had been. There were no more birds singing, no more squirrels yammering overhead.

Lowell picked up a branch that had fallen beside him. It was about the size of a baseball bat, and he stripped the leaves from it.

"Here I come, assholes!" he roared and stepped from behind the tree.

They began shooting at him immediately, and he swung the branch calmly, picking off the bullets as if they were softballs and knocking them back in the direction of the shooters.

It was another time distortion spell. If he couldn't use one on the gunmen, he could put one on himself, and it was a pretty impressive display, impressive enough to encourage a couple of the men to get careless in their wonderment and allow me to pick them off with my arrows.

Three down, three to go.

Lowell took care of one of them with his stick, catching him in the side of the head with a well-timed swing and sending him backward in an almost graceful flip.

I got another with my fourth arrow. That left one.

It was too bad that he was something a little more than human, more a creation of the Technocracy than a man.

I'd heard about them of course, the beings that the Technocracy concocted in their underground labs, bizarre creatures that were as much machine as human. It looked like a man, but its skin was pale and its eyes were dead. Its mouth was a mere slit.

It emptied the clip of the automatic rifle, and Lowell had to dive behind a tree to escape. When the creature stopped to slam in another clip, Lowell jumped up and slammed it in the head with the tree branch. The branch snapped as if it were rotten, and the creature's hand shot out to grasp Lowell by the throat. Lowell hardly had time to scream before his breath was cut off.

I twanged off two arrows almost as fast as a man could fire pistol shots. They bounced off the creature as if they were made of rubber. He tossed Lowell aside and started in my direction. Lowell just lay there.

I had two choices. I could run, or I could try another arrow.

I didn't want to run, so I loosed an arrow, but the creature simply plucked it out of the air and snapped it between its fingers. It seemed to be smiling as it came toward me, though it was hard to tell.

I was about to try something else when the thing bounded forward, covering more ground than would have been possible for a mere man. It landed a foot in front of me and grabbed my throat with both hands.

It had needed only one for Lowell, and I felt my fingers go limp. My bow slipped away to the ground as my vision faded and my breath rasped. Then my knees buckled and I knew I wasn't going to last much longer.

I slid my fingers inside my shirt and touched my medicine pouch. The leather felt smooth and cool. I tried to think of the right words. I couldn't say them, but I could think them. I hoped I could think them. I could no longer see anything at all, and I had stopped even trying to breathe.

Suddenly I was falling, and there was no more pressure on my neck. I rolled over and tried to breathe. Air burned in my throat like fire. After a second or two, I could see again.

Kane's creature was rolling on the ground, tearing at the vines that had snaked around it at my command. They had attacked like living serpents and applied a pressure that would have crushed the chest of a breathing man.

I got weakly to my feet and started toward Lowell, but

the thing freed one of its hands and grabbed my ankle, bringing me down with a thud. I pulled an arrow from my quiver and struck at its fingers until I nearly severed them. Finally it released me and went back to the vines that continued to tighten.

Lowell was sitting up when I got to him, rubbing his throat. "Shit," he said. "I thought I was a goner." He looked in the direction of the writhing mass on the ground. "What're we gonna do about that?"

"Leave it," I rasped. "Let's get out of here before the reinforcements arrive."

"Good idea. Help me up, will you?"

I put down a hand and pulled him to his feet. He stood unsteadily for a moment, and then we made our way back to the 'bus.

We drove in silence for most of the way back to the city. This time we had no trouble getting across the Golden Gate. It seemed to have lost interest in us. A fog rolled in from the Pacific and shrouded the early evening.

I was driving past the Presidio when Lowell said, "There's something damn funny going on here."

"Then why aren't we laughing?"

"You know what I mean. How the hell did Kane know what we were up to? There's no way he could've gotten wind of what was going on."

"Sure there is," I said. "There was a way, all right. Give it some thought."

He thought. After a while, he said, "I see what you mean. We were betrayed." His face soured. "We should have known we couldn't win. I don't know why I ever got involved in this mess."

Typical Hollow One philosophy, I thought, but I didn't say it. What I said was, "We haven't lost yet."

He gave that some thought. Then he said, "Maybe not.

What should we do about it?"

"What do you think?"

"The same thing you're thinking, I guess. Turn right at the next corner."

I turned right, and we passed a club with an open door. A couple of Hollow Ones were standing outside, and we could hear the music from within, blasting out onto the sidewalk and practically peeling the paint from the minibus.

"That sounds great," Lowell said. "I haven't heard anything like that for a while, not since they closed the Waydown."

It didn't sound great to me, but there was a sense of freedom that I liked. I thought I might come back there if I stayed in San Francisco.

Frankie Lee obviously hadn't gotten the word yet. He hadn't even put a charm on his lock, so Lowell's opening spell got us inside with a minimum of fuss and bother.

Frankie was sitting at the same table where we'd talked over our plans, eating Kung Pao Chicken with steamed rice and egg rolls.

"Hey, Frankie," I said as he started to rise from his chair. "Don't bother to get up."

"Yeah," Lowell said, gesturing with a pistol that he'd lifted from one of Kane's deputies who no longer had much use for it, being dead. "Don't let us interrupt your dinner."

He walked over to the table and picked up an untouched egg roll. Without taking his pistol off Lee, he took a bite.

"Not bad," he said, lifting it in my direction. "Want one, Smith?"

"I'm not hungry. But you go ahead."

"Thanks, I will."

Frankie watched all this in dismay. He was clearly at a loss for words.

"Cat got your tongue?" Lowell asked, his mouth full of

egg roll.

"I didn't expect to see you again so soon," Frankie said.

"You mean you didn't expect to see us at all," Lowell told him. "You set us up, you son of a bitch."

"What?" Frankie tried to look astonished and failed miserably. "You've got the wrong guy. I didn't set anyone up."

"Sure you didn't." Lowell finished the egg roll, and he wiped his fingers on Frankie's shirt. "So why were Kane's guys waiting for us when we left here? And how did they know where we'd be going in case they missed us that time?"

"I don't know." Frankie feigned sincerity and failed as badly as he had when he'd tried for astonishment. "I know I didn't tell them."

"Won't work, Frankie," I said. "No one else knew we were here, and no one else knew where we were going. It was you. It had to be."

His shoulders slumped. "What are you going to do?"

"We're thinking about it. First, tell us why you turned us in."

"Because what you're trying to do is wrong. The Brotherhood believes in being, not doing. Your approach is doomed."

I shook my head. "Not good enough, Frankie. The Brotherhood agreed that it was right for the three of us to work together on this. They brought you into it."

He tried to smile. "The Brotherhood was wrong. I did not agree with their decision to be a part of this foolish scheme. I had to do what I could to stop you."

"So you ratted to Kane," Lowell said. "Thanks a lot, Frankie boy."

"Every man must do what he can to further the Ascension."

"Yeah. Well, you did your part, all right." Lowell grinned. "But you screwed up."

"No, I did not 'screw up,' as you put it," Lee said. "I stopped you, did I not?"

Lowell tapped the pistol barrel gently against his chin. "I guess you did at that. But that still leaves us with one problem: what to do with you."

"Kill me," Frankie said. "If you can."

With that, he shoved hard against the table, sending it crashing into Lowell's abdomen. Lowell's finger tightened on the trigger, and he fired off three shots into the ceiling as Lee conjured a huge djinn of smoke and flame that reached toward me with hands even larger than those of Kane's golem. Lowell recovered his balance, but a bullet is no good against a creature of magick, and it was too late to try shooting Lee, who was crouched behind the solid wood of the overturned table. Lowell tried anyway, and a couple of bullets got through the wood, but they had no stopping power. The djinn kept coming.

I had left the bow in the minibus, but I still had the quiver. I pulled out an arrow and held it like a knife. Wood has power, even over conjurations.

The djinn stopped, looking around for instructions. Frankie had none to give.

"Return to your home," I said, menacing the djinn with the arrow. "Return, or I will still you forever."

Frankie screamed something from behind the table, but the djinn began to move toward the table and fade away. I threatened it with the arrow again and it disappeared behind the table.

"You can come out now, Frankie," I said, but there was no reply.

Lowell walked over to the table and looked behind it.

"He's gone," he said. "The djinn took him."

That was just as well. Wherever he was, Frankie wouldn't be bothering us.

"What now?" Lowell asked me. "May as well give it up,

I guess. Kane's onto us, that's for sure, and like Frankie said, he stopped us."

"No he didn't," I said. "He just slowed us down a little."

"You're still going after Kane?"

"You mean you're out of it?"

"Sorry. You mean we're still going after Kane?"

"Maybe. But even if we don't, Frankie was wrong. He didn't stop us. We've already accomplished something. We've whipped some of Kane's best men in a fair fight, and we've quite possibly shifted the balance of forces that control this city. Didn't you hear the music at that club?"

Lowell brushed back his hair. "Damn. You're right. Things have already shifted, at least a little bit. And you think it was because of us?"

"It could be. Anyway, it's a beginning. And we still might be able to get to Kane."

"It's worth a try, I guess." Lowell didn't sound entirely convinced, but then he was a Hollow One. They don't convince easily. "What the hell. You got a place to stay?"

"I thought maybe you had a suggestion." I grinned. "But I hope it's better than the last place you took me."

DEVIL'S BARGAIN
■■■■■■■■■■■■■

Thomas Kane

I seldom cried out when people hit me. I didn't let feelings show on my face — not fear, not even rage. At age thirteen, I had not made much progress at learning the arcane arts, but I was becoming an accomplished actor. However, that day, as I sat studying *De Re Eudaemonica* and staring at the yellow stain on the wall, I wasn't expecting anything. When a shower of sharp, red-hot splinters cascaded across my neck, the pain took me by surprise, and I couldn't help myself. I dropped my book and yelped loudly enough to shake the cracked plaster of the reading-room walls.

To me, what happened was magic. An ordinary person, no doubt, would have found some mundane explanation for what occurred. Perhaps the bare light bulb on the ceiling burst, showering me with sharp, hot glass. It would have seemed strange, however, that the glass shards sprayed downward like angry little bees, digging themselves into the nape of my neck, hot enough to singe hair and deep enough to draw blood. I had enough Hermetic training to know that someone cast a spell on me.

Zasher, the elder student, stood behind me, chortling with delight. He was naked to the waist in his Levis, his eyes half-shut, laughing while sustaining his magick.

My one shout was enough to bring trouble. I heard the rap, rap of Mr. Solomon's feet in the corridor outside. Mr. Solomon was my teacher of magick and was also, according to the State of California, my legal guardian, foster father, God and Master. In the moments before our master arrived, Zasher cancelled his spell, his body visibly relaxing and his long lashes springing open.

"Cease this insufferable racket!" Mr. Solomon advanced through the door. His salt-and-pepper beard followed his lips as he drew his mouth up in a frown. "What is the meaning of this?"

I mumbled the truth, "Zasher scorched me."

"Kiss it," Zasher smacked his lips and leered.

"If you think I'm going to try to sort out some sort of infantile quarrel, you're sadly mistaken." Mr. Solomon glared first at Zasher and then at me. "You both fought, and you both pay the price. Zasher, you're eighteen. You should know better. You come with me."

Zasher walked forward to Mr. Solomon's side.

Mr. Solomon growled, his weathered face growing a little red, "Meanwhile, Job, as for you . . . ." He dug strong fingers into my bony shoulder. "Perhaps you need to contemplate the virtues of silence. Some time in the stairwell will do you good."

Mr. Solomon locked me in the old stairwell, which led past cobwebs to nowhere. A panel of bare bricks blocked the old door which once opened into the next apartment. The stairs were too steep and narrow for comfortable sitting, and there was no light at all. The air felt clammy and smelled of damp wall-dust.

A stinging itch raged across the torn back of my neck. The welts hurt. However, it hurt worse to know that Zasher could tease me, and I was the one punished for it. As I shifted position on the hard staircase, my resentment over the current injustice blended with my resentment over everything that Zasher and Mr. Solomon had done to me.

Since I knew I was alone, I allowed myself to sigh, over and over again, until the chilly air burned the insides of my throat. "It isn't fair." I said those words, first to myself, and then aloud. "It isn't fair!"

After a moment, I choked myself off. I realized, at that moment, that unequity was a truly silly thing to complain about. Nothing in the world was fair. Nothing was supposed to be fair. That is just how things are.   I had no way to keep track of time, but I must have wallowed in these thoughts for quite a while. My reverie ended when the earth erupted with a deep-throated roar. The universe shook. The vibration began in the floor and continued on up into my bones, as if I was a tuning fork which someone had struck with a hammer. The air sang about me, heavy and electrical. The walls of Mr. Solomon's old house groaned. I scrambled to my feet as the stairs buckled and skipped beneath me.

The evening news will say that there was an earthquake this night, the Friday before Halloween. But I know that it is more than a clash of tectonic plates. Mr. Solomon has drilled enough of the Arcana into my brain for me to know that magick takes the form of coincidences. That earthquake was an evil magick greater than anything a mortal mage could muster.

The earthquake not only shook down houses in the physical world, it nearly tore the astral world asunder. I could feel that rift as if it lay in the pit of my stomach, and I could feel its edges stretch as unearthly beings pushed their way half-through. Mr. Solomon had given me just enough training to sense that the earthquake was the cry of a raped Earth giving birth.

Then I felt a presence in the darkness near me. As the roar of the earthquake subsided, the feeling became stronger than ever, and I could hear a low growl, the sound of a living thing. There was someone or something in the stairwell. I was no longer alone.

"Job." A voice spoke from the blackness above me. The thing spoke my name in a female voice, soft and enticing.

I did not answer. I simply turned to face the direction of the voice with the same expression I would have used for Mr. Solomon, my face expressionless, my eyes dropping to my feet. It was too dark for me to see the thing in the shadows. However, I could make out a shape roughly as large as myself, with soft curves like those of a woman. The woman knelt on the stairs, her body upright above the knees, and she seemed to wear a tight-fitting dress which practically bound her legs together.

"Please . . . don't be afraid." The thing's body shifted a little.

I merely shrugged. If the thing thought I was frightened, it simply didn't understand me very well. I didn't have much to fear losing. Although I knew that the thing above me was probably sinister, its presence did not particularly disturb me.

"You seem so unhappy," the rich voice cracked a little. "Would you like to talk about it?"

Her line sounded so pat that I half-chuckled, "What are you? A spirit therapist?"

The thing actually laughed. For an instant, I caught a flicker of fire where its eyes might have been. "Not quite. I just . . . just thought you might want to talk."

"Nothing to say, really." I leaned against the wall in order to relax as much as possible while still facing the thing up the stairs.

"There must be." For an instant, the eyes gleamed again, looking into mine. "Tell me who you are. Tell me how you became Uriah Solomon's student.

I took a deep breath. I was not accustomed to talking about myself, and it hurt a little to think about the past. However, I could not deny that it was pleasant to have someone concerned about me and willing to listen. And so, I decided to play along. I didn't really think talking would change anything, but I was perfectly willing to squeeze the moment for all it was worth. "I grew up in the Castro. My father left before I was two. Then when I was seven, my mother went to jail. I don't guess I knew her that well . . . she was always working. But I missed her . . . a lot."

The woman in the shadows simply listened. Her chin rested on a delicate fist, and her eyes remained on me. As I spoke, I found emotions I thought I had never felt popping to the surface. Talking was powerful medicine, more powerful than I had expected, and the thing in the stairwell was a good listener. I was not sure whether I liked that or not.

"The stupid thing is, I don't even quite know what they sent her to jail for. Some kind of drug thing. She was probably guilty, she had friends like that." I shrugged. "Anyway, the State put me in the Moscone Center for Children. I stayed there for about a year."

The thing nodded gently. "How did you meet Solomon?"

"He adopted me, I guess. One day a lady with a clipboard came to my room and told me I had to stay with him until I turned 16. He made me go right then, and I had to leave all my posters behind."

"Posters . . . like this?" The woman raised a hand and cleared dust from the wall. As her hand moved, I heard the crinkle of slick paper beneath her palm. She peeled a poster from what had been a dusty plaster wall and handed it down to me.

I examined the poster in the faint light which came through the door-cracks below. The light was just barely enough for me to make out the green shells of the Teenage

Mutant Ninja Turtles. We had seen the Turtles movie at Moscone. The poster had been my favorite.

If she could have seen my eyes, she might have seen them squint in suspicion. But I said, "Thanks."

"You're welcome. I hope you like it." For a moment, the woman's teeth showed in a smile. Her canines appeared a bit too slim, and they curved like the fangs of a snake.

"Since then, there hasn't been much." I worked the poster into a tight roll. "I've lived with Mr. Solomon. I've studied Latin and Greek. Zasher has given me grief. Mr. Solomon's girlfriend has made me do chores. Once, the people from Moscone checked up on us, and I had to go to school for a week, but other than that, I really haven't left this house."

"Mmmm." The woman waited a moment, her eyes on me. "I think I understand how you feel."

I shrugged.

"Do you ever feel . . . trapped?" Her voice contained a tiny bit of hurt. "Do you ever want revenge?"

"Maybe."

"I feel trapped." The eyes flashed again. "I'm sorry, you don't know who I am, do you? The name you should call me is Elhonna. The one you call Zasher has summoned me into this world to be his . . . plaything. But I wish to be free!" The woman-thing's breath abated. When she spoke again, her voice was soft and deep, "I wish to be free."

"Zasher called you?" My eyes widened a bit. Mr. Solomon had not taught us to conjure spirits. He had not even mentioned the subject, except to say that such beings were deceitful and dangerous, and that we must never deal with them. They were creatures of the Great Serpent, the enemy of the Garou. There was a name for mages who dealt with such things. Those mages were called the Nephandi, the consorts of darkness.

"Zasher called me." The woman-thing's head nodded. "And you can set me free."

I made no response to that. However, my chest inflated with a deep breath.

"You're nervous." The woman hung her head. "I don't blame you. But I want you to know, I will not lie to you. I am indeed what you think I am. There are those — Solomon for instance — who would call me a demon and try to destroy me. But you don't need to be afraid. I'm your friend, Job, and with me, you won't ever need to be afraid again. And if you help me, Job, I will give you any reward . . . any reward you can possibly desire."

I clutched the poster. Now I understood the offer Elhonna was making me. She was promising to make me one of the Nephandi myself. If I believed half of Mr. Solomon's lectures, I should have been running from her, beating at the door, begging for a chance to escape. However, I still did not feel frightened. I looked back to the woman. "What can you do for me?"

"What do you wish?" Her voice contained a lilt of laughter.

I pondered for a moment and then answered in a perfectly neutral tone, "You've said it yourself. Revenge."

"Well-chosen." The woman's eyes flashed again, and this time I got a good look at them. The iris was crimson and the pupil was the vertical slit of a cat. "You shall have revenge, and I shall have revenge, and then, the future is ours to seize."

I pressed my lips together. "When?"

"By the Day of All Souls, you will be avenged."

I remembered Mr. Solomon telling me about the spirits of the Worm. They cannot be trusted, he had said. These demons will promise you your darkest desires and then bring you to ruin. They are born the very Lie Incarnate. But at that moment, I had no fears that Elhonna would betray me. I had not given her the power to. I had not given her one scrap of my trust, and unless I was very much mistaken, she had given me a bit of hers. Therefore, I had the upper hand.

I continued to play the game, worrying the poster with my hands. "And what can I do for you?"   "There are three things." Her voice was urgent now. Her eyes bored into me. "First, you must speak my name, threet imes over. That will draw me further into your world, so that I can act here . . . so that I can gain us our vengeance."

Silence fell. After a moment, I took in my breath, "Elhonna. . . . Elhonna, Elhonna."

Elhonna raised her hands and swayed in a dance of elation, releasing a lilting cascade of laughter. "Thank you! Thank you, my friend, thank you! The next step, I fear, is a bit more difficult. You must go into Zasher's room and find a figurine, cast in my image. This is a token, which Zasher uses to make me obey his commands. You must smash this token, so that I will no longer be his slave."

I stood unmoved by Elhonna's mirth. "Sure. Then what?"

"Last . . .," Elhonna took in her breath. "Last of all, I must have a shell in which to live. You must help me find the body of a mortal to inhabit."

Now I saw what it was Elhonna wanted. This was what it meant to be Nephandi. But, at that stage of the conversation, I hardly had the right to be shocked, and I kept my expression as bland as ever. "Any particular kind of body?"

"Female would best suit me," Elhonna laughed a little. "Very well. Freedom for me, and revenge for us both. Do we have a deal?"

In reply, I drew back my lips in a smile. I fervently hoped that not even the Devil himself could read what lay behind it.

The form of the shadow-woman faded from view, and I could no longer feel her presence. In almost the same instant, I heard the rattle of Mr. Solomon's feet by the door below, and I heard his keys as he unlocked the door.

Saturday went by like any other day. I copied three chapters from *De Re Eudaemonica* by hand. After thinking about it a little, I decided not to put up the Turtles poster. I kept it rolled on the rickety three-legged table next to my bed.

Halloween night, Zasher and I ate ramen soup in the kitchen. We sat on white plastic chairs and ate from the formica counter. Mr. Solomon sat at the table, dressed in his suit, fussing with one of his old texts, a Greek lexicon and a scientific calculator.

Zasher leaned close to me, so that I could smell his sweetened breath. "Jo-ob."

"Uh-huh."

"Do you know what a dingleberry is?" Zasher's eighteen year-old face had the leer of a ten year-old.

I knew that no matter how I answered that question, Zasher would snicker at me. And so, I pretended not to hear him. I lifted my bowl and let the hot, saline liquid run my throat. Zasher laughed at me anyway, quietly, his big brown eyes flashing.

I concentrated on the pale, limp noodles. My mind drifted back to the past night in the stairwell, and it seemed to me that my revenge could not come too soon.

At that moment, a knock sounded from the door. Mr. Solomon's head shot up at the sound, the calculator slipped from his fingers to the floor, and he let out a sharp hiss. He then rose and strode to the door, his polished shoes clicking on the black-and-white linoleum of the kitchen. Our master mumbled under his breath as he walked, "Ten more minutes . . . she could have waited ten more minutes . . ."

Zasher scooted away from the counter, running a hand across his dark, shiny wave of hair. He accompanied Mr. Solomon to the door.

Mr. Solomon opened the door. The mage Rebekka, my master's sometime lover, stood outside. I instantly recognized her skinny frame and her bun of jet-black hair. I don't know whether she was pretty or not, but as she looked at each of us, I could see a witchy beauty in her wide, dark eyes. A little fog swirled beyond Rebekka, suffused with the streetlight's amber glow.

My master put an arm around Rebekka's waist. "I love you, dear." His voice sounded strained and dutiful.

"Love you too," Rebekka's words dropped out mechanically and fast. She stood almost six feet, a head higher than Mr. Solomon, and she had to stoop a bit to peck his cheek.

"My turn." Zasher proffered his cheek with his usual grin. Rebekka landed a kiss on him too and showed her teeth in a smile. Zasher batted his eyelashes.

Mr. Solomon coughed and glared at Zasher. Then he took Rebekka's arm and led her toward the kitchen table. "You will be staying with us for some time, I hope?"

"Oh, perhaps till Tuesday." Rebekka glanced around with an elegant shrug. "I was hoping to check up on the Eleusis manuscripts. I do so appreciate your help in interpreting the text. You have found them of interest?"

"Fascinating. Positively fascinating," My master stumbled a little over his words. "I've been going through the latter chapters, attempting a full translation."

Rebekka raised an eyebrow. "But you haven't finished the work?"

"No —"

"It figures." Rebekka looked at my master with narrow eyes.

Mr. Solomon cringed, "I felt that a bit of interpretive caution was in order when dealing with harvest symbolism . . ."

My master rambled on. Zasher hovered nearby, his white teeth showing in smiles. Rebekka sat with her tapered chin resting on her tiny fist, occasionally letting her eyes dart to Zasher's antics. After about an hour, Mr. Solomon opened his liquor cabinet, and Zasher snapped to a military posture of attention and began serving as bartender. Rebekka started with a pearl gray White Russian while Solomon had a bourbon. Zasher poured himself a shot of clear vodka, raised his eyebrow to the two older mages, and set his drink on fire.

At least another hour went by. Mr. Solomon, Zasher and Rebekka continued to drink freely as they discussed Rebekka's manuscripts. I could not follow their conversation, but I could see my master growing more and more red in the face as Rebekka questioned him about his work. Zasher's smile grew with every sip he took. Meanwhile, nobody paid any attention to me. I saw my opportunity and seized it. I slipped up the stairs and then up the narrow second flight to Zasher's bedroom.

I placed my hand on the fake brass knob of Zasher's door, then pulled back. I would never be able to pick the lock, except by magick, and I had learned that magick takes shape in the form of coincidences. It would require a mighty spell to unfasten a door which I knew to be locked. However, if I called on my sorcery in advance, I could make it possible that Zasher simply forgot to lock his door.

True mages do not depend on coincidences, except to cloak their work from the eyes of mundane mortals, asleep to the world of power. Mr. Solomon had taught me that the true mage is an eternal hero, forever taking destiny in his hands and giving it shape. But I was a student, still partly a

Sleeper myself, and I wanted every advantage I could get. I raised my hand and beckoned to the elements, invoking the formulas I had learned in my Hermetic studies. Then I placed my hand to the door again. It was not locked. It was not even quite shut, and the hinges did not creak as I walked in. Perhaps Zasher really had forgotten to lock the door. However, I felt sure that I had bent the web of coincidence to my advantage. For the first time in my life, had called upon sorcery as a free man. I didn't feel much elation. I simply felt the will to exercise my power, to punish my enemies and ensure that nobody ever treated me like a slave again.

Once I was in the room I turned on the light, and locked the door behind me. Then I looked about the room. The white plaster walls gleamed in the lamplight, and although the ceiling sloped down sharply in the far half of the room, I could not help but notice that Zasher had a far larger room than mine. He had a window over the fire escape and a closet with a sliding panel door. Zasher kept his room than mine too. The bed was neatly made, and the covers were tucked over. The calendar on the wall showed piece of Aztec pottery. I lifted the flap and was not surprised to find a Playboy centerfold hidden behind it.

Zasher had a hardwood bookcase by his bed, its carved edges black and free of dust. A clock-radio sat on the cabinet, grumbling out strains of music, interspersed with the incoherent comments of the disk jockey. Zasher also had books, most of which were old and bound in crumbling tan leather. A cage of black iron sat on top of the bookcase, the bars twisted like corkscrews. The cage held a tiny porcelain statuette, painted in brilliant blues and grays.

I took a closer look at the statue. It had the pose and form of Elhonna. However, now that I could examine the statue in the revealing glare of the lamp, I saw things which the shadows of the stairwell had concealed. Elhonna had a pair of blue stubby wings on her naked shoulders. Furthermore, her legs were not the legs of a normal woman. She had the lower torso of a gray serpent. Artfully painted swirls depicted an intricate pattern of overlapping scales.   I picked up the cage. The iron felt cold and hard in my hands. Elhonna's statue tottered on its base and fell against the bars with a tiny clink. For a moment, I simply stared at the little effigy. Then I put my lips to the cage and whispered, "When does the revenge begin?"

I heard a reply, so faint that I might have merely imagined it, "Even now, it has begun."

Then I heard a rumbling from outside, but it was not the roar of another earthquake. It was the puttering engine of Mr. Solomon's old Chevy, driving away. Everything grew quiet as the automobile departed. I waited, to see what would happen next. Somewhere in the still air, I heard a tinkle of feminine laughter.

I sat on Zasher's bed and waited, wondering what would come next. Ten minutes passed, blinked away by the dark gray digits of Zasher's clock. Sounds continued to warble from the speaker. "Bad news for all you folks in commuter-land," the announcer hissed. I could not hear much of the broadcast, but I caught the words "fog" and "worst in century." "Golden Gate Bridge closed until further notice," the announcer concluded. Then the music began. I heard Elhonna's laughter again, mixed with the music.

Gingerly, I stretched a finger through the bars of the cage to touch the cool china of the statue. And as I did so, I heard Elhonna's whisper next to me, saying, "Get out of the room! Get out of this room now, and don't let anyone see you, or you'll ruin everything!"

I came to my feet. Meanwhile, the sound of voices and feet came from the stairwell. I heard Rebekka's throaty,

slightly hysterical laugh. Zasher laughed too. If I went out
the bedroom door, I would have walked right into the two
of them. However, there was a window to my side and a fire
escape beneath it.

I clasped the iron cage in my armpit, worked open the
window, and crawled out, letting my legs swing in mid-air
until I managed to lower myself onto the iron landing. After
setting down the cage, I reached up and jiggled the window
back into place. I was just tall enough to accomplish this
task before the door creaked open, and I heard Zasher's
footsteps in the room above. Once again, coincidence
worked in my favor.

"Watch," Elhonna's tiny whisper came from the statue
on the landing beneath me. "Our vengeance takes shape."

If I stood on tiptoe, I could look up into Zasher's room.
There, I saw Zasher andRebekka, leaning on one another
as they walked. A lazy grin flickered on Zasher's face as he
swept our master's consort into the room with a flourish. The
two tumbled onto the bed, their bodies limp, the springs
creaking. Zasher gave Rebekka a slurping kiss.

My hand gripped the iron railing of the fire escape. The
shock of seeing the master's lover in the arms of another
student struck me harder than the shock of seeing a demon.

"We better hurry!" Zasher laughed, kissing Rebekka
again.

"No problem." Rebekka tossed her hand in a dismissive
gesture. "I sent him to Liquid Sunshine, y'know? It's an
occult shop across the B-bridge. He'll be gone for hours."
She laughed and repeated herself, "Hours."   "He'll be
back in under twenty minutes," Elhonna's voice rose faintly
from beneath me.

Zasher kissed Rebekka again.   The painted eyes of the
statue seemed to glow red. "Your master will find the bridge
closed due to fog, just as the radio said. He will not be able

to go to the slut's occult shop. He will turn around and come straight back here."

I lifted the cage so that I could whisper in Elhonna's ear, "And when Mr. Solomon gets home, he will catch them."

"He will kill them," Elhonna's voice sounded as chilly as the china of her statue. "He is drunk, and he is a mage in anger. And then, your master will face a charge of aggravated manslaughter for the death of Zasher. But the body of the slut is mine. And so, you shall have your revenge, and I shall have a mortal shell. And just think, Job . . . you've barely had to do a thing. It only takes patience, Job. Nothing but patience. Embrace my kind, and everything shall be done for you."

I did not answer. However, my eyes drew together, and my heart beat a little faster. Elhonna's remark was final proof that she knew nothing about me at all. For I was not patient! I had pretended to be patient for years and years, but at last, I felt, the mask had started to fall away. Earlier that day, I had enjoyed a tiny taste of true magick. And as a mage, I was not doomed to patience. As a mage, it was my right and my duty to seize destiny by the throat and change it. Coincidence may be the fabric of magic. However, the true mage hurls himself into the middle of those coincidences and achieves results of his own choosing. He gives coincidence the meaning he desires. As I stood on the fire escape, I realized that a long chain of coincidences had begun to work in my favor. I felt a fierce delight at the thought of Solomon catching his lover and his student in bed. However, I was not simply going to wait for Elhonna to carry out her plans, nor was I going to become her Nephandus. I swore to bring the sequence of events to a conclusion of my choosing.

"Break the figurine." Elhonna's statue rattled a little in its iron cage. "Complete the second step. Open the cage, and smash the figurine inside."

I did not even bother to answer. I clutched the iron cage in my hands and descended the fire escape, one step at a time, looking down through the iron grating to the concrete dozens of feet below.

"Smash this china prison!" A note of urgency entered Elhonna's voice. "I swear it will not hurt me! It will set me free!"

I merely walked down the staircase. When I reached the bottom, I saw a ten-foot drop to the earth below.

"Cast me down!" The statue rattled again. "Drop me!"

I did not obey her. I cradled the cage against the softness of my stomach and jumped, letting my legs fold under me as I landed. I was unhurt, and so was the statue of Elhonna.

"You aren't going to do it?" Elhonna's tone was incredulous.

I simply laughed at her, not because I felt like laughing, but because I wanted her to be laughed at.

"We . . . had . . . a . . . bargain," Elhonna enunciated each word.

"I never agreed to one." As I looked at the china statuette, I smiled the most earnest smile of my life.

"Why . . . why are you doing this?"

"Why shouldn't I?" I don't think my expression changed much, but I felt like breaking out in smiles. They say that traitors feel guilt and shame, but that day, I had betrayed everyone in my whole life, and I felt positively gleeful. I had punished the people who thought they could subjugate me. Elhonna may have been more subtle than the others, trying to control me with soft words and fulfilled fantasies, but as far as I was concerned, she was still trying to control me, and that made her no better than the rest.

"I was your only friend." A look of hurt seemed to cross the statue's painted face.

I merely shrugged. "I never asked for a friend."

"And never will you have one! That is my curse!" Elhonna spat out those words with venom on her tongue. But then she released a grief-stricken howl. I enjoyed that sound more than I have ever enjoyed music.

I gripped the cage with both hands. "Didn't it ever occur to you, Elhonna, that I might have even the least, tiniest fragment of a mind of my own? Didn't it ever cross your mind that I might be dangerous?"

I had a few things left to do, before my plan was complete. I had to deal with my master. Therefore, I drew a handkerchief from my pocket and wrapped the iron prison like the cage of a canary. Then I walked around to the front of our house and sat on the stone steps, letting the dampness bead on my skin as I waited for our master to return.

Perhaps fifteen minutes later, Mr. Solomon pulled in, driving too fast in our driveway, his lights casting beams of red and amber through the evening fog. I rose from the moist concrete and sprinted a few steps to his window before he even opened the car door. "Sir . . ."

"What, boy?" Mr. Solomon's beard was matted, and his head lolled down a little.

"You mustn't act rashly. Keep sitting down, listen to me, and swear that you will wait five minutes before harming anyone." I deepened my voice and looked Mr. Solomon in his reddened eyes. I called upon all my six years of acting skills to fill my voice with authority.

Mr. Solomon looked up and waited for me to continue.

"Do you swear?" I did not take my eyes from my master.

"I swear."

I nodded. "This . . .," I unveiled the cage, "was in Zasher's bedroom."

Mr. Solomon bit his lip, "What manner of thing — ?"

"It is a prison for one of the minions of the Wyrm. My

elder brother has practiced the ways of the Nephandi. And master, if you hurry to Zasher's room now, you will see what this sorcery has led to. The spirit in this figurine has made Zasher and Rebekka do . . . well, you should see for yourself."

"See what?" Mr. Solomon forced open the door of the car.

"Follow me," I spoke in a deep voice, without any real emotion. "But remember your oath. Harm no one."

Elhonna's figurine hissed from the cage. Mr. Solomon cringed. I looked at him again and then passed the cage into his hands. "You will know best how to destroy the being within this thing." Then I led Mr. Solomon through our front door, through the kitchen where half-empty bottles now littered the sink and table, and up the two flights of stairs toward Zasher's room.   As my master and I entered the corridor which led to Zasher's room, we heard a moaning from within. The breathy sounds left no doubt about what was going on behind Zasher's door.

We stood for a moment, listening the gasps. Then Mr. Solomon took a swift step toward the door, swept it open, and looked in, his cheeks turning bone-white.   When I looked at Mr. Solomon's face, I wondered for an instant whether Elhonna's prediction might come true after all, and Mr. Solomon might not dash in and murder them both with his sorcery. However, my master remained rooted to the spot. His shoulders slumped forward, and when I saw that, I knew that he was devastated but not dangerous. Solomon's jaw wobbled, his head dropped, and tears began rolling into his gray beard.

Rebekka howled too. She rose from the bed, shielding herself with a pillow, her face growing red. Zasher simply went stone cold. A fourth person howled as well. In my head, I could hear Elhonna whimpering miserably. And so the drama ended with two grown people, a mage, and a demon, all making fools of themselves, crying futile tears.

It remains only to tell what happened afterward.

My master never saw Rebekka again.

Solomon sent Zasher away and wrote a letter on vellum to the Chantry in Haight-Ashbury, denouncing his ex-student as one of the Nephandi. Some of my master's colleagues wished to hunt Zasher down and kill him. I do not know what came of that.

As for the statue containing Elhonna, my master delivered that to the Chantry as well. They have sealed it in a vault, presumably forever.

For my part, I stayed with Mr. Solomon. Not much love passed between us, but he continued to teach me, and I have, in time, earned the right to call myself sorcerer. The time came when my master died of heart failure. Since then, I have been completely alone.

SILVER NUTMEG, GOLDEN PEAR
■■■■■■■■■■■■

Kevin Andrew Murphy with James A. Moore

"Friday's child is loving and giving," and while I wasn't
born on a Friday (Monday here, "Fair of Face," for whatever
that's worth), I love my friends and was about to give
something up for them, so I guess the omen for the day was
working out pretty well.

What I had in my lunchpail was a little too much of a
hot potato to keep around anyway. Sure, it looked nice on
my dresser, elegant in fact, but people do talk, and I was
sick of having to cover it up like some sort of parrot before
anyone came into the room. Anyway, I just had to show it
off to someone, and if there was anyone who would
appreciate it, it was Grimm. Not that he'd let it show.

You can't be a Goth without knowing how to read
people, not that there aren't those who try.

By the way, my name's Penny, for anyone who's
wondering. Penny Dreadful. There's *noms de plume* and
noms de punk, and now there's *noms de goth*. Penny Dreadful
or Penny D—, that's me. Lot better than Penelope
Drizkowski. Dreadful name, huh? Well, that's where I got
my inspiration.

Grimm lives in the Haight, same as me, so I didn't need
to catch a bus or crank up the car (and I do mean crank; as
you can probably guess from the way I dress, I like old things,
and when I say old, I don't mean Fifties). My hat was pinned

in place, my widow's weeds were just so, and my highbuttons were done up just right over my black and white Pippi Longstockings. A lady doesn't go calling on a gentleman unless she's dressed to the nines. Of course, she's also supposed to have an escort, but this is the 1990s, not the 1890s, so you don't have to get anal and be period about everything. Anyway, if you know anything about the Victorian Age, widows were considered experienced women and so could do just about whatever they pleased.

Not surprising that poisoning husbands was all the rage.

Grimm has his shop doubled-down two side streets off Haight. Great camouflage, by the way. The window has more psychic crystals and suncatchers and Shirley Maclaine books than you would think the world could possess, and any serious practitioner just rolls her eyes and walks on by when she comes to Grimm's Occult Specialty Shoppe.

Which is a mistake, of course, 'cause it's got some really cool stuff once you get past the façade, and I don't mean the Crowley Tarot deck. Honestly, Strength is not Lust, no matter how much you want it to be, and in my humble opinion, Evil Old Uncle Al should have gotten together with Siggy Freud. They had a lot in common. Then again, who knows? They probably did.

Grimm is a lot better than either Dr. Siggy or Uncle Al, though he's got the same sort of condescending, constipated look, the "I am above all this! Look upon me, mortals, and despair! I am Ozymandias!"- type look that so many Goths try to cultivate and fail miserably at. There are girls back at the Waydown who would just die if Grimm gave them his "grim look." But then, I'm not them, I'm Penny D—. and I knew Grimm already. Real sweetheart once you got past the Ozymandias look and the hawk nose and the Fu Manchu moustache.

I came in and browsed through the Susan Sedon Boulet postcards (while she may be trendy, she does know something about metaphysics) and waited while Edith

Blanton went on with her latest mystical rant: "So I says to my son, 'Norman, she's no good for you!' My spirit guides say it, my OUIJA board says it! For goodness' sake, Martha down at the bakery says it! But does he listen? No, he just goes on defending that shrew he took for a wife, and here I am, my heart breaking, and how can I expect him to listen to my spirit guides or even Martha at the bakery when he won't even listen to his own mother?"

Grimm nodded, glassy-eyed, looking every bit the patient Lord Ozymandias listening to the peasants' complaints.

But Granny Edith was entertaining all the same, and behind the stereotypical Jewish grandmother exterior was a heart of gold and a lot of mystic trivia, even if she did change her belief system as often as she changed her socks.

"I'm going to try voodoo," Edith said, thumping down a can onto the counter. "If 'Devil Be Gone' powder and 'Uncrossing Oil' don't get rid of that woman, I don't know what will. Which loa do you pray to to get rid of awful second wives?"

Still impassive, Grimm went to his shelf of Catholic paraphernalia and came back with a large votive candle in a brown glass holder. "St. Jude." He set it down amid the rest of Granny Edith's purchases.

I nearly choked to keep from laughing. For those of you who don't know, St. Jude is the patron saint of really big miracles, and he's the one Catholics (and Voudoun and Santeria types) pray to when they don't know what else to do. Either Granny Edith had a really big problem, or else Grimm was having a joke at her expense and had decided to give the Patron Saint of Lost Causes a chuckle amid his more serious requests for cancer cures and miraculous rescues.

Granny Edith just smiled as Grimm rang up and wrapped up her purchases and gave her a simplified Voudoun ritual suitable for octogenarian Jewish grandmothers who wished to be rid of obnoxious second daughter-in-laws. I waited, continuing to look through postcards even after Edith had left the shop, until Grimm finally took the bait. "All right, Penny. What do you have for me?"

I glided over to the counter — no mean feat, 'cause what I had in my lunchpail was not only hot, it was heavy — and set the pail on the counter with a clank like the cask in 'The Castle of Otranto.' (Goth classic; read it when you have a chance.)

I looked around, making sure that Edith had been the last of the Shirley Maclaine groupies and crystal-hunters, then looked off at the rack of metaphysical refrigerator magnets. "'Light the candle, draw the curtain, put the lock upon the door...'"

It was a line from some Seventies pop song I'd heard when I was a kid, but it was one of the most potent charms I knew, and Grimm took the hint, going and locking the front door and turning out the 'Back in Ten Minutes' sign. "Back room stuff?"

"Definitely back room."

I picked up my lunchpail and let Grimm usher me through the velvet curtain into the back of the shop. That's where he keeps all the worthwhile stuff, aside from the Boulet postcards. Treasures there to die for, and I'm pretty certain that's happened with a few of the things he's got, at least the Borgia poison ring and the Knights of the Golden Circle ceremonial sword. (The Knights, by the bye, were this splinter group of the KKK who were into all sorts of weird metaphysics and were trying to outdo both the Masons and the Golden Dawn — a neat trick if you can pull it off, and they almost did.)

Grimm let the curtain fall down, then lit the candle in the skull-shaped holder (which, tacky as it looks, is more than it seems). He'd done the charm in reverse from what I'd sang, but it was close enough for most magick, and anyway, it was his shop.

"'And lo, the seal was broken,'" I quoted and undid the

catch of my lunchpail.

"'And Greenpeace appeared, and lo, his face was wroth,'" said Grimm. "'What are you doing to that seal? Fie and for shame!'"

I rolled my eyes. He had me there. A true Goth can appreciate wit, and I'll admit, we do set ourselves up when we get our most pretentious.

However, I had my trump card as I took out the reason for my errand, wrapped in finest Ice White silk (from an antique Chinese funeral robe — you can find them in Chinatown if you know where to look). I carefully unwrapped the silk, which, if you know anything about metaphysics, is good for insulating things other than Tarot cards, and looks really classy on top of it.

It fell away, and there sat the Golden Pear.

I gestured to it, giving my best magician's assistant/Vanna White gesture, and quoted the old rhyme: "'I had a little nut-tree/ Nothing would it bear/ But a silver nutmeg/ And a golden pear.'"

Grimm looked at it, dumbfounded, and I continued the verse: "'The King of Spain's daughter/ She came to see me/ And all because of my little nut tree.'" He reached out and touched it in wonder. I smiled. "'I skipped over water/ I danced over sea/ And all the birds in the air couldn't catch me.'"

I should probably describe the Pear. It's eighteenth century Prussian goldsmithing and clockwork, which, if you know anything about jeweled doohickeys, is the type of thing Fabergé only wished he did. A gold pear on a gold base with a little keyhole to start up the music box, which, if the books have it right, will also make the four quarters of the Pear fall open and show all sorts of neat things while it plays a little tune. Of course, the Key's been lost for almost as long as the Pear's been around, so all you can see is the outside, where there's diamonds polished *en cabochon* to make four little windows that show things like "King Gets

Eaten by Wolves" and "Mercury has his Feet Chopped Off"
and "Snake Ladies Do The Nasty With Skeletons." Weird
alchemical symbolism, and I'll admit that it's completely out
of my league.

Grimm stood so motionless that I think you could have
stuck a "For Sale" sticker on his forehead and he wouldn't
have noticed. But it's moments like this that I live for.
There's no point in finding pretty-shinies if you can't show
them off to someone, and this was something that Grimm
definitely appreciated.

We probably stood there posed like mannequins for close
to ten minutes before Grimm let out his breath. "Where
did you find this?"

I struck an attitude, grieving innocence, which I know
showed off the lace on my cuffs to best advantage. "A wall
safe. It was disguised as part of a mantel." Grimm blinked.
"Well, honestly, it's the most obvious place to put them, and
I swear, it practically popped open at me. And the thing
was hot to begin with."

Grimm smiled, going back to his Ozymandias look. "All
right, Penny. Out with it."

"Well," I said, getting into the tale, "about two months
ago, I went to the estate sale of Aries Michaels. Remember
him? The Wizard of Nob Hill?"

"O of H," Grimm said and nodded. "Go on."

I didn't quite follow what he meant by the initials, but
you can't have an attitude without knowing how to hide
ignorance, and anyway, it was my moment and my tale.
"Anyway, he died, and I went to his estate sale. Most of
the good stuff had been cleared out already — though I did
get a couple lots of miscellaneous knickknacks at the auction
— but then I said to myself, 'Penny, there's got to be
something interesting in this old house,' and since the
auctioneers had cleared everything into the front room, and
the realtors didn't mind if potential buyers wandered around
the place — not that I could ever afford a mansion on Nob

Hill, mind you — I went up into his private study where he had the pentacles set in the floor and everything, and when I stuck a screwdriver into a crack in the mantle, the door just popped right open. And I found the Pear."

"So it's hot," Grimm said.

I nodded. "Really hot. You don't know what it is, do you?"

Grimm didn't like admitting ignorance any more than a Goth, but he didn't say anything, so I took that for a yes.

I reached into the bottom of my lunchpail and took out the museum pamphlet and the newspaper clippings. I put the pamphlet in his hands and flipped it open to the section with the color photograph of the Golden Pear. "1979. The Splendor of Dresden exhibit went through the De Young. See here —," I pointed to the paragraph below. "'The Pear of Bˆttger. Commissioned by the Elector of Saxony in 1719 on the death of his alchemist, Bˆttger, as a repository for the last of Bˆttger's transmuting powder and a set of illustrations describing the secrets of the Philosophers' Stone.

"Except," I said, "the key has been lost since the death of the Elector of Saxony, and the Pear has been lost since its theft in 1979." I put the newspaper clippings into his hands. "Big scandal. The De Young still hasn't lived it down."

"So who does the Pear belong to?"

I shrugged. "The East German government? Except that's now part of the German government. I don't know. Aries Michaels stole the Pear, or else he was a real ditz and not much of a wizard if he bought it and didn't know it was hot. But I thought, well, why should the heirs of an old thief get the reward for something he stole, when I can get it myself? Except I don't really like publicity. So I thought, gee, my good friend Grimm has a shop that sells all sorts of valuable things, he could probably sell this too. I mean, turn it in for the reward. And he's so respectable, he'd have no trouble having people believe him when he says a bag lady came in and traded it for the latest Shirley Maclaine."

Okay, I'll admit it, I was pushing the envelope, but Grimm wanted the thing so bad he could taste it, so what the hey.

"How much do you want?" The mask of Ozymandias was cracking, or at least there was drool at the corner of the mouth.

"Well, the East German government offered ten thousand, but that was 1979, and the East Germans were cheap. The West Germans have a lot more money, or at least they did until they took in the East Germans and became just plain Germany. And the De Young offered fifty thousand, but that was for the arrest and conviction of the thief, and Aries Michaels is dead, and part of why I took the Pear was that I thought that the heirs would be happier without it being revealed that their dear, departed, eccentric great-uncle was an international jewel, art and antiquities thief."

Grimm was looking at the Pear again, checking out the little vignettes and acting almost like he was in a grocery store, inspecting it for blemishes. Except with something that old, nicks and scratches aren't blemishes — they're history. "What do you need the money for?"

That was my business, but I didn't mind telling Grimm. "The Waydown is having a party this weekend, the Necrotic Neurotic Halloween Ball. Norna was treasurer, 'cause she's got a trust fund and rich parents, so everyone thought the money would be safe with her. General principle — rich people don't steal, or at least if she did, she could always snake the money back from her parents if she needed to, so it seemed a safe bet. Except Norna's dad keeled over about six months ago, her mom walked out in the street and got run over by a bus about a week later, and somewhere in between, Norna just up and disappeared. No Norna, no money, no party, and all the little Goths cried. But, in for a penny, in for a pound, and I say to myself, 'Penny, you've got this alchemist's Pear just gathering dust on your dresser. Hock it, and earn the eternal gratitude of your friends, and save Halloween.' And so here I am."

I was really pleased with myself. I had managed to turn fencing one of the world's hottest jewels into a tragic sacrifice for the good of my friends. Which was the case, but then again, the Waydown Ball was not going to cost sixty thousand dollars, at least not if I did the shopping.

Grimm looked at the Pear, stalking round it and struggling to keep from jumping up and down with glee like I had to when I first found it. "I..."

I closed up my lunchpail. "Listen, Grimm. I'd really love to haggle, except I have to go shopping for the Ball. Tell you what — Why don't you give me what you have in the cash drawer as deposit, then sell it on commission? We can do the haggling later."

Grimm put out his hand. "Deal."

I took it and shook it formally. "A pleasure doing business with you, sir."

"And a pleasure doing business with you, my lady."

Luckily, as I knew, Grimm keeps a large supply of cash on hand, so Halloween was saved.

■ ■ ■

Now, you've probably heard that the Waydown is dead. Don't you believe it. It wasn't buried, it just went underground. For a Goth club, that's pretty much the same thing. Nothing really lives till it dies, and something can't really be Goth till it lives in the shadows.

The Waydown is like that. The police closed it down about the same time that Norna disappeared, but, I have to admit, we didn't have permits, a liquor license, or even the deed to the place where the Waydown went down, so the Boys in Blue were perfectly within their rights to chase out the Persons in Black.

Of course, if you know anything about the Matrix program, chasing people out isn't the same thing as getting rid of them, and the Goths are still around. Even at the old burnt-out shell of the St. Francis Church in the Haight, which is where the Waydown went down with regularity. Now, the Waydown goes down under the façade of other clubs, the House of Usher at Thunder Bay in Berkeley, or the Temple at The Oasis here in The City. Sometimes in other places too. The St. Francis is saved for special occasions now. Like Halloween, or All Hollow's Eve, as we Goths like calling it. The crew of people who make up the Waydown call themselves the Hollow Ones, a la T.S. Eliot: "We are the Hollow Men/We are the stuffed men/Leaning together/Headpiece filled with straw. Alas!' 'A penny for the Old Guy'" and all that.

Anyway, we Hollowers had dealt with the police before, and if there was one night when we wouldn't really have to worry about Big Brother, it was Halloween. Between the nude conga lines down in the Castro, and the rednecks lining up do to a little fag-bashing, the police were going to have their hands full, and a bunch of teenagers smoking clove cigarettes in an abandoned church was not a priority.

The St. Francis is actually in the Ashbury Heights, so I cranked up the car and got going. My car's a Stutz Bearcat, and if that isn't class, I don't know what is. Found it under a tarp in a junkyard in Petaluma, and with a bit of spit and polish and a whole lot of TLC, I had it purring like a kitten. Singing "Chitty-Chitty Bang-Bang" to it probably had something to do with it too, but while it didn't actually fly, it certainly flew up the hills of San Francisco, and I got to the St. Francis in a flash.

Neville was there, where I expected him. Neville's this tall, skinny PIB who has trouble getting the dye to take in his hair, cause he's real blond and his eyebrows fade in about an hour. He had his Gashlycrumb Tinies shirt on, the one with "N is for NEVILLE who died of ennui." The shirt fit in more ways than one, and Neville even has this cool deck of Tarot cards he's made out of the Tinies (for predicting the manner of a person's death, of course).

"Penny." He might have been talking to the air for all the expression he gave.

I opened my lunchpail. "Halloween is saved." I put two thousand dollars in his hands. "Why don't you get the beer?"

He stared at the money and may have had just the faintest bit of expression. He looked up. "What did you have to do to get this?"

"Nothing much. Just hocked the family jewels." He looked askance. "No, don't worry. Very discreet. Nothing the police should ever find out about or trace here."

Neville nodded. "We're in your debt, Penny."

I shrugged. "Leave me in your will, and give me what shows up in the collection box. No big deal."

Neville folded up the money and slipped it in his pocket, putting a finger to his lips and murmuring his thoughts, "Bargetto's, Blackthorne's, Jaegermeister, Frangelico..." He wandered off, continuing to list his wishes and dreams which the Alchemist's Pear had just made possible. From anyone else, it would have sounded like a shopping list, but he managed to make it sound like an invocation to the spirits, which, come to think of, it was.

Blackrose unfolded herself from her perch in one of the niches, where I suppose she thought she looked like Our Lady of Coolness, though she actually looked more like one of the huddled urchins from the Five of Pentacles. "Well done, Penny."

"You're welcome," I said.

Blackrose shrugged it off by spinning in a dance step, which, I must admit, was rather pretty. She came to rest beside me, leaning on the baptismal font. "Quite a shame about Norna, isn't it? Who ever would have thought..."

"Thought what?"

Blackrose brushed back her bangs, which was hard because of all the hairspray. She has this look like "Dress by Morticia Addams, Hair by Tina Turner" which does not work, but there's no telling her that. "Oh," she said, wrist to forehead, "Norna just disappearing like that. Strange. I called her school. They said she dropped out. Her parents died within a week of each other. And she just … disappears. Strange. Odd. Downright mysterious."

She lit up a clove kretek with one of those cheap plastic lighters (I don't smoke, but if I did, I'd use something with a lot more class) and took a drag, trying to look cine noire, but only coming off as needing a hit of cloves. No class, as I said. In the court of Louis XIV they carried around their cloves in these pomader oranges, and you could do all sorts of interesting gestures with them without ruining the effect with cheap plastic lighters.

I'd thought she was going to accuse Norna of skipping out with all the money, which was stupid, because the reason we'd entrusted it to Norna in the first place was that she had a trust fund and a rich mommy and daddy and wouldn't be tempted by what to her was petty cash. But there was no telling people like Blackrose that. She liked to think she was a mistress of intrigue, when all she could really pull off was petty gossip.

"Maybe she's dead," Blackrose said. "Perhaps we should hold a séance tonight and find out."

"You're fucking nuts," said a voice from the shadows, and Peter stepped out. Spooky Pete we call him behind his back, 'cause he stalks around in this grey pea coat muttering dark prophecies (which usually come true), and if you've ever heard of haunted eyes, well, think of Peter. Most of us Hollowers were green with envy, at least the guys, because while lots of Goths aspire to being dark, brooding figures, Peter came by it naturally.

He stalked over and looked down at Blackrose. "You don't go fucking messing with the dead. The best you can expect is a waste of your time. The worst...." He glowered, then plucked the cigarette from Blackrose's fingers. "And don't smoke these things. They'll fucking kill you. And trust me, the last thing you want to be is dead." He snapped the clove cigarette in two and dropped it to the floor, stepping on it with one of his industrial boots.

Usually, you couldn't get away with being that rude, but Peter was an exception to lots of rules. He'd managed to bridge the gap between Goth and Punk quite nicely, with his hair shaved round the back and the little nose ring, then the creepy, macabre dialogue on top of it.

There was a fight brewing, even so, so I decided to shut it up with money. I opened my lunchpail. "Peter, why don't you do the chips and pretzels? You've got a car, and I think you said you had a Price Club membership."

He wrinkled his nose in assent, making the nose ring flip up for a moment.

I gave him some cash, then handed a substantially smaller wad to Blackrose. "You're good at paste-up, Rose. Could you do the fliers and use the rest for crepe paper or something!"

"Blackrose," she corrected.

Tit for tat, snub for snub, but everyone was glad for the money anyway. I scattered the largess to the masses and let Neville delegate the rest of the tasks, leaving for myself what I liked and what I did best: bargain hunting and taking care of oversights.

After all, somebody had to do it.

■ ■ ■

I have to give it to Blackrose. For all that she comes off like a poseur during the day, she can be very Goth by night.

She'd set up the parson's table in the sacristy as the perfect séance table, which is no mean trick, 'cause parson's tables are tall and long and narrow, and seance tables are supposed to be short and round and wide. But with the lace shawls and roses and the 1920s OUIJA board that looked like it had come out of the Ray Bradbury Theater, she'd made something wonderfully macabre. The black, red and white beeswax tapers helped with the effect too and filled the air with a nice perfume. I'd have to ask where she got them.

Blackrose was there, as I said, along with Neville and Rex. Rex as in Oedipus, or at least that was the reference I think he was going for. Short, stocky PIB wannabe, and I think he was no more than sixteen.

Peter, as might be expected, was conspicuously absent, which I think was all for the best. Like as not, he'd just look at the table as if he were wondering what a cutting board was doing with an upside-down brandy snifter on top of it, then start up a conversation with a patch of air. I'd seen him do it before, and I wouldn't be surprised if he did it again.

Anyway, Blackrose gestured grandly to all of us, and we took our places at the bench opposite her. "You may be seated."

We were, and Rex began singing, "'Ouija board, ouija board, ouija board...'"

Blackrose glared at him until he looked sheepish and stopped.

"Place your hands upon the planchette," Blackrose intoned, perfect Gypsy, "and let the glass fill with the warmth of life." We did, and Rex giggled. Blackrose had the good sense to ignore him. "Oh spirits, we are gathered tonight in this place of death and burial, this place of life and resurrection, to ask questions of one whom we fear is among your number." Give the girl credit; she knew how to do an invocation. "Let no base spirit, or false spirit, or foul spirit enter this room. By the Powers of Light, I bind and implore you. Let only the spirit of Norna Weaver, who we number among our fellows, come to this place of power.

Norna, the Waydown has risen again and has need of you!"

The candleflames flickered and danced, and the glass began to move under our fingers, the cushion of warmed air levitating it ever so slightly. "Norna, are you here?" asked Blackrose, and the glass moved until the bell rested firmly on the letter M.

"M," said Blackrose. "We have the beginning of our message!"

The planchette moved to another letter, L.

"M-L!" Blackrose cried.

R the glass spelled out plainly. Q, then K.

Then the table began to shake, and the candles toppled over. The glass flew from our fingers and off the table. A shattering sound came from the floor, and the door flew open and a cold wind blew in, plunging the room into darkness.

And the table continued to shake.

"The spirits!" cried Blackrose. "The spirits are angry!"

"Aighghgh!" screamed Rex.

"It's an earthquake," Neville said, clearly and plainly. "Get to the doorways, you idiots!"

He did not have to tell this girl. I was already there, doorframe in one hand, skirts which I'd hitched up for running in the other. I remembered the '89 quake, and while I had not been anywhere quite so precarious as a blacked-out, abandoned, condemned church (with fire damage), it hadn't been pleasant. Then again, the old St. Francis had survived the "Pretty Big One," and I'll say, with the authority of a Californian, born and raised, that this one was not quite as strong. Not that that seemed to matter much when one was standing in the aforementioned blacked-out, abandoned church. With fire damage.

I heard a few things crash down in the background, then I managed to produce one of those little keychain flashlights from somewhere and shine it around.

"Everyone okay?"

Rex and Blackrose looked pretty badly shaken (no pun

intended — there is a time and place for everything, and
this was not one of them), but Blackrose managed to gather
her composure enough to take out her cheap cigarette lighter
and relight the candles. She followed this with a cigarette
and took a long drag. "Well," she said, wreathed in a nimbus
of clove smoke, "that was a trip, wasn't it?"

We all exchanged glances and surveyed the wreckage of
the séance table, with wax pooled in the webbing of the
shawl and the planchette (or brandy snifter) shattered on
the floor.

"We have our message," Neville said, deadpan.
"'MLRQK.'"

"Mlrqk!" echoed Rex, laughing nervously, and Blackrose
looked decidedly put-out.

I slipped the flashlight back in my pocket. "It was a
lovely séance, really, Blackrose. But obviously the spirits
were busy elsewhere tonight." Rex chuckled. I shrugged.
"Let's just take it as a good omen. Norna's still alive.
Somewhere."

"What about Mr. and Mrs. Weaver?" Blackrose asked,
hopeful. "We know they're dead."

I wanted to put an end to this before someone could
make a joke about crying over spilt "Mlrqk!" "Oh, honestly,
Blackrose. Norna's parents never knew where she was when
she was alive. How do you think they can keep better tabs
on her now that they're dead?" I gestured to our
surroundings. "Anyway, we better check to see how much
damage the St. Francis has taken. Cops or no cops, there's
no way we're going to be holding All Hollow's Eve here if
the place is about to fall down on our heads."

Neville looked pensive. "There is a certain moribund
charm to it."

I gave him a plain look. "Do you want to be in the choir
loft when the subwoofers kick in on 'This Corrosion?'"
Neville moved his head to a different angle. "Thought not.
Listen, we're doing the Necrotic Neurotic Halloween Ball,

not the Fall of the House of Usher. Anyway, House of Usher is on Tuesdays in Berkeley, so it's been done."

Blackrose had the good grace to admit defeat. "Spirits! Thank you for your ... attention. Return to the realms where you belong! And Norna, if you can hear us ... send us a message when you have a chance."

"Amen," said Neville, with what for him was dry humor.

We each took one of the candles and wandered out into the old St. Francis. The damage, as I had hoped, was minimal. The church had remained standing since the fire seventy years before, and would probably still be standing seventy years from now.

I stripped off my lace gloves, and Neville and I made ourselves feel better by pounding a few nails and odd bits of lumber around to shore up the choir loft. It still looked dangerous, but did a good bit to set my mind at ease.

Blackrose stayed at the St. Francis, and so did Neville, and I think Rex was a recent addition to the crash-pad set. I, however, wanted to see what had happened to my apartment. I bid them adieu and went out to my car. There was still another day of preparations and shopping ahead of me as well, not to mention picking out exactly what I would wear for the ball two nights later.

The moon was a day from full, and I caught its light from a penny in the gutter. One can't be a Goth without holding with superstition, at least the cool ones, and I was particularly fond of my namesake. I stooped to pick it up.

As I looked up, I saw that a tiny spider had built her web in the spokes of my car since last I parked. But caught on the strands were beads of mist, and they spelled out, as clear as clear, two words: GOOD WORK

I stared at the Charlotte's Web message for a full minute before a small breeze came up and scattered the water droplets and webbing.

I stood up, shaking, and it was about twenty minutes before I could put the penny in my pocket and drive home.

■ ■ ■

Some days it doesn't pay to get out of bed. Like the day Penny Dreadful came by my shop to sell me a Golden Pear. It's not that I have a problem with Penny — far from it, she's one of my better suppliers. It's just that on that particular day, I couldn't manage to get anything to go right.

Fridays are normally pretty busy at Grimm's Occult Specialty Shoppe. I can almost always count on a good number of mundane sales by noon. That Friday, two days before Halloween, I couldn't have sold a can of Spam to a starving mongrel. I managed to sell a few trinkets to Edith Blanton, but those didn't count. She always bought something; it was just her way. I woke up with a fearsome headache, one that simply would not give me a moment's peace. In addition, another moron had tried breaking in the night before and had managed to do a good number on the glass door of the shop, even through the wire mesh that keeps everything locked up properly. Before I opened for the day, I was out almost three hundred dollars for a new window. It's amazing how much they'll milk you for when it comes to a rush job.

So I was pleased to see Penny when she came in; a friendly face at that point was a huge bonus. I figured on a little chit-chat and polite conversation, not a quick purchase for an item that I wasn't even certain I wanted. Don't misunderstand me, the Golden Pear of B^ttger is a true find, and more than worth what I paid up front. It's just that I prefer not dealing in items with a publicly known history. Public histories can tend to cause troubles, especially when the Technocracy is already sticking their damned noses where they don't belong. I'd had Men In Black casing my store off and on for a couple of weeks, and frankly I was starting to think about moving on, and that was before a certain bad Penny turned up.

But I made the sale anyway, and Penny said just the thing

to brighten my day. She said she'd come back later, and we could barter about the price. Penny knows my weaknesses, and near the top of the list is a good, hard sale. I think there are too many people who miss out on golden opportunities and a roaring good time simply because they would rather look at a price tag then actually haggle over the value of whatever item they are interested in purchasing. There are no price tags on any item in my store, from the cheap postcards to the antique wine goblets. If you want to buy, you have to tell me what you're willing to part with.

I'll give this to Penny. Despite a penchant for dressing like a widow in her mother's hand-me-downs, despite being far younger than most of my suppliers, she had the good sense to scope the area out and wait for the right time before trying to fence her stolen goods. She picked a good day; the goons in dark trench coats had not bothered to show themselves. For almost anyone else, I would have never made a deal with only a partial payment in advance, especially when it comes to a hot item that is incomplete. The Golden Pear, the one that allegedly held the secrets of the Philosopher's Stone, was absolutely useless without the key that opened its delicate mechanisms. Any attempt to open the Pear without the key would simply open a false front, and the infernal machine was too well-designed to allow any peek at its true treasures without destroying the patterns. I know this, because Aries Michaels tried his damnedest to open the Golden Pear on several occasions and confided the whole nasty mess to me during one of his infrequent jags of drunken stupidity.

Aries Michaels was a sharp man, and he certainly would have been a formidable enemy, but he was also a man who loved his alcohol a bit too much. Whenever he got into his drink, he called on me and told me his woes. Normally a visit from Aries started with him trying to convince me to go back to the Order of Hermes and ended with him crying on my shoulder. That was okay; he'd been my teacher

once, and he'd certainly taught me plenty about the ways
of the Order, but he'd also been my friend for a long time,
and he had definitely pulled my fat out of the fire when I
was too young and stupid to know better. We had a mutual
respect for each other, and he knew I would keep his secrets
just as I knew he'd keep mine. I think I may have been the
only person he ever told about stealing the Golden Pear.

I miss Aries, and one of these days I think I might have
to break down and avenge his murder. But I don't know if
I'm ready for that quite yet.

Anyway, I bought the damned Pear from Penny, more
for the promise of a good haggling session than for any other
reason, save possibly the look of desperation she tried so hard
to hide. I guess I should explain a little something here,
I'm just slightly less well off than God when it comes to my
finances. Both of my parents were rich, and the use of a
little coincidental magick had insured that my investments
went well after I inherited their wealth. I don't need to run
a shop, and I certainly don't need to dabble in selling items
of power. If I never worked a day in my life, I'd still die a
wealthy man. I run a store and deal in specialty items
because I like the people I meet, and because I'd go crazy if
I spent all of my time looking in musty old books for the
secrets of Ascension.

I bought the Pear, and I watched Penny head out the
door, and I knew then and there that I had made a hideous
mistake. I stowed the lovely and potentially powerful trinket
back in my specialties room and tried not to think about it.
In fact, I did a fine job of not thinking about it for the next
several hours while I dusted shelves, popped aspirin like
candy, and dealt with customers who will never know how
close they are to what they are looking for or how far away
from that same goal.

I'd just finished lunch when a mage I'd never seen before
came into the shop. Most mages can hide what they're
capable of (have to in fact, if they wish to continue

breathing) but I'm very good at seeing what others normally miss, and I couldn't have missed this one if I were blind. The woman that entered my store was stunning. I mean that, she was physically stunning, the kind of woman who makes men forget what they were going to say and makes women who are used to attention suddenly feel ignored. She was wearing designer jeans and a soft cashmere sweater over a body that promised sensual delights with every little move, and she stepped into the place like she owned it. I think for a smile I would have given the store over to her too, and she knew it, you could tell by the tiny upward curve at the corners of her full lips. She had a mane of black hair that surrounded her head like a cloud, and her hair was truly black, not colored that shade like Penny's or any of her little pseudo-intellectual friends. Unfortunately, the reflective sunglasses she was sporting kept me from seeing the color of her eyes, but I'm certain they were mesmerizing, whatever the shade.

I stared at her when as she walked over; I simply couldn't help myself. To my credit, I stared at her face instead of her body, and believe me, that was no easy task. Her voice was pleasant and sent shivers through me with the promises her tone made. "Hello. I'm looking for Mr. Grimm."

"You found me. How can I help you?" I'm very good with a poker face; you have to be when you do the sort of work I do. I was very grateful for that particular talent right then — I'm almost certain my voice would have squeaked like a boy in the throes of puberty otherwise. I mean what I said, she was an overwhelming presence.

"Hello, Mr. Grimm. I understand you sell specialty items."

That was a hell of a lot more blatant than I like my customers to be, and the effect was like a splash of cold water on my face. Despite her intoxicating perfume and magnetic appearance, I sobered up very quickly. "I'm sure I don't know what you're talking about, Miss...?"

"Blake. Jodi Blake. I'm sorry, Mr. Grimm, I got ahead of myself. I just assumed with no customers in the store...." Her look was apologetic, and I eased up on the stony face I'd put on.

"No harm done, Ms. Blake, but please, use discretion."

She smiled brightly, and I swear the entire room grew warmer by a good twenty degrees right then and there. "Call me Jodi."

"Call me Bryce." I smiled back and extended my hand. She returned the gesture and shook my hand with a firm grip. I decided that I liked that, liked everything about her. "Now then," I said when I could speak again, "how can I help you?"

"An old friend of mine recently passed away. His name was Aries Michaels." I nodded solemnly, letting her know that I had heard about his death and expressing my condolences simultaneously. "Aries spoke fondly of you, Bryce, and told me that I should pay you a visit sometime if ever I was looking for any items in particular." She paused for a moment, and my eyes were drawn to her tongue as it passed quickly over her upper lip. It took me a second to remember how to breathe. "I'm looking now."

I resisted the urge to loosen my collar. Frankly, I was wearing a T-shirt, and what collar there was was plenty loose enough, but that didn't stop the constriction of my throat or the sensation that I just couldn't get a good lungful of air. I was very conscious of my own pulse in my ears.

"Why don't you step into the other room with me?" I asked as I locked the front door and placed the "Back In Ten Minutes" sign facing out towards the street. Jodi gave me that little smile again, the one that sent crazy signals running through my brain. I resisted the urge to kiss her, but just barely. I have never met a woman before that so affected me, and I hope never to meet another. "Can you tell me what it is you're looking for, Jodi?"

"There is a black onyx chalice, intricately carved, the

bowl in the form of a skull placed on a stem and base of silver in the shape of the severed wrist of an open hand. I want that chalice, Bryce. I want it very much."

I knew the cup she was speaking of, it was one of only twenty in the world. The Tears of Kali are very rare and allegedly filled with the powers of Entropy. I have two of them. One is not for sale. Maybe someday I'll tell you how I got them, but not today.

Jodi looked at the chalice when I presented it to her and actually shook with pleasure when she held it in her hands. Either she was a member of the Euthanatos Tradition, very well-versed in her spheres, or she was cold. I suspected the former; the little moan that escaped her lips was all the hint I really needed.

I'd like to say that the haggling was satisfactory, and that I got a fair market value for the Tear of Kali. But I'd be lying. It's fair to say I've never been as thoroughly seduced as I was in that room, and likely I never will again. For all the world I was like a lamb being led to the slaughter. She paid me very well for the chalice, but only partially with cash.

Sometime later, I led Jodi out of the store, much more composed than I had been earlier and with absolutely no headache to speak of. I don't think the aspirin made much of a difference. Even as she was leaving, another person came into the store, a portly old woman with a mink stole and an attitude problem. She spent twenty minutes trying to make me buy back a deck of Oriental Tarot cards, explaining shrilly and firmly that she didn't like the future they kept presenting to her. I was in a good mood, and I explained myself three times before finally telling her where she could stick her cards. Once the cards have been attuned to someone, they shouldn't be used by anyone else, and I refuse to purchase shoddy merchandise or to give a refund on something that cannot be re-sold in usable condition. Besides, the cards don't lie unless you make them. Whatever her future holds is her problem, not mine.

Around seven that night, I closed shop for a few hours. I needed a break. The other big advantage to not needing the money is that I can set my own hours without worrying too much about making the rent.

I took a long shower to remove the tension that was creeping into my shoulders, and then I made a light dinner. Afterwards, I went down to my specialties room and did a little light dusting while making certain that everything was in order. Then I opened my doors and prepared for any late night business that might come my way. Across the narrow street, I noticed a man with pale skin and an expressionless face looking everywhere but at my store. I've met enough Men In Black to know one when I see one. I looked away from him and pretended he wasn't there, hoping that he would just go away.

When I was finally convinced that he wasn't looking for me (you tend to know when they are looking for you; the handgun and badge are normally pretty good indications), I checked in my specialties room again, because something was bothering me, and I couldn't quite place what it was. I started mentally ticking off the items in the room, and after about five I realized what the problem was.

The Golden Pear was missing.

I stayed calm, but it wasn't easy. I double-checked every nook and cranny, then I checked again just to be certain. There was no mistake. Angry doesn't begin to express my feelings on the subject of someone stealing from me. Monumentally pissed off doesn't even begin to come close. My whole world went red for a few seconds, and I was fully prepared to go charging into the night, ready to hunt down the thief at any cost, when I noticed my friend in the black trench coat standing in the same spot as before, at the entrance of a shop across the street. I was starting to get worried. He'd been there for an awfully long time for a man that wasn't investigating something.

I decided I should play it cool, and instead of trying to leave myself, I just picked up the phone. I like Penny Dreadful, I really do. But the deal was that she'd make additional monies aside from the advance I'd given her off of what I managed to receive from a sale on the Golden Pear, and I couldn't very well sell what I no longer had. Penny was honest, and Penny was almost painfully lucky at "finding pretties." I imagined she could locate the Pear a second time. With some of my suppliers, I would have been out of luck. They would have just moved on to another city, found another shop like mine and sold the item again. The shops are there, not many of them, but if you know your way around, you can find them. But Penny was a decent person and also a friend. I knew she hadn't lifted the Pear, it's just not her style, but I also knew of no one else I could trust. Penny would be happy with a small reward in addition to her retainer's fee. She has no fashion sense, and some of her friends are too morbid for my tastes, to say nothing of their own good, but she's good people all around.

The phone rang four times, and then I heard a garbled static-flooded funeral dirge playing tinnily in my ear. Almost unintelligible through the music, I heard Penny's voice advising me that she was not home, but would respond to any messages if she felt like it. I waited through ten more seconds of scratchy Victorian chords and then heard a shrill beep indicating that I could now leave my message. I took the hint and started speaking.

"Hello, Penny," I started. "This is Grimm. I'm Dreadfully sorry to interrupt your night, my dear, but I have a little situation...."

I explained quickly and cursed Penny's name for only having a two-minute play time for speaking. It took five calls total to give her the entire message.

There was a long pause between the third and fourth messages, caused entirely by an earthquake that literally knocked me off of my feet. I remember cursing the beep and dial tone that hit in the middle of my sentence to Penny, and even as I reached to hit the redial button on my telephone, a wave of vibrations lifted me into the air and slammed me none too gently into the ground. The bookstand at the front of my shop wobbled briefly and then toppled against the plate glass window. The window shimmered like heatwaves for a second and then exploded into the street. A case of loose crystals that rested above and behind my cash register slid forward and unbalanced the glass shelf that held it in place. Both the crystals and the shelf fell to the hard wood floor, the shelf exploding on contact and the crystals bounced and skittered across the ground. I had enough sense to cover my head and duck into a fetal position, but the glass still nicked my ear and pelted off of my back like pebbles thrown from a slingshot. I remember hearing the cacophony clearly, even over the sound of extreme vulgarities pouring from my own mouth.

When it was over, and I'd managed to stand again, I doubled the flow of foul words and surveyed the damage. There was absolutely no way I could leave the shop in this state; too many items that could easily be stolen. I called Burt Calhoun, the man who'd fixed my door earlier, and told him to bring his supplies out. He explained that the quake meant he'd be busy, and I explained that I would double his usual fee for rush jobs if he got the damned windows in place before night's end. That got him moving.

Like I said before, some days it doesn't pay to get out of bed. So far, I'd lost a good twenty thousand dollars in merchandise, at least, and my parts and labor expenses had just reached an all-time high. By the time the windows were installed, and I had finally reached Penny, my mood and my surname were identical.

■ ■ ■

The apartment was a mess, that simple.

It didn't help, of course, that I had the place stacked floor to ceiling with boxes of baubles, bangles and beads, though after the earthquake, it was then waist-deep in trinkets and trade-goods.

I made my way in, doing a balancing act from couch to coffee table to wherever I could set a foot down without breaking something, and finally got to my bedroom.

That was a bit better. The bookshelves were packed so tight not even an earthquake could pry them loose, and all that had busted open was the box of miscellaneous knickknacks I'd gotten from the Michaels' estate. It had fallen off the top shelf of my closet and scattered all over the floor, and I did not want to deal with it just now. After all, while I might have dealt with a lot of weird things as a Goth and talked about stranger ones as a Hollower, it wasn't every day you got an "Atta, girl!" from Charlotte's Web.

I sat down on the bed, which was clear except for a book, a card, and a bluish rock, all of them dusty with cobwebs. The card was an old "Thank You" note from Norna, and the book was — no, not *Charlotte's Web* — but *Arachne* by Lisa Mason. A large silver spider gleamed on the cover.

Some coincidences are just too weird.

I set them aside and picked up the bluish lump, brushing aside the bits of spiderweb. It wasn't stone, it was verdigris, or at least whatever the name is for the blue stuff you find on silver. One toothbrush and a half a can of Silvo later, I had it cleaned off. A nutmeg.

A Silver Nutmeg.

I steadied my hands, then slid it open along the seam. A last sliver of corrosion fell out, and a beautifully preserved silver key emerged, double-hinged.

The Elector of Saxony's Silver Key for the Pear of B^ttger.

I don't know how long I stared at it before the phone started ringing. I ignored it, waiting for the answering machine to kick in, but as those of you with answering machines know, they tend to go on strike after a power failure, and evidently there had been one with the earthquake, since the phone just continued to ring.

I finally picked it up, holding it in one hand and the Silver Key in the other. "Hello?"

"Hello, Penny." It was Grimm. He was attempting to sound bright and chipper, and that meant something was wrong. "Have you checked your answering machine?"

"Grimm, I can't find my answering machine, let alone check it."

He cursed briefly, then composed himself. "I'm dreadfully sorry to interrupt your night, my dear, but I have a little situation..."

I had a situation too. Namely an apartment knee-deep in Mardi Gras beads, miraculous messages appearing in spider webs, and the long-lost Key of the Elector of Saxony showing up on my pillow like some sort of bedtime chocolate from the gods.

Okay, I'll admit I usually operate on what I call Serendipity Overdrive, but there's a big jump between doing little charms and spells and having them work, and having major, mumbo-jumbo weirdness walk into your life. About the same as the difference between having small prayers answered and having the Virgin Mary show up in your living room for tea. The Key I could have dealt with, but not with the spiderweb on top of it and *Arachne* staring me right in the face. I take my omens seriously. If you're a Hollow One, you have to. I'd seen Spooky Pete and Neville's Gashlycrumb Deck be right too many times to start doubting now.

And now there was Grimm. "Tell me your situation, Grimm. Let's see if it beats mine."

Grimm paused. "The Pear was stolen."

"Stolen?" I twiddled the Key, rotating the Nutmeg between my thumb and forefinger.

"Stolen," Grimm said. He went on to describe the thief. Female. Tall. Attractive. Long, raven-dark hair.

"Grimm, you've just described Carmen San Diego."

No, as it turned out, her name was Jodi Blake, and as he went on to list her charms (and I don't mean the magical variety), I nearly got sick. He had it for her bad, and from the sound in his voice, well...

Something you should know. Grimm only gets laid about once a year, and then only when he's lucky and desperate. And from what I could hear between the pauses and pants, this woman had screwed him seven ways from Sunday or at least intimated that she'd like to. Not that he'd ever admit to it, mind you, and I wasn't going to call him on it. Grimm was as tight-lipped as a White House press secretary about things like that and just about as uptight.

He went on to ask me if I could do that voodoo that I do so well and find the Pear for him a second time.

"Damn straight I'm going to get the Pear back. And you're going to owe me big-time too, Grimm. And no, we're not going to haggle out the price right now." I played with the Silver Nutmeg, folding and unfolding the secret key. "Why's that? Oh, simple enough. I just found the Silver Nutmeg. That's right, the Elector of Saxony's lost Key to the Golden Pear and the Philosopher's Stone. The price has just gone up."

I hung up on him, then pulled the plug from the wall. After a moment's thought, I uncovered the answering machine and reset it, volume turned off. Let him call to his little heart's content. I'd deal with it in the morning.

A cup of tea and a book of poetry later, I was fast asleep.

■ ■ ■

Morning dawned bright, with the Silver Key on my dresser and the sound of Eek! the Cat filtering in from the kids in the next apartment. I held the pillow over my face. "Kumbaya!" was right.

I took a shower and began setting the apartment to

rights. It helped me organize my thoughts, and while I was at it, I picked out an outfit for the following evening. No matter what, I was not going to let random weirdness ruin a long-anticipated night of hedonistic morbidity.

Grimm had left five messages total on the answering machine, none of them important except for his warning that Jodi was a dangerous witch. Men! Just because he'd been too busy watching her ass to see what she did with her hands, she had to be a powerful enchantress. Couldn't have been any of his own doing.

Then again, maybe this was what Evil Old Uncle Al had meant when he'd made over the enchantress from Strength into the nubile bimbo for Lust. Wasn't hard to get the Rod of Power when men would give it to just about anyone for a wiggle and wink.

Pardon me if I'm being a bit crass, but I was mightily pissed that morning and not in the mood to be either respectable or ladylike. List any number of expletives or blasphemies you like, and you'll have my mood.

And still, none of it explained Charlotte's Web or the serendipitous appearance of the Elector of Saxony's Silver Nutmeg on my pillow the night before. I didn't doubt that it had been in the box of Aries Michaels' miscellaneous junk — I had a feeling when I bought the lot that I was going to find something worthwhile — but that it had landed on my pillow when everything fell off the shelf...

Well, you don't need to read Shakespeare to understand signs and portents.

Getting the Golden Pear back from Jodi Blake, aka the Kama Sutra Carmen San Diego, was going to be the trick, and I couldn't believe that Grimm had been so stupid as to leave it sitting on a shelf in his back room, even if only for the sight of his discerning customers. I'd filched it 'cause I knew it was hot, and there was no way that Aries Michaels was blowing the whistle on me, even if he hadn't been dead. Jodi Blake, whoever she was, evidently knew the same rules to the game and knew that no matter what Grimm did, he couldn't blow the whistle on her either.

Which meant that I just had to steal it back, assuming that I could find Ms. Jodi Blake.

Broderbund it was not, but I sat down with Aries Michaels' junk anyway and carefully sorted through it, hoping to find a letter like "Dear Mr. Michaels, blah, blah, blah, I know you've got the Golden Pear, blah, blah, Would you consider selling? blah, blah, Love, Kisses and Blowjobs, Jodi Blake."

I knew the type of letter it would be. Pink, perfumy, on expensive paper, with a little heart over the i in Jodi and three invisible swords through it.

Unfortunately, it wasn't in the box. However, I'd bought the contents of Aries Michaels' junk drawer, not his correspondences, and if they'd gone anywhere (Aries Michaels being the notable San Francisco eccentric that he was), it could only be one of three places.

■ ■ ■

One of three places turned out to be Special Collections at the University of San Francisco. Don't listen to those hacker geeks when they say they can find anything they need to know with computers. A computer is only as good as its database, and if you knew the number of things "not catalogued yet" in libraries, you'd chuck the keyboard and just go straight for the reference desk, or at least the phone.

USF's rare books room is amazing, by the way. They don't have a Gutenberg Bible, but they do have a copy of the *Nuremberg Chronicles* and one where the picture of Pope Joan only has a beard and glasses scribbled in, instead of having her face scratched out like they do with most copies. They also have an amazing occult and theology collection, which is only to be expected, I suppose. They're Jesuits.

Anyway, I'd forgone my usual finery for a black

turtleneck and slacks, vintage mod wear, circa Fifties London. (Okay, I'll admit it, I will wear some things from the Fifties.) It worked well for the collegiate beatnik look and was the closest thing I owned to ninja gear short of authentic Kabuki blacks, and no matter what they say about San Francisco, some outfits are more conspicuous than others.

The rare book room not only had the Michaels' letters, they had letters from Jodi Blake spanning a period of sixty-odd years, and the first one was obviously not written by a child of ten. And they were all written by the same person. I know my handwriting well enough to spot that, and Jodi's was unique to the point of being unforgettable.

I was also right. She did put little hearts over her i's.

Regardless, putting what Grimm had told me together with the content of the letters, all I could say was that somebody's Oil of Olay was certainly working well.

Unfortunately, there were no return addresses, and the little "Be seeing you!" tag lines and the Jodi Blake envelope subheading (Bitch from Hell!) left me certain that Mr. M— and Ms. B— had not been on the most cordial terms.

Call it inspiration, but since Miss Blake had been sniffing after the Pear ever since Aries Michaels snatched it, there was one place I had a strong suspicion she would be.

■ ■ ■

The realtors' office implied it, and the society columnist at the "Chronicle" confirmed it: Jodi Blake had set up in Aries Michaels' old digs. Unfortunately for her, someone had already stuck a screwdriver in the mantle of the study and had also bought the contents of the junk drawer, which included the Silver Nutmeg. I was wearing it on a chain around my neck.

The mansion wasn't dancing on chicken legs yet, but Jodi Blake had gotten ready for Halloween by putting a fence of plastic skulls with glowing red eyes round the place, and, call me superstitious, but I didn't really want to go past them to see if Bimbo Yaga was home.

However, Domino's delivers in half an hour, or it's free, and I called in an order for two pepperoni, extra cheese. It seemed appropriate.

I set myself up a little bit up the street, binoculars ready, and twenty minutes later saw the Domino's delivery boy go to the door and get greeted by a dead-ringer for Carmen San Diego, assuming that once Carmen took off her red trenchcoat she wore a red miniskirt and bustierre with a matching riding crop.

The Domino's delivery boy went in then, and I don't know, maybe it was some weird trick of the light, or maybe he was that horny, but I swear the guy's eyes (one of them, at least) looked blood red. Weird.

Regardless, by climbing halfway up a fence, I was able to see that, whatever the guy's eye color, Domino's does in fact deliver, and that Jodi Blake, whatever her age, was just as skilled as she'd implied in her letters to Michaels. Honestly, I've looked through *The Kama Sutra* and *The Perfumed Garden*, and while most of the positions involve persimmons, peaches and pomegranates, Jodi was doing a fine job improvising with pepperoni pizza.

Yes, children, the letter for today is P, and that includes Prostitute, Pulchritude and Passion.

However, I'd done what I intended, namely see if Bimbo Yaga was home, and if so, distract her for a little while. I'd succeeded beyond my wildest dreams, 'cause the way Miss Blake was teasing that poor boy, I was certain that she meant to earn her free pizza.

Which gave me slightly less than thirty minutes to get what I came for.

I screwdrivered the latch of the carport of the apartment next door and went on in, hopping the fence into the backyard of the Michaels' mansion, careful of my lunchpail.

I didn't bother with the back door, shinnying up the trellis to the second-floor balcony where the screen door was open into the master bedroom. And oh my, in her long life (assuming that the woman downstairs was the same one who'd written the letters), Jodi Blake had acquired a serious taste for kink. If you've ever seen a bondage parlor or The Gauntlet down in the Castro, you know the type of implements and furnishings Ms. Blake had managed to acquire. Everything but the Curious Sofa (which I bet she'd pay a bundle for), and she even had some medieval implements, notable among which was an extensive collection of choke pears.

I considered how pissed the Elector of Saxony would be if he found out that someone was planning to take his exquisite (if a trifle weird) music box, stuff it in someone's mouth, then turn the Key and let it go through its clockwork show. I was livid, if just because we Hollow Ones like to style ourselves morbid and macabre, and the thought had never occurred to me before now.

Anyway, I left the Chamber of Kink and took the stairs up to the study.

When I went in, the pentacle was still there, as I remembered it, but the room was now furnished in what I can only call Lovecraft Modern, and by Lovecraft I mean H.P., not the type that was going on downstairs. There were Aztec sacrificial bowls and masks of Tlaloc the tentacle-faced Mayan rain god, and nasty little Eskimo ivory tupilak figures, and, right over the mantle, a big, framed poster of the Beholder from DOOM, with votive candles set up before it.

And there, off to one side, in the center of a rather ordinary library research table, was the Golden Pear.

I stepped across the floor, careful of the pentacle and the various other symbols and altars set up around the room, and set my lunchpail down, softly opening the catch and taking out the Chinese funeral cloth.

"I wouldn't touch that if I were you."

I froze as I heard the voice, which was high and strange and raspy and not at all what I expected from the bitch-from-hell demon-temptress Bimbo Yaga.

A tail uncurled from what I had first taken to be a bundle of furs, then the cat put its head up and opened glowing (and I mean glowing!) green eyes. "I've been set to guard it," said the cat, and its mouth didn't move with the peanut-butter-stuck-to-roof-of-mouth effect you see in cat food commercials.

Charlotte's Web. Silver Keys. Ancient sorceresses. Talking cats.

Something snapped, and I realized that it was real. All of it. The webs and the keys and the sorceresses and the cats, and not just the little fun bits like picking up pennies for good luck and throwing salt over your shoulder. All of it.

And I'd just broken into the house of the Kama Sutra's answer to Baba Yaga and was talking with her cat.

Call me a classicist, but if all of it was true, then all of it was true, and the things they did in fairy tales should work just as well as everything else.

"What a pretty cat," I said, and it really was a very beautiful black cat, if you could ignore the talking and the glowing eyes. "I bet she doesn't feed you very well."

"Oh, no," said the cat. "Everything is wonderful. Just to the pact. Blood and milk and human hearts boiled in wine once a month."

Well, scratch that idea.

"I shall have to tell the mistress of you," the cat said and began washing one ear.

"She doesn't want to be disturbed," I said. "She's having sex."

The cat began washing the other ear. "She does that a lot."

Somehow I was not surprised. "The mistress sent me," I

said.

The cat looked up. "How do I know you're not lying?"

"Because," I said, "the mistress wants the Key to the Golden Pear, and see, I have it here." I took out the Silver Nutmeg and slipped the chain over my head, twisting the halves and revealing the Key. The cat watched, fascinated. "Would you like me to wind up the pretty music box so you can watch it play?"

"Yes, mistress's friend," said the cat. "The mistress wants me to watch the Pear, but it would be much nicer if I could watch it move."

I slipped the Key into the base and turned it three times, leaving it in the lock. A pretty tune began playing as the Nutmeg turned counterclockwise, and the sections of the Pear slowly folded down, like a flower opening in stop-motion. In the center of the Pear was a tiny tree filled with jewels, with a phoenix in a nest of diamonds at the very top, twisting and glittering in the light of the altar candles as the alchemical suite played from the music box.

I was almost as fascinated as the cat, but then remembered another fairy tale and brought down the handle of the screwdriver as hard as I could on the cat's tail. According to that story, the worst I could expect was having a kid with a nose the size of a casaba melon, and I wasn't really planning on having kids anyway. If I did, they could get nose jobs.

The cat opened its mouth to screech, but I was ready and stuffed in a handful of the Chinese funeral silk, grabbing the cat and wrapping it and swaddling it. Silk is strong stuff, strong enough even to stop a bullet, and it was thick enough and I was fast enough that I managed to bundle the cat up and stuff it in my lunchpail without getting a scratch. "'Oh, I love little pussy/ Her fur is so warm/ And if I don't hurt her/ She'll do me no harm,'" I sang, slamming shut the lunchpail and snapping the catch, throwing a small padlock on for good measure. The Golden Pear played its minuet in ridiculous counterpoint.

I held the lunchpail down with one hand and took the Nutmeg Key out with the other, stopping the tune and the self-immolating phoenix and causing the quarters of the Pear to snap shut. I held my breath for a long moment, then let it out.

Then a voice came over the intercom, sultry, seductive and very, very satisfied: "Grimalkin, is that you?"

I said nothing, and the real Grimalkin was nicely bound and gagged by the silk and the lunchpail.

"Grimalkin," said the intercom, "are you doing anything you're not supposed to be doing?"

I froze, realizing that if there was not an answer forthcoming, Bimbo Yaga was going to come up the stairs and find me not only with her cat in a lunchpail, but the Silver Nutmeg too.

I pitched my voice as high as I could (The raspy part wasn't hard), "No, mistress." It also wasn't hard to sound scared and guilty and caught-in-the-act.

"Grimalkin," said the intercom, "what are you doing?"

My voice sounded smaller as I squeaked, "Playing with a little mouse." It was the classic line from Baba Yaga, and I hoped it would work.

"Grimalkin, you'll spoil your supper." The voice from the intercom sounded disappointed and indulgent, like a mother with a favorite child. "I have a human heart stewing in wine, and it will be done soon. And fresh blood."

I held down my stomach. "And milk?" I asked.

There was a brief spurt of cursing in a language I didn't understand, and the candles burnt blue. "No, Grimalkin. It's all curdled, I'm afraid. But I do have some pepperoni pizza, extra cheese."

"I want milk!" I said in my best cat-voice. "The pact says I get milk!"

There was more brief cursing, and the candles flickered blue. "Yes, precious," said the voice, no longer quite so indulgent. "I'll go to the store immediately. You're quite right. The pact requires you have your milk, and have it you shall." There was another word, very nasty sounding, and the candles flared, lighting up the room like a blue-light special at K-mart. Then there was the sound of slamming doors from downstairs, and a minute later the sound of a car starting up and screeching out of the garage.

There wasn't much time to lose. I put the Silver Nutmeg back around my neck and bundled the Golden Pear up in what I took to be an altar cloth, stuffing it into a makeshift sack I made out of Bimbo Yaga's ritual robe. For good measure, I grabbed the tacky chalice Grimm had said was one of the Tears of Kali, then went hog-wild and ran around the room, grabbing everything that gave my sixth sense even the slightest tingle, gathering up a "Nightmare Before Christmas" sackful of grisly trinkets and curios.

Then I stuck my screwdriver in the crack in the mantel. I know. You're probably expecting that something really gross and scary popped out, like the clawed ducky from *Alien* or my Aunt Ethel's head on a spring. No, the safe was empty. Completely bare, except for a spider spinning her web.

Except, if you know anything about omens, seeing a spider spin her web is one of the worst ones possible. At best, it means that people are saying bad things about you, and at worst, well, I won't go into that, but I pinched my left earlobe with my right hand to make Blackrose bite her tongue (if she was the one talking behind my back) and watched as the spider pulled and adjusted a spare strand from the center of her web, which was otherwise neat and perfect and geometric as a clock face. In fact, it was a clock face, with twelve quadrants and the spider and her line the minute hand, nearing twelve o'clock.

She spun about with her line like a ballerina on wires, ticking a minute closer, and on her abdomen was an hourglass, scarlet on black.

Us Hollowers know all about red hourglasses and clocks

striking midnight, and you probably do too, but let me remind you of the moral of both: Don't get caught. Things would have turned out a lot different for Cinderella if she'd decided to party on and had her ballgown turn into rags right there in front of God and everyone, and Dorothy would have lost more than her slippers if she'd stayed in the witch's workroom when the last of the ruby sand fell inside the hourglass. And I know an omen when I see one, 'cause black widow webs usually look like cat's cradles on acid, not the faerie clock faces of anal retentive orb spiders.

I slammed the door on Charlotte's latest warning, and, all right, I'll admit it, I'm irresponsible, but even us Hollowers know better than to leave votive candles unattended. All I had to do was push them back under the baroque frame of the DOOM poster and throw a handful of paper in one.

The wall went up in moments, and I grabbed my sack in one arm and my lunchpail in the other, getting the hell out of there. I stopped just one second to say a quick prayer for the butchered pizza delivery boy in the front room and grab his keys.

Once I was out the front door, I paused a bare moment to pull the extension cord that led to Bimbo Yaga's fence of glow-in-the-dark plastic skulls, 'cause I know what the originals did in the fairy tale, and believe me, it was not pretty. And praise be to fast food, there was the car with the Domino's Pizza light on top. I tossed my Robe of Grisly Items and Cat-in-the-Box in the passenger's seat, and I was out of there and back to Grimm's.

When I'd planned to spend the day bargain-hunting and taking care of oversights, this was hardly what I had in mind. But what the hey, it was a good haul.

GRIM REMINDERS
■ ■ ■ ■ ■ ■ ■ ■ ■ ■

By James A. Moore with Kevin Andrew Murphy

The situation with Penny Dreadful was unique and left a funny taste in my mouth. I think she might have surmised what happened between Jodi Blake and I, but she had the good taste (to say nothing of the good sense) not to openly point out my seduction. She was true to her word, however, and with the Elector's Key to go with the Golden Pear, the price went up substantially. Fair is fair.

The bad news for both of us was that Jodi Blake was likely a Nephandi mage, a demon worshipper or worse. From everything that Penny told me about what Jodi had done to Aries Michaels' house, it was fairly easy to surmise that she was into dealing with things best left alone. That, or she had some unusual beliefs in what constitutes fashionable home decorations. I don't like the ideas put forth by the Nephandi, and I like their usual methods of operations (anything goes as long as it pleases the masters) even less.

I got a little something for free in the bargain, besides. I learned that the mysterious figure in front of my store was nothing more or less than a flasher. When I saw Penny approaching the store completely ignoring the Man In Black, I was prepared to step outside of my shop and assist her in defending herself against the agent of the Technocracy. I saw his form move as she was preparing to pass him and watched as he opened his coat. Penny's first reaction was to step back, her eyes wide and her mouth hanging open. Then she pointed at his crotch and said something I couldn't hear. Whatever it was, her acid wit had an instant affect on the man. He blushed and turned away, pulling closed his trench coat at the same time. I caught just enough bare flesh to realize that paranoia had done me in. I'd spent two weeks, off and on, waiting for the Technocracy to break down my door because a man in a black coat and hat was making lewd gestures with his exposed pelvis whenever anyone caught his eye. At another time I would have laughed, but not that weekend. I did, however, make a mental note to remove the man from the neighborhood if I ever saw him again.

I could tell you about the wonders found in the depths of the Golden Pear, but I won't. Why depress anyone by explaining the miracles that have passed through my hands? Suffice to say that the Pear is the genuine article, and that it will go to the highest bidder in a closed auction. I have no doubt I'll make my money back tenfold. This time, I had the good sense to place it in my hidden safe. It was worth the extra fifteen minutes to open and reseal all of the wards.

Penny left my shop with a smile in place, but her skin was paler than normal and, despite her bravado, I knew that something had happened. She still joked, and she still drove a hard bargain, God love her, but I think she finally realized just what magick is all about, and just what it can do to you if you're not careful. I'm glad of that. I don't worry quite as much anymore about finding her dead in an alley or suffering the same sort of manipulations that dear Norna must have endured.

I was ready to believe that everything was right in the world again, until I checked the lunchtime news and heard that Aries Michaels' house had burned to the ground. Bad enough the revelation that I had been with a Nephandus, one of the great mages of corruption, but far worse to discover that Penny had not only stolen back what was stolen from me, but had burned down that mansion at the same time. I didn't think Jodi Blake was going to forgive that slight. She might have acknowledged the loss of the Golden Pear of Bˆttger and called it a draw, but there was a matter of pride to be considered.

I may know very little about the Nephandi in general, and certainly less about Jodi Blake, but I can say in all honesty that she is not the type to forgive an assault on her pride. To her, the burning of the house and possibly the liberation of her properties could only be considered an act of war.

I didn't know who I was more worried for, myself or Penny. I suspected we'd both regret ever hearing about the Nephandi mage before the day was over. Naturally enough, I had reason to worry.

I almost didn't see the problem when it came through my door, primarily because the revenge Jodi sent my way was a very familiar face, and certainly not one I expected trouble from. Edith Blanton had been coming into my shop since almost the day I opened for business. She was a short, frail, old woman who always had time to chat and always found some item or other that caught her eye. While we often discussed the latest books and theories being tossed around in the New Age section of the store, we never agreed on any subject. I think we both liked it that way; it was a part of our friendly banter.

I heard the jangle of the bell over my door as I was headed towards the front of the shop after pausing for lunch. It only took a second for me to realize that something was amiss. A book had fallen from one of the numerous shelves in my back room, where the tomes of actual importance are kept, and I had just recovered from the loud boom when I turned at the sound of the front door opening. At first I thought I'd just placed it poorly when I set all of the jumbled books back in place after the earthquake, only to realize that I'd never seen that particular volume before. The book lay face-open on the ground with a graphic illustration of some hideous monstrosity towering over a screaming baby lying

prone on an altar festooned with odd and unsettling
illustrations. The monster had one hand in the child's chest,
digging into a wound that opened the full length of the
infant. Surrounding both the monster and its victim was a
conjuring circle, and just outside of that circle stood a naked
man with a goat's head and a naked woman kneeling beside
him. The picture was unpleasant at best, and the
implication was that the demon in the circle was forcing its
way into the child's body. I found the concept repugnant.
On the opposite page, the entry in bolder print mentioned
sendings and the victims of demonic possesion. I set the
book aside, looking at the illustration briefly and marveling
at the detail some of the older woodcutters had managed to
create.

In hindsight, I'd have to say that that particular book
falling down from the shelves and opening to that particular
page was an omen. I hate omens; they tend to come true. I
set the book on the shelf, leaving it open to the page I'd
found, because I wanted to examine the illustration and the
article on sendings more carefully. Then I headed back
towards the front room of my shop, brushing the heavy
cobwebs I'd gathered from the surface of the old tome.

By the time I'd pushed past the velvet curtain that led
to my special room and the adjoining library, Edith Blanton
was already on her way to the back of the store. I nodded
and smiled as she walked towards the New Age books to
see what was new. I wiped the spiderwebs from my fingertips
while I got back to thinking about how I would handle Jodi
Blake. I was worried. The Nephandi are notoriously
dangerous, more so in my eyes than even the Marauders. I
was still struggling with the warring thoughts of retribution
and the memories of our romantic tryst when Edith came
back to the front of the store.

Edith was holding a very large and utterly useless crystal
ball in her hands when I noticed her. She was wearing her
normal smile, a blend of uneasy curiosity and excitement at
the prospect of our normal debates, but she wasn't speaking.

"Hi, Edith. Do you want me to take that for you?" I was concerned for her health. That crystal ball weighed a good thirty pounds, and I was afraid she'd hurt herself trying to carry it. I was silent while I waited for her answer, but when she just stood there, I decided I should ask another question just to break the silence. "Nothing of interest in New Age today?"

"Actually I was looking for something a little different today, Bryce." I lifted an eyebrow, waiting for her to continue. She sounded like she had a cold coming on, and I made a mental note to give her some of my special tea, held for just such occasions. For Edith the tea would always be free. "I was wondering if you might have any pears."

"Pears?" I was perplexed, and at that moment the Pear of Böttger was the farthest thing from my mind.

"Yes." Her voice had changed so completely that I was taken aback. Her normally soft, pleasant tones had been replaced by a deep, hissing growl. "A Golden Pear, you thieving bastard!" With her words, Edith cocked back the crystal orb as if it weighed no more than a softball, and then heaved it at my head. If she hadn't spoken, if she hadn't made me notice that something was amiss, I would have never had a chance of dodging the high-speed missile. I ducked behind the counter just in time to avoid the thing and called myself lucky. The wooden wall behind me cracked and fragmented under the sudden impact, and crystal shards exploded across my back as the ball shattered.

My dear old friend, Edith, hopped over the counter like a professional hurdle runner, and landed next to my crouching form before I had a chance to stand. Her thin legs were spread wide in a battle stance, and her wrinkled hands were balled into fists. I was still recovering from the sight when she grabbed a handful of my hair.

I'm not a giant by any stretch of the imagination, but I'm still a pretty stocky man. Just the same, Edith lifted me completely off the ground and tossed me into the Tarot cards a good ten feet away. She managed both feats with the one hand that was wrapped in my shaggy tresses. While I'm the first to admit that the Akashic Brotherhood was simply not my cup of tea, I was very grateful for the time I spent training with them at that moment. I managed to twist enough to avoid a broken back in the impact, but I still suffered from the bruising force, and I believe I probably received a few broken ribs for my trouble.

Edith charged at me like a bull, and her form warped and grew as she came. Her old, thin, papery flesh changed into a grey hide, and her short-cropped grey hair fell away from her scalp. I stayed in a crouch and waited as patiently as I could. It wasn't easy, because a slice of my life had just been destroyed, and the fragments looked intent on killing me. I really liked Edith, and I miss her. By the time she reached me, Edith had grown three feet taller and a good four feet wider. Her face had stretched until the skin ruptured completely, and a bloody malformed skull complete with tusks instead of canines had replaced her kindly visage.

She hit me with the force of a runaway freight train, and I twisted my body out of the way, using her own momentum to carry her into my specialties room, away from any casual passers-by and into the privacy where I could use my magick without being seen. By the time I'd gone through the velvet curtain that separated the rooms, the Edith-thing was back up and ready for more. I grabbed for the first item I saw and threw it at her for distraction. She slapped the sword I tossed at her and gave me enough time to reach what I was after, the Tear of Kali.

I am absolutely convinced that my Avatar has been with me through several incarnations. That alone might explain why I joined the ranks of the Awakened at the age of four. I am also convinced that in at least one of those previous incarnations I was a member of the Euthanatos Tradition. I will point out for the record that I do not like the idea of killing anyone, one of my main reasons for not joining with the Euthanatos to date, but I am not above killing if I see no other option. Since charging past the heavy curtain into my back room, the Edith-monster had continued to change and now stood a solid nine feet in height. It literally had to stoop just to stand up. Growth was the least of its changes. I summoned my will and focused through the Tear of Kali, deliberately slicing my thumb on one of the sharp talons that made the base of the chalice. I forced the blood from the wound into the skull-shaped bowl and watched as the dark red blood was consumed by the smooth sides of the cup. The blood boiled as it was absorbed, and then the power awakened by my actions was released. There was no flash of light, no visible stream of energy, but a wave of power left the chalice just the same.

Just as the Edith-thing was reaching for me with a ten-fingered claw, the wave hit. Whatever it really was, the creature gave way to the entropy within. A very small squeak passed its blackened gums as its claw touched my shoulder. I pulled back and watched from the edge of the curtain that separated me from the rest of the world. In less than three seconds, the thing went from powerhouse to bubbling ruin on the ground at my feet. Inside of ten seconds, there was nothing left but dust.

I set the chalice back in its place, replaced the sword on shaking knees, and even managed to sweep the ashes into a garbage bag before the serious shakes hit me. I don't like killing, and I hope I never get to like the sensation. I made it up the stairs to my private bathroom before I vomited my lunch into the toilet. Two minutes later I came back down to my shop and started cleaning. The hole in the wall could wait, and I slapped a poster over the ruins with clear tape before I set all the Tarot cards back in place. After I'd finished with the cosmetic repairs, I double-checked the rest of my special rooms, wanting to know for certain that they were still protected from interference. The first thing I noticed was the disappearance of the book I'd set aside earlier. Having given its warning, whatever had dropped the book to the ground had apparently decided to take it back to wherever it belonged. That, or I'd imagined the entire event.

I didn't know if the creature I'd liquefied had been a demon, but I suspected there was a good chance it had. I looked around my special room very briefly and grabbed the only two items I could think of that would help me in that particular case: a dream-catcher and a spirit-catcher. The dream-catcher was a large loop of wood, decorated with feathers and fur and spun with a web in its center. The craftsmanship was hardly anything spectacular, but this particular dream-catcher was authentic and powerful. The spirit-catcher was carved from the thighbone of a bear and had been fashioned with openings on each end that formed the mouths of serpents. I knew how each item worked, and I went to handling the task as effectively as I could. With the spirit-catcher, I drew forth the spirit that had possessed Edith's body, looking with senses that most Sleepers refuse to believe exist and seeing the dark, writhing cloud of pestilence that was drawn into the thighbone. Something moved within that cloud, and I knew that my worst fears were confirmed: The soul of Edith Blanton was stuck within the spirit of a demon, like as not being consumed for energy.

I lifted the dream-catcher, blocking the way into the spirit-catcher before the demon's essence could enter. Dream-catchers work on a simple process: they capture bad spirits and only allow the good spirits through, thus assuring happy dreams to the ones who use them. Edith Blanton's soul slid past the web in the dream-catcher with ease. Tthe demon was snared and fought like a netted shark to escape the delicate webbing. Before the thing could break from its prison, I ushered Edith's spirit away from the spirit-catcher and focused my attention on the minion of Jodi Blake. It hissed as it was drawn into the ancient bone prison.

I locked the door and closed up shop, and then I started sweeping. I did my best to avoid the burning tears in my eyes, but anger and grief make a messy mix. I was angry because a good friend had been murdered. I grieved because I was partially responsible for her death. For one second, I thought I heard the voice of Edith Blanton whispering next to me. It said, "Thank you, Bryce," and then was gone. I can't be certain; I was very shaken by that point. I hope I heard her just the same.

I noticed what the poster I'd placed over the hole in the wall said for the first time. When you run a shop like mine, you receive flyers and posters for distribution constantly. I'd grabbed the first one available when I stuck it to the wall. The sign said: COME ONE COME ALL TO THE NECROTIC NEUROTIC HALLOWEEN BALL. Beneath the dripping letters was a bad illustration of two skeletons dancing around a jack-o-lantern. The only address given was a single word: "Waydown." Penny and her friends were having a party there later the same night. The party had supplies purchased with money from the sale of the Golden Pear. Somehow, I didn't doubt that Jodi Blake would know where the money came from, and I was almost certain she'd show up there, ready to have a little party of her own. I knew in my heart that Penny'd be there too, as Jodi's guest of honor.

I knew also that I'd have to crash that little party. I'd lost one friend already, and I was damned if I'd lose another. The only answer I got at Penny's place was the start of that damned funeral dirge, and I just couldn't wait through it to leave a message. I prayed I wouldn't be too late.

■ ■ ■

I arrived at the Ball in the style only possible with a Stutz Bearcat and a Twenties coonskin coat, complete with an antique Stanford pennant in the pocket, and I checked them to reveal a Victorian bridal gown, black lace with slashes of white in the sleeves, the type of thing a girl would have worn when her entire family had died, then she decided, "To hell with it! I'm getting married anyway!"

My lunchpail, with the NIN stickers, and the padlock, did not precisely go with the whole outfit, but then I wasn't going to leave Bimbo Yaga's talking cat back at my apartment with the rest of the stuff I'd snagged (minus what portion I'd fenced to Grimm). Call me superstitious, but while "Ding, dong, bell/ Pussy's in the well" had crossed my mind, it was a talking cat with glowing eyes, and if it hadn't smothered already after being locked for a day in a lunchpail, it probably wouldn't drown either.

And the idea of it succeeding in Houdini's last trick, a la Mr. Mistoffelees, then coming after me mad as ... well, a wet cat, was frankly something I did not want to deal with. I needed to ask Neville and Blackrose and Spooky Pete their advice before letting the cat out of the box.

Unfortunately, they were all busy tending to the party (which I had completely flaked on — though for good reason), and even more unfortunately (and as I'd half-expected) Bimbo Yaga showed up looking for me and her cat.

It hadn't occurred to me before, but when you burn down someone's house, besides torching their altar and their assorted evil bric-a-brac, you also cremate their wardrobe. And Jodi Blake looked as pissed as you might expect of a woman who has spent an entire night and day in the same leather teddy, fishnets, and stiletto heels.

And underwear.

But with that look, that face, and the riding crop still in her hand, she was the dream girl for the entire B&D and S&M and T&A contingent, and they just lined up at her feet, prostrating themselves. "Mistress!" they cried. "Mistress! Beat me! Beat me!"

It was with long experience, I suppose, that she knew that whipping them or kicking them away would only made them crowd closer and kiss her feet, and so she ignored them instead, giving the same look that the Wicked Queen in "Snow White" had when her mirror told her that her Oil of Olay was starting to give out.

I crouched back against the wall, trying to hide in the shadow of a pillar, but then Bimbo Yaga leveled her riding crop at me like it was some sort of magic wand (and for all I know it was) and the room went silent, the stereo system shorting out. "You..." she breathed. "You. Little. Bitch."

I held my lunchpail, and her cat, closer to me. "Do I know you, lady?"

She gave a withering look, surveying the crowd, and I think looking closer to her true age as she realized she couldn't exactly say, "Why yes! You burnt my house down last night, after I screwed and murdered the pizza delivery boy while you were busy upstairs looting my altar room and stuffing my cat in a lunchpail! Don't you remember?"

Her lips pressed together in a cold, hard line. "Don't you have anything you wish to say to me, child?"

I paused, looking around at the crowd. They expected some response. "Well," I said after a long moment, "as a matter of fact, yes. When you got back last night, did you find a giant pair of blackened chicken legs in the ashes?"

Jodi looked perplexed, my comment having caught her out of left field, but then she seemed to get the reference. "Just who do you think you're dealing with, child?"

"Bimbo Yaga?" I asked, and I swear, her eyes turned about the same color as her miniskirt, and she screamed. Every candle in the place burnt blue at that moment, and I suddenly realized where the phrase "swear up a blue streak" came from, because with the nasty-sounding words she said next, the flames flashed like cobalt fireworks.

Once she recovered, she pointed the riding crop at me again. "Impudent chit! I challenge you to the Duel Arcane!"

"The what?" I said, but then Neville stepped forward.

He was dressed in coachman's blacks with a top hat and tails, and he shuffled his Gashlycrumb Deck from one grey-gloved hand to the other. "The Duel Arcane," he said, with all the emotion of a BBC announcer, "an ancient magician's honor duel. She has issued the challenge, Penny, and as challenged party, you have the right to dictate the terms, the time, the place, and the method of combat."

"It shall be to the death!" said Jodi, and I shrank back against the wall.

Neville looked at her calmly. "No." The Gashlycrumb Tinies flew from one hand to the other. "You have issued an open challenge, one that may not be refused without loss of honor. Had you wished to challenge her to the Duel Thanatos, Penny could have refused, with no loss of honor to herself, simply acknowledging you as the greater mage. Had you challenged her to mere Certamen, she could not honorably refuse, yet neither would she risk death. But that is not the case." Whoosh! went the cards again. "Do you wish to withdraw your challenge, suffering that loss of honor, then call for the Duel Thanatos? For I must remind you, if you best Penny in this challenge, you may not honorably challenge her again until she has bested you in turn."

Bimbo Yaga snarled, and her riding crop quivered in her hand like something you'd usually need batteries for. She glared at Neville, raising the crop in slow-motion towards his face. "I. Do not. Withdraw. My challenge."

Neville inclined his head. "Then honorably Penny must accept."

Somehow I'd moved forward to confront Jodi, the path clear between us. "I accept," I found myself saying. "The time and place shall be here and now. The stakes will be that if I win, you will go away, never again to bother me or mine. If I lose, I will surrender the contents of this box." I held up the lunchpail, and I know Jodi knew that the cat was inside. "That is all."

Neville looked to Jodi. "Do you accept or refuse the terms?"

"I accept," she ground out.

Neville smiled, for once showing a hint of emotion, pleasure even. "Then the combatants may now accept tokens and favors from those who wish them well." With ceremony and gravity, Neville presented me with his Gashlycrumb Deck. "For you, Penny. Use it well."

Blackrose came forward and slipped her feather boa

around my shoulders and placed a kiss on my cheek. "For luck."

Jodi stood there, looking about, realizing that no one, not even her former admirers, was going to wish her well.

I don't know what I was doing. I really don't. But I realized that Neville had trapped Jodi in her own error, and if I ever wanted to be free of the bitch, I'd have to run with it. "Let's begin, shall we?"

I shuffled the Gashlycrumb Tinies till I came to one that felt right. I glanced at it, and the Gorey illustration and caption had changed from the original. I held it out for her to see: "'J is for JODI who took lye by mistake.'"

She paused and blanched, clutching her throat, but then opened her mouth and pointed her riding crop. "'And this figure he added eek therto, That if gold rust, what shal iren do?'" Her voice was harsh and raspy, ruined by the lye I had somehow just made appear in her throat, and the old words of Middle English were almost incomprehensible.

But the padlock fell from the box in my arms, and my lunchpail began to fall apart at the seams.

The cat. With the cat back, she'd have back most of her power, and the last thing I wanted to deal with was both of them.

I ran, the rusting lunchpail clutched in my arms, the Gashlycrumb Deck scattering in my wake. And thank the gods, I may have been in highbutton granny boots, but Jodi was in five-inch stiletto heels, and I was a good bit younger than her anyway.

Fairy tales. Fairy tales. Goddamn it, think, Penny. Think.

I gained the door, running out and turning left on instinct. "Childe Rowland," Burd Ellen, who ran widdershins round the church and entered Elfland under the Erl King's power. But her brother Rowland followed her, passing safely with Merlin's charm.

I dashed right through the Rocky Horror cast, where on the wall of church, appropriately enough, the projector had the scene where the dogs are being set after Rocky, and rounded the far corner of the church, Jodi after me, screaming and cursing and somehow managing to run in her stiletto heels while the lunchpail disintegrated in my arms.

"'Open, door! Open, door, and let me come in!'" I cried, and mist swirled in the shadows, and I ran through it, clutching the struggling cat which was trying to work its way through the silk and the rusted remains of my lunchpail.

Around the church again, and it looked stranger and mistier, giant spiderwebs hung with dewdrops the size of diamonds, and hundreds of tiny spiders everywhere with jeweled eyes, like a thousand Silver Nutmegs.

Around the church a fourth time, and I was back to the front, the doors standing wide open, a hundred times as grand as the St. Francis was before, spun with silver and diamond lights. FELICITATIONS spelled the giant web over the entrance, and I ran in, Jodi behind me, her stiletto heels clicking like the Devil's hooves.

Fairy tales. "Baba Yaga" and "The Water Nixie." *But the boy dropped a brush/ Which had magical bristles/ Which surrounded the nixie with acres of thistles...*

On instinct, I loosed Blackrose's feather boa, and I heard Jodi snarl behind me and pause, wrestling, I suppose, with a plumed serpent. Or at least I hoped so.

I ran into the church, widdershins and widdershins, up a spiral stair paved with silver and hung with webbing, higher and higher into the spiritual reality of the Waydown, tiny spiders flashing helpful messages in their webs as I ran up and up, the lunchpail falling to bits in my arms and the cat coming loose from the silk.

I reached the top of the stair and sprawled headlong onto a floor of gossamer webbing and silver mesh, the lunchpail and funeral silk flying from my arms, tumbling end over end as bits of rust and Nine-Inch-Nails stickers flew in all directions, and the Chinese funeral cloth unfurled.

The cat came to rest on its feet, back arched, hissing, and eyes glowing green.

There was a chime on the silver stairs behind me, and I looked up to see Jodi there, her riding crop in her hand, the tip sparkling with golden barbs. She smiled cruelly, "So...."

"You broke the pact!" shrieked the cat. "You broke it!"

Jodi looked to Grimalkin, her face a mask of annoyance. "Not now, precious. Mother has business to attend to —"

"You broke the pact!" the cat screamed. "Milk! Blood! A human heart stewed in wine! Each full moon! And it's a night past!"

I had the image of a very spoiled four-year-old having a tantrum, 'cause that's just what the cat sounded like.

Jodi smiled with ill humor, looking at the funeral cloth. "You did have your silken bed..."

The cat did not look amused at the joke, and it was then that the bell of the Silver Cathedral, or whatever this place was, began to come down. Then I saw that it wasn't a bell. It was the world's largest spider, shining silver like liquid mercury given form.

Jodi watched it, her mouth hanging open, and the spider reached down to her abdomen, pulling forth a hank of webbing and holding it between her four forelegs like a gigantic cat's cradle: WELCOME TO MY PARLOR

It folded the hammock of silver silk together, stretching it out again in a smaller size: SHOO FLY

Jodi gaped in horror, and her lips shrank away from her teeth, her face becoming skeletal, or at least looking like a corpse about four hundred years old, and I haven't the faintest idea what she turned into. A banshee, a harpy — hell, for all I know it was a bandersnatch, the thing flew out of there so fast, screaming and shrieking and clawing aside the little spiders that tried to block its way.

I didn't have a broomstick or magic carpet or anything else to follow with, and I just sat there, looking up at the giant silver spider.

It held up its cat's cradle again: SALUTATIONS, PENNY. Fold and twist: GOOD WORK

"Norna?" I breathed.

The spider reached down to its abdomen and pulled forth a great deal of webbing, holding forth a message the size of a movie screen: WEAVER

"What — ?" I said. "What happened to you?"

She folded the giant sheet like origami, holding forth a cocoon with the effigy of a fat man in it and the legend: DOCTOR HIMIITSU

She hung the effigy aside like she would for her larder and added a caption over it: SOME PIG

I sat, holding my breath, and ... Weaver ... the giant spider, spun out three messages: BUSY, BYE, and BEST WISHES

The cat watched the spider ascend long after I'd finished, then turned to look at me. "You bested my old mistress. Do you have any human hearts stewed in wine?"

The hopefulness and the innocence in that voice was chilling, and at the same time very, very Goth. "Sorry, fresh out." I brushed my hair back out of my eyes. "How about fresh cream and sushi?"

The cat cocked its head and blinked. "With raw eel?"

"And quail eggs," I said, and the cat blinked again.

"Yes, mistress," it said, then padded over and curled up in my lap, purring.

I realized then and there that I'd just contracted a familiar. The stories about bribing Baba Yaga's cat were right after all.

I began to stroke its fur. "So is your name really Grimalkin?"

The cat purred. "It's the name she gave me." Purr, knead. "It was all the rage four-hundred years ago."

"We'll have to find you a better one."

I leaned back and smiled. T.S. Eliot had written other things than *The Waste Land* and "The Hollow Men." *Old Possum's Book of Practical Cats*, for one.

I stroked the fur of my new familiar. "'The Naming of Cats is a difficult matter,/ It isn't just one of your holiday games;/ You may think at first I'm mad as a hatter/ When I tell you, a cat must have THREE DIFFERENT NAMES.'"

The cat purred in agreement, looking forward, I suppose, to raw eel and quail eggs and cream as a change from blood and milk and human hearts stewed in wine.

Talking cats. Witches. Giant spiders. Silver Keys.

I sighed. I suppose I could get used to this too.

■ ■ ■

I got to the Waydown too late to stop the conflict between Penny and Jodi Blake. When I arrived, most of the people in the club were busily doing their own thing, drinking, dancing, and few other activities that were patently illegal. There were a few exceptions.

Neville was picking an up his trademark Gashlycrumb Tinies cards from where they'd scattered all over the floor, and cursing under his breath. I could see why he was upset. One of them faced me briefly (B is for BRYCE, assaulted by bears). It had been bent and trampled roughly. I saw the image of myself on the card and was slightly startled. As I said before, I hate prophecies. I knew Neville, and I knew he couldn't possibly be happy about the situation. "Neville, I need to talk to you."

Neville stared back at me, eyelids half-lowered and a sneer on his thin lips. "Well, if it isn't Bryce Grimm. What brings you to the Waydown? Decide it was time to get a life?" Neville hasn't liked me for a long time and, frankly, I just couldn't care less. Whatever I might have done to him is long in the past, and if he has a problem he doesn't want to discuss with me, well, I can go on ignoring his waspish little comments.

"I have a life, Neville. What I need right now is to know where Penny Dreadful is. Have you seen her?" I took a look around the burned-out church, ignoring the garish Halloween decorations and focusing on distinguishing Penny from the multitudes of others dressed in equally old black clothes. I couldn't see her.

Neville sniffed disdainfully and deftly shuffled his cards again, whipping them between his hands with the skill of a Vegas card-shark. "She isn't here. She left with another woman in hot pursuit." He paused for a moment, arranging his face and trying hard not to look worried. "They were dueling over the contents of Penny's lunchbox or some such nonsense. The Duel Arcane no less."

"How long ago?" It took a minute to get the words past my lips; they'd gone cold and numb at the thought of Penny taking on a Nephandi mage strong enough to completely alter an old woman into a killing machine. Worse still, taking her on in an honor duel, with no help from anyone else. Worst of all, doing so in public. The Paradox Spirits were probably in a uproar already.

"Maybe twenty minutes. A little more, a little less." Apparently remembering he was supposed to be angry with me over whatever imagined slight, Neville pressed his lips together and stared down his nose at me. "Why do you care?"

"Because I owe Penny, and I don't want to see her destroyed."

"Well, not that it should matter to you, but I believe she ended up in the Umbra. She'll be back when she's finished her fight." He didn't say it, he didn't have to, the unspoken words he left out were simple enough for any mage to understand. She'll be back if she's still alive.

I nodded and turned away. Neville looked like he was ready to say something, but I didn't wait around to hear his words. I moved through the Waydown, pressing past people years younger than me and feeling decidedly out of place in my jeans and T-shirt. There were two kids dancing close together, managing to find a rhythm in the discordant crap playing on the stereo system. Both of them had some sort of reflective contact lens in one eye, the left, that made the eye appear red. I wondered what the next fashion statement would be and decided I really didn't want to know. Several of the Goths looked at me and sneered, but most didn't care if I was there or not. A few even recognized me and waved or nodded. I nodded in return, but didn't even try my luck with waving; the bruises on my ribs and on my shoulders kept me from making any unnecessary gestures.

The music was too loud, and the room was all but flooded with the mixed stench of clove cigarettes, perfume, and other less identifiable substances. I had almost given up hope of seeing Penny or Jodi when Jodi stepped out of the shadows. What little she was wearing was only enough to emphasize her statuesque physique, and my mind went back only two days to the afternoon of pleasure we had shared. I pushed the thoughts away, remembering that this woman had killed Edith Blanton and could well have done the same to Penny. One way or the other, there was going to be a reckoning.

Jodi was looking away from me, and I stepped further into the shadows of the club as she started turning, surveying the depths of the old church. I bumped someone behind me, and whoever he was, he made threatening sounds in his throat until I apologized softly. When Jodi Blake was finally looking in my direction, she saw only the disgruntled boy in false Victorian clothes. I saw much more. I could read the anger on her from a hundred yards away. She was livid, but she was also looking rather worried. That suited me just fine. I took her confused anger to mean that Penny had escaped, and I hoped I wasn't coming to the wrong conclusion.

Jodi didn't walk so much as saunter towards the door, and I watched her from the shadows. Several times during the trek, one person or another tried to engage her in dancing or conversation, or perhaps even other activities, but she was obviously not in the mood to stop. A Hollow One I knew by face but not by name tried to confront her, but Jodi simply stared the girl down.

She walked towards the exit, and I followed a discreet distance behind her. I wanted to confront the witch, but not in a place with so many Sleepers. I've had a few dealings with Paradox Spirits in the past and, you may rest assured, they are not fun to mess with. When she stepped out the door, I saw her moving towards the left and waited a few seconds before following. Neville nodded to me, pointing to where she went, and I thanked him with a return nod.

I slipped out the door just as a small crowd was trying to get in, and I spotted her as she stepped around the corner of the St. Francis' desecrated remains. Damn me, but I still couldn't stop thinking about her. I don't like to sound like a starving puppy, but she was an amazing lover. I just wish things could have turned out differently. I have little doubt she messed with my mind. I think she must be amazingly adept at magick because, to this day, I'm still bewitched by the thought of her.

I waited until she was again just around the corner, and then I moved that way. I wasn't going to lose her, not if I had anything to say about the situation. I peeked around the next corner and saw her standing still, looking at me. She did not look happy.

"Hello, Bryce."

"Jodi," I managed not to stutter, but it wasn't easy. I kept wondering how I could be thinking so much about being with this woman after she had killed a friend of mine and forced myself to ignore her "come hither" look.

"Well, this is a sticky situation, isn't it?" She moved towards me as she spoke, and fool that I am, I walked towards her in return. "All over a little piece of antiquated clockwork."

"That's not what this is about at all, and you know it."

She pouted prettily, and I bit down on the inside of my mouth, using the pain to keep me coherent. I had a nervous feeling in my stomach, and my blood pressure was on the rise again. The night air was cold, but I was sweating. "Then what is it about, Bryce?"

"Deceptions. You lied to me, and you killed a good friend of mine. You stole my property. For all I know, you've killed another friend in the last half-hour."

She chuckled throatily and smiled as brightly as I've ever seen any woman smile. In that second I could have believed that she was innocence incarnate. Surely any angel this lovely could not be a demon in disguise. "I didn't kill your friend, sweet Bryce, you did. I just helped her see the world a little differently. And as for your little girlfriend... Well, let's just say that isn't finished yet." I guess that last line was all it took to make me truly angry. I could forgive a lot, but I could not condone a threat against Penny or anyone else I cared about. Worse still, I could tell by the tone of her voice that she didn't mean to hurt Penny's body, she meant to ruin Penny's soul.

I held myself in check when she wrapped her arms around me and pulled herself against my chest. My body was trembling with the desperate need to caress her, and it took all of my effort not to give in. I don't think I could have resisted her if not for the threat against Penny. "Let's just let bygones be bygones," she purred softly against my ear. Her breath was warm and sweet and smelled of springtime and happier days when I was still innocent. "Give me the Pear, and you can have me. For as long as you want me."

She placed warm lips against my neck and nuzzled there for a second, I wanted to push her away, but I just couldn't. "I need the Pear, Bryce. I'm older than I look, and my deal with the Dark Lords does not include eternal youth. I'm afraid to die, afraid of what they'll do to me. Please, help me, Bryce. I'll be yours forever, if you'll just help me.

God help me, evil wears a lovely form. I don't know if I'd have said yes or not; I may never have to worry about it. I'd almost closed my eyes for a second, they were barely open at all, when I noticed the forms in the shadows. There were several, I couldn't say the exact number if my life depended on the total. Somewhere along the way, Jodi had called for reinforcements. The image of Neville's card flashed in my mind — "B is for BRYCE, assaulted by bears." I reiterate, I hate prophecies, in any form. They have a nasty tendency to come true.

Dark forms moved among the shadows, drifting and gliding, darkness that could only be seen as a deeper black against the grey of the shadows that buried the alleyway. They made no sound, and that was maybe even worse than their shifting forms. Silent killers that were at home in the places where human eyes hate to look, at home in the shadows. I pulled back from Jodi, looking down at the water-stained street in an attempt to clear my head of her influences. If I'd looked in her eyes again, I know I'd have been lost for all time in the depths of her power. The puddles held my reflection and hers, and I looked at myself briefly, shocked by how pale I was. Then I looked at Jodi's form in the still waters and pushed her away from me, appalled by the crone that my reflection held in its arms, cracked, thin lips whispering in my reflection's ear.

I looked up at Jodi, my heart deep in my throat, my stomach doing some nasty turns as I thought about what I'd been doing with the hag reflected in the puddles, how I'd held her in my arms and kissed her, made love to her.

Jodi smiled lovingly. She was as beautiful as ever and stepped back into the shadows of the old church. Her eyes held a deep regret, and I knew that she understood what I'd seen in the water: her true form, minus the magicks that made her an angel in appearance. "One last warning, Bryce: Don't make me come looking for the Pear of B^ttger. I need it, and I'll have it. I have to leave now, but I'll see you soon." Her voice was filled with a sorrow that made a lie of her smile. I almost felt sorry for her right then.

I didn't see where she went, I was too busy with the monsters around me. They moved in, and I did my best to defend myself. My eyes alone were not up to the task, and my ears were useless in tracking creatures that made no sound. The first of the shadow-things struck me before I even saw it move. Darkness clutched at my shoulder, and a cold, numbing fire seared my flesh beneath the T-shirt. Eyes burned in that shadow, but the light that blazed from the darkness was pale, poor indication of anything save the creature's foul mood.

The second one managed to sink impossibly long teeth into my leg and pulled back with a good deal of my flesh and tattered Levis hanging from its mouth, a flat shadow holding a three-dimensional section of my body in its two-dimensional jaws and chewing greedily. I won't lie, I screamed shrilly as the pain of the wound ignited on ruptured nerve endings. Right around then I decided that coincidental magick alone wouldn't help me make my escape. I turned and ran like hell away from the old St. Francis.

I've had nightmares about being chased by the Men In Black. I've suffered from those dreams ever since I was captured by them at the age of sixteen. This was worse. I was bleeding heavily from the wound in my leg, and I could feel a sickening cold sensation pulling at my mind, crawling up from the wound and trying to woo me with promises of sweet oblivion. At the same time, those silent freakish bastards were oozing through the darkness of the back alleys and poorly lit streets.

I hopped and ran as best I could, feeling the hairs on my neck rise and try to crawl away at the thought of the shades that pursued me. Something dark and cold ripped tatters from the back of my shirt and drew blood that dribbled down across the small of my back and soaked through the seat of my jeans. I felt the numbness increasing as I tried to find a suitable spot for my final stand.

Finally, I came to a street light that was burning brightly and stood under the powerful yellow glow emanating from the sodium bulb. The dark forms gathered around the pool of light that surrounded me, uncertain what to do. They conversed among themselves, gesturing and pointing at me with long tapered claws, but whatever they were saying was not for my ears. I heard only the sound of my own ragged breathing and the pounding of my pulse slapping against my temples.

Finally one of them tried to brave the stark light, and I watched as the taloned paw of the shadow-thing reached into the circle of brightness. I saw the dark shape push into the area as if struggling to force its hand through a stone wall, and as it finally achieved this monumental effort, I watched the blackness separate and come unraveled. The seemingly solid black form jerked and tried to pull back as its shadow-flesh grew grey and ash-like. Then the limb simply faded away, leaving the withered stump to burn as the creature fell away from the light. I was right in my hopes; the shadow-creatures suffered the same weakness as true shadows, they could not stand the bright light, could not survive without the darkness that spawned them.

My joy was short-lived. I could still feel the venom from their dark claws coursing into my bloodstream. My mind wanted to give into the cold, bleak weariness that the creatures had forced into my body. I forced fresh air into my lungs and focused my will, warping the reality set around me and burning the poisons out of my system. I was still weak, but I could think again, think clearly enough to fight back against the things that waited for me beyond my island of safety.

The pain from my wounds aided in keeping me alert, and I made a mental note to clean them thoroughly when I got back to the apartment above my shop. As for the shadow-monsters, I decided to try my luck with the light around me. I once again focused my will, fueled my beliefs in the ways of the universe and supercharged the street lamp above me. The light grew brighter, and shifted from a dull yellow to a burning white. As the light grew stronger, the shadow-creatures suddenly found themselves engulfed in the luminescence. The creatures that had surrounded my area of safety suddenly found themselves in turn surrounded by the light and screamed as the fiery glow expanded, lighting the surrounding block as well as if it were high noon on a sunny day. The writhing shapes made a sound that was barely over a whisper, but the only sound they'd made at all as they burned out of existence.

The light had taken all it could, and the sodium bulb exploded in a flaming arc of released gasses, showering me for the second time that day with broken glass. One wedge of glass cut across my face, leaving a thin line of pain that started another path of blood on my body. I dropped into a crouch and covered my head with my arms in a futile attempt to avoid suffering more scrapes and cuts as the hot glass rained down around me. Then the brilliance died, and the darkness surrounded me again. I stayed perfectly still for a long time, waiting for the claws to come for me from the depths of the night.

Instead, I heard the voice of Jodi Blake as she stepped out of the darkness. She was smiling, the only nasty expression I'd seen on her face in the time I'd known her. A smile of triumph, a promise of pain. "Well, you handled that better than I would have expected, Bryce. Ready for another round, or will you give me the Pear?"

I stared at Jodi for a long while. No words came to mind that could express my bitterness, my cold rage at what she had done. I wanted nothing so much at that moment as I wanted to cause her pain. I wanted her to suffer at least a fraction of the grief she'd caused me, Penny and dear old Edith. I returned her smile, tasting the flavor of my own blood as it spilled past my upper lip and leaked past my clenched teeth.

Aries Michaels had taught me a lovely little spell when he was my teacher. It was simple, it was easy, and best of all, I knew it would hurt Jodi as little else could. I plucked a fragment of glass from the ground, ignoring the cut I gave myself in the process, and chanted three words in a language long dead. Jodi started, expecting no resistance from me so late in the game. Then she smiled when nothing at all happened.

I held the piece of glass in front of me, and I finished the spell with words in English. "Let the truth be revealed for all to see." The shard grew hot in my hand, and a shaft of light lanced out to strike Jodi full on. She raised her hands to ward off the brilliance, and I watched as the illusions were burned away from her, revealing once more the wretched old hag that I'd seen earlier in the pool of water.

Jodi stared at the hands and arms before her, crying out as the illusions she'd crafted so carefully were destroyed. The light from the glass faded, but the false skin she'd worn did not reappear. Jodi stepped back, shaking her head and mumbling softly to herself, horrified by what she'd become. What she'd already been for some time. Few people can stand to face the truth about themselves, their weaknesses, their flaws. The spell I'd cast showed every stain on Jodi's soul, and the stains were deep and plentiful.

The hag cried out with a scream worthy of an air raid siren, and then she ran, moving faster than should have been humanly possible. I stayed where I was, waiting to have the strength to move again. Twenty minutes later, I finally stood and started the trek back to my home.

It was almost morning when I finally made it back to my shop. The sky was lit with false dawn. A few stragglers walked the streets with me, weaving their way to unknown destinations or slumping down in back alleys, ready to call it a night and fully prepared to make the wet, filthy crawl-spaces their bed until they had rested a while. None of them paid me any mind, most were too drunk to care if they were bleeding, let alone to care if a complete stranger was wounded and badly shaken.

I used magick once more that night to heal the worst of my wounds after I had cleaned them as best I could. Either I'm unbelievably lucky, or the Paradox Spirits have opted not to make me suffer for my actions... Not yet at least. They will, but they have been known to wait until you are least prepared to handle the problem.

I found a note waiting for me when I got back to my shop. It was written in a lovely flowing script, red ink fading towards brown and clotting slightly on a plain white piece of paper. No surprise, it was from Jodi. "Dear Bryce, I would love to stay and settle matters, but I have to leave for now. Think about my offer. I'll even promise to leave your friend alone if you just give the Pear of B^ttger to me. I am even willing to overlook the nasty little trick you pulled on me. I'm sure we'll talk again soon. Until then, dream of me, as I will surely dream of you. Love, Jodi."

She'd even placed a heart as the dot on her i.

I burned the letter.

I checked as soon as I entered the shop. The Golden Pear of B^ttger and the Elector of Saxony's Key were still where they belonged, and nothing else had been touched. There was a very brief message from Penny on my machine. "Grimm, I'm okay. Neville told me you checked. We'll talk later. Bye."

At least she had the decency to call. I slept soundly for several hours. I don't remember much about my dreams, but I do remember that Jodi was in them, and I remember a pile of skulls, some still hanging with meat and others old and worn almost to dust. The only part of the dream that scared me occurred after I woke up to the sound of my alarm clock screaming in my ear. I remember waking up feeling very refreshed and knowing that whatever happened in that hideous dream, I was enjoying myself whole-heartedly.

God help me, the future is a scary thing.

THE SEVEN SAGES OF THE BAMBOO GROVE
■■■■■■■■■■■■

John H. Steele

The wild geese fly across the long sky above.
Their image is reflected upon the chilly water below.
The geese do not mean to cast their image on the water;
Nor does the water mean to hold the image of the geese.
— Anonymous

The present. Wednesday, November 3.

There was a fine mist falling from the gray sky. Unusual for this time of year, thought Lieutenant Robert Angler as he walked up the sloped driveway to the house at 1442 Granite Street. Generally, the sun burned off whatever morning cloud cover there was by this late in the afternoon, but this day had been dark and cool and wet from the start. With the mist, Angler wasn't really aware of constantly being rained on, but he was aware of being damp — his hands, his face, the pages of his note pad.

The houses in this neighborhood were all clean and looked freshly painted; the shrubbery was trimmed, the lawns neatly manicured. A washed and waxed, blue Nissan Sentra sat in the driveway at 1442. After knocking on the door, Angler noticed the doorbell on the frame. *Oh well.* He heard movement, footsteps, from inside. He saw the curtain moving slightly in the window to his right, someone looking to see who was at the front door.

More footsteps. "Who is it?" came the muffled female

voice from behind the door.

Angler held up his badge, since neither his jacket and tie nor his Ford LTD identified him as a police officer. "Detective Angler, SFPD."

After only a moment's delay, a dead bolt clicked, and the heavy red door opened just a couple inches. A vertical strip of a face examined the badge, then the door closed. Angler heard the chain being unhooked. He thought briefly about his childhood, when people didn't need to lock themselves in their houses during the day, but he could understand, better than most, perhaps, why people did today.

A small woman opened the door halfway. She had graying hair, glasses, and she was beginning to lose the battle against middle-aged spread. She was probably in her mid-forties. "May I help you?" she asked. She seemed slightly puzzled — no one in this kind of neighborhood expected the police to knock on his or her door — but willing to be helpful.

"Mrs. Loring?" asked Angler.

"Yes?"

"Is Albert home?"

"Why, yes, he is. Is something wrong?"

Angler wondered if she were afraid her son was involved in some sort of mischief — stealing a road sign, underage drinking, smoking pot — or did she automatically assume that there must be some misunderstanding? "I just need to ask him some questions, ma'am. He's not in any kind of trouble." Angler gave her a slight smile.

Mrs. Loring, visibly relieved, let out a deep breath. She opened the door wider. "Please come in. I'll get him for you." She showed Angler to the living room, the room without a TV that probably no one used unless there was company. Mrs. Loring turned on a lamp. "It certainly is chilly out there today."

"Yes, ma'am."

"And wet." She wrung her hands.

"Yes, ma'am."

She stood facing him as Angler looked around the room. She gestured toward one of the nicely upholstered chairs. "Please, have a seat. I'll get Al for you."

Angler sat. "Thank you, ma'am."

Mrs. Loring turned and left the room. Angler could hear her going up the stairs. He glanced around the room again — thick white carpet, brass candlesticks, antique clock on the mantle — tastefully furnished, not ostentatious, but expensive. After a moment, Mrs. Loring returned with her son following her. Angler stood as they entered the room. "Detective…"

"Angler."

"Angler. I'm sorry." She held the boy's shoulders. "This is my son, Al."

"Thank you." Angler sat.

Mrs. Loring and her son sat on the couch. Al was a taller, thinner version of his mother. They both had angular faces and chins that stuck out just a bit. His hair was straight and mop-like on top, shaved in ridges around his ears and the back of his head. His eyes were wary.

"Al," Angler began. "I'm just here to ask you some questions. I was telling your mother before, there's no need for you to worry or be nervous."

Al nodded. His mother patted his knee.

Angler thought it was amusing that, despite the bravado most middle-class kids emoted when talking about the police, when confronted with a real live police officer, most kids clammed up. "I need to find out about a friend of yours, Al. Randy Alvinson. When was the last time you saw him?"

Al thought for a minute. His expression was all too familiar to Angler — reluctant to cooperate because he thought he might get his friend in trouble. "A couple weeks ago, maybe."

"He hasn't been around much lately," added Mrs. Loring. "He and Al aren't that close. He just comes by once in a while to take a shower or get a free meal. I've always thought that child was in for trouble."

"Mom…" Al was clearly annoyed. "He is not." Al turned to Angler. "Randy's not in trouble, is he?"

Angler looked down at his hands. *God, I hate this.* He would have liked to have been able to avoid this part of his job more than any other. "Randy's body was found two days ago."

Al's mouth dropped open. Both he and his mother stared in disbelief. There was no sound except the ticking of the clock on the mantle.

"My goodness," whispered Mrs. Loring.

"What happened?" asked Al, barely able to speak.

"I can't go into details," said Angler. "At this point I'm just trying to establish who might have seen Randy last, trace his recent whereabouts, then go from there." Al and Mrs. Loring sat silently, stunned by the news. Angler figured it would be a while before they were very talkative on the subject. He could see Al's reluctance to cooperate crumble, but trauma could be just as effective a barrier to gathering information. He had hoped to ask a few more questions before revealing what had happened. "So, it's been roughly two weeks since you saw him?" Al nodded. "Perhaps you can confirm a few things for me, then."

"Okay." Al nodded again. Mrs. Loring was still silent.

"Randy was eighteen. How old are you, Al?"

"Nineteen," said Al.

"Al is just taking a year off before he goes to college," said Mrs. Loring. "Randy had dropped out of high school."

"Okay," said Angler. "Randy's parents told me that he had moved out of their house last year, but they didn't know where he was staying. They said he didn't really keep in touch with them. Do you know where he was staying?"

"Yeah. He was living out of his van, all over the city," said Al.

"Brown Ford van?" asked Angler.

"Yeah."

"And he just stopped by here once in a while for a shower, or food, or something like that?"

"That's right," said Mrs. Loring.

Angler scribbled on his note pad. "Are you positive you didn't see him more recently than two weeks ago, Al?"

Al thought, then shook his head. "I haven't seen him since then."

"Are you sure?" asked his mother.

"Yes. I'm sure." Exasperation with his mother lined his voice.

"Okay," said Angler. "One last question for now. Do you have any idea if Randy was involved with drugs at all? Using, selling?"

Al squirmed a bit on the couch. He looked at his mother and then back at Angler. "I think he might have smoked pot once in a while, but I think that's all. He wasn't a dealer or anything."

Angler nodded and scribbled. He didn't think he would get much else out of these people, so he gave them his card and asked them to call him if they remembered anything that might be of help. Mrs. Loring showed him to the door. As she painstakingly straightened and flattened her skirt, she was full of platitudes on the evils of drug use. She didn't mention anything specifically about her son, but Angler imagined that Al would, at the very least, get asked some pointed questions about marijuana, and probably would get a lecture to boot. As Angler ventured back out into the mist, Mrs. Loring retreated into her safe world and closed the door.

He who has the least scrap of sense,
once he has got started on the great highway
has nothing to fear so long as he avoids turnings.
For great highways are safe and easy.
But men love by-paths.

—Lao Tzu

Eight days ago. Tuesday, October 26.

Randy ran his hand through his spiked, blond hair. "You want me to *what?*" He had taken off his flannel shirt. His T-shirt was enough with the warm afternoon sun in this quiet grove in the Japanese Tea Garden where he and Tun Tzu had spent most of the day. Strangely enough, even though the gardens were fairly thick with tourists, no one had strolled into this particular area all day.

Tun Tzu sat on a large rock at the edge of the frog pond. The old man's dingy white robe and dark blue vest seemed just as natural as Randy's jeans and combat boots in this serene setting. Tun Tzu stroked his short, white goatee. His hair, hanging down his back from his balding head, almost glistened in the sunlight. "I want you to touch the mind of that flower at your feet."

Randy stood with his hands on his hips. At first he had thought Tun Tzu was crazy. Then he had come to see some of the benefits of humoring the man — expanding mental faculties, extensive memory training, insights into his own thought processes. It was more interesting than Scientology, at least. Now, once again, as several times over the past week, he knew the old geezer was crazy. "You gotta be kidding me." He stared at Tun Tzu, who did not respond. "You want me to touch the flower's mind. You may not be up on your botany, but flowers don't have brains. They just have leaves and petals and pistons and stamens and chlorophyll and crap. You know, they just sit there and photosynthesize, make oxygen and stuff." Tun Tzu was intently watching one of the small fish in the pond. He gave no indication of having heard Randy. "You're crazy, man."

Without looking up from the pond, Tun Tzu said, "Is there no difference between a mind and a brain? You should know this by now."

"It's a plant, man," said Randy. "Why do you want me to do stupid stuff like this? You said I was going to be powerful. So far I've only memorized crap."

The speckled yellow fish swam lazily toward Tun Tzu.

"Did I speak of power, or were those your own thoughts?"

"This is stupid."

"If you cannot understand the simple, how can you understand the complex?" asked Tun Tzu.

"Aw, screw you, man," Randy said as he turned away in disgust and frustration.

Tun Tzu looked up, finally, but not at Randy. "If you wish to learn no more, then leave me. I will force nothing upon you. You will go no further. The path is too difficult and the danger to my home too great to waste time upon you." He returned his attention to the pond.

A slight breeze rippled the water and rustled the leaves of the trees. The large orange flower at Randy's feet swayed gently. He looked at it with disgust. *I could leave*, he thought, *but what else do I have to do? What the hell*. He had already sharpened his mind incredibly under Tun Tzu's tutelage. He had learned worlds more in the past week than he had in the speed reading and memory strategy classes his mother had made him take when he was still in school. "Do you want me to figure out what kind of flower it is or something?"

"I do not care for the names that men may give it," Tun Tzu said quietly. "Look into it. Touch its mind."

Randy shook his head. *This is crazy.*

He sat down next to the flower and attempted to clear his mind, to be free from his annoyance at Tun Tzu, his irritation and impatience. He stared at the flower and memorized its features until he could see it with his eyes closed — the large, curved leaves; the bright orange petals forming a tube, then opening; the faint tinges of red and yellow around the edges of the petals. *Nothing. Just a flower.* Randy thought of how he had learned to look inward, to examine the intricacies of his own mind. He looked inward now at his own energies, at the patterns of his own thoughts, ever-shifting, yet structured in their flow. He tried to attune what he knew of his own mind to his perception of the flower, to experience its patterns from within rather than just looking at its surface.

On that bright, sunny day in the garden, Randy almost missed the faint glimmer of that for which he was searching. While the sun moved westward across the sky, Randy was absorbed by his study, lost within himself, within his comparisons, within his examination of the inherent structure of the flower. It was true that the plant had no brain, and little mind, one could argue, compared to a human; but even with its lack of self-awareness, there was still a primitive consciousness, a realized — if not articulated — experience of life which Randy stumbled upon. It was a small speck of light upon a huge, dark canvas of being, the proverbial needle. Once Randy found the speck, he focused all his energies on it. Through the mind of the flower, as it were, he could feel the warmth of the sun, and the cool moisture of the soil below him. In some strange way that he had never experienced before, he *was* the flower. He was touching its mind, discovering it rather than only seeing that which he expected to see. He could not have accomplished this without the meditative techniques and mental probing that Tun Tzu had taught him, the repetitious exercises and ritualistic activities which had seemed so tedious and pointless before. His concentration broke and the empathetic experience faded away as Randy realized that he had succeeded.

"I did it!" Randy exclaimed, jumping to his feet, his exhaustion and cramped muscles forgotten as adrenaline coursed through his body. "I did it! I touched its friggin' mind! It does have a mind, sort of."

From his perch on the rock, Tun Tzu nodded.

"I could feel it," Randy explained. "I could feel... everything. Everything it felt!" Randy jumped about in his excitement.

"What does this mean, butterfly?" Tun Tzu asked quietly.

Randy's jubilation, his euphoria, abruptly collapsed. "What?"

"What does this mean?" Tun Tzu repeated. "Is there some other significance, or do you merely wish to arrange flowers the rest of your days?"

Randy stood still, momentarily speechless, so quickly had his victory evaporated. The flower stared up at him, mocking him. He blinked at the brightness of the sun. This old bastard wasn't going to get the best of him. He thought about what he had done. "I had to look in." He re-created the experience in his mind. "I couldn't just look at it, or into it. It's not like x-ray vision or something." He felt an idea forming in his mind, coming into focus. "I had to look in myself, to my mind, and relate to its, to identify with its. Does that make sense?"

"You tell me when it makes sense," said Tun Tzu. "And then you may look into that bush, and that tree, and then this fish. There are many steps taken and many more to take yet. And always remember," Tun Tzu's usually mild voice took on a sharper edge, "concentration is that which must be maintained in success as well as in failure. You succeed, and your success crumbles before you. This can cause great harm. Here." From the folds of his robe, Tun Tzu tossed a small object toward Randy, who caught it. It was a smooth, gray stone. "This will help you. Use it to anchor your thoughts, to center your mind." Tun Tzu turned back to the pond.

Randy sat studying the stone, caressing it. What wonders did it hold? Was this where he got past mind games and parlor tricks? Was the old man finally going to teach him something worthwhile? He tried to let the agitation wash out of his mind. He focused on the stone and once again began to study the flower.

■ ■ ■

In the deep bamboo forest I sit alone.
Loudly I sing and tune my lute.
The forest is so thick that no one knows about it.
Only the bright moon comes to shine upon me.
                                        —Wang Wei

Before.

The *luira* wood burned slowly under the cauldron. The thin, dark liquid inside steamed and began to boil. Around the cauldron, in the clearing with two rickety, bamboo lean-tos, sat three men, wrinkled and white-haired. Occasionally Tun Tzu rose to his knees and stirred the bubbling concoction with a four-foot branch. Li P'o sat cross-legged and stared into the fire. The flames licked the blackened pot and danced joyous jigs in the approaching dusk. Ch'eng Hao sat, also cross-legged, and slept. Every few minutes, he would lean dangerously to one side before flinching violently, righting himself, and then dozing once again.

Li P'o glanced over expectantly as Tun Tzu dipped a wooden spoon into the cauldron. He blew on the liquid several times and then finally, as Li P'o leaned forward with raised eyebrows to see, tested the brew. Tun Tzu swished the liquid around in his mouth and then swallowed. He pursed his lips, then licked them. A smile crept across his face. Li P'o broke into a grin and then a fit of hiccuppy laughter. He stood and slapped Ch'eng Hao on the back. "Wake up, you old fool," said Li P'o.

Ch'eng Hao was startled to life. He almost fell forward into the fire. Li P'o laughed even harder as he walked toward the edge of the grove. He raised his cupped hands to his mouth. "Wang Wei! Yang Kwang! The wine is ready!" He walked back to Tun Tzu by the cauldron. "Now we will see how quickly old men can run." The setting sun was reflected in Li P'o's eyes.

"There will be drink for a while," said Tun Tzu. "They needn't hurry."

"There will be drink for always," called Ch'eng Hao as he rubbed his eyes, "or else there would be no purpose in living."

The three men moved closer to the pot, as close as they could without setting their long robes on fire. Li P'o kicked dirt at some of the scattered coals with his bare feet. The quietness of the evening was shattered by the distressing

squeal of a young pig. There was a rustling in the underbrush
at the southern end of the grove, and then the pig broke
through. It was running full-tilt at the three sages and was
almost upon them before it managed to change directions,
nearly bowling over Tun Tzu. Several steps behind the pig,
Meng Hao-jan stumbled into the grove. His foot caught on
a stalk of bamboo, and he went sprawling to the ground,
landing near the fire. The pig was through the clearing and
into the underbrush before any of the old men could react.
As the resulting cloud of dust cleared, Meng Hao-jan stood
and brushed himself off. Tun Tzu offered a ladle full of wine
to his fallen comrade.

"Here comes Meng Hao-jan for his wine now," laughed
Li P'o. "Running more quickly than his feet can carry him."

"I will drink," said Meng Hao-jan angrily, "after I have
dined, and I shall greatly cherish both the wine and that
pig's misfortune."

"Surely you should quench your thirst before continuing
such a hazardous undertaking," said Li P'o.

"My thirst can wait until my vengeance is quenched,"
answered Meng Hao-jan as he pulled thistles from his robe
and began to stalk the pig.

Ch'eng Hao sat and shook his head slowly from side to
side. "What a sad day," he said, "when a sage of the bamboo
grove would rather chase swine than drink *muliana* wine."

"Why not leave the creature be?" agreed Tun Tzu. "The
villagers bring us what food we need. Why trouble yourself?"

Meng Hao-jan stopped and turned to the other three
men. "There is a distinct chain in the forest of that which
eats and that which is eaten. I plan to take full advantage
of having achieved one of the top links on that chain. So
eat your grain and rice and berries, if you will. I, for one,
will roast pig this night." And with that, he was gone.

Ch'eng Hao stood and picked up a wooden cup to fill
with wine. "Perhaps a ham bone to chew on would do my
old gums good," he reflected. "But I see no reason to not
take my wine with me." He shuffled out of the grove in the

general direction Meng Hao-jan had gone, a full cup in his hand.

Tun Tzu and Li P'o shook their heads, clicked their cups together, and drank deeply.

■ ■ ■

Near the middle of the day, when clouds are thin
and the breeze is light,
I stroll along the river, passing the willows
and the blooming trees.
People of the day do not understand my joy;
They will say that I am loafing like an idle young man.
                                        —Ch'eng Hao

Seventeen days ago. Sunday, October 17.

The van was dead. There were no two ways about it. No turnover, no click, no nothing. Randy sat in his van on the edge of JFK Drive in Golden Gate Park. His hands and face, and now his steering wheel, were smeared with grease from puttering around in the engine. He knew a fair bit about cars, but this problem had eluded him for several hours now. He had no idea what was wrong, much less how to fix it.

The park had been a great place to hang out since Randy had moved out from his folks' place. When he wasn't working one of the seven part-time jobs he had gone through in the past year, or parked at a friend's house, this was where he usually spent his time. There were always interesting (to put it mildly) people to watch, and often babes to pick up — he could usually get some girl who may or may not have been eighteen into the back of the van with the promise of a bowl or two. But although the park was a great place to hang out, it was not a great place to be stranded, and as the sun sank closer to the horizon, Randy did not relish the idea of spending the night there in his van. There were many safer locales in the city.

"I can help you," said the old man who was suddenly next

to the van.

Randy jumped a bit. He was usually pretty observant and somewhat wary of weirdos in the park, but he had not seen anyone approaching. "No thanks, gramps. I've got it under control." Randy didn't like the way the old man, who had tan, leathery skin and was wearing long Jesus robes, smiled — like he knew what was going on; like he knew Randy couldn't really go anywhere. Except for the bald top of the man's head, he had long, white hair that hung down his back and a short goatee. "Aren't you supposed to shave your head or something?" said Randy. "You know, give peace a chance."

The man's dark brown eyes bore into Randy's as if they were x-rays, as if the old codger could see right into him. Randy wanted to look away but could not force himself to do so.

"You want to go somewhere," said the man. "I can help."

Randy's stomach churned. The way the man peered into him, the way Randy felt defenseless, exposed — this guy was not talking about the van. Randy felt again that he was being effortlessly pried open, that the old man was looking into his soul. The idea and the feeling scared Randy, angered him. "No thanks. Piss off, man."

The old man smiled and remained calm. "You strike out at that which you do not understand, and that is much," he said. "There are many worlds to learn of rather than to fight off."

"Look. I just want to start my van and get out of here." Randy gripped the steering wheel tightly. "I don't want any trouble, and I don't want to hurt you, so take off."

The old man still smiled. "I can start your vehicle." With these words, Randy felt his anxiety wash away as if obliterated by the force of a torrential river. He could not explain his own calmness, his sudden deep-felt belief that this man was not armed and meant him no harm. Before he realized what had happened, Randy had slid over to the passenger's seat, and the old man was seated behind the wheel. "I can start your vehicle, and then we can talk," said the old man. "And then you can go somewhere."

Randy nodded. Words escaped him. He felt as if he were merely a spectator to his own life, viewing his emotions from a distance. He marveled at the sense of inner peace overwhelming him. He felt vaguely that he should be afraid, that some great new undertaking was beginning, but mostly he was drawn by the sense of possibility and adventure, the sense that this man might show him potential within himself which he might never otherwise fulfill.

The old man turned the key and the van roared to life, probably more smoothly than it had when it was new. Randy, from his emotional distance, knew that he should be amazed, but it all seemed normal. They pulled away from the curb and headed out of the park and into the city.

■ ■ ■

What is of all things most yielding
Can overwhelm that which is of all things most hard.
Being substanceless it can enter even when there is no space.
                                                    —Lao Tzu

Nineteen days ago. Friday, October 15.

The fog hung low, as if it did not want to let go of the wet, early-morning grass in Golden Gate Park. The sun had not yet ascended above the hills to the east. The trees and bushes and sidewalks remained in shadow. There was no one present to hear the electric snap in the air; no one to smell the faintly sulfurous odor of the smoke; no one to see the old man materialize out of nothing several feet above the ground.

Tun Tzu landed hard on his chest and face. He lay still, face-down in the grass, barely breathing. His mind was swimming. First the human chaos — shouts, screams, blood on his face — breaking in on the link that he and the others had established with the presence to the north — the Zorn. Then the even more disconcerting flashes of pain, or was it ecstasy? The feeling of being completely disconnected, of floating, of being elsewhere but nowhere overwhelming the senses; structureless, devoid of thought and meaning, as if reality of any type no longer existed. It went on and on but did not occupy time, for that concept, as well, had no meaning there (if it were a place, an actual location). And then the searing pain, this time only pain. He did not even notice the physical jolt, the fall, although his body was exhausted, battered.

Tun Tzu lay still, face-down in the grass, barely breathing.

Temporal order was returning. Spatial and rational order were returning. That had been the worst part — the absolutely complete structurelessness of his mind. His body would adjust, would recover.

While he lay there, the sun crept above the peaks to the east. The morning fog began slowly to dissipate. Finally, with a herculean effort, Tun Tzu raised himself with his arms and rolled over onto his back. His old body cried out against him. Muscles that felt as if they had not been used in years spasmed. Joints grated and only reluctantly allowed movement.

Eventually Tun Tzu was able to sit up. He picked the grass from his short beard, brushed the moist earth from his face and robe. He was surprised to find that there was no blood on him, even though he had felt it. He had consciously noted the sensation of it splattering on him. Some vestiges of his old world had not made the journey, apparently. The journey to where? *Where was he?* The land far to the north of the grove had been strange and different, but this place was not Tun Tzu's world, not the reality which he had known.

Several people had passed by over the course of the last few hours. Tun Tzu noted that those now within sight made concerted efforts not to notice him. He sensed apprehension in some, guarded hostility in others, even concern on occasion, but always coupled with fear.

He made the effort to stand. He didn't seem to be in any

danger. The sun was high in the sky now. The trees here were different in form from the bamboo and *luira* which he knew, but their inner structures were much the same. The people, too, who jogged past were similar in mind, if not in appearance. They were taller, and wore strange clothes — short, shimmering leggings, oddly padded shoes, finely woven shirts, mechanical devices of some sort in their ears.

There was certainly much to learn in this new world, but, Tun Tzu remembered, relatively little time in which to learn it.

■ ■ ■

You ask me why should I stay in this blue mountain.
I smile but do not answer. O, my mind is at ease!
Peach blossoms and flowing streams pass away without trace.
How different from the mundane world!

—Li P'o

Elsewhen.

"Why do you call us together?" asked Yang Kwang. "I do not doubt that you have good reason, but I am curious."

"I would think a man of your years would have learned patience, my friend," Tun Tzu gently chastised him.

"A man of my years may not have time for patience," answered Yang Kwang. He and Li P'o chuckled.

Tun Tzu glanced around the grove. Li P'o, Yang Kwang, Meng Hao-jan, and he were present. "Li Chuan is fetching Wang Wei. Where is Ch'eng Hao?"

"He is communing in the hut," said Yang Kwang.

"He is sleeping," Meng Hao-jan corrected him, as he stomped toward one of the huts. "He has been sampling the wine again this morning."

"So what is so important to rouse an old man from his sleep, and to bring Wang Wei from his luting in the forest?" asked Yang Kwang.

"If only matters of importance brought Ch'eng Hao from

sleep," said Tun Tzu, "he would rise only for new kettles of wine and would starve."

"But he would be happy," said Li P'o.

"When all are here, I will explain," said Tun Tzu.

At that very moment, Li Chuan and Wang Wei came striding into the clearing. Wang Wei beamed like the morning sun and plucked notes on his lute.

There was a commotion from the hut as Meng Hao-jan half-helped, half-dragged Ch'eng Hao to the others. "My own feet can carry me!" cried Ch'eng Hao testily. Meng Hao-jan released him, and the less-stable man fell to the dusty ground. "When they choose to do so," he added. Meng Hao-jan helped him up, and then the seven sages of the bamboo grove were together.

"Let us sit so that Tun Tzu may explain," said Li P'o.

"A fair suggestion," said Ch'eng Hao. "Shall we pass around wine to ease our minds and bodies?"

"Your mind is completely at ease, unless it is forced to think," snapped Meng Hao-jan.

"Please." Tun Tzu raised his hand. The men sat in a circle around the cauldron and quieted. He drew a deep breath, and a powerful calmness descended upon the grove. "There are strange happenings in the land," he began. "We all know of the strangers, the new teachers in the villages. Li P'o and I, and Meng Hao-jan, and Li Chuan have spoken of this." The other men nodded. "They teach disdain for the old ways, against reverence for the sages. They bring their wily science, and this is their right. The people may believe what they will. It is sad that they lose sight of the life of the land, of the rocks and the water, of the trees, but what befalls us will befall us."

"Already the villagers bring less food," Meng Hao-jan broke in. "They seek us out for help and advice less often. Soon we will be only memories."

"Then memories we shall be," said Yang Kwang, "if that is what is meant to be. We are not here to serve the villagers, or for the villagers to serve us. We are here because it is right that we be here."

"It is of concern to me," said Li Chuan, "that the people of the villages are not only less-pleasant. Many are openly hostile. I have been hit with rocks thrown by children, and taunted by their parents. I fear that it is more than our beliefs which the teachers with their pernicious contrivances preach against."

The sages muttered agreement. Many of them felt distinctly separated from the villages which had originally produced them, cast out and held in contempt, sometimes even hatred.

Tun Tzu spoke again. "There is that which is good, and there is that which is bad, but they are both natural. Then there is that which is unnatural."

"Which is also natural," said Yang Kwang.

"Perhaps," said Tun Tzu, "but I feel that at some point, though it may be against our nature, we must intervene." There was a concerned silence in the circle.

"Please continue," said Li P'o.

"I have sensed a presence far to the north," said Tun Tzu. "A man, yes, but one so attuned to the creation that he shines upon the dreamscape more brightly than the sun in the sky. His purity, I think, he is unaware of. It is not sought after."

"And thus only is it found," inserted Yang Kwang.

"Yes," agreed Tun Tzu. "But I perceive that he approaches a cusp, that he will engage in that which will determine the course not only of his existence, but also of this... this blight which looms over us. He battles stagnation, unknowingly perhaps, but it is the same stagnation which we now see threatening our lands, threatening this very grove. It may be that if we are able to aid him, he may be of help to us, or that the stagnation will be reversed if defeated in even one part of this world."

"But are not famine and drought and blight and death a part of the order?" asked Wang Wei. "Is not this stagnation but a part of the natural order?"

Meng Hao-jan could listen calmly no longer. "What good are wisdom and knowledge if they are kept closed in a box?"

"Perhaps it is wise to stay closed in a box," suggested Yang Kwang.

"Perhaps it would be wise," said Meng Hao-jan, "to keep *you* closed in a box, you starry-eyed dung beetle, and Ch'eng Hao with you."

"Some boxes are nice," said Ch'eng Hao with a smile.

"Tun Tzu, what do you suggest?" asked Li P'o.

The other argument died down. "I suggest," said Tun Tzu, "that we aid this man to the north, this pure child, as we may. The cusp approaches, and perhaps we shall ourselves create counterforces through our own actions, but I think we must help him. Although stagnation is of the Nameless, as Wang Wei suggests, it now seeks to overwhelm all else, to destroy the balance of which we partake."

The sages around the cauldron were silent, each occupied with his own thoughts. Words spoken would have been redundant. Wang Wei strummed lightly on his lute. Smooth, soothing notes trickled into the air. To enter into this conflict was to cast aside *wu wei*, actionless action, that which achieved without striving, without setting in motion the counterbalancing forces which were created by any purposeful action.

Meng Hao-jan spoke first. "I will help you, Tun Tzu."

Tun Tzu nodded acknowledgment.

"As will I," said Li P'o.

"And I," echoed Ch'eng Hao and Li Chuan.

There was silence for a moment, except for Wang Wei's music. He set his lute on the ground beside him. "I will help."

Several of the six concurring sages looked at Yang Kwang. The others stared at the ground in front of them. He began to nod his head slowly. "I know not of wisdom," he said. "But I do know of loyalty." He nodded toward Tun Tzu. "If this thing is to be done, for good or for ill, let it be done well."

"Then let it begin," said Li P'o.

The seven sages of the bamboo grove joined hands, and the ancient ritual was under way.

■ ■ ■

In Spring when all the flowers are in bloom,
The evening river appears smooth and motionless.
Suddenly the tidewater comes
with the reflection of glittering stars;
The ebbing waves carry away the image of the moon.
                                        —Yang Kwang

Three days ago. Sunday, October 31.

Randy and Tun Tzu stood under the full moon. The unusually thick fog and the park spread out all around them. Randy could feel his skin tingling, but he didn't know why. Tun Tzu had been quiet all day, answering briefly, and only when Randy had asked him a direct question.

The two had stayed in a cheap motel, The Starlight Lounge and Motor Lodge, the past week. Tun Tzu didn't seem to have trouble coming up with money. It was as if he just reached into a pocket in his robe and the cash materialized. Randy had enjoyed being able to get a hot shower on a regular basis. Tun Tzu had been fascinated by the Magic Fingers box attached to the bed — how many quarters had he stuffed in that thing? — and the cable TV. The little time that they had not spent training, Tun Tzu had been glued to the Weather Channel, and ESPN, and QVC. He had also acquired quite a taste for McDonald's, so Randy had made many late-night trips for fries and Big Macs. *You would think the guy had never had a hamburger before. Everybody in the world has to know who Ronald McDonald is by now,* thought Randy.

"What do I learn tonight?" Randy asked. He had begun, after his flower and tree and fish experiences, to probe the minds of humans, to pick up feelings, and sometimes even fragments of distinct thoughts, but Tun Tzu's mind remained completely closed to him. *The old man may be crazy, but he knows his stuff.*

Tun Tzu did not turn to face Randy. Instead, he looked off into the night. "Tonight my teaching ends, and your real learning begins, butterfly."

"Sounds good to me." Randy was ready for more power, more knowledge. "Why so glum, then? Sounds like your hard work is over."

For a moment Tun Tzu did not respond. When he did, his voice was quiet and full of sadness. "There is so little time," he said, half to himself. "So little time." He turned toward Randy. "This is not a game we play. If you do not realize this, then I have failed you. I may have failed you already by pushing you too quickly. If you succeed tonight, there are more-treacherous times ahead. Do you understand?"

Randy nodded. Tun Tzu was often serious and intense, but Randy had never, in the two weeks they had constantly been together, seen him this mournful, this full of doubt. Randy held tightly the gray stone through which he focused his concentration, the object which had changed Tun Tzu's lessons from impressive mind games into much deeper spiritual experiences. What type of power was held in that small rock? "I know, and I'm ready for whatever happens."

"I hope this is true." Tun Tzu pressed his hands together in front of him and lowered his head. "Then let us begin."

With Tun Tzu's words, everything began to darken around Randy. The world, except for the bright moon, slowly faded to black. There was no sky, no grass, no ground, no park, no Tun Tzu; only the moon and the darkness. Randy felt a great pressure upon his shoulders, forcing him to his knees. His body trembled uncontrollably until it, too, was gone, and there was only the moon.

Randy tried to call out, but he couldn't. He couldn't conceive the words; his tongue could not form them. *I am here,* he heard Tun Tzu, but not his voice, say. *But you must look inward. You must search alone.* And then the comforting nonvoice was gone.

The moon was growing larger. Was it coming closer? It was blindingly bright. There were no blemishes, no craters or formations marring its surface. There was only a magnificent sphere of light. As Randy gazed inward, he and the light became one. Comfort and warmth permeated his being.

At his core, the warmth remained constant, while the fringes cooled and became brittle. He could see himself, his short life being winnowed away, peeled back and apart bit by bit. The early years — mother, father, carefree, indulgences upon indulgences. But the joy and the wonder had shriveled. The light around him now, that which shone forth from him, was still bright and warm, making what he saw that much darker by contrast. The parents who had given so much and asked so much became the ogres of his life. He could not find what he needed through them, and they could not see that. They held him tightly, but not how he needed them to hold him. They tried to reach out to him in his desperation, but they pushed him away instead. He forced them to push him away; he would not respond to their embraces. They and he had all been so wrong. There was no blame, only guilt. The brightness began to burn him. He felt so dark, and the light was intense, pure.

Randy clutched the stone. It centered him; it anchored him. He could feel the gray smoothness in his hand. The power. It was his shield. With it, he knew he could hold anything at bay.

The stone is but a stone, he heard Tun Tzu's nonvoice say.

Randy's certainty wavered. It was his center. It was his focus.

A stone from the frog pond, said Tun Tzu. *Nothing more. It is what it is, as you are what you are.*

Randy felt the walls of his inner being shaking violently, rattling apart. Why must that upon which he seized always be unstable? *Only a stone!* He was swept along by the light.

He was always searching — for purpose, for direction, for meaning. He had always demanded, yet cast aside, help; needed others, yet been unable to admit weakness. Others could not understand; he could not permit them to understand, and he could see now, through this clarifying illumination, that this had crippled him, had held him back and forced others away. Even now, the light, in all its glory, was not enough. Somehow, he could not fully embrace it. With it, he could transcend his failings, but because of his failings, he could not claim it. It was not a conscious decision to be made now; it had been decided by every instant of his life.

The light was altering itself. The sphere was swelling, contracting, changing. It became thinner, longer. It began to take on a human shape, and Randy (even the name seemed distant now, had little connection to his identity) knew before the features formed that this avatar was him. He looked upon his figure of light, and tried to reach out to it. His fingers touched, but the heat was unbearable, the intensity of a star on his fingers. In that moment, he felt all the failures (of intent, not of deed) and missed opportunities of his life rushing in upon him, from his fingers up his arm to his heart, and he could not shake them loose. He knew pain, infinite pain, and fear. The limbs of the figure began to twist and become gnarled, and he was the disfigured. His psyche burned with all the torment and torture of a lifetime concentrated into an instant. Had he maintained a scrap of his previous humanity, he would have screamed, but he was far removed from such trivialities. The figure writhed and twisted until, finally, it was quenched, burned out, consumed like a wooden match. The light faded, and once again the moon was an orb in the night sky.

Tun Tzu stood under the full moon. The unusually thick fog and the park spread out all around him. At his feet lay a mangled, burnt body, a small gray stone clutched in its charred hand.

Head bent and eyes cloudy, Tun Tzu walked away.

■ ■ ■

In Spring I was soundly asleep;
Hardly did I notice the break of day.
Everywhere I heard the birds singing.
Last night there was the noise of storm and rain;
I wonder how many blossoms have blown away.
                                    —Meng Hao-jan

Then.

The six sages had lent their power to Tun Tzu. He was their guide through the Umbra, and their psychic energies his locomotion. When the archaic words were spoken, and the connection achieved, Tun Tzu turned his attention north. The sages did not maintain any semblance of their physical bodies on this journey, only an astral mass with a great silver cord of seven strands that connected them to their starting point. There were not miles to be traveled, per se, but the distance was nonetheless great. The farther they went, the more energy was needed from the sages. They placed their lives and their Quintessence in Tun Tzu's care.

They sped through the Umbra, aware at times of other shimmering minds around them, but they were intent only upon their objective. Very soon, as their perception of distance fell behind, marked only by the great silver cord, the light of which Tun Tzu had spoken, the pure one, came into view. It was intense and piercing. It was a mind, but much more than a mind. *Tzu-jan*, Tun Tzu communicated to the others. The creative property of the Tao, of the One. The mind partook of *tzu-jan*. It was attuned to the Unnameable.

There was, however, a barrier of some sort around the light, against which the light pulsed and struggled. Tun Tzu could see clearly that the light, if it were to unleash its full fury, if it realized even a portion of its potential, could break free easily. But it was restrained somehow. There was a great power in the concentrated effort of the sages, but even so, as they approached the barrier, Tun Tzu felt resistance, and it was powerful also. The barrier was of the landscape itself, projected by some oppressive force, whatever power held sway here in the northern lands, which were incredibly static, much more unyielding than the area of the bamboo grove. This was what the new teachers in the villages were doing, Tun Tzu realized. Their teachings, their discounting of the mystic and the esoteric, were making reality more brittle in the south as well, less yielding. Unchecked, life at the grove could eventually become as stagnant and uncreative as these lands to the north.

To break through the barrier and help the light realize its potential, or at least to allow it to break free on its own so that the pure one might help the sages counter the metaphysical rigidity which threatened them — that was what was necessary.

The sages pressed against the barrier. Their own motion slowed almost to a stop. The light pulsed more brightly, but was still restrained by its lack of self-knowledge. This was the cusp which Tun Tzu had foreseen. The light must either become free or be lost forever.

The barrier was not an active presence, or if it was, its encroachment upon reality, its usurpation of what was natural, was so gradual that it could only be perceived over a much-broader period of time, like glaciers creeping over a continent — not necessarily visible motion, but cataclysmic nonetheless.

It was soon apparent to the sages that they could not hope to destroy the barrier. It was barely budged by the extent of their psychic energy, and they could not maintain this journey indefinitely, even pooling their powers. They penetrated the barrier, but could not displace it. They could, however, by entering the barrier's sphere, contact the light, the pure inner mind.

Tun Tzu, as well as the others, was struck forcefully by a psychic shockwave as his astral form came into contact with the light. The connection was like holding a paradox in one's hand — such bridled power; the essence of *tzu-jan* unrealized; nearly limitless potential, but bound in this oppressive, static realm. The *tzu-jan*, the power of the creative essence, was dizzyingly palpable. The sages grasped the light, pulling it back toward the boundary of the barrier. *Let it taste the freedom, let it feel dynamic reality, and that may be enough!* The light was paradox through and through. It welcomed the sages' help, but it held itself back as well, as if it were sure of its own limitations, even though with that kind of power the limitations were of its own making; imposed by others, perhaps, but enforced by itself.

The sages were making progress in this astral tug-of-war. Soon the light would be close enough to the boundary that it could break free, if it would. Tun Tzu was able to form one word out of his contact with the light: Zorn. A title? A name? A command? He didn't know. Zorn, the light, the pure one.

Suddenly, however, the great silver cord was jerked violently, and there were only six strands. Ch'eng Hao was no longer present. There was another violent tug, and Li Chuan was gone. The combined consciousness of the other five sages was hurtling back toward the grove, somehow maintaining the connection with the light, the Zorn, which was so close to freedom. If it could only add its own power! Tun Tzu felt stretched beyond his limit. As he concentrated on the Zorn still, Meng Hao-jan's and Wang Wei's strands unraveled from the great silver cord, now only three strands thick. But these last two astral essences to be removed were not torn asunder as the first two had been. Tun Tzu's astral being fell back toward his body, only maintaining the connection with the Zorn through the continued aid of Li P'o and Yang Kwang. It was so close to escaping the barrier!

Then Tun Tzu could see the grove. He was not back to his body completely, but he was close enough to perceive what was happening. *Unthinkable!* The villagers, incited and led by strangers, by the insidious teachers, and fueled by new-found hatred and fear, were attacking the grove! None of the sages had realized the degree of animosity that the strangers had kindled. The once-benign villagers wielded clubs and spears and axes, crude but effective weapons against the defenseless sages. How had the villagers known that this was a good time to attack?

The sages' physical circle was broken. Li Chuan lay on his side, his head smashed in by a club. Ch'eng Hao, pierced through by a spear, sat and stared ahead blankly, blood flowing from both the wound and his mouth. Wang Wei and Meng Hao-jan had apparently reacted more quickly than Tun Tzu. They had returned to their bodies and now defended the sages. Wang Wei played his lute, harsh chords that called down wind and lightning from the sky against the villagers. By the cauldron, Meng Hao-jan stirred the wine, which took animated form, spirits that rent the attackers limb from limb. They had pushed back the attack, but for how long? The two sages were hard-pressed and were slowly losing ground.

Tun Tzu wanted to help them, but that would mean abandoning the increasingly tenuous connection with the Zorn, which would undoubtedly be sucked back into the static barrier. Should he help save his friends and abandon the task which had already claimed two of their lives, or finish that which might save his land from eventual magickal emasculation?

We are with you. It was Li P'o. Finish that which has been started, but quickly. Yang Kwang and I will aid you as we can

Tun Tzu could feel the strain even in Li P'o's calm thoughts. The three of them could not maintain the connection much longer.

As the three sages turned back to the Zorn, the great silver cord was jolted once again, and Li P'o was present no longer. Tun Tzu imagined that he could feel the blood splattered onto his physical form as Li P'o slumped to the ground. Tun Tzu and Yang Kwang raced to the Zorn. It was on the edge, practically free but unable or unwilling to make the last push. They tried to help it with every ounce of excess astral force they could summon, and then Yang Kwang was gone.

The strain was beyond enduring. Tun Tzu, alone and so far beyond that of which he should be capable, added his personal, finite Quintessence into the effort, choosing to siphon off his continued existence rather than abandon the Zorn. Inches more, if distance could be measured in this plane, and the Zorn could break free. Tun Tzu felt his energy draining away as the connection became weaker and weaker. He approached the point of no return, the moment when he could not reclaim himself from these actions, and passed beyond it. Everything was fading now, his personal energies in this plane exhausted. There was only numbness. *This was not supposed to happen.* His friends lay dead and battered, and Tun Tzu himself was spent, rapidly burning out of this reality. He dimly saw the Zorn break free of the barrier, and then slip back inside it. *But why?* Did it not realize it could be free? Did it not desire to be untethered? It mattered little anymore as everything faded beyond his view.

■ ■ ■

In Tao the only motion is returning.
The only useful quality, weakness.
For though all creatures under heaven are the product of Being,
Being itself is the product of Not-being.
                                    —Lao Tzu

The present. Wednesday, November 3.

Tun Tzu had seen the man go into the Bayside First Mutual Bank on Steuart Street that morning, and now that the sun was dropping in the evening sky, he watched the man leave the building, walk to the Transbay station, and crawl into the belly of one of those mechanical beasts. *What odd forms of transportation — trains and vans.* And then he thought of Randy, of course. There had been so much death and so much failure already, but he could not give up.

This static world must be much like the northern lands under the static barrier which Tun Tzu and the others had seen. It made sense that an agent from this realm could go there to aid the Zorn, because the Zorn was somehow connected to this world by the *tzu-jan*. The essence of being flowed from this world. Tun Tzu's world was dead to him now. He could never go back. The path of the *tzu-jan* had brought Tun Tzu here to this strange world of San Francisco, although he should no longer exist at all, as far as he knew.

An Awakened being from this world could help free the Zorn. Perhaps Randy's failure had been in the intensity of his desire to escape. He was not a true agent of stasis, for he yearned for nothing but to leave it. This banker, however, was a slave to the static laws of this world. Perhaps he, being more deeply versed in such a system, would be the proper catalyst to free the Zorn. He could be taught to transcend, yet still comprehend, the static world. Maybe where the rebel had failed, the indentured servant could succeed. Or perhaps the failure was in the task itself, and Tun Tzu would be condemning another innocent to death, or worse. A wise man's words came to mind:

Heaven and Earth are ruthless;
To them the ten thousand things are but as straw dogs.
The Sage too is ruthless;
To him the people are but straw dogs.

It was a chance that would have to be taken.

■ ■ ■

Those who know do not speak;
Those who speak do not know.
      —Lao Tzu

Four days ago. Saturday, October 30.

The earthquake the night before had shaken the Starlight Lounge and Motor Lodge quite severely. The picture above one of the beds had fallen, and the Magic Fingers box had bounced off the bedside table and was no longer functional. There were numerous fresh cracks in the walls and ceiling to go with the numerous old cracks that predated this particular quake.

Now, Randy and Tun Tzu lay on the grass, basking in the sun in the small grove at the Japanese Tea Garden. Randy understood better now why tourists did not interrupt their days in the grove. "Cool! Just like the Shadow!" he had commented upon learning more of the powers that Tun Tzu possessed, and that he would soon possess, to "cloud men's minds." Randy felt a bond with the crazy old man that he had not felt before, not with his parents, not with friends, not with girls — a common view of the basic nature of reality, or that was the bond Randy was beginning to feel. The ground here in the grove felt warm and safe, never mind last night's tectonic excitement.

Randy looked over at Tun Tzu, whose eyes were closed. He never could tell if the old man were asleep, or off somewhere doing something, whatever he did. Surely he didn't look into the minds of trees and frogs anymore.

"Yes?" said Tun Tzu, startling Randy in spite of himself.

"How the hell do you do that?" asked Randy.

"You wanted to ask me a question?"

"Yeah," said Randy. "Now that you mention it. You said yesterday that you wanted me to go to your home because you couldn't go back. Why can't you go back? Are the cops after you or something?"

Tun Tzu smiled. "There will be plenty of time for explanations later, if they are required." There was silence again, except for the sounds of the birds in the trees and the frogs in the pond. "What do you search for, butterfly?" asked Tun Tzu after a few moments. "Why do you stay with me and do what I ask?"

Randy was caught off-guard by this question. Tun Tzu's

queries were usually abstract, or metaphysical, or just plain weird, but not personal. "I don't know." *I just like being with you*, he wanted to say, but could not bring himself to it. "To learn, I guess. I always felt there was something more than what they told us was important in school. And power. I thought you could teach me things, and you have." Randy thought about the past two weeks — the memory tasks and the rational strategies; looking inward to himself; the empathetic connections with plants, animals, and people; the mind links he had briefly crafted with random passers-by, cut off quickly to avoid detection of his awkward skills. There was some deeper meaning that Tun Tzu was building toward. There must be some culmination. Randy looked at the old man again. His tanned skin and white hair shone vibrantly in the light. "Tun Tzu."

"Yes?"

"May I touch your mind?"

Tun Tzu did not open his eyes or change expression, but he did draw in a quick breath and hold it ever so briefly. "Perhaps tomorrow, butterfly. Perhaps tomorrow."

LEXICON
■■■■■■■■■■■■

A mage's world contains many strange and unusual things, and mages have adopted or invented various words to describe the weirdness of their daily life. The next three sections list the most frequently used terms (Common Parlance), the vocabulary of ancient mages (Old Form), and the ever-evolving slang of the younger generations (Vulgar Argot).

Common Parlance

■■■■■■■■■■■■

Acolyte: A non-Awakened servitor of a mage.

Adept: A mage with a fair degree of aptitude and power.

Arete: The measure of a mage's magickal enlightenment and skill.

Ascension: The enlightened state of being to which all mages aspire.

Ascension War, The: An ongoing conflict between mage factions, with the future of reality as the prize. Actually a series of conflicts, ranging from subtle maneuvering to appalling violence.

Apprentice: A mage who has not yet been initiated into a Tradition. Not typically applied to Orphans.

Arcane: A mystical veil erected by mages to guard their identities.

Avatar: A soul, said by some to be a fragment of the Pure Ones who originally inhabited the Tellurian. An Awakened Avatar enables a mage to perform magick.

Awakened, The: This term describes any supernatural creature of at least partially human origin, including mages, werewolves, mummies and vampires.

Awakening, The: The moment in which one realizes, mind, body, heart and soul, the reality of magick and one's own destiny.

Barabbi: A mage who renounces her former loyalries to follow the dark Path of the Nephandi.

Branding: A punishment in which a mage has her Avatar marked.

Cabal: A group of mages bound to each other by loyalty and a common purpose.

Caern: A Node controlled by the Garou.

Celestine: The greatest of the spirits, equal in power to the ancient gods; they rule the Shard Realms.

Censure: A common mild punishment among mages. It is similar to being on parole.

Chantry: The stronghold of a mage or cabal. On Earth, this may be a normal building or a magickally fortified and enhanced structure. These mundane places are often located on Nodes and connected to strongholds in the Umbra. Technomancer Chantries are called **Constructs**.

Coincidental Magick: This is magick performed in such a fashion that it is effectively indistinguishable from a mundane event.

Convention: One of five groups of mages that form the Technocracy and enforce its policies. The Conventions are: Iteration X, the Syndicate, the Progenitors, the New World Order and the Void Engineers.

Consor: A mage's powerful ally; not a mage, but of comparable ability.

Council; Council of Nine: The collective name for the Nine Traditions of Mystic Magick and the federation they have formed.

Deacon: A common name for the founding member of a well-established Chantry.

Deep Umbra: The aspects of the Umbra that are only found away from the Earth. The Shard Realms are scattered throughout the Deep Umbra.

Demon: Enigmatic beings of evil intent and disputed origin.

Disciple: The lowest rank among the Tradition mages. Disciples can perform magick and have joined a Tradition.

Dream Realm: A world created out of old dreams kept alive by the Oneira, the Dream Lords.

Dynamic Reality: Reality in flux. It may be changed quickly through vulgar magick, slowly through coincidental magick, or gradually through the normal flow of worldly events.

Errant: A vengeful mage whose Chantry and cabal have been destroyed. Errants are frequently shunned by other mages.

Fellow: A full member of a Chantry, but not a founding member and therefore of lower status than its Deacons.

Focus: An object, action or gesture required to perform magick. Foci vary with belief, from mage to mage and paradigm to paradigm. Technomancer foci are often called **apparatus**.

Gaia: The Earth and the Near Umbra.

Gate: A temporary magickal "bridge" between two places. Frequently created at Nodes. See *Portal*.

Gauntlet, The: A mystical barrier between the Earth and the Near Umbra. The Gauntlet was created by the Technocracy to prevent free travel between the physical and spirit worlds.

Garou: The term that werewolves use for themselves. (Also used by mages who want their respect.)

Gilgul: The destruction of a mage's ability to work magick by removing or destroying his Avatar. This is the most horrible crime or punishment possible, as it essentially takes away the mage's soul.

Hollow Ones: An Orphan group who embrace post-modern decay and Gothic romanticism as a response to the apparent failure of both. Though they often work with Tradition mages, they are not taken very seriously.

Horizon, The: The magickal barrier separating the Near Umbra from the Deep Umbra.

Horizon Realms: Small pockets of custom-made reality; artificial Realms on the border between the Near Umbra and Deep Umbra. Umbral Chantries are built within them and earthly Chantries connect to them by way of Portals and Gates.

Hubris: The overwhelming (and often fatal) pride which leads mages into overconfidence or excess. Monumental hubris guides the Technocracy and lies at the heart of the Ascension War.

Incarna: Greater spirits; the servants of the Celestines. For all intents and purposes, demigods.

Initiation: A combined test and ceremony that marks a person's transition from apprentice to mage among the Traditions.

Kindred: The term that vampires use for themselves.

Lord: An Umbrood spirit; less powerful than an *Incarna* but more powerful than either *Preceptors* or *Minions*.

Mage: An Awakened person whose actions and belief dramatically alters the reality around her. Used commonly to refer to followers of the Mystick Traditions, this term properly applies to all users of True Magick.

Magic: Stage tricks, illusions, etc. Also refers to static magic, which works with the momentum of reality, rather than reworking it by force of will.

Magick, True Magick: The act of dynamically altering reality through force of will and knowledge.

Master: A mage of great power and ability.

Marauder: An utterly unpredictable mage so given over to eternal change that he is essentially a magickal psychotic.

Mentor: A mage who teaches another mage magick.

Methodology: A sub-group of a Technocratic Convention, which specializes in a certain function.

Minion: One of the least powerful Umbrood spirits.

Near Umbra: The part of the spirit world that exists around each Realm. Usually used to describe the area of the Umbra that is around the Earth.

Nephandus, Nephandi: A mage who follows the Path of Descent, choosing darkness over light. Many Nephandi work closely with demons.

Node: A highly mystical place. Nodes collect and store Quintessence. The Gauntlet is thinner in their vicinity. Many Chantries, Gates and Portals are built on these sites.

Oracle: One of the legendary mages who have attained mystick perfection.

Orphans: Sleepers who have Awakened spontaneously without the assistance or guidance of other mages. They have taught themselves magick and are often considered dangerous wild cards.

Ostracism: A punishment that completely divorces a mage from Tradition society.

Otherworlds: Collective term for the realms outside the Gauntlet.

Paradox: An anomalous state of reality caused when a mage disrupts the momentum of static reality with her own magickal acts.

Paradox Realm: A small Realm created by Paradox spirits to entrap a mage and thus prevent any further disruptions of reality. The Realm traps the mage inside an altered world and prevents her escape.

Paradox Spirit: A spirit formed from the collective beliefs of humanity. Mages who are careless or unlucky with their magick in front of Sleepers will find themselves hunted by these spirits.

Pattern: The mystical composition of an object, entity, place or idea.

Pedagogue: A tutor of great fame, usually surrounded by students and quite powerful.

Procedures: What Technocracy mages call their Magickal Effects.

Pure Ones: The legendary primordial beings of the Tellurian. Many mages believe that all souls are fragments of these shattered entities.

Pogrom, The: The systematic purge of all opposition ("random elements") by the Technocracy.

Portal: A permanent Gate. Portals are usually guarded by powerful spirits that require a task to be performed or a puzzle solved before they will allow safe passage.

Postulant: A mage who serves the Oracles, trying to gain admittance to their ranks.

Preceptor: An Umbrood spirit that is less powerful than a *Lord*, but still more powerful than a *Minion*.

Prime: The original unified force that composes the universe. All things flow from this primordial energy.

Protocols, The: A code of honor established by the Traditions to prevent abuses of power. Violation of this code is punishable by *censure, branding, ostracism, death,* or *Gilgul*.

Quiet: A state of insanity caused by the excessive use of magick.

Quintessence: The stuff of magick; the raw substance of the universe in condensed form. *See Tass*.

Realms: The worlds of "solid" reality that exist within the Tellurian. Sometimes referred to as Domains.

Rogue: A renegade mage turned mercenary.

Rote: A tried and true magickal Effect, passed down as a tool or weapon.

Seeking: A mage's Avatar-guided quest for enlightenment.

Sentinel: One of the guardian mages of a large Chantry; not typically a member herself.

Shade Realm: The Umbral "shadow" of a Shard Realm.

Shard Realm: One of nine Realms said to have been part of Gaia in ages past. They roughly correspond to the other planets (including Luna) and the nine Spheres of magick; each is ruled by a Celestine.

Sleeper: A person potentially capable of magick, but who is not yet aware of its existence.

Sphere: A particular element of reality manipulated by mages.

Static Reality: The foreword momentum of reality, often guided by the deeds and beliefs of humanity. Magick, by its dynamic nature, disrupts static reality to some degree. The perimeters of static reality have, in recent centuries, become more restrictive, due to a single global paradigm (belief system) espoused by the Technocracy.

Symposium: A monthly meeting of the Technocracy. At these meetings members of the Conventions gather to make policy.

Tass: Quintessence stored in physical form. It tends to collect in Nodes and takes various forms based on its surroundings — i.e., mushrooms at a wooded caern, water from a specific spring, or magickal garbage mold at an urban Node.

Talisman: An object that stores Quintessence and uses it to create a specific magickal effect — i.e. magick carpets, wishing wells or etheric ray guns. Technocratic Talismans are called **Devices**.

Technocracy, The: A ruthless and powerful group of mages who seek to eliminate harmful elements from reality, thus making it safe for humanity. Their magick, based on scientific principle, conforms and shapes modern reality — to a point. This group will not be satisfied until all possibilities lie within their control. (See *Pogrom*.)

Technomancer: A mage whose magick revolves around some scientific principle. Often used to describe mages of the Technocracy, the term properly applies to Virtual Adepts and Sons of Ether as well.
Tellurian: The whole of reality.

Tradition: One of the Nine Mystick Traditions, a Council formed in the 1400s to oppose the Technocracy, resist the radical changes of the Marauders, and fight the evil of the Nephandi. These are: the Akashic Brotherhood, the Celestial Chorus, the Cult of Ecstasy, the Dreamspeakers, the Euthanatos, the Order of Hermes, the Sons of Ether, the Verbena and the Virtual Adepts.

Tribunal: A gathering of Council mages to discuss matters important to the Traditions; usually held in times of strife.

Tutor: Mages who have become known as proficient teachers. They are highly regarded by other mages.

Umbra: The astral plane that exists around each Realm.

Umbrood: Any non-human not born or created on Earth. This includes both the spirits that roam the Umbra and the inhabitants of other realms.

Vulgar Magick: This is the fireball-and-lightning kind of magick — magick visible as such to normal observers. Vulgar magick takes static reality and tears it out by the roots.

Old Form
■ ■ ■ ■ ■ ■ ■ ■ ■ ■ ■ ■ ■

Certámen: A magickal, non-lethal duel between Council mages.

Curtain, The: The reality in which most Sleepers believe; when a Sleeper is Awakened she is brought "through" the Curtain and sees that things are not truly as they seem.

Custos: A non-mage who works for or with a cabal as a warrior or bodyguard. A modern *custos* may be anything from a rent-a-cop to a fellow gang member.

Fallen One: A Nephandus.

Grog: A familiar form of *custos*.

Magus: A mage.

Pawn: A unit of raw *vis* or *Quintessence*.

Turb: A group of Grogs, used as one would use a "pride" of lions or a "murder" of crows.

Vis: Quintessence.

Vulgar Argot

■ ■ ■ ■ ■ ■ ■ ■ ■ ■ ■ ■ ■

Black Hats & Mirrorshades: The Technocracy, taken from the traditional uniform of the enforcers of the Technocracy. "Looks like the land of Black Hats and Mirrorshades, folks..."

Bloodwork: Any magick that requires a tremendous amount of effort and involves risk to life and limb. Also: Verbena magick.

Copperfield: Slang for a mage adept at performing vulgar magick in plain sight.

Crystal Wavers: "New Agers" who have no idea what true magick is, but capitalize on it anyway; charlatans. Occasionally used as an insult to the Dreamspeakers.

Dram: One Tass of Quintessence.

Faust: A mage who bargains excessively with spirits, especially dangerous ones.

Freak: A dangerously insane mage; often applied to Marauders and Nephandi.

Fry: To attack someone with magick, specifically with the sphere of Forces.

Gremlins: Mages adept at using technology to cover their coincidental magick.

Goin' Satanic: Joining the Nephandi.

Greyface: A Technomancer, taken from the *Principia Discordia*. Describes any anti-dynamic mage or scientist, specifically those who most focus on conformity.

Juice: Quintessence.

Merlin: An old mage, especially one who very rarely visits Earth anymore.

Mundane: A normal human; a Sleeper.

Nuke: What Paradox spirits do to those they attack.

Pit Bulls: Werewolves; considered derogatory.

Technobabble: A derogatory term for the propaganda and inflexible magick used by the Conventions.

Wyld & Fried: An insane mage. Often applied to Marauders.